THE VERITY: PART ONE

MJ LAWRIE

COPYRIGHT

This is a work of fiction. Names, characters, and incidents either are the product of the author's imagination or are used fictitiously. Any resemblance to actual persons, living or dead, events is entirely coincidental. For more information, address:
hellomjlawrie@gmail.com

For the man who raised me. Who gave me my dark sense of humour. Who taught me how to be strong, independent and loyal. And who also taught me how to handle my whisky. Thank you for always being there for me and for accepting me for who I am. This book is for you, Dad. My very own Elder Eight. I wouldn't be me without you!

CHAPTER ONE

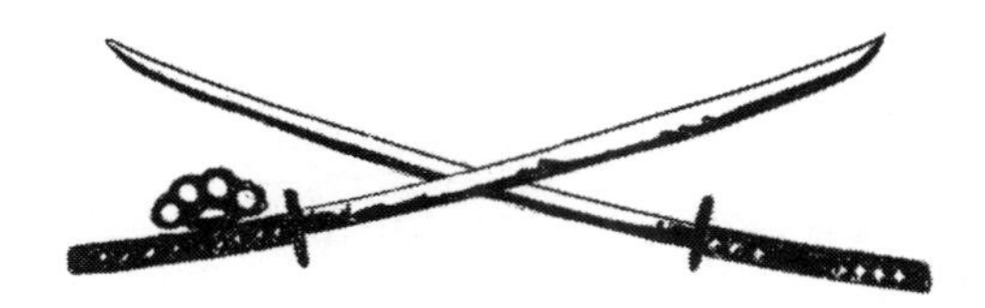

A rare and welcomed gust of wind sweeps my long, auburn hair across my face. I scrape it up into a ponytail, gathering the thick mass of curls and tying it with string to keep it out of my eyes.

Crouching behind this brick barricade and keeping well out of sight is torture. Hiding, it goes against every instinct I have. My muscles twitch with the need to move and the more I think about what's coming, the harder my heart continues to beat and the more I struggle to keep from fidgeting.

I risk a sneaky peek over the barricade and have yet another scout of the area. There's not a single living tree in sight. Just their grey, brittle husks remain. The buildings are pretty much gone now. Only their bare metal frames and crumbling brickwork have been left behind. I can't remember the last time I saw a bird fly in the sky or a wild animal of any kind. I saw a dog once. I think. It ran off before I could get a proper look. Back home, we have livestock. Cows, chickens and sheep. But everything out in the wild is just... gone.

Well, almost everything.

'When are they gonna give the starting signal?' I whisper eagerly, glancing into the distance to a hill about a mile away. There, on its peak, is a large canopy with a dozen people sheltered beneath its shade. They're all watching me and the five others by my side as we remain crouching low, taking shelter behind this wall. 'I'm desperate to get out there,' I add. 'I don't know about you guys, but I can't wait!'

'Scarlett. This isn't supposed to be fun!' Tee hisses at me, jabbing her elbow into my ribs. With an enormous smirk, I murmur a less than genuine apology. 'And will you stop grinning like a lunatic!' she snaps. 'This is serious stuff. It's not a game.'

'Yeah, yeah,' I reply, rolling my eyes and wiping the beads of sweat from my brow. 'I know. I'm taking this perfectly seriously, as I always do. Keep your knickers on, Tee.'

'Never mind my knickers. Guide your concern to the mission.'

Q-Tee, my best friend. My sister, really. She swishes her long, brunette ponytail in annoyance and glares at me. She definitely has some Japanese heritage in her family tree. Of which I'm very jealous. Such a great culture.

Well, it was.

Tee usually has a smile that can make the coldest of hearts melt. Her eyes sparkle with kindness and her spirit just wraps you in love. She's a tall, slender and very elegant girl who always holds herself with grace. Even now, crouched behind a wall in this blistering heat and wearing all her leather battle gear, she does all those things. But today, her usual smile is nowhere to be seen.

Her hazel eyes are wide and dry. She hasn't blinked for far too long. She never does when she's in hostile territory. Even though I know that her heart is beating like crazy and that she's fighting the urge to throw up, she's ready to fight. Ready to kill.

The bow on her back makes her lethal. Her skills and accuracy with that thing are unreal. I once saw her use an arrow to put out the flame on a candle at one-hundred feet. Didn't even graze the wax.

Awesome.

Well, she has been using it since she was five.

I was the same age when I held my first sword.

I shot my first crossbow at six and learned to ride a horse while wielding both weapons at seven.

Our job is to kill.

We're very good at our job.

But unlike Tee, I *love* my work.

'It will be fine, Tee. Please. Blink,' I encourage with a squeeze of her shoulder. 'The way you're staring at me is making me nervous.'

'You're nervous?' she says in an uncomfortably high-pitched whine. 'You can't be nervous! You never get nervous!' She slams her hand over her eyes. 'We're all gonna die.'

'No one's gonna die. Right guys?' I look to the other four for some support in calming her down.

Flash nods far too eagerly. His eyebrows are so high, they're almost lost in his hairline and his body shakes as if he's freezing. Despite the dozens of beads of sweat trickling down his face. He's a skinny guy with extremely blonde hair who has the dullest blue eyes I've ever seen. Even duller today. Probably the result of a sleepless night. Even with no sleep behind him, he still moves faster than anyone I've ever known. Guy runs like the Devil is chasing him.

Most of the time, that's precisely what *is* chasing him.

Titan nods too, but much more confidently. He's a big guy with dark skin and short black hair. He's built like a tank and could probably crush your skull with his bare hands. But he's so gentle and sweet, he never would. He glances at Flash, careful not to show the slightest bit of the worry I know is boiling away underneath that calm exterior.

Worry. Not fear.

Because Titan's out here with the man he loves and losing Flash? Well, for Titan that would be worse than death.

He grips Flash's hand so hard, his fingers lack any colour. And Flash holds him back just as tightly.

Tee sees and gives a fretful little whimper.

Not getting any support from those two, clearly.

I look to Cass instead. A jittery archer is the last thing we need and he's always been a strong sense of reason for us all. No matter how much shit hits the fan, he never loses his cool.

'It'll be fine,' Cass agrees, as I knew he would. He places his hand on Tee's other shoulder and she relaxes ever so slightly knowing she's protected by us both. Cass's dark brown, permanently tousled hair, hangs over his grey eyes. He emanates calm. Control. Competence. But his strong jaw fails to make it into the reassuring smile I know he's trying his best to give her. She doesn't notice his disingenuous grin.

But I notice.

I also notice how his lean and muscled frame is tensed.

He's a good foot taller than me. Strong, athletic, quick and extremely lethal.

The perfect person to have by your side out here.

The perfect person full stop really.

'As long as we all do what we're supposed to do, everything will be fine,' he assures her. 'Scarlett isn't nervous. She never gets nervous. She's excited. Because she's an idiot and enjoys this madness.'

'An idiot that could kick your arse,' I remind him.

'In your dreams,' he replies, with the slightest hitch in the corner of his mouth.

'Alright. Fancy a bet?'

'What do you have in mind?'

'Whoever gets a lower kill count has to give the other a back rub.'

'Your back rubs are like slow punches along my spine,' he complains, eyebrows raised.

'Yeah,' I shrug. 'But yours are really good. And since I'll be winning anyhow, my crap back rubs are completely irrelevant.'

Cass gives a low, amused chuckle as Tee continues to glare at us both.

'We are about to face death. And you two are joking like it's any other day!' she scornfully hisses. 'Winder, will you tell th-'

'Is the sun falling to earth?' Winder groans, interrupting us and wiping the sweat from his face with the back of his hand. 'Because it really feels like the sun's getting closer. Did we miss the memo of yet another disaster trying to wipe us out, or what? I'm sweating like a pig.' His brow furrows and his eyes glaze slightly. 'Do pigs sweat? I mean,

I've personally never seen a pig sweat, but people say they sweat.'

'I don't think pigs actually sweat, Winder,' I reply with a shrug and checking my dagger is secure in my leg holster. 'It's an expression. Like... raining cats and dogs.'

'Don't even get me started on that expression,' he laughs. 'What the fu-'

'Guys!' Tee pleads. 'Do you have any idea what we're about to face out there? Can you at least try and take this seriously?'

'Oh, Tee,' Winder sighs, slinging his arm over her shoulder and almost pulling her over under its weight. 'You worry about stuff way too much. Everything's gonna be fine. For sure. We've got this. We've *always* got this.' He starts scratching at his neck, picking off strands of his hair that are stuck to his skin. 'I shouldn't have cut my hair today. It's itching the hell outta me.'

'I still can't believe you shaved it all off.' I lean over and help pull out the long stray strands of ginger hair from beneath his collar. 'I can't get used to it.'

'Long hair's too much in this heatwave. Why they're insisting on doing this today is beyond me,' he complains, looking up at the spectators on top of the hill. 'Pretty damn sure it's the hottest day of the year. When are they gonna give the signal? We're gonna melt if they leave us out here for much longer. I say we just go over, clear the area and go home. It's my turn in the shower first, and I'm hungry as hell.'

'We go over when they signal. Not a second sooner,' Cass says clearly. 'And no one is having a shower until you clear up the mess you made in the bathroom. Your hair was all over the floor when we left. And the only reason you're hungry is that you lost a bet with Scarlett and had to give her your breakfast this morning. You know you can't beat her in hand to hand combat. She's too fast. You can never catch her.'

I laugh mockingly at Winder, who decides the best response is to shove his finger up my nose.

'Gross!' I hiss, slapping his hand away.

'Guys! Seriously!' Tee pleads. 'Can we focus?'

'I'm too hungry to focus.'

'You had a whole apple this morning,' I remind him.

'An apple isn't filling. It's-'

'Guys!' Tee snaps again with much more severity. 'I mean it. You focus... or... or...'

'Or?' I ask.

She narrows her eyes and crosses her arms. 'Or I'll tell the boys about the book you have stashed under your mattress.'

'Book?' I scoff. 'What book?'

'You know precisely which book I mean.'

'I have no idea-'

'Ya know... The one with all the steamy se-'

"Tee!'

'I think it's called, "*Secret diary of a call-*"

'Alright!' I snap, feeling my cheeks redden. 'I get the point. I'm focused, okay? Totally focused. C'mon.' I smack Cass on the arm. 'Let's take another quick look. See if anything's changed.'

Together, we peer over the barricade, careful to be quiet and unseen. The top of our heads barely pokes above our cover as we scan the area.

Ahead of us is an old three-story building made of red brick. It was once an old factory of some kind. The door is boarded up with a thick piece of wood and the two windows either side of it are sealed with metal sheeting. The panelled windows above are all shattered and missing their glass, leaving behind rusty metal window frames. Unlike the rest of what surrounds us, this structure's still standing, which is precisely why this location has been chosen. There are rusted, burnt-out shells of five old lorries precisely where they were abandoned just over half a century ago.

'So...' Cass whispers in my ear, and I know he has a grin from ear to ear. 'About this book...'

'Mention it again, I'll kick you so hard between the legs, you won't be able to sit for a week.'

He's chuckling to himself as we turn back to the others.

'What does it look like out there?' Tee asks nervously.

'Well, it's still an old factory,' I reply. 'Just as it was ten minutes ago. It's still three stories high. Just as it was ten minutes ago. And it still looks completely sealed. Just as it was ten minutes ago,' I tell her, for the third time.

'I meant are there still six targets?' she asks exasperatedly, pinching the bridge of her nose and closing her eyes. 'You are such a sarcastic cow, Scarlett.'

'Yes. There are six Class Threes visible,' I laugh, nudging her with my elbow. 'Probably not part of the original assignment. More than likely, they just wandered over. The factory is our mission. We need to kill the six Class Threes first before we attack it.'

'And then?' Titan asks. 'You and Cass are up for the Red Coat positions so we're following your lead, right?'

There's a pleading tone to his words. I understand why. Out here, you follow orders, or you make them. And it has to be perfectly clear who does what. Can't have people bickering about what we should or shouldn't do. Which is the purpose of this whole exercise. Deciding who will do the leading. But for the last seventeen years, Cass and I have always taken the lead. In everything. Where we go. The games we played as children. Battle formations.

And no one ever complains because without sounding big-headed, Cass and I are the best. It's life and death out here. And a wrong call or a bad choice can end someone's life. That's a burden not many people want to bear.

But like I said, Cass and me? We're the best. And the others trust us completely. As they should.

No one's died on our watch.

Yet.

'So...' Tee says, as each one of them shuffles a little closer to Cass and me. 'What is the plan?'

'We stick to our usual formation. You two,' I point to Titan and Flash. 'You're scouts and second wave. Tee, you're our eyes and our bow. Stay up high. Me, Cass and Winder on the ground up front. Three-point formation. This is our final assignment, guys. We get one shot. We mess this up... it's over. In every sense of the word.'

'That's a crap pep talk,' Winder scoffs.

'We've been training for this since we were five. That's twelve years of experience. Twelve years of solid training. Twelve years of blood, sweat and tears. All leading us here. There's nothing else to say. Today is the day. Today will define the rest of our lives. So, we play by their rules. Show them what we can do. Earn our ranks, survive, and go home. Got it?'

'Got it,' they all agree.

'Good. How's that for a pep talk?'

'Much better,' Winder nods approvingly.

I peer over the top of the wall again. 'Titan, Tee and Flash... when Cass, Winder and I make our move, you go around the outside of those lorries. Use the vehicles as a barrier between you and the six targets. Tee, that third lorry there?' I make sure she knows exactly where I'm pointing. 'You climb up on its roof. It will give you a good vantage point. Titan and Flash, do your scout of the building and get back to us as soon as you can with what you see inside. We need to know how many targets we will be facing, and their Class. Steer clear of the six targets outside. We'll deal with those.'

'Sure thing.' Titan nods.

'Tee, how many arrows you got?' I ask.

'Twenty,' she replies. Her hand pats the quiver full of arrows at her hip. Her other rests firmly on the string of her bow across her chest.

'How many targets did you think we'd be facing?' Winder laughs.

'Well, I might miss,' she says, not taking her unblinking eyes off me as she talks to him.

'You never miss, Tee,' I remind her.

'Well, she did once,' Winder teases, jabbing my shoulder where I have a scar from one of her arrows. Tee makes a high-pitched kind of whine and chews on her lip.

'Ignore him,' I insist. 'Everything will be alright. Just stay up on that lorry. Your assignment is with your bow. That's it. Under no circumstances are you to fight with anything other than your bow.'

'I don't have anything *but* my bow,' she whispers, her cheeks flushing with embarrassment. 'Should I?'

I shake my head, but internally I'm groaning.

Why the hell didn't she bring her sword?!

I pull out the dagger from my holster and give it to her instead. 'Take this. Just in case. We all agreed, you're going for a Green Coat so they need to see your skill with a bow. That's all. They see that, you'll be put up on the wall for sure.'

'You sure you guys aren't mad?' she asks. 'Me being on the wall means I won't join your unit.'

'For the hundredth time. Of course not,' Cass insists. 'The wall needs you more than we do. You're the best archer in the army and your place is up on that wall keeping us all safe.'

As she nods and takes a deep breath, Cass settles his eyes on me.

'Thank you,' I mouth, before he flashes me a wink. Putting her up on the wall was his idea. That way, she doesn't have to be out here fighting. She can stay home and protect everyone there instead. She's capable of being on the ground. Sufficient with a blade. And brave. Stupidly so. But being out here terrifies her. And fear leads to mistakes. And mistakes can get you, and others, killed. We all care about her too damn much to let that happen.

'If you start running low on arrows, signal. I'll get more to you,' I tell her. 'We won't know what - or how many - are in that factory until Flash and Titan do their scout. Keep your eyes open and watch our backs. We have one straightforward objective. Clear the specified area quickly and efficiently of any and all targets.'

'And don't get eaten alive by them.'

'Yes... Thank you, Winder. When the six targets are down, and when we know what we're dealing with inside that factory, we head to the door and open it up just enough so a couple of them can fit through at a time,' I tell them while they all nod. 'They'll funnel out towards the light. Now remember guys, because two of us are gunning for the Red Coats, this mission will be harder. I imagine we'll be facing a few more targets than the other units have had to face. They're gonna wanna see our skills. See us prove ourselves. So please, no loud noises. No yelling. The targets will be slow as long as they're not stimulated.'

A high-pitched whistle travels through the air. We look up to the hill and see the spectators all standing in a line watching us.

'That's the signal. It's go time,' I whisper, giving Cass another whack on his arm in excitement before turning to the others. 'Tee...'

'Get to the lorry and stay there. Blink. And don't miss. Got it.' She nods.

'Flash, Titan...'

'Go peek in the windows and see what's inside the factory while you, Cass and Winder kill the six targets outside,' Titan replies. 'Understood.'

Tee gives me a kiss on the cheek. 'Love you. Be safe out there and kick arse. C'mon fellas.' She heads out, Titan and Flash following close behind.

'Six Class Threes,' Cass says as they head off. 'Piece of cake.'

'Boring.' I roll my eyes. 'I'm looking forward to seeing what's inside that factory.'

Not that I don't love the Class Threes. I mean, a target is a target, and no target should be taken lightly. But Class Threes are slow. Cumbersome. A little dull.

The group of spectators watching over us are scoring our skills with a weapon and our ability to adapt to the ever-changing environment that a post-apocalyptic world inhabited by millions of these creatures create. Today determines our rank for when we join the army in a few days' time. It's the final of sixteen tests we've had to endure this past year. Our last year of a training programme that started the day we were born and ends when the youngest member of the unit turns seventeen.

That's me. The group's baby. And today is my birthday.

'Hands in.' I hold out my hand. Cass lands his palm on top of mine. Winders lands on top of his. 'Just like any other day. No holding back. No showing off. We go in, and we all come out.'

Cass wraps his fingers around my hand and grips it tightly.

'Don't do anything stupid, Scarlett,' he tells me.

'You know me.' I grin excitedly.

'Yes. I do. So, I'll say it again. Don't do anything stupid.' His slight smile doesn't match the seriousness of his eyes. 'Killing you would really suck.'

'Please,' Winder scoffs. 'If Scar gets bitten and turns into a target... we're all screwed.'

But despite the joking, there's a heavy tension between us. People have died in these tests. And worse. Been bitten and become one of... *Them*.

'Remember our promise. We get bitten, we get put down. No hesitating. We don't wait for anyone to turn. We just do it. None of us wants to be left like that.' I nod to the creatures behind us and the boys nod in agreement. 'Death or glory.' I repeat the motto drilled into us for as long as we can remember.

Death or glory, Cadets.

Death or glory.

'Their death,' Winder adds.

Cass nods his head. 'Our glory. Let's do this.'

CHAPTER TWO

We climb up on the brick barricade and reveal ourselves.

I look down at the six putrid vermin below. Their naked, decaying bodies are slow and rotten. Their arms dangle. Their heads loll. Their feet drag behind them and their gurgling carries on and on.

They're so disgusting.

How they were ever human is beyond me.

They still have no idea we're here, even though we're all in clear view. After flashing me a quick wink, Cass walks along the wall to the left, then Winder makes his way to the right.

I stay in the middle, my full attention on Tee as she climbs up the side of the lorry to gain her high ground. Once in place, she has her bow poised and is ready to work. Her mechanically operated weapon uses pulleys and cables that help her deal with the heavy weight at a full draw. It's made from materials we salvaged from out here in the wild. The white feathers on her arrow are flush against her cheek and her eyes never stray from the six targets below.

I watch Flash and Titan silently heading around the back of the building to see what's inside.

To my right, Winder has his battle axe ready. A crescent-shaped thirty-inch long blade on one side and a square hammer on the opposite. It's heavy. Big. But he's more than strong enough to wield it and it's utterly devastating to those he swings it against.

To my left, Cass.

His weapons of choice?

His two Haladie daggers.

A pair of double-edged daggers that consists of two curved blades attached to a single hilt. Usually, there would be a third blade coming out from where his knuckles would be, but Cass replaced them with a flat, thick lump of metal so he can deliver one hell of a punch. They're a dream for stabbing and slicing while moving quickly. And the chunk of metal at his knuckles shatters skulls beautifully. Cass is a wonder to behold with them on the battlefield. It's almost like he dances as he kills.

Everyone is in position. I glance at the boys either side of me, and we all nod our readiness before pulling up our face masks. They're little more than large wrappings of black cloth. They cover our mouth and nose to ensure no blood from the targets enter our bodies, so we don't get infected and turn into the very thing we're here to kill.

Each of our masks has been decorated. They're our own version of war paint.

Winder's has the biggest grin drawn on to it, with big red lips and huge white wonky teeth. Tee's has a simple smile with comically drawn zig-zag teeth and rosy cheeks. Cass has a very realistic wolf mouth, snarling, with blood dripping from its fangs.

I drew that one. It's awesome.

And mine? Mine boasts the golden grin of a samurai with long fangs.

I'm a bit of a samurai fangirl. Ever since I was eight, after I read about them in a book I found in an abandoned library truck, I've been obsessed.

Titan and Flash refused to let us draw on their masks, fearing any backlash from our commanders back home. They have the simple army issue brown ones.

Miserable sods.

Reaching over my shoulders, I draw my weapons from my double back harness.

My two katanas.

Each one is a gorgeous, forty inches in length. Twenty-eight of which are made of the finest steel, forged into two thousand and forty-eight layers. The handles are tightly wrapped in black silk cord. The tsuba is a circular, iron beauty carved with white doves in flight. The one I hold in my right hand has a black steel knuckle-duster welded to the handle. An extra recently added by Cass, Tee and Winder in celebration of my birthday.

I love my katanas.

But what I love even more... is using them.

I give a high-pitched whistle, breaking the silence of this deserted wasteland. It echoes off the walls of the factory and draws the attention of the six Class Threes ahead of us.

'Hey, ugly!' I call over, careful not to be loud enough for whatever's inside the factory to hear me. 'Hungry?'

Slowly, they turn and look straight at me. They start chomping at the air. The gurgling of their still liquefying insides rattle in their throats as bile, pus and blood bubble from their mouths.

'That's it. We have some lovely auburn female.' I gesture to myself. 'Or perhaps you prefer some ginger-'

'Strawberry blonde!' Winder corrects me, slightly offended by my use of the G-word.

'Some strawberry blonde male. Or perhaps a bossy brunette?' I add with a nod to Cass.

'Funny,' he grumbles, twirling his haladie between his fingers.

The feet of each target drag in the dirt, and their arms sway heavily by their sides as they move. I jump down, giving my blades a playful spin in my palm and reacquainting myself with their weight.

I don't need to. I know them as if they're my own limbs.

The boys jump down too and we begin closing in on them. Whistling and calling insults to dead ears. Now the targets are distracted, Flash and Titan, along with their single swords, can get to the factory unchallenged. The small pack of six walking corpses fracture. One goes to Winder. Two to Cass. And three to me.

It's my lucky day.

'Scarlett...' Cass warns, as I start to giggle with glee. 'Don't do anything reckl-'

'WAHOO!' I run towards my marks, kicking up dust and spinning my swords as I go.

Their instincts to eat kick in and they move quicker. Louder. As I reach the first, it swipes out for me. I use an old crate and jump up high into the air, somersaulting over it and slicing my blade clear through its neck as I go. Its body falls flat and its head rolls across the dirt, but the mouth still chomps. The other two turn as I land. I spin and skid half a foot or so and wait for them to come to me.

As I wait, I stab the severed head through its temple, silencing its snapping jaws for good. As the next one reaches me, I slice through its neck with a swift swipe. But not all the way through. It stands there like an open Pez dispenser, arms still reaching out and mouth still moving. It turns so it can see me and I can't help but laugh a little at the sight of it trying to figure out if it should walk backwards or forwards in order to reach me. My fist slams into the side of its head. The iron knuckle-duster makes its skull shatter around my fist. It sways, and with a kick, I send it down, never to get back up. The third comes at me teeth first. I thrust my blade up beneath its jaw. The tip comes out the top of its skull. The target is still blinking. But stops when I pull my weapon straight through its face.

It crumples to the ground.

Three corpses of corpses surround me.

With a flick, I clean my steel of as much of their congealed blood as possible before checking on the boys. Cass ducks and weaves between his two, slicing their throats and stabbing them in their temples with grace.

Show off.

Whereas Winder uses the hammer side of his axe to slam his fat target to the floor and then brings down the curved blade executioner style, severing its head from its fat body. He then lifts his hammer and – *splat.*

'That was easy,' Winder shrugs.

'Cos that was the warm up. Where are Titan and Flash?' I ask. As if on cue, they suddenly start sprinting towards us.

Flash is stumbling over his feet in his haste and Titan keeps glancing over his shoulder. 'Well... that can't be good.'

'How many?' Cass asks as they reach us.

'Dozens,' pants Titan. 'Too many to count. And the floors above have caved in, so they're all on the ground floor.'

'It's a test. I know they said it was gonna be more difficult cos we want Red Coats, but they wouldn't make it impossible for us,' I insist. 'They said fifteen at most.'

'Well I don't know what to tell you, Scar.' Titan shrugs angrily at the slightest inclination that I don't believe his words. 'I lost count after thirty. There are loads!'

'You gotta be kiddin...' Winder whispers before looking at me and Cass. 'We can't take on thirty! They'll eat us alive! *Literally!*'

But Cass and I are already preparing, wiping our blades clean with the hem of our brown leather coats, leaving a thick trail of black blood behind.

'Guys... you can't be serious?' Winder's eyebrows are raised and unsure. 'Thirty?'

'We have to. If we forfeit, we'll be reassigned to a new unit and retested,' I reply. 'If we can't pass this thing with a team we've been working with for more than a decade, we sure as hell ain't gonna do it with a bunch of other failed Cadets, are we?! We stick to the plan. But Titan *and* Flash will both work the door, and we kill whatever comes out.'

Cass nods. So does Titan and Winder.

Flash, on the other hand, looks like he's about to soil himself.

'I can't work the door, Scar. I can't.'

'You ain't got a choice,' I reply. 'Titan won't be able to hold the weight of thirty monsters pushing against it on his own, so you gotta help him. We need to make sure only a handful come through at a time so we don't get swamped. I'll tell Tee what's happening.'

'You let Tee stay out the way! Why not me?' he argues like a child.

'Tee is an archer. She's exactly where she needs to be and if we asked, she'd do the door. But your skills with a bow are not as good as they are with a sword, and you chose to specialise your training with a sword, not a bow. If I remember rightly, because *"only girls stay out of the fight and hide on high ground"*. So quit complaining and get to work. I'll tell Tee-'

'I'll tell her!' Flash insists, before turning and sprinting in her direction. I can't believe it when he starts scrambling up the side of the lorry.

'Bloody coward,' Cass mutters.

'He's scared,' Titan apologises. 'Maybe if he stays up on the lorry-'

'What? He'll poke the targets with his sword?' Cass snaps. 'For god's sake, Titan. Your boyfriend *is* a goddamn coward. Never mind he's leaving us one man down, if he stays up there, he'll fail.'

'I can work the door alone,' Titan insists. 'Flash can hang back. He can catch the stragglers that get past you guys. He'll get a score that way, and he'll be less likely to get hurt. Please?' He looks at Cass and receives no sympathy or understanding at all. So, instead, he looks at me. His big gentle eyes plead for my support. For my understanding. For me to help protect the man he loves.

'Fine,' I say, not able to cause the guy any more worry. At least this way, Titan's head will be in the game rather than worrying about Flash. 'You boys get in position. I'll get Flash down and tell him to hang back and kill the ones that might get past us. But, if that door gets too heavy, you tell us. You don't struggle and end up getting yourself killed, understand? A single whistle and we'll get to you.' He nods as I run over to the lorry where Flash is still scrambling up the side. Tee is watching him, looking utterly dumbfounded. 'Get down here!' I hiss at him angrily.

'No.' His voice is a quaking mess. He's uncoordinated, not even managing to climb the side of a simple lorry. All his training has abandoned him and terror has taken control. That's not his fault. But it still pisses me off.

I grab his ankle to try and pull him down. 'Get down here! We're being evaluated.'

'I don't care!'

I pull down my mask and look up at him. 'Flash, you can't hide from this! You refuse to fight, they will fail you! They'll punish you for cowardice and reassign you to another unit. One made up of other failures. You'll be lashed before you're sent out here with strangers to die. Do you hear me? They don't want cowards in their army, Flash. They'll find a way, any way, to get rid of you. Get down here!'

'There's too many,' he argues, kicking my hand away. 'You didn't see what I saw. We're all dead if we face them. Get off me, Scarlett! I don't wanna die!'

'Never mind the targets. Get your arse down here, or I'll bloody kill ya!' I grab his ankle and yank. He kicks at my knuckles hard but misses my hand and the sole of his boot slams into my face instead. White hot pain shoots across my nose and I see spots. I stumble back as he watches me in horror. I feel my nose and look at the tips of my fingers where a good amount of red now drips down them.

'Oh no... Scar... I'm so sorry.'

'You bloody idiot!' I bark, my insides filling with a cold fear that I rarely ever get. 'You absolute twat! Look what you've done! You've made me bleed!'

There's a hell of a high-pitched shriek from inside the factory. Inhuman and evil wouldn't even come close to describing it. What's worse are the several others that follow. All of the targets inside the factory can smell my blood. The slightest whiff is like a hit of adrenaline for them all.

'Get on the lorry,' Tee orders in a panic, reaching down to me. 'They'll tear you apart! You're bleeding! Scarlett, get on the lorry!'

'I ain't a coward. Unlike that fool.' I turn to the others. 'BLOOD!' I yell, holding my hand up. No point being quiet now. I'm a great big bloody steak, and those human-eating monsters probably haven't eaten in years. They can smell blood for miles. They're all gonna be coming for me.

'SCARLETT!' Cass bellows, running towards me. 'GET ON THE LORRY!'

We all watch as the board of wood covering the door to the factory starts to bulge and crack. The starving creatures inside screech louder as they go mad for the smell of my blood.

'TITAN! GET AWAY FROM THE DOOR!' I bellow. He stops and starts backing away. 'NOW, TITAN! MOVE!' When it begins to splinter, he turns and sprints towards us, desperate to get as far from the entrance as possible.

'Scarlett, you have to get on the lorry!' Tee argues. I look up at her still reaching for me and shake my head.

'You may need more than your twenty arrows. Don't miss, Tee. And you...' I point to the pathetic excuse of a soldier who has finished clambering up the side. 'Keep down so the others up on the hill can't see you hiding up here. If I survive this, Flash... you and I are having a conversation. If I don't, I'll make sure I bite you first.'

Cass and Winder have run to my side to try to stop the flow of blood coming from my nose.

'It's too late!' I snap, pushing them away. 'They've smelt it. Just focus on the fight! We're being evaluated.'

'Screw the evaluation. They're all coming for *you*!' Cass barks. 'Get on the lorry!' He grabs my waist and tries to lift me up. I slap him away. 'For god's sake. You can fight from the lorry, Scarlett.'

'I'll get a bad mark if I do that. And any shot of getting a Red Coat will be gone.'

'You'll risk your life for a sodding coat?!'

'Better believe it.' I wipe my nose, pull up my mask and ready my katanas. 'I'm getting that Red Coat if it kills me. Mark my words. Boys, get in your positions. Tee, get your bow ready.'

'You keep your aim focused around her,' Cass adds sternly to Tee. 'They're gonna be going for her more than us. You keep her safe. You hear me? You protect *her*.'

'I will, Cass. I promise.'

I hold out my hand. 'Death or glory.'

'Their death,' Winder says, putting his hand on top and looking at Cass anxiously. Cass continues glaring at me, clearly considering if he could just knock me out and throw me on the lorry. But he adds his hand to the pile.

'Our glory,' he adds.

We break.

Tee gets to her feet and readies her bow. Winder takes his position to my right. And Cass leans in close, his nose almost touching mine and his angry breath landing on my skin.

'Do - not - die, Scarlett. I mean it. You die, I will bloody kill you.'

'You better.' I grin.

He tucks a stray strand of hair behind my ear. His eyes look deep into mine, and I see fear in them. A fear for me. For my life and my safety. A fear of losing me.

'Together,' he says. 'We do this together, and we come out of this together.'

'Always, Cass. Always,' I reply, resting my hand over his as it settles on my cheek. Only for a moment. Then we let each other go. And we prepare to fight for our lives.

The makeshift door holding back the undead shatters. They pour out. One after the other, all falling over themselves before scrambling up and heading this way.

It's a stampede of monsters, all bumping into each other as they head bloodthirstily towards us.

Towards me.

Their hollow shrieks go on and on. Not one of them needs to take a single breath. Their arms dangle by their side's as they run but the smell of blood has really riled them up and filled them with whatever passes for adrenaline. Their jaws are open wide. Flesh and bile are dangling from their rotten but razor-sharp teeth.

'Here they come,' Winder sings, readying his axe.

'ATTACK!'

We run straight at them, ducking and weaving between their snapping jaws and clawing hands. The air moves as they miss me. I skid. My feet slide across the dried dirt and I lean as far back as I can, dodging an outstretched hand and set of teeth. My Katana slices through its ankles, making it fall. Straightening myself, my other blade goes through its temple. But there's another. And another behind that. The boys move forwards, stopping some that are desperate to get to my blood.

But plenty get past.

As I hack, and slice, and stab, and jump around, the targets fall. And they don't get up. They never do when they taste my steel. Cass, like me, can hurl himself about. Our gymnastic and evasive techniques are our greatest weapons, and we've spent thousands of hours honing them together.

Winder uses brute strength as his main form of attack. His hammer smashes skulls and takes out legs. A whoosh passes my ear as one of Tee's arrow's goes straight between the eyes of a Class Three behind me. Before it lands in the dirt, I snatch the arrow free and tuck it into my waistband for later. The boys do the same with any that hit a target near them. The pristine white feathers make them easy to see. If she doesn't hit the right spot in the very centre of their brain, they just keep going. Destroying their brains are the only way to kill them.

But Tee is a fantastic shot, and rarely misses.

I carry on, sending one blade through a sternum and my other through a forehead. Swipe, don't retract. Destroy as much of the brain as possible.

'SCAR!' Winder bellows, pointing over my shoulder before returning to his fight. Behind me, an enormous specimen swings its thick arms at me, hitting me square in the chest and sending me flying a good six feet through the air. I slide across the floor where I land at Winder's feet with a groan. He offers his hand and yanks me up, swinging his axe, blade side first, over my head and swiftly decapitating two that were directly behind me. I plunge my blade through the gut of another approaching our side. I pull up, slicing it in two. For some, their flesh, although thick and leathery, act as nothing more than a bag to contain their liquefied insides and brittle bones. It's tough to cut through it, but with enough practice, it's possible. And I've spent my whole life practising.

We all have.

'Are you loving this?' Winder asks, bringing down the hammer edge on another target. 'Because I am *loving* this!'

'Hell yeah, I'm loving this!' I roar with laughter. He shoves his collected stash of arrows into my waiting hand and charges off, swinging that brutal weapon as he does while laughing. A target swipes for me. Its hands scratch at the air as I lunge back. Nearly too far. I thrust the tip of my katana's blade into the ground over my head and use it as leverage to push myself back up.

Swipe.

And off comes its head.

Stab.

Right between the decapitated head's eyes.

There's a path to Cass who has a fistful of arrows. I run to his outstretched hand as he offers them to me.

'Seven!' he boasts, shoving his dagger into another one's temple repeatedly. 'Make that eight! That Red Coat and your back rub are totally mine!'

'Nine. Suck it!' I brag, before I carry on running past Titan who's dealing with the odd one that manages to get past us. I reach the lorry. 'Get the hell down here now!' I order Flash. He shakes his head as he trembles all over, lying on his belly with his hands over his head. 'If you don't get down here and fight, you'll be reassigned. Is that what you want? GET DOWN HERE!'

'Oh for goodness sake,' Tee hisses, letting loose an arrow. 'Just leave the git and focus on you and the boys.'

But I try once more. 'Flash, if you don't fight for yourself, then fight for Titan. Help him!'

Nothing. So I give up.

I thrust the arrows into Tee's outstretched hand. 'How many targets left?'

'Seventeen,' she replies quickly before returning to the task at hand and letting loose a steady stream of arrows. 'Get back out there.'

Seventeen? Damn. There's no time to waste. With a quick glance to the hilltop, I spot a group heading our way. Their horses are kicking up the thick dust as they run. I get to Cass, whose hands are going so fast, he's almost a blur.

'They're sending in reinforcements,' I tell him, pointing to the incoming cavalry.

How rude.

They only ever intervene if they think we don't stand a chance.

'What? Why the hell are they-' *Stab. Slice. Kick.* 'Doing that? It will invalidate the test.' He pushes me out the way and decapitates a Class Three as I behead another coming up behind him. 'Like hell am I going through all this again!' His attention diverts to Tee. 'TEE! SEND A SHOT! TELL THEM WE GOT THIS!'

She aims her mechanical bow high, straight at the oncoming stampede of would-be saviours. She lets loose an arrow with green feathers which soars for maybe two hundred meters and lands a reasonable distance in front of them as she waves her arms in the air wildly. They slow, and thankfully, stop their approach. They've got the message. Green means we're good. Stashed away in her quiver is an arrow with red feathers. But we won't use that. No matter what. That's a *"we need help"* arrow.

'DOWN!' Cass bellows. I land on my knees as he swipes his blade clear over me. I hear a screech followed by a thud. I reach up, taking his elbow so I can launch myself at a skinny but vicious little bastard mid-leap. It collides with me instead of Cass's back, and we land in a pile on the floor. It opens its mouth wide, but instead of my neck, it gets my steel in its mouth. I don't need to drive it through, it's that desperate to reach me it ends up decapitating itself just above the jaw. I lean to the side, avoiding its blood, and roll it off my body before getting back on my feet.

'This is so much fun,' I chirp. 'We should make them frenzied every time.'

Cass gives an eye roll and we carry on. Blades flying. Decapitating, slicing and destroying target after target as a shower of arrows fall from Tee's direction, landing exactly where they need to land. I don't know how long we fight. It feels like hours, but it's probably only been fifteen minutes or so. And as the final Class Three meets its end, I sheath my katanas, lower my mask and catch my breath.

'That was... AWESOME!' I cheer, turning to the others while laughing victoriously and wiping my still bloody nose with the back of my hand. 'Seriously! How much fun was that?'

Everyone is absolutely covered in sweat, black goo and dust as they lower their masks. Winder beams with me, Cass too, although reluctantly. We all enjoy the relief that it's done. But a low gurgling noise draws our attention to the side of the factory where one last target claws across the ground, legless and missing one arm. Its teeth are still chomping at the air.

Winder gives Cass his axe to hold and makes his way over. Looking down at it, he lifts his black boot and slams it hard into its skull before returning to us with a smug grin.

'Ten,' he boasts.

'Eleven,' Shrugs Tee with a shy smile, slinging her bow over her shoulder as she joins us all.

'Fourteen,' Cass says in triumph, wiping more of my blood from my face with his thumb.

I pat his shoulder. 'Seventeen,' I sigh happily, with a less than sympathetic grin.

'No way you got more than me!'

'Guess we'll soon find out.' I lower his hand and nod to the group heading towards us on horseback, no longer rushing, but trotting at their leisure. Elder Eight is up front. I spot Titan helping Flash off the lorry and dragging him back towards us, whispering harshly in his ear.

'Who won?' Winder calls out.

'Need you ask?' Elder Eight replies with a laugh as he approaches. I take the reins of his mare as he climbs down to give me a firm shoulder squeeze. 'Good job, Cadet 5-3-6. Kill count of seventeen. That's the highest achieved for a final test. You broke the record! Very impressive.'

As he turns to congratulate the others, I stick out my tongue to Cass who looks thoroughly pissed off.

Elder Eight is our commander. We've been with him since we were five years old after leaving the orphanage to start our training. He's in his late forties with no hair on his head, but a comical, jet black handlebar moustache. He's more muscle than man. His handshake is firm enough to make the bones in your hand grind together, and he's a wicked fighter. He uses a broad-sword. And he taught me everything I know.

'What the hell was with this one?' he asks, gesturing to Flash who lingers behind his horse. 'Scuttling up that lorry? What happened? It was a bit of a blind spot for us. We couldn't see him at all.'

'He did fine, Elder. I assure you. He killed,' I reply easily, glad that they failed to see his cowardice. 'Flash... I mean, Cadet 5-8-5, was on the lorry momentarily to try and get a head count. He remained at its base to protect Tee. I mean, Cadet 6-2-3.'

Cass furrows his brow at my blatant lie. But it's a necessary one. Those who fail or give an unsatisfactory performance are reassigned. Which means they're removed from their unit and forced to do it all again with a new unit comprised of other failures. They don't tend to survive because no one on the team seems to have a bloody clue. Imagine a group consisting of Flash's facing that lot!

'You drew blood, Cadet.' Elder Eight gestures to my throbbing nose.

'One of the targets elbowed me,' I lie.

'Careless...' he tuts. Flash avoids my stare as I lie through my teeth for him. If saving his back-side has cost me any marks... Class Threes will be the least of his problems. 'And I told you to wear your standard uniform today. We got Grey Coats here ya know. You're supposed to be makin' a good impression.'

He looks me up and down and shakes his head. But I love my outfit.

The grip on my old Nike high top shoes are still fantastic, despite them being a good fifty years old. Much better than the thick, heavy military boots the others insist on wearing. The dark red high tops and the big black tick are more than unique. They're one of a kind. Maybe the last in existence. They're one of my best finds out beyond the wall. I discovered them in what remained of a young teenage boy's bedroom. Proudly placed on a shelving unit along with a pile of video games and nudie mags.

Winder took the mags.

Above my shoes, from my ankle to my knees, are strips of thick cream leather, similar to a bandage, wrapped around my calves. A style I adopted from the great samurai of ancient Japan. They protect my skin from the monster's teeth. The brown leggings and the black tank top is standard cadet uniform. Those and the knee-length brown leather coats we all wear.

But the rest, that's all me. My style. My own version of armour.

I hacked off the sleeves of my coat years ago, much to the annoyance of Elder Eight, but I found them too constricting when fighting. Cass made me a pair of thick leather arm cuffs a few years back, which unlike the tight leather sleeves of the coats, move with me, so I'm still protected. But this morning, he surprised me with a new pair as the other ones were getting a little... well, they were falling to pieces. My new ones fit snugly from my wrist up to my elbow and give me protection against bites and scratches. He carved the word death into one, and glory into the other.

'I'm a better fighter when I'm comfortable,' I argue, defending my wardrobe choices.

'If you say so. Fantastic shooting, 6-2-3. As ever.' Elder beams at Tee, who turns pink as she accepts his compliment with a quiet giggle. 'The Green Coats will be lucky to have you, I'm sure.' That makes her smile even more. She longs for the safety of the wall. A Green Coat would make her beyond happy.

'Any chance the Red Coats would be glad to have me?' I ask.

Shaking his head and chuckling away to himself, he looks at the boys. 'And you two...' He puffs out his cheeks in appreciation for the boy's skills. 'I have to say, very impressive. Quick. Tough. Very effective.' He looks at us all in turn with a clear sense of pride in his young cadets. 'Your unit is the best I've ever seen in face to face combat. You work together like you're one organism and it's a thing of beauty. Don't ya agree, fellas?' he asks the three men who have slowly made their way towards him, still on their horses. Their black coats boast their position.

'Absolutely,' the youngest one replies with a cocky grin. He must be in his early twenties. He leans down and shakes Cass's hand. 'Your reputations precede you. I thought they were exaggerating your abilities. I was told to look out for the one that fights with two bladed weapons. They said you're the best. Congrats on breaking the record.'

'Sorry, mate.' Cass nods at me. 'You're looking for Scarlett. Not me.'

'Oh.' He looks at me like I'm something he can't figure out as Cass retracts his hand. 'I didn't have binoculars. I thought... but you're a girl.'

'That I am.' I reply.

'I was expecting a guy.'

'They usually do.' I continue to smile, my mouth filling with venom.

The Black Coat looks between Cass and me.

'So, *she* was the one that got a seventeen kill count? Not you?'

'Yep,' Cass replies, looking at me with a mixture of pride and annoyance. 'She's very enthusiastic about her work.'

I feel my face redden.

'I bet she's enthusiastic,' the Black coat says quietly with a slimy grin, looking me up and down.

'I could enthusiastically kick your teeth in if you keep undressing me with your eyes.'

'You think you could take me?' he laughs loudly.

'Better believe it.'

'I think I'd like to see you try.' His eyes linger on my chest.

'I suggest you rethink that,' Elder interjects, resting his hand on Cass's shoulder before he can go for the guy. 'She could easily kick your arse, Black Coat. You wouldn't last a minute.'

'We were just playing, right, Cadet?'

'Oh yeah,' I scoff. 'Playing.'

'You can go,' Elder orders his entourage. 'Pack up the canopy and get ready for the journey home.'

As they turn to leave, the Black coat can't resist. 'You did well. Ya know. For a girl.'

Elder pats me on the back as I watch them all leave. 'You did superbly, Kiddo. No matter what is or isn't between your legs.'

'Thanks, Elder.'

'You need to complete a sweep of the area.' He gestures to the factory. 'I suggest you and Cass head inside. Make sure it's clear.'

'We'll give you a hand,' Tee offers. But Elder stops her and shakes his head.

'No. Just them. Off you go, Cadets.'

'Alright,' I agree. 'Tee, Winder... you go around the back of the factory. Make sure it's clear. Cass and I will check inside. Flash, Titan, gather the bodies up and burn them.'

'We can help with-'

'You can do as she's told you to do, Flash,' Cass warns him, barging into his shoulder as he passes. I have to jog to catch up with him.

'Don't need to be such an arse hole, ya know,' I scorn, once out of earshot of the others. 'Flash didn't behave that way intentionally. He panicked.'

'If I were an arse hole, I would have told Elder Eight the truth. That Flash booted you in the face as he attempted to save his own skin. That he made you bleed as a stampede of the undead were a few feet away in that factory of doom. And then hid away behind Tee the whole evaluation. He's useless. Dead weight.'

'He's family.'

He scoffs as we come to the door of the factory.

'Just because he's family, don't mean I have to like the idiot.'

We peer inside. It's empty. Save for a large container with the doors bolted shut slap bang in the middle of it. Thick metal support beams are keeping the building up, but the floors above have rotted away so we can see right up to the roof which has half caved in. Rays of sunlight light up the interior.

'You were reckless today.'

'Let's check the inside of the container,' I sigh, hoping to avoid yet another telling off.

'Case and point. Why do we need to check the sealed container?'

'Because Elder Eight just sent us in here. The two-people wanting to earn a Red Coat. Chances are the Elders put the bloody thing in here as an additional test.' I go ahead as he picks up his speed to follow. 'And how exactly was I reckless?'

'Wahoo...?' He looks at me with disapproval. What's new. 'Who runs towards a group of human-eating monsters with a grin and cheers "*wahoo*"? You didn't wait for us, you just charged off. And you still stood front and centre, bleeding all over the place!'

We reach the container.

'This may come as a surprise to you, Cassius, but I'm more than capable of fighting the fight. Bleeding or not.

I don't need you or anyone else to help or protect me. I may *just* be a girl, as that arrogant Black Coat just reminded everyone, but I can handle myself. Better than most.'

'You being a girl has nothing to do with it. I don't want to watch you die. That's all.'

'I ain't going nowhere.' I promise.

We draw our weapons and press our ears against the door.

'I can't hear anything. You?' I ask. He shakes his head.

'I should report you to Elder Eight,' he says gruffly, making me laugh. 'Not that he'd reprimand you. Teacher's pet.'

'Report me for what? For not being a coward? For killin' seventeen Class Threes? For leading a successful mission with you? He said I did good. Why don't you report yourself to Elder Eight for having a stick up your backside instead?'

'You know what?'

'What?'

'You're so bloody annoying.'

'Likewise.'

He gives the door a hard kick. The clang echoes within the four walls. We listen. Silence.

'Ain't nothing in there.' He concludes, turning and taking a step towards the door and back to the others. 'The test is over. C'mon. Let's finish clean up and get home. I'm knackered.'

'But there might be something useful in it,' I argue, looking up at the crate. 'It's sealed for a reason. It could be books or clothes or... or... seeds,' I add, in a desperate attempt to convince him to open it.

'Seeds?' he repeats with a disbelieving raise of his brow. 'You know there ain't seeds in there.'

I shrug. 'There could be. And it could still be part of the Red Coat test. We really should open it up.'

He folds his arms across his chest. 'You're going to open it no matter what I say. Aren't you?'

I reply with a mischievous grin I know he loves to see, despite himself. I know him way too well. The corner of his mouth twitches as he concedes.

'Fine.' He heads back. 'But you behave like this is a game. This is life and death, Scarlett. One wrong move and you could end up a target.'

'Well, if I do, then I trust that you will be there to put me out of my misery and ensure that the last words I hear will be a good old fashioned "I told ya so".'

'You think it would be that easy? For me to just kill you like that?'

'Sure... why not?' I shrug.

He shakes his head. 'You don't seem to realise that those Class Threes were once human beings. They were someone's kid. A parent. They're-'

'Boo-hoo, Cass. Whatever or whoever they were... they ain't that no more. They're soulless, human-eating beasts. And if I ever turn, I fully expect you to chop me up before I get a chance to kill you or anyone else. As far as I'm concerned, as soon as they got bit, they died.'

'That simple, huh?'

'That simple. Don't deny you don't love the fight just as much as me. I see it in your eyes. I hear it in your voice. You and me? We were made for this. And we love it. Don't we?'

He holds my gaze a little longer than necessary. 'Ready?' he asks finally, nodding towards the crate.

'Always.'

He slides the large metal bolt across the door to unlock the container and slowly opens it up, careful to keep the exit clear in case anything does decide to crawl or sprint out. It creaks as it opens. The thick rust is objecting to every bit of movement. If there were anything in there, the noise would have it coming at us. There would be screeching and scuttling. We relax. But Cass is clearly far from done with his lecture.

'I do enjoy the fight. But I also fight smart and carefully. You don't. You charge in and treat it like a game.'

'Can you just get to the point of this lecture please?'

'My point is, Scarlett. One of these days, your carelessness is gonna get your arse in a situation that requires someone to save you. And when that day comes, you better hope-'

Suddenly, the metal doors fly open. One whacks Cass in the head, knocking him down in a daze. The other, I narrowly miss, but the large bolt slams into my ribs phenomenally hard and sends me flying through the air completely winded. My katana skids across the dirt, out of reach.

As I hit the ground, I cough and gasp as the metallic taste of my own blood fills my mouth. But my attention soon shifts to what's walked out of the container.

It's no Class Three.

It's a bloody Class Two!

It stands more than six feet tall with razor-sharp teeth. Its lips have rotted off, leaving nothing behind but bone.

A Class Two target is solid muscle. It's like punching a wall. They're strong and can move twice as fast as any human and ten times faster than a Class Three. The ones we faced outside stumble and stagger about. These don't. They're focused and co-ordinated. They have some form of intelligence but zero humanity. I've faced a couple in my time, but always with the full force of my unit by my side.

Never alone.

Is this really part of the test? To kill a Class Two?

It looks down at Cass who can barely lift his head and starts to head towards him. Its fingers flex, ready to start tearing at his flesh. I spit a mouthful of blood onto the floor, hoping to lure it to me instead. It stops and sniffs the air before turning to look at me.

'Hey!' I call, desperate to get it away from the barely conscious Cass. 'You smell that?' I spit more blood. It growls and faces me. 'Come and get it. This way. That's it. Good human-eating monster.'

'S-Scarlett... run!' Cass stammers, trying to regain his senses.

'No chance.'

It sprints towards me, it's mouth open in an endless hollow shriek. I try to reach for my katana over my shoulder, but the whack to my ribs has made it impossible for me to move my arm enough. It opens its mouth and goes for my neck.

'Ahhh... crap.'

I do the only thing I can think of, and shove my leather cuffed arm in its mouth.

'Try biting through that, Bitch.'

Its teeth are firmly lodged in my armour. With my free hand, I pull up my mask. I don't want anything to go in my mouth.

That would really be game over.

I thrust my forehead into its face. But that does less than nothing. I lift my legs and kick it hard in the chest. It lets go of my cuff, stumbles backwards and regains its balance before crouching low and pouncing high into the air. It reaches where the ceiling of the floor above would be if it hadn't collapsed. I roll out the way as it comes in for its landing. In a quick move, I tackle it and pin it beneath me, grunting against the pain in my ribs as I do. As it lunges at me teeth first, I grab its head as it starts clawing at my body, but it can't get through my leather coat.

They may be hot and heavy. But they really are the best type of armour against these creatures.

I slam its head into the ground again and again and again, but still it growls and snarls. Its arm swipes through the air and hits me straight across my face, knocking me onto the floor. I roll over and try to get up, but it grabs my ankle and I fall. As it claws at my leg, I kick and kick, slamming the sole of my shoe into its face over and over. With each whack, I hear a crunch and a squelch. Its fingernails hook into the leather wrappings around my leg, and it starts dragging itself up my body.

Bloody hell...

I have to get away from its teeth. I turn and claw at the ground, dragging myself away, when I see the most beautiful thing I've ever seen lying just ahead of me.

My other Katana.

I reach out. My fingernails brush it. With a growl, I push harder and wrap my fingers around its hilt, ignoring the pain in my ribs.

Now it's really over.

For it.

In a quick move, I spin round, lift the blade above me and thrust it straight through the top of its head and down its throat. With a final yell, I give every last bit of my remaining energy into one last upwards heave, showering myself with bits of skull and brain.

'Urgh. That's so gross.'

Someone starts slowly clapping. I look to the door and see Elder Eight, as well as a couple of Black Coats, standing there looking very proud. He folds his arms across his chest, gives me an approving nod, turns, and then they all leave.

I knew it. It *was* a test.

Breathless, I roll the Class Two off and lay on my back clasping my side. I pick off the bits of zombie skull from my hair and lower my mask, desperate to get some more air into my lungs. Cass stumbles to a stop beside me in a frantic panic, rubbing his head and falling to his knees.

'Oh shit. That was a Class Two! They put a bloody Class Two in a bloody container for us!'

'Seems so,' I wheeze.

'Are you okay?' he asks.

'Oh yeah...' I cough, still laying on my back and clutching my ribs. 'I'm Brilliant, Cass. Fantastic. You? How are you doing?'

'Can you get up?'

'Sure, I can.' I shrug.

'Then why are you still on the ground?'

'I'm just waiting for you to come and save me from this situation I seem to have found myself in.' I pat his arm. 'In your own time, buddy.'

He eases me up, laughing to himself. 'You're such a sarcastic cow.'

'I know. One of my many charming attributes. I have to say, thanks for my birthday present.' I gesture to the thick leather arm cuffs that just saved me. 'They came in very handy. Barely a scratch, look.'

He wraps an arm around my shoulder. 'You are very welcome. So,' he says, grinning from ear to ear. 'Seventeen kills and to top it all off, a Class Two. Tell me, have you enjoyed your seventeenth birthday, Scarlett?'

'Are you kiddin?' I smile. 'It's been the best birthday ever!'

CHAPTER THREE

Fifty years ago, the world ended.

And how it ended, well, those details have always varied depending on who you ask. Much like anything I suppose. Personally, I don't really care. I tend to live in the here and now. In my opinion, it doesn't matter what lies in the past. Today is what matters. Especially in a world where you spend your days fighting the undead and where every second could be your last.

But if I'm ever asked what I believe about how the world descended into a desolate wasteland filled with starving human-eating monsters, I repeat the story that Elder Eight told me when I was six years old, sitting on his stoop while he stitched me up after a rather messy training session with Cass and his haladies.

It all started when most of North America disappeared under the sea. Millions of lives were gone in the blink of an eye. It was the biggest wave the world had ever seen. The ice caps had melted. Global warming had reached its peak and Greenland, the U.S and half of Canada disappeared with no warning. There were no signs that this disaster was coming and no hope of survivors. Four hundred million people sank beneath the waves that day.

But that was just the beginning.

Four days later, a streak of red light illuminated the sky. And everything got very, very warm. We lost communication with the world. TV's, radios, phones and the internet just stopped working. The southern hemisphere had been hit by some kind of solar event. No one really knows what happened to them all over there. But the fact that no one saw daylight for another two weeks, because the atmosphere was too thick with ash and smoke, meant that whatever it was, it wasn't survivable. When the sun finally broke through, the radios crackled to life. Those still alive were told that South America, Africa and Australia had been destroyed.

Half the world's population had perished in a matter of days.

Three and a half billion people were just gone, leaving the rest of the world to stumble about blindly in panic and grief.

Plant life began to die. Trees became brittle. Grass became dirt. Animals withered and died.

We had made the world sick. Humanity had mined it, boiled it and raped it of everything it had. And soon, what was left of the world's human population got very hungry.

Cibus was created.

The mass-produced pill was to be taken three times a day and provided stimulants for energy, vitamins for thriving and a suppressant for that pesky hunger.

Cibus was to be humanity's saviour. You can still see it advertised on a billboard a few miles down the road from home.

But it wasn't our saviour. Not by a long shot.

Soon after the distribution of Cibus, there were reports of cannibalism, extreme violence and butchery carried out by those incapable of adjusting to life without a steady supply of food.

But no fear.

The army, or what was left of it, would fix it.

Settle down and take your pill.

But the Army wasn't prepared. No one was. How could they be when the attackers - still with flesh in their teeth - continued to charge with a chest full of bullet holes?

The streets ran red with blood.

Literally.

People were torn apart by other people... and eaten alive.

This wasn't just hunger.

It was Cibus.

The suppressants had the reverse effect and drove people mad with hunger. Hunger beyond reason or understanding.

The stimulants made their body clock stop. They didn't age. They just rotted.

Slowly.

The so-called *vitamins* attacked the blood and changed it. Cut them, shoot them, and instead of blood, a thick, black substance would ooze from their wounds, clotting almost immediately.

They stopped being people. They stopped being human. They stopped breathing.

And they just... wouldn't... die.

Unstoppable, un-killable, dead, human-eating monsters. And they were everywhere. To make it worse, their bites are contagious. If they sink their teeth into you, you become like them.

But not everyone turned when they took the pill. Certain blood types reacted differently. Some stayed human. Others turned into what we now call Class Threes. Slow but determined creatures which drag their limbs and hobble from foot to foot. Then there's the Class Twos. They became strong. Fast. Solid.

And then... Class Ones.

Although rare, Class Ones are something else entirely. Not one of them is the same. A Class One destroyed an entire town. A *whole* town! The buildings. The people. All on its own. It stood thirty feet tall, so the story goes.

I personally have never had the pleasure of facing a Class One. No one I know has. I hope one day I will. That would be a great kill under my belt.

The cities fell first. London, Manchester, Birmingham and Liverpool burnt to the ground two days after the outbreak. That was on humanity though. The army bombed them in a desperate attempt to kill the monsters.

Didn't work.

There was no evacuation either. Hard to say which side lost the most.

Survivors gathered in farmlands and small towns away from cities and tried their best to survive. To wait for someone to do something. For someone to save them.

And then the message came. It travelled over the radio for days and days.

'Come to The Haven.'

The message was followed by coordinates.

The lost and lonely travelled far to reach this so-called *"Haven".* What they found was exactly that.

A family by the name of Sands owned a large section of land in the east of England. They'd created the one and only safe place left in the country. Humanity would have died. We would have disappeared entirely if it wasn't for them. And for one man in particular.

Harvey Sands.

He accepted everyone that turned up. No one was sent away. Everyone was fed. Clothed. Given safety.

As long as they followed his rules. He was a godly man and believed that everything that had happened was some kind of Armageddon. His town was his very own Noah's ark.

No murder. No blasphemy. No sex out of wedlock. Love thy neighbour and all that jazz.

So, unless you wanted to get kicked out and left to fend for yourself...

All hail the great Lord Sands.

To some, Harvey Sands turned into a messiah of sorts. They followed his law to a tee. And insisted that others did too. He played the part well and called himself "*God's representative on earth*". His devout followers became known as The Grey Coats.

Grey Coats are the law keepers. They're recognisable by their grey jackets that reach their knees and boast a decorative V with wings either side, sprawled across their backs. Their coats have hoods so large, they cover their faces. We never see under the hood. We have no idea who they are or what they look like. They are the best of the best. The most highly skilled fighters we have. Most are selected at the age of ten and whisked off to be trained independently. Or as I call it, brainwashed. Grey Coats are militant in their duties. Fanatical almost. They choose you. Not the other way around. They asked me to join seven years ago when I turned ten. But I said no. Rather than fight, they dish out punishment for the slightest indiscretion anyone makes, and they take immense delight in doing so. Not the type of people you want to piss off.

The survivors needed protection, supplies and most of all hope that one day they'd reclaim their country.

So, Harvey Sands, along with the help of his faithful Grey Coats, created the Sainted Army. Back then, members of the Sainted Army were volunteers.

They started by building a fifty-foot-high and four-foot-wide wall that stretches on for twelve miles around the town dubbed "*The Haven*". Within which, the survivors built homes, cared for the land and each other. They regrew grass. Replanted trees. Looked after the animals and reproduced. All the time, following the stringent laws set forth by Harvey Sands and enforced by his Grey Coats.

But beyond the brick and metal of the high wall, was death in the form of sixty million zombies.

Harvey Sands was in his forties when all this happened. He died twenty-three years ago and his son Malakai took his place. Malakai enjoyed the devotions that diverted from his father straight to him but he wasn't happy with the small army of volunteers that helped protect him and scout for supplies. I mean, who willingly wants to go out there and get eaten alive? So, the law of Donation was created. Of course, this was instructed to the new Lord

Sands direct from God and fully enforced by the growing number of Grey Coats he had at his beck and call. All happy and willing to punish anyone who dared disobey him.

Every first, third and fifth child birthed by the same woman is to be donated to the Sainted Army.

Yep, that's right. Donated!

More like torn from the hands of a sobbing woman who had spent nine months growing a baby, only to hand it over to a life of blood, sweat and eventually, a brutal and ugly death.

As soon as they're born, off they go to live in the military orphanage until they turn five. Then they're placed into a unit of six and shipped off to The Academy, where they spend everyday training together until the youngest member turned sixteen. After that, the unit undergoes a year of evaluation, demonstrating their skills so they can be assigned a rank worthy of their abilities.

And in the Sainted Army, there are four ranks.

The Canaries are recognised by a black coat with a yellow bird stitched onto their lapel. They used to search for survivors. Now they scour the country for supplies. They started as volunteers. Now, most are criminals sent out to live beyond the wall for months at a time as punishment. Most never return, which I think is probably the point.

Then there are the Green Coats.

They protect the wall and watch the borders.

Typically, they're archers. They stand guard and shoot down anything that gets too close to the wall. They tend to be female, as it's seen as one of the weaker ranks of the army by a few sexist and ignorant idiots, so most men refuse to pick up a bow unless they have to.

Black Coats go out in groups to hunt these monsters and search the surrounding area for supplies. They go out beyond the wall for a few hours at a time and never go too far. They're the foot soldiers. The real army.

Six Black Coats make up a unit.

And then there are the Red Coats.

It's the rank given to the one soldier who excels at skill, leadership, and capability. They lead all the Black coats who graduate with them.

It's the rank assigned to the best of the best. Save for the Grey Coats, of course.

The evaluations end on the youngest members seventeenth birthday.

That's me.

That's today.

And then we join the real fight.

Our mission is simple. Rid our country of every single zombie out there and keep everyone with a heartbeat, breathing.

We haven't heard anything from another country since the last ferry arrived with four hundred survivors on board over fifty years ago from Ireland.

We're all that's left now.

Two thousand and sixty-three people huddled together in the corner of Suffolk, England.

And we share our country with sixty million human-eating monsters. Otherwise known as Targets, Class Ones, Twos, or Threes, and to a few, good old-fashioned zombies is the preferred title.

Two weeks ago, Malakai died.

I heard he fell down the stairs. But if anyone asks, he was led away by an angel.

And that leaves us with Lord Noah Sands.

The twenty-one-year-old son of Malakai.

From the moment I was born, it's the one thing that has been drummed into me, into all of us, every single day.

The oldest man of the Sand's family is Gods representative on earth, and we must all follow his sacred word.

The Verity.

It's the name of our way of life. The name given to the laws we must follow. The name of the order that governs us. That Noah Sands Governs. If we ever forget what the sacred word is, we simply pull out our Verity book. We're instructed to keep it on us at all times. The small leather-bound book we were given when we left the orphanage is similar to what some called the Bible. But this one has empty pages so that new laws can be added to it. There's a great big V on the front with elegant silver wings behind it. The same as the emblem the Grey Coats wear. Our cadet numbers are in the top right corner.

Mine has blood stains on the pages and a stab mark from a stray sword.

Plus a few doodles I drew of me decapitating targets.

Noah Sands is now in charge. He demands the same amount of respect and devotion as his father and grandfather did before him. The Grey Coats are as loyal as ever to The Verity and in turn, to Noah. But what differs now is Noah's interest in the Sainted Army. And in my personal opinion, a distinct disinterest in the religious path set forth by his predecessors. Even before his father died, he's been a constant figure and influence on the Elders on how we're trained. His family never bothered, but Noah is one hell of a skilled swordsman. I've seen him with a sword.

Very impressive.

I think he carries on the ruse of his faith only to keep order and control over the Grey Coats.

But that's just my own opinion.

Tee, Winder, Cass, Titan, Flash and I were all donated to the Sainted Army within six months of each other.

I'm the youngest. Today, I turned seventeen.

What a way to spend a birthday!

We're issued with a number when we're born. Not a name. We never learn where we come from. Never meet our parents. We live away from the civilians. We're our own family. We named each other. Care for each other. We love each other. Some more than others.

Titan and Flash are lovers. A way of life that is strictly forbidden. But in my opinion, love is love, so it doesn't bother me. It's the only thing Flash has ever been brave about. Loving another man.

Tee and I are sisters. We share a room, and clothes, and secrets. She's hands down the sweetest girl in the Sainted Army. Anyone will tell you. Which is why I chose the name I chose for her. She really is a Q-Tee.

Winder and Cass are brothers. Best friends. Comrades.

And we are all, family.

Each morning, we gather and offer silent prayers to the wellbeing of God's representative on earth.

For Noah.

For The Verity.

I personally sing, *put the lime in the coconut,* on repeat in my head and think about what I'm gonna have for breakfast.

What a load of old crap.

God does *not* exist!

No one is speaking on his behalf.

But Noah has big ideas for the Sainted Army. He's determined to win back our country. So, I'll play along. We all play along. It's hard to believe in any kind of god when you see what's happened to the world and the people that lived in it. I've not met a soldier yet that believes in god, but we all play along. Not only through the fear of the Grey Coats and their wrath, but also, to keep our place behind the safety of the wall. We lose that, we're dead.

I get to kill zombies with my friends by my side. I get to survive. So...

All Hail Lord Sands... or ya know... *"Put the lime in the coconut"*

CHAPTER FOUR

Cass reaches down and starts pulling me to my feet.

'Here,' he says, helping me to steady. 'Let me help you.' I stagger as he brushes off the dust from my legs. I spit the last of the blood from my mouth and take a deep, painful breath. 'I told you we shouldn't have opened it.'

'We were supposed to open it.' I look at the Class Two and point at what's left of it. 'They put it in here as a test. Elder Eight was watching us the whole time. Well, he was watching me kick its arse. He was watching you have a nap. Can you believe it, Cass? I killed a Class Two all on my own!'

His stern glare has little effect on me. I can't tell if he's pissed at me being right, or us almost dying. Either way, I'm pretty chuffed.

'Where are you hurt?'

'I'm fine,' I tell him, waving my hand dismissively. He lifts my top nonetheless so he can run his fingers over my ribs. I wince and hiss various swear words before batting him away. 'Will you stop pawing at me?! I said I'm fine.'

'I think one's broken.'

'I'm just bruised, Cass,' I insist. 'Like I said... I'm fi-'

'You are not fine!'

With a tut and a roll of my eyes, I step away, which makes him growl quietly under his breath. Something that always makes me laugh, and him growl even louder. 'Maybe there's something else in the container. Let's check it out.'

'What? Because one Class Two isn't enough? Are you *trying* to get yourself killed?'

'Err... no. I'm just doing my job. Maybe you should stop trying to cop a feel and do the same?'

'You wish I would cop a feel,' he scoffs. 'There's nothing else in that container. We need to get back to the others.'

'Not until we check that container,' I reply simply, shrugging my shoulders and taking a step past him.

He blocks my path. 'You're not going over there.'

'You gonna stop me?'

'Yep.'

'I'd like to see you try.'

'Okay then.' He prods my side and I double over, trying not to heave at the pain he's inflicted. The furious look I throw him as I peer up at him through my hair has him looking smug.

'You took a whack and your rib is probably broken. *I'll* check out the container.'

'I'm more than capable.'

'Yeah... perfectly capable,' he mutters, watching as I slowly ease myself up straight. He makes his way towards the large metal box, spinning his haladie in his palm. 'So, you think this was part of the test for our Red Coats?'

'Of course it was.'

'Seems a bit drastic, shoving a Class Two in a box.' He reaches the container and opens up the door fully, his haladie ready and raring. 'No more targets,' he reports, heading inside. His feet shuffle as he walks around it.

'Well?' I call over. 'Is there anything else in there?'

His head pokes out the door. 'Oh yeah... there's loads of stuff in here. Seeds, books, clothes. Scar... there's chocolate!'

'Really?!' I ask, excitement clear in my voice.

He walks out and kicks the door shut.

'No. Not really. It's empty, you daft cow.'

'You utter git,' I grumble, resting my hand on my ribs and filling with disappointment. 'You know I love chocolate.'

Still chuckling away to himself, he returns to my side, picking up my second katana from the floor on his way. 'C'mon. Let's get back to the others.' He gently returns my swords to their harness and takes a second to examine my face. I feel the warm trickle of blood still falling from my nose. With the sleeve of his leather coat, he wipes it away, letting his thumb rest on my cheek a little longer than necessary. As soon as I feel my cheeks redden, he swiftly lets go and nods to the defeated Class Two. 'I'll drag that out to the fire.'

'Damn right you're dragging it out,' I add, watching him head towards the motionless Class Two. 'Since you did sod all killin' it.'

'You're going to a doctor when we get back. Your ribs could be broken.'

'If I report an injury, I'll get marked down. So no. I won't be doin' that.'

'If I tell Elder Eight you're hurt, he'll drag you there himself. Everyone knows you're his favourite.'

'Are you threatening me?' I watch him as he grabs at the Class Two's ankle and slowly hauls it across the floor towards me.

'CADETS!' Elder Eight yells from outside. 'WHAT'S THE HOLD-UP?'

'Coming, Elder,' Cass calls back as he stops in front of me. 'A broken rib isn't something to ignore and your face is bruised and bleeding. You need medical attention.'

'I'm not risking a single mark and if I report an injury, it will affect my score. Not a word. You hear me? Or you'll be sorry, Cassius.' I jab a finger in his chest and square up to him. I have to tilt my head up and he has to lower his to meet my stare. Our noses touch and he seems to find it a little amusing. 'Real sorry,' I add in a low warning.

'Is that so?' He leans further over me, accentuating the height difference and making me crane my head back so far, my foot has to shift back so I don't fall.

'Yes. I mean it, Cass. If you tell anyone I got hurt, you'll regret it.' With a firm shove, I push him away and straighten myself up.

With a small chuckle, he carries on walking out of the warehouse with the corpse trailing behind. 'Ohhhh, I'm shaking in my boots. C'mon future Red Coat, let's go home.'

With a triumphant grin, I follow him out.

Future Red coat. I love the sound of that!

The journey back to The Haven is uncomfortable. Elder Eight, along with the three Black Coats, are riding just up ahead, leading us all home. The others who were up on the hill, various Grey Coats, Red Coats and a couple of Elders, left as soon as the assignment was over.

My stallion, Hanzo, isn't a smooth ride on his best days. Usually, it doesn't bother me. But with my ribs in this much pain, it definitely bothers me now. He's a temperamental but beautiful beast with deep, dark brown hair and a white stripe straight down his face. And no one other than me can ride him without getting bucked off.

'You doing alright?' Cass asks, trotting beside me on his stallion, Midnight. He has the deepest black coat that shines blue when the light catches it just right. Cass glances at how my hand gingerly holds my side.

'Just tired.' I brush his concern off, lowering my hand. 'I checked. Nothing's broken, now shhh. Before someone hears.'

'You're going to the doctor when we get back,' he says with that annoying matter-of-fact tone he dons so often. 'I don't care if it marks you down. Your health is more important. And then you'll-'

'I said I'm not going.'

'We can tell them that you fell *after* the evaluation.'

'I said no, Cass.'

'And I said I don't care.'

I take the reins and pull back so Hanzo stops. Cass grunts and carries on knowing all he'll find now is silence and a fair amount of eye rolling if he stays. As he usually does when he knows I won't back down. And I never back down.

He simply carries on and travels beside Winder instead, and when Tee appears beside me, we trot on.

'How's it going?' I ask her.

'Great.' She beams, her eyes doing a full three-sixty of our surroundings. 'I'll be glad to get home and wash the day off me.' She brushes off the layer of dust settled on her coat and continues watching the land around us warily.

We follow what used to be the motorway to get home. Our horse's hooves clip and clop as they walk along the four-lane carriageway with cracked tarmac and abandoned husks of cars pushed to the side. The buildings around here were knocked down years ago to use for the great wall surrounding home. Anything of use inside - furniture, clothing, medical supplies - absolutely anything remotely useful, was hauled into The Haven. So now, there's nothing left for miles but a hilly wasteland and countless human-eating monsters wandering around aimlessly.

'You still planning on putting your number in for the lottery tomorrow?' I ask Tee, crossing my fingers out of sight in the hope that she's changed her mind since this morning.

She nods, a tinge of embarrassment flushing her cheeks. And I inwardly sigh and slump at the idea.

And wail.

And swear.

It's a miracle I keep my composure, but she needs my support. Nothing else.

'It's a silly thing to do. I won't get picked.' She watches me, waiting for a reaction. 'You think I'm a sell-out,' she claims when she doesn't get one. 'I want a Green Coat, which means leaving your unit to stay up on the wall. And now I want to enter the lottery so I can leave the army. You think I'm-'

'I don't think you're anything but my best friend and my sister,' I clarify. 'And I certainly don't think you're a sell-out, Tee. You're not the only girl putting their number in the lottery. I think you'll find I'm the minority here. It's completely up to you. If winning the lottery will make you happy, then I'll support it a hundred per cent. I mean... if I had it my way, you wouldn't. But that's just me being selfish. I can't imagine not seeing you every day.' I look at our hostile surroundings. The miles of dead land. The ruins of old buildings. The nothingness. 'Just think, you'll be giving up all this.'

'Will you please put your number in with me?' she asks for what must be the hundredth time.

'Tee, I've already-'

'Scar...' She reaches out and takes my hand. 'I'm begging you, please put your number in with me. If there's a shot at one of us getting out of this life-'

'I don't *want* out of this life. I love this life.'

'That's what scares me. You enjoy being out here fighting those things way too much. I'm terrified that your... er... enthusiasm-'

'Stupidity,' Cass counters.

'Will get you killed,' Tee concludes sadly.

'I am exactly where I want to be. Where I'm needed. And if anyone wants to try and take my swords from me and replace it with a ring? Let them try. I could do with a laugh.'

'I wish I were as brave as you. Every time I come out here, all I can think about is that it might be the last. I don't want to turn into one of those things.'

'Listen.' I give her hand a big squeeze and make sure she sees my eyes, because I am not messing. 'I promise you, with every fibre of my being, that you will not die. You will not turn into one of them. And if you don't win the lottery, you'll be safe up on the wall. And me and the boys will see you every evening when we have dinner in the great hall. I promise. Either way, you're going to be as safe as a soldier can be! Plus, me not putting my number in only increases your chances of winning. Less competition.'

She sighs, retaking her reigns and giving up trying to convince me to enter the lottery. Her eyes land on Winder who is digging around his backside, pulling out his underwear.

She openly sneers, 'Are you searching for gold up there, Winder? Cut it out. No one wants to be seeing that!'

The boys ahead of us chuckle to themselves before Winder turns to face us, his underwear now free of his arse.

'Do you think he was up there with the others today?' he asks.

'Who?' I reply.

'Noah Sands, obviously.'

I scoff and shake my head. 'No way. Noah is far too important to be put in harm's way like that. The Grey Coats would have been out in force if he were up there.'

'That's a shame,' Tee sighs. 'I've always wondered what he looks like. Actually, come to think of it, probably best he wasn't there today.' She glances down at her dirty and sweaty body. 'I'm not exactly looking my best.'

Winder looks to Tee. 'If Noah was up there today, he'd fix the lottery so you would win for sure, Tee. You're adorable. Even all sweaty.' She blushes as he compliments her. She always blushes when he compliments her. And he is always doing it. 'And even if Scar did put her number in and win, he would probably demand a do-over,' he adds.

'Hey!' I snap. 'What's that supposed to mean? What's wrong with me?'

'Nothing. You're fine. But you kind of have that look...'

'What look?'

Cass turns and smirks. 'The kind of look that says – say or do the wrong thing, and I'll cut your head off so I can play football with it.' They all give a small chuckle. 'Tends to put people off.'

'Could you imagine Scar being a doting wife?' Winder asks Cass.

'Hell no! She's too mean. And always covered in zombie guts. It's like her perfume. Rotting flesh and congealed blood.' Cass sniffs the air as the others laugh. 'No offence, Scarlett.'

'Oh. None bloody taken. Sod you lot. I'm a delight. And I don't smell.' I give myself a whiff and almost gag. 'Well, today doesn't count. It's a heat wave, evaluation day and we all stink. So...'

Elder gives a high-pitched whistle and points to the east where there's a Class Three stumbling towards us from behind an old building.

He turns on his horse and looks at me. 'You still bleeding?'

I wipe my hand under my nose and there is still a little wet blood there. I groan and nod, gripping Hanzo's reigns before giving him a kick.

I'm attracting the creature. So it's my duty to put it down. As I ride, my ribs cry out in pain. The sound of hooves descending on me make me turn. I expect to see Cass. But it's Elder Eight.

'You alright?' he asks, looking at my side.

'Fine, Elder.'

'Your riding is weaker on your right. You injured?'

'No, Elder.'

'Kiddo, tell me-'

I unsheathe my sword, kick Hanzo, and we take off at a gallop, leaving him in our dust. It's an easy kill. A swift swipe results in a head removal and a quick skewer stops its jaws from chomping. I return to Elder who waited patiently for me to finish. He holds up his hand and I stop. The others are continuing on, but watching us.

Elder looks pissed. 'You have an injury and you're hiding it. Why?'

'I have no injury, Elder.'

'I only saw part of the fight between you and the Class Two. Were you injured before I got there?'

'No,' I insist coolly.

'Protecting someone?' He gives a single scoff as I remain quiet. 'If I see ya claspin' your side again, you're goin' straight to the doctor when we get back. Got it?'

'They'll mark me down-'

'Then ya shouda thought about that before gettin' hurt.' After a moment's glaring, he adds, 'If it's still hurtin' ya tomorrow mornin', come see me. I'll see if I can help.'

'Will that affect my mark?'

'Not if I keep my mouth shut it won't, no.' He nods to the others. 'Go. And ride easy.'

'Thanks, Elder.'

He grumbles before riding on.

After an hour of mindless chatter and aching arses, The Wall comes into sight and we all give a collective sigh of relief.

It's really done. We've finished our final assignment and our time as Cadets is almost over.

Soon, we'll be real soldiers and we'll trade these Brown Coats in for our official army ranked colours.

Our horses all pick up their pace. They're as keen as us to get home for some rest and food. In the middle of The Wall is a large iron door which can only be opened from the inside. On each door, made of cast iron, are two gigantic V's with a set of elegant wings behind them.

The emblem of The Verity.

These doors are the one and only entrance into The Haven.

The Green Coats work the pulley system, opening the gates for us. The loud grinding of the gears puts my teeth on. We ride in and they seal behind us. We're welcomed back home by the cheery applause of the people who live here as civilians. They always gather when Cadets return from their final assignments. Littered about are Grey Coats, patrolling the crowds. Everyone glances at them nervously, careful not to hold their gaze for too long. They're brutal bastards who seek out any criminal activity and see to it that the guilty are punished. I use the phrase "criminal activity" loosely. I've always resented the fact that we feel more paranoid than protected when we see them. After all, they're supposed to be protecting us, right? From each other. From ourselves. From the dead. But it's hard to trust a group of people whose faces we never see. Who seek out punishment more than guilt. Who wears a thick leather whip at their hip stained with blood. As they slowly walk through the crowd, those the Grey Coats pass lower their heads and keep their eyes firmly down. One wrong word. Hell, one wrong look, you'll soon feel the lash of that whip. Civilian. Cadet. Black Coat or Red Coat. It doesn't matter. The only authority they answer to is Noah. And to a certain degree, the Elders. They can't punish an Elder.

But they can – and do – punish the rest of us.

Happily.

You couldn't have two more different landscapes. Inside the wall, everything is looked after with the utmost care and devotion. There's green grass and lush trees. Flowers and berries. It's like riding through a fairy tale. Everything is sacred here. The food is grown away from the public, and it's all fiercely audited. Not a bean is grown without it going in a ledger. Nothing is wasted, and no one goes hungry. Unfortunately, it's nearly all root vegetables. Goddamn radishes are the nastiest thing I've ever eaten.

We have livestock. But we don't eat meat. All leather is from animals that died naturally or from items found out beyond the wall. It's all about healing the world and respecting nature. Which is why burning any form of fuel, or producing any kind of pollution is forbidden. Hence the horses. We see remnants of the technology that the world once had. Televisions. Computers. Machinery with hundreds of buttons and huge furnaces that would pour tons of smoke out into the atmosphere. Even enormous winged structures that used to fly and drilling rigs that went miles underground, pulling out oil!

All of it played a part in the death of the world. So now we let it rot. After we took what we needed of course.

The civilians that we pass live in the main town in the centre of our walled-in fortress, in huts and cabins. They have the babies, farm the land, collect the water, and anything else that doesn't include training and fighting the undead. Although they clap and cheer, celebrating that we've managed to survive, they avoid looking at us. Each one that holds a child's hand has donated at least one of their offspring. I could have passed my mum and dad a dozen times, and I would never know. Other than my auburn hair, I have no distinguishing characteristics that could be any sign of where I came from. Hazel eyes. Not overly tall or noticeably short. No birthmarks or abnormalities. But I'm yet to see anyone in the town to match the odd red my curly hair boasts.

They never look us in the eye. We could be theirs, and they harbour a certain degree of shame about giving us away. The life of a donated child is hard. Relentless. Brutal. Some of us don't even make it through training. Some don't make it out of the orphanage.

But I love my life. I love the fight.

I wave at the kids. They wave at me. They're too young to know what lies ahead for them. What lies beyond that gigantic wall and heavy, metal door. They don't know about the monsters as we do. They don't know that one day they'll have to donate a child of their own to a life of fighting. At least if they see us smile, wave, happy... perhaps it won't haunt them as much as it haunts their parents. So that's what we all do.

'That woman's here again,' Tee says quietly, her gaze flitting towards a tall lady with long brown hair and the same features as her. She lingers by the wall regularly when we're out, as if waiting for our return. Tee smiles and waves at the woman we all think is her mum. As ever, the woman lowers her head and disappears into the crowd, dragging a little brown-haired boy after her. Tee keeps her sweetness and waves at the kids. Her ability to maintain a brave face is inspiring. I know she would love nothing more than to throw down her bow and go dig up some potatoes. She'd be a great wife and such an amazing mum. But we don't have that choice. We can't marry until we retire. And retirement age is forty. Not many of us reach that. And even if we do, no way we'd hand over a kid to a life of this. So hardly anyone from the military marries.

This is our lot. End of.

Well... except for the lottery of course. Which is why Tee's so anxious about the whole thing. It's a girl's only way out of this life, and her one and only chance to have a family of their own without handing over a kid. Win the lottery, you're excluded from the law of donation. You get to live a domestic life with the man himself as dear husband.

Lord Noah Sands.

It would be her dream come true. It's many of the army girl's idea of a dream come true.

We follow the soldier's road, which avoids the town and leads straight from the gate to the Military Village.

No civilians are allowed down this way. We pass others training or getting ready to head out on various missions. They all acknowledge us, and we acknowledge them.

Once the horses have been fed, watered and stabled, we head back to The Academy. The building we call home. Fifty years ago, it was a great and extremely luxurious hotel, complete with indoor and outdoor pools, something called a spa, and various courts for playing racquet sports on. Now, the outdoor swimming pool is where we lift weights. The tennis court is where we practice with heavy weaponry. And the indoor pool is a gymnastics training area. This four-story, three hundred and twenty-eight bedroomed building made of dark-red brick and lead tiles, now serves as the home of five hundred Cadets all going through training.

Ten Elders spend their days passing on their specific skills to us all. Archery, swordplay, gymnastics, and a dozen other fighting techniques. The left-wing houses ages five to ten. The right-wing, ten to sixteen. And the cadets aged sixteen to seventeen live in the north wing as they undergo a whole year of evaluation.

Boys on one floor. Girls on the another.

The various Lord Sands that have been and gone in the last half century - along with the Sainted Army - extended the safe zone right up to the sea, taking in small village after small village. Now we have some good thirty-odd square miles of safety surrounded by the great wall on one side and the ocean on the other. The Academy is the centre of the Military Village. It's where we sleep, gather to eat, meet for assemblies and even witness public punishment. In the forecourt is a large stone pillar stained with blood. There's one in the civilian's village too and by all accounts, it's a lot bloodier than this one. I've never been lashed, but Cass has. After some Cadet grabbed Tee's backside, he punched him in the jaw. Knocked out two of his teeth. But that wasn't what earned him ten lashes, the scars of which still linger on his back. It was what he said.

"What the hell do you think you're doing?"

That one word – *Hell* - led to his public flogging.

Lesson learnt.

Don't swear in front of anyone you don't trust. Blasphemy is not tolerated!

But beating up a groper? Crack on.

Some of the windows of this once magnificent building have been smashed, others simply rotted out of their frames. We had to take out the revolving doors ten years ago when they jammed and no one could get in or out. The entrance is just a massive hole in the wall now. But you have to walk up a lovely flight of marble steps to get to it. So that's nice I suppose. The guttering's a mess, so the building's pretty damp and at least four of the chimneys have fallen off the roof.

But today, it looks very different. Reminds me of a pig wearing a dress.

The front forecourt outside The Academy has been tidied and decorated with blue and red bunting. The broken windows have been boarded up. The debris from years of neglect have been swept away and potted rose bushes have appeared all over the place. They even have little ribbons attached to them. Cadets pass us in droves as they carry on their work, tidying and fixing.

'Hi, Scarlett,' they greet.

'Afternoon, Scarlett,' they say.

'Well done on your final assignment, Scarlett!'

I nod and give a brief hello to them all. Every face is familiar but I wouldn't say I know all their names.

'Wow. They would crawl up your backside if they could,' Tee laughs.

'It's just my kill count they admire. Not me,' I remind her. 'Where did they find all this crap?' I laugh, looking at the stupid attempt to try and make this place look half decent. 'I asked for a new blanket last week cos mine's threadbare. I was told there wasn't one. My pillow's so flat it's like sleeping on a sheet of sodding paper. But this stuff?' I gesture to the rustic red carpet currently being rolled out the front door. 'They can find this stuff alright.' I laugh as I watch the middle-grade cadets sweep the dusty floors and wash the grime from the remaining windows. 'What a joke.'

'We have to make an effort,' Tee says simply. 'It's a big deal, this visit. I mean... *Noah Sands* himself is coming! He deserves better than this.' She gestures to the crumbling mess. It's the least looked-after building in the place cos everyone here is far too busy training to stay alive to look after it properly. And we have far too low a standard of living to give a damn anyway.

'This is our home. If it's good enough for us, it should be good enough for him.' I head over to one of the younger cadets who is at the top of a ladder. It wobbles unsteadily beneath him as he scrubs a second story window with gusto. I grip it tight and make sure it's steady so he doesn't fall and break his neck. 'Alright up there?' I call.

'Yeah. Oh! Scarlett! Please don't trouble yourself. I'm good up here. This work is beneath you.'

'Beneath us all,' I mutter, returning my attention to Tee who takes hold of the other leg. 'All this fuss. Washing windows, sweeping floors, for what?' I lower my voice and lean in so no one else can hear me. 'He ain't divine, Tee. He's no more a spokesman for God than I am. And if he weren't a good leader, a good fighter, and dedicated to defeating the targets, no one in the Sainted Army would give a damn about him. He's just a man.'

'He's not *just* a man, Scar,' she says scornfully. 'Now his dad has died, Noah Sands is the leader of The Verity! He's-'

'If you say God's representative on earth, I'll bloody slap you,' I warn.

'Of course not. You know I don't believe in all that nonsense. But, Scar, Noah and his family are the only reason we're alive.' She sighs, her eyebrows raised as if she's said this all a hundred times over. She has. As well as all the Elders. I rest my hand on my hip and let her have at it. 'They literally saved us. And Noah has singlehandedly increased food production with his new system of farming. Cadet fatalities have gone down since he added extra curriculums to our training like field medicine and evasive tactics. He deserves our respect.'

'Alright, Tee. I get it. Noah's fab-'

'And...' She ain't done. 'He just lost his dad and has been thrown into this new position of power.'

'I don't think he really minds-'

'If that wasn't enough...' Oh wow. She's really on the defensive. 'He's got to go through the process of the lottery to get a wife so he can further the Sands bloodline which is a huge responsibility on him and whoever is chosen.' She pauses and looks at me with a wrinkle on her brow. And I know exactly what's coming. 'You should really put your number in.'

'No.'

'I just think-'

'Tee, I-'

'The winner gets to have a home! Have a family! Have a real marriage! It's every girl's dream.'

'Not mine.' I shrug. 'I have a family. A home. And I'm married to my work. To my swords.'

'You're being ridiculous,' she snaps. 'And stubborn.'

'And you're being an annoying bitch!' I bark back, my voice echoing around the courtyard making her blink at me in surprise. 'I don't want to put my number in the sodding lottery. I don't want to be chosen to be Noah's sodding wife and that's the end of it! I don't get a say in much. But I get a say in this. And it is not happening. I will not be shoved into a pretty dress and used as a breeding mare.'

'Alright. Calm down. I'm sor-'

'But you keep on! You haven't stopped badgering me about this bloody lottery since we were kids and I am sick of it. You want to marry him? Crack on, Tee. Just leave me out of it. Got it?'

The cadet above us glances between us, wet sponge still in hand. Various others have all stopped to spectate too. And Tee keeps blinking at me, startled at my sudden outburst. It's very rare I lose my temper with her. And those doe eyes make me feel rotten to the core for speaking to her so harshly.

'I'm sorry,' I sigh, reaching out and taking her hand in mine. 'I shouldn't have spoken to you like that. I'm just really tired of people telling me what I should do, ya know? I just want to join the army and wear a Red Coat. Look. I'm sure Noah's nice enough. And I hear he's not bad looking either. But I want to fight. Not stay home and raise his kids. That's your dream, Tee. Not mine. I couldn't think of anything worse. To be taken away from my home and everything I know. From the fight. From-'

'Cass?' she adds with a knowing look. I narrow my eyes at her with a warning as she shows me her cheeky little grin, forgiving me for my outburst.

'I could say the same about you and Winder,' I retort.

'We get our coats before we find out who wins the lottery,' she says slowly and through her teeth, ignoring my words and scowling fiercely. Sore subject that. Clearly. But her eyes are drawn to something behind me, and her scowl disappears, only to be replaced with wide and worried eyes. 'Oh no. Scar... look.'

'What?' I turn to see what she's looking at. 'Oh bugger.'

Flash is talking to Titan, looking at me nervously as if preparing himself to come and talk to me. But it's Cass storming up to him from behind that has Tee worried.

'Cass!' I warn, letting go of the ladder and heading towards them. 'Cass, don't you dare!'

Too late. He spins Flash round by the shoulder and slams his fist straight into his face. Flash hits the ground hard, clasping his nose and looking up at him absolutely terrified.

'Cass! Stop!' I yell, running over.

Cass towers over him and points a finger in his face. 'You nearly got her killed, you selfish little bastard! What did you think you were playing at?'

'Cass, mate! Let it go!' Winder says, grabbing his elbow as he pulls it back again ready for another strike. Titan could floor Cass with ease. But he doesn't. He just kneels beside Flash and helps him to sit.

Cass pulls his arm free and tries to land another punch, but I jump between them.

'Enough!' I order. 'Stand down.'

'He almost got you killed!' he says furiously.

'You need to keep it down,' I warn in a hush, looking around the forecourt. Everyone has fallen silent and is watching us. 'He screwed up. He knows that. But it's not worth him getting reassigned over. And, he won't do it again. Will you, Flash?'

He shakes his head as he clasps his bleeding nose.

'See? It's all good.'

'It's all good?' Cass hisses. 'ALL GOOD?' he roars, shaking his head. 'Nah. It ain't good till he learns his lesson.' He charges forwards again, his furious eyes squarely on Flash still on the floor. But I stand in his way and shove him hard in the chest, making him stumble back.

'You take one more step towards him, I'll shove my foot so far up your arse you'll be tasting rubber for a week,' I warn. 'We have enough to be dealing with out there, without turning on each other in here.'

He looks me up and down and turns his anger on me instead. 'What were you doing holding up a ladder?'

'Don't you start on me.'

'Go and sort your ribs out,' he orders, pointing towards the house. '*I'll* deal with Flash.'

'What's wrong with her ribs?' Tee gasps, rushing over and fussing.

'Nothing.' I brush her off. 'I'm fine.'

'Get your backside to the doctor before I drag you there myself.'

'Just shut up, Cass. You're starting to get on my nerves.'

'SCARLETT! DO AS YOU'RE TOLD!'

'Don't you talk to me like-'

'I GAVE YOU AN ORDER!' He storms up to me, showering me with spit and towering over me so I have to lean back a little to stop his face touching mine.

'You done?' I ask calmly.

'Go. Or I will make sure Elder Eight knows exactly what happened today. Flash... that container... your injury. All of it. You'll be marked down. So go, or else. Am I making myself clear?'

'He's right. If you're hurt-' Tee takes my arm. I yank it back.

'I know that what happened with me today scared you. And that you're angry at Flash for what he did. I know you're behaving this way because you care.' I step closer to Cass, so my face is in his. But he doesn't step back and now our noses are touching. 'But if you ever talk to me that way in front of people again... actually...' I slam my own fist into his face, and he joins Flash on the floor, clasping his bloody nose. He looks up at me furiously.

'Problem?' A Grey Coat calls over with an amused chuckle. 'Need help with the little lady, Cadet?'

'No,' Cass replies with a snarl, wiping the blood away with his sleeve. 'I think I can manage.'

I lean over him, my finger now in *his* face. 'Don't you dare talk to me that way ever again, Cassius. In private. Or in front of anyone else. Don't you *ever* threaten me or my ranking in order to get me to do what *you* want, ever again.

If you do... I'll break more than your nose. Am *I* making *myself* clear?'

The courtyard is silent. Not even the Grey Coats intervene. After all, I'm not breaking any laws.

'Yeah,' he growls. 'Crystal.'

'Good. I don't need your protection. For you to defend me. Or your misogyny. I'm not a defenceless little girl that needs rescuing. It was me that saved your arse today and don't you forget it.' I turn and head inside the house. People scurry out of my way as I pass.

He's such an asshole.

I storm through the enormous entrance lobby, barging into those who don't move aside quick enough.

They glance at my swords as I pass and keep quiet.

A wise move, given my mood.

The stone floors are heavily marked and cracked from years of abuse by our military boots. The walls are peeling paint and faded floral wallpaper. Above my head - four stories high - is a huge domed ceiling with a rusty chain dangling from the centre. The crystal chandelier fell off decades ago. Killed two Cadets, according to Elder Eight. There's a small crater in the floor where it landed.

You can see each level above us. The landings are like long balconies surrounding each wall. Most of the bannisters have rotted away so you don't wanna get too close to the edge. It's a hell of a long way down if you do. There's a grand staircase straight ahead which leads up to the first floor and there are hallways, stairways and passageways leading every which way. This place is a bit of a maze. But I've lived here for as long as I can remember, so I know it all like the back of my hand.

As I walk down the halls, up several flights of stairs and through various corridors, I quietly mutter to myself about the prat I left on the floor downstairs.

Who does he think he is? How dare he talk to me that way.

Urgh.

No one gets under my skin like Cass does. And that really pisses me off. That he can make me this annoyed and angry.

Prick.

I finally reach the hallway that leads to the room I share with Tee. Our own little slice of solitude. Which we share. Joint solitary, if there is such a thing.

Room 148 on the third floor at the very front of the house. We get the sun in the morning. Lovely way to wake up. Beams of light searing into your eyeballs. We don't have curtains. Obviously.

I can't wait to wash. To get out of my clothes and into some joggers and a tank top. Something comfortable and breathable. Oh, to lay on my bed and sleep. Yes. Sleep.

No. No sleep.

Standing outside my door are two men.

Grey Coats.

Their large hoods cover their faces, as ever. Their plain black jeans and military boots are exactly the same. They stand with their arms folded across their chest, staring straight ahead. The winged V emblem sprawled across their backs.

I stop dead in my tracks. 'Ahhh... bloody hell,' I whisper. This is the last thing I need. I just want to wash and go to sleep. Not deal with this. They haven't spotted me. I back away, hoping to leave unseen.

Someone behind me clears their throat. I jump and spin to see another Grey Coat at my back.

'Oh... Mr Grey.' I nod in polite acknowledgement, clutching my chest from shock. I hate how they move so quietly. They're always sneaking up on people. Truth is, I have no idea if any of them are men or women. We never see their faces. We just call them all *"Mr Grey"* on account of their jackets.

'Language, Cadet. You know the laws against blasphemy.'

'Commander,' I reply with a small bow. 'I didn't realise it was you.' Of course, the one to catch me swearing would be the leader of the Grey Coats. 'I'm so sorry. It was a slip of the tongue, I assure you.'

'I suggest you learn better control of your tongue then, Cadet,' he says dryly.

'Is this visit about today's assessment?' I ask with forced enthusiasm. And a bit of hope. Surely, *he's* not here. Not today. Please not today. I look to the door of my room where the two men are still standing guard.

'You know why we're here.' He nudges me forwards towards my room. 'You're wanted.'

'I take it there's another *Mr Grey* in my room waiting for me then?'

The Commander just gives me another gentle nudge.

'Crap,' I whisper. 'Is he in a good mood at least?'

'He's always in a good mood,' he replies tiredly. 'Especially when he gets to see you. In you go, Cadet. He doesn't like to be kept waiting.'

I take a deep, weary breath. 'Don't I know it,' I grumble, heading towards my room.

Mine and Tee's bedroom consists of two twin beds, which are on opposite sides of the room. A large desk lies in the middle, where Tee makes her arrows. All around the room, various weapons are strewn about. Knives. Axes. Arrows and the such. No guns though. They're forbidden. Even if you are lucky enough to find one out in the wild – which no one has for over a decade – they're too noisy and too dangerous. One shot and it attracts the dead for miles. Similar to blood. And one missed shot could kill a fellow soldier. So, no guns.

There's a wardrobe where Tee and I store our selection of uniforms. We share all our clothes. We're the same size, and apart from my kicks and leather wrappings, we wear the same thing every day. Black tank top, brown leggings, our brown leather coats and joggers for our down time. There's a door to the left which leads to the bathroom. And standing by the window straight ahead, looking out at the forecourt where everyone is busy with their preparations, is another *Mr Grey*, still with his hood up. The door is closed as soon as I enter, leaving us alone. He doesn't turn. He stays looking outside with his hands cupped neatly behind his back.

'I'm amazed you let him speak to you like that,' he says, still not turning to look at me. 'Most of the Cadets here idolise you. The rest are afraid of you. Not him though. *Not Cassius*.'

'I think my right hook proved that I didn't let him speak to me like that.' I take off my harness and throw my weapons on my bed. 'How are you? I wasn't expecting to see you today-'

'What is it about him? Why are you friends with such a rude, arrogant person?'

'He's not-'

'I watch him boss you about. Who does he think he is?'

'I'm too tired for your jealousy today... *Mr Grey*. And definitely too tired for a lecture.'

'A lecture?' he scoffs. 'You're sounding a little insolent there, Cadet.'

'Apologies. I've just had a really long day. Final assignment and all that. Maybe you could come back later?'

I wait.

He stays.

I sigh.

He's not going anywhere.

'Do you mind if I clean up? Like I said. It's been a long day.' I head into the bathroom after he gives a single nod.

We have a steady water supply here. For washing anyway. It's not clean enough to drink, and it's icy. But it's more than welcome in this heat. Not so much in the winter when the pipes freeze up. I peel off my leather wrappings from my legs and shrug off my brown leather coat, wincing as I move my right side.

I lift my top to inspect my ribs. There's an impressive amount of purple and blue. I feel each rib. I'm more stiff than anything else. But it's just bruising. Nothing's broken.

He's followed me in and is leaning against the door frame, watching me.

'I heard you did really well today.'

'You did, huh?' I lower my top and turn. I rest my hands behind me on the sink as we face each other. 'What are you doing here? I thought you lot weren't supposed to arrive until tomorrow.'

'I grew impatient. Knowing I was going to see you again, I couldn't wait until tomorrow.' He strolls towards me and rests his hands on my hips.

'You should be more careful. You being here is a huge risk.'

'I'm perfectly safe.'

'For me, *Mr Grey*. It's a huge risk for me,' I remind him, looking at how he holds me. 'You won't be the one publically flogged and banished to The Canaries if caught with a man in her room, unchaperoned, with his hands on her person. And besides, I thought we agreed that this was done with. These little meetings. My training's done now.'

He lowers his hood and smiles his *oh so charming* smile. His short dark hair is perfectly groomed. His face is entirely clean-shaven and his clothes are perfectly ironed. He's clean and smells of soap, all of which makes him stick out like a sore thumb compared to the rest of us at The Academy. He tucks a few loose strands of my knotty, dust-filled hair behind my ear, rubs off some dried blood from around my nose with his thumb and looks longingly at my lips.

'*You* agreed this was done with. Not me. And for the record, I would never let anyone flog you or banish you. Ever. Have you missed me even a little bit, Cadet?' he asks.

'It's been a week since we saw each other. And I've been training like crazy. I haven't had the time to miss you.'

'But have you missed me?'

'Do you want me to have missed you?'

He laughs and firms his grip on my hips. 'You're as beautiful as ever, Cadet 5-3-6.'

Now I laugh, knowing I'm an absolute filthy mess. 'And you're ever the charmer, Noah Sands.'

CHAPTER FIVE

Noah leans in. His soft lips start working my neck and his body shifts closer.

Oh bugger.

I told him! I made it clear that the kiss we shared was a mistake. When I lay my palms flat against his chest and gently push him away, he groans.

'Take it you haven't changed your mind then. Still don't want me?' he complains.

'Noah, you're here to pick a wife. You think kissing me is the best idea right now? Your duty requires you to marry, and mine requires me to-'

'Die.'

'Fight.' I correct him. 'I need to focus on my job. And I don't want to be in the way of you and your new wife. We're friends, Noah. That kiss the other week was a-'

'Look, I know what you said, and I respect that.'

'Is that why you just helped yourself to my neck with your lips?' I ask him with raised eyebrows. 'Because you respect my decision?'

'I just wanted to talk to you.'

'Then talk without kissing. But if you don't mind, make it short. I'm exhausted. I need to wash. I'm covered in Zombie guts. My ribs are killin' me. And I ache like crazy.' As he looks to the floor sadly, I feel guilty. 'How are you doing?' I ask. 'Losing your dad and all, gotta be hard. Anything I can do to help?'

'Not really. But let me help you. Here.' He turns me and starts rubbing my shoulders. 'Purely platonic, Cadet,' he chuckles. I watch him in the little shard of mirror Tee glued to the wall when we moved into the room. He sees me looking, waiting for him to open up.

'Fine,' he sighs, avoiding my gaze. 'I'll share. I'm alright. Dad was old-fashioned, rigid, cold and firmly stuck in his ways, but losing him was harder than I thought.' He shrugs. 'But, there is something you can do to help me through this awful time of grief.' He returns his mouth to my neck and traces soft kisses all along my skin.

He's persistent if nothing else.

'I think you and your *Mr Greys* outside should get out of here before someone sees you. Tee could be back here any second.' I move a little, but he just guides me back.

'No, she won't,' he says. 'I've made sure no one can come up here.' He's not getting the hint and getting much more handsy.

'Noah... why have you come here?' I ask, gently guiding him away from me. 'Cos I've told you, that kiss was a mistake. So, if that's the only reason you came to see me, you wasted a trip.'

'Spoilsport,' he groans, backing away and fighting a smile. 'I actually came to talk to you about the lottery. I want to ask you something.'

'Oh yeah? You want the low down on all the girls who are putting their number in?' I tease.

'Are you coming to the lottery opening tomorrow?' he asks.

'I am.' I untie the string holding up my hair and let it loose. The amount of dust that comes out is surprising. As I shake free the thick mass of curls, I create a cloud of grit around me. Meanwhile, Noah's whole face has lit up with excitement. 'What are you smiling at?' I chuckle.

'You're putting your number in?'

'What? No, of course not,' I reply, laughing at how ridiculous that would be. 'Why would I?'

'Err... because we've been...'

'In all the years we've been friends, we've kissed twice. Two kisses does not a wife make, Lord Sands.' I continue ruffling my hair to try and clear it. I pull out my fingers from the nest on top of my head. Gross. There's goo in it.

'Would being married to me be so awful?' he asks shortly.

'I didn't say that. I'm sure it would be great. You'll make some girl very happy.'

'Then put your number in.' He shrugs. 'And I could make *you* very happy.'

'But that life ain't for me. I mean... could you imagine me as a wife?' I laugh at the ridiculousness of the idea and toss my brown cadet jacket in the sink. But I feel his eyes boring into my back. When I turn, he's not smiling. Far from it.

'Is it *him*?' he sneers, nodding over his shoulder to where he was standing at the window when I came in. 'Is *he* the reason you won't be with me?'

'Please tell me you're not being serious.'

'I thought we had a connection. All the time we've spent together...'

'Training. We train together. We have a laugh, and yes, we've kissed. All of two times, Noah. But you know that we're just friends.'

'I'm just asking, *Cadet*. Is it the fact that you don't want to be *a* wife? Or that you don't want to be *my* wife that's stopping you entering my lottery?'

'Both,' I tell him, taking a seat on the toilet and pulling off my kicks. I pour out the dirt I've collected into two little piles on the floor.

'I don't want you talking to Cassius anymore.'

'Excuse me?'

'You heard me.'

'He's in my unit, Noah. That would be impossible. Look. You don't see me sneaking into your mansion by the sea, demanding this that and the other. I have never once asked you for any special treatment or favours. You asked me to keep our friendship quiet, and I have. Also, Cass and I are none of your business.' I drop my shoes and look up at him leaning against the door. I've let my annoyance take control. Not a good move. Not with him.

'So, there is a you and Cass?'

'As far as we're two best friends-'

'You two kissed?'

'No. And even if we had, Noah, it would be none of your business.'

'It would be my business because I would be forced to punish you both for breaking the law. Soldiers are not permitted to be intimate.'

'*We've* kissed.' I remind him. 'You gonna punish us too? Listen, nothing is going on between Cass and me. He is *not* the reason I'm not putting my number in. If I became your wife, I'd have to leave the army. And I won't. You know that.'

'I love you,' he says plainly.

'You... you... what?' I stand and stare at him mouth open. 'No. You don't.'

'Yes. I do, and I have from the moment we met.'

'Stop it.'

'No. I thought I could just be your friend. But then we kissed. And I want more. I want to be with you. Properly.' He charges over and takes my hands in his. With a huge grin and eager eyes, he tells me, 'I choose *you* to be my wife.' He waits as I seem to misplace the ability to speak. He's acting like he's handed me a great gift. But he should know it's a gift I don't want. 'Can you stop looking at me like a fish and say something?'

'Oh my god.'

'I love you, but don't you swear at me.'

'Why are you doing this?' I pull my hands free and step back. 'What's wrong with you?'

'Why am I doing what? Giving you the life of your dreams? The chance to have a family and not spend your days fighting for your survival?' he snaps. 'I want us to be together. No one will know I've fixed the lottery for you to win.'

'Noah... I'm really sorry-'

'Don't. Don't you dare,' he warns, pointing a finger at me angrily. 'I'm giving you what every girl would kill for so don't you dare turn me down.'

'Every girl but me. You know what I want. This!' I gesture around me. 'When we met, I was crystal clear about what I wanted. I couldn't have been any clearer! You understood.

You helped me train so I could be the best and earn my Red Coat.'

He's getting angrier and angrier. Like a kettle on a stove. And he's starting to whistle. This is a nightmare. An absolute nightmare. Of all the people to upset...

'Can you seriously say, that after all this time, you feel nothing for me?' he says through gritted teeth.

'As a friend and as our leader, of course I do. But as a husband?' I shake my head. 'If I'd have known you felt so strongly... I never wanted to be put into a position where I'd have to hurt you.'

'You don't have to hurt me. Just... put your number in.'

'I can't do that.'

'WHY?!' he bellows, slamming his fist into the wall making me jump and step back. I've never seen him angry. And he's left a great big hole in the wall now too. 'It's because you want *him*! *Cassius.*' I reach out and take his hands in an effort to calm him down. He swallows hard, afraid to hear some unspoken truth that simply isn't there and avoids making eye contact with me. I take his perfectly smooth and pristine face in my scarred and calloused hands. I look him right in the eye and make sure I speak as kindly as I can because hurting him is the last thing I want to do.

Or should do.

'Noah... I don't want to marry because I want to be in the army. I want to fight. I want to be a Red Coat. Cass has nothing to do with it. To be honest, *you* have nothing to do with it. It's all about the job. Please believe me, Noah. You're a great guy. You have a huge job to do yourself, and you deserve someone that will help and support you in being the great leader you are. That will devote their whole life to you in a way that I never can. You'll find a woman who will look after your heart. That will give you children and cook your meals. And while she's doing that, you'll have me to help you in the fight out there beyond the wall.'

'You could do both.'

'No. I can't. You know that. The law forbids an active soldier to marry. I can't be in the army and be a wife. Your family made that rule. If we break it, then you'll have to extend that right to everyone. Which you won't.' I run my hand down his arm as he looks to the floor. There. I think that he's accepted my choice. I turn back to the sink to finish washing up.

'I order you to put your number in.'

Slowly, I turn to gauge him. And yep, he's being deadly serious. There's a firm finality in his face. He could fix it so I'm chosen. I know it. He knows it. He could make me his wife. He could make me anything he wanted.

'A-are you being serious?'

'You will put your number in,' he says coldly. A flash of anger sparks in his eyes and the air gets colder, I'm sure. 'I will force you to put it in.'

'You'll force me?' I ask in disbelief. 'What does that mean? You *can't* force someone to marry you.'

'Is that right? And how will you stop me exactly?'

'The Elders would never allow-'

'Let me stop you right there.' He rests his finger over my lips. 'You tell anyone about us... You tell anyone that we knew each other before the lottery announcement, I will kill whoever's ears are unfortunate enough to hear your words. Do you understand me?'

'Why are you being this way?' I ask, desperation a little too clear in my voice.

'You will put your number in or else, Cadet.'

'This isn't you. You're not a cruel man.'

'Perhaps I am a cruel man,' he says slowly. 'Perhaps I've been too kind with you. Maybe a lashing would knock some sense and respect into you. Is that what you want?'

'You want to have me lashed for refusing to marry you?' I reply.

'You always tell me I'm a good man. I'm just not good enough for you, is that it?'

'No! You are a good man. You have great plans for the army. I know you'll do great things and I want to help you achieve them all. I'm your friend and your servant, Noah. Give me an order, and I'll follow it. As I always have. My sword is yours. I'm on your side.'

He rests his hand on my cheek. 'You mean that?'

'Of course,' I reply nervously.

'Then kiss me.'

I go rigid as he looks at my lips. 'W-what?'

'I'm giving you an order, Cadet. You said you would follow it. Kiss me.'

'My sword is yours,' I reply in barely a whisper. 'Not my body. I will not kiss you, Noah. Not like this.'

'I said... kiss me,' he orders through gritted teeth.

'I-I want you to leave now, please.' I back up. Desperate to get some space between us. 'I said I want you to go!'

He suddenly lunges at me, slamming his mouth onto mine and pushing me back. I try to yell, but his forceful kiss steals my voice. My lower back slams into the sink as he forces his tongue into my mouth. He takes hold of my waist, keeping me held in place. His palm rests over my bruised ribs and I groan in pain. I push against his chest, my hands finding nothing more than his immovable frame of what could be made of perfectly sculpted stone. He doesn't budge an inch and for all my skills, I panic. I've never been touched this way before. It's nothing short of a violation, I feel sick with it. I've been punched. Kicked. Shot with an arrow. I've faced monsters. But this? This has me cold on the inside. This has me scared.

I slap him hard across the face.

It gets him off. But I've just struck the most powerful man alive. And now my sense of violation shifts.

To fear.

What I've just done is a death sentence right there.

I step back, too in shock at what's happening and his sudden change in personality to think of anything to say or do. He checks his lip. There's a little blood there.

'You hit me.'

'I'm sorry,' I whisper. 'Noah, I didn't mean-'

Slap.

I get a hard-backhand right across the face and get sent down to my knees with spots in my vision. He stands over me pointing his finger in my face and such hatred in his eyes.

'If you ever raise a hand to me again, I will have you executed,' he warns, as I remain on the floor with my head down and blood dripping along my chin from my split lip. I daren't move. I daren't say a word. I stay perfectly still, not even wiping the blood away. 'How dare you,' he says in a low, menacing tone that chills me to my very core. 'How dare you strike me. I am of God. I am your leader. Your commander. Your-'

'I thought you were my friend.'

'If I didn't love you and only held you as a friend, I would have you strung up from the neck and thrown from your window this very minute for striking me.'

'I'm sorry,' I repeat quietly. 'I shouldn't have struck you. But-'

'But?' He reaches down and lifts my chin with his finger. I look up into his dark eyes. 'But what? What possible reason could you have for striking me?'

'You didn't have my permission to touch me that way,' I force myself to say. 'Just because you are who you are, doesn't mean my body is yours to touch as you please.'

'Is that right?' He grabs my arm, pulls up his hood and hauls me to my feet. 'I'll show you exactly what I can do to your body if I wish. It's time you learnt some goddamn respect.'

He pulls me out my room so fast, my feet trip over themselves. The other Grey Coats step aside and follow us as he leads me down the stairs.

In the lobby, Tee, Winder and Cass are in the middle of regaling our final assignment to a crowd of younger Cadets, all of which are watching them with awe and hanging on their every word. Cass sees me being hauled out.

'HEY!' he yells, charging after us. 'WHAT DO YOU THINK YOU'RE DOING?' He runs after us, outside, down the steps and plants his feet between me and Noah, and the lashing post. 'What's happening?' Cass demands. 'What did she do?' He looks at me with an angry frown. 'What did you do?'

Noah won't speak. His voice is too well known. So he slams his fist into Cass's face and steps over him as he falls on the floor. Noah shoves me into the arms of another Grey Coat.

'Tie her to the post,' he says quietly, his voice shaking with anger. The Grey Coat nods and leads me to the post by my elbows. I look back at Noah over my shoulder as my hands are fastened around the stone pillar so I'm hugging it. He follows and stands close.

'You do this... that's it,' I warn him. 'Me and you are done.'

He leans his face in close to mine. 'The box is opening tomorrow,' he says. 'Put your number in. And I will stop this.'

Behind him, everyone is gathering. Winder's helping Cass to his feet but it takes both Winder and Titan to hold him back. If Cass tries to stop this, my lashes get doubled and he'll receive twice more than me. We all know the rules.

I look back to Noah and my stubborn streak takes over completely. Now I'm not locked in a room alone with him, and he can't touch me intimately without my permission, I'm not so afraid.

'What will it be, Cadet? A wedding ring? Or the lash of my whip?'

'Shove your wedding ring where the sun doesn't shine. I'll take the lashes any day. I hope you enjoy this. Cos it's the last time you'll ever get to touch me.'

He grabs the back of my top and tears it right down the middle before running his fingers softly down my spine. I shudder in revulsion.

'No. It won't be. I was going to take you for a moonlight picnic on the beach tonight to celebrate your birthday. But I guess this is the gift that you have chosen.'

'Like I said. I'll take the lashes.'

Holding out his hand, he takes a few steps back and a Grey Coat hands him a brown leather whip encrusted with years of our collective blood soaked into it.

'TEN LASHES FOR DISOBEDIENCE,' The Commander calls out on behalf of Noah.

I glance around me. The Cadets stand tall and rest their hands over their hearts. A sign of respect. We all know these punishments are cruelty. Not discipline.

Tee darts through the throng of people and is swiftly grabbed by a few standers by.

'Tee, close your eyes. Cover your ears. Don't look, you hear me?'

'NOW HOLD ON A MINUTE!' Elder Eight hollers, charging towards me. Two Grey Coats block his path. 'YOU GET YOUR HANDS OFF HER.'

'Stand aside, Elder. This is Grey Coat business,' The Commander calls out dismissively.

'That's *my* Cadet!' he roars. 'I demand to know what she did. Disobedience? There's no Cadet more loyal and dedicated to the fight. How did she disobey?'

'It's okay, Elder,' I tell him, keeping my eyes firmly on him. 'It's okay. Please. Just... don't let Tee see.'

He still pushes the Grey Coat for a reason.

'Tell me what she did!'

'None of your concern,' The Commander replies. Noah unfurls the whip and slaps it against the ground. The crack it creates echoes all around us and the crowd jumps. Tee howls like a wounded animal. It hasn't even started yet.

'Elder Eight,' I plead. 'Tee. Don't let her see this!' He turns and goes to her side. His face is red with fury but he wraps his arm around her. I bury my face into my arms and get ready. Winder and Cass join Tee and Elder Eight. She buries her face in Winders chest and covers her ears as he holds her close. But everyone else looks on.

Crack.

I close my fists tight and seal my mouth shut as the whip meets my flesh.

I will not scream.

I will not whimper.

Crack.

It's a hot searing pain that throbs as soon as the whip leaves my skin.

Crack.

I peer over my arm. Cass's jaw is rigid and Elder has hold of his wrist in case he decides to try and intervene.

Crack.

Everyone flinches.

Crack.

But no one looks away.

Crack.

No one says a word.

Crack. Crack. Crack.

Noah storms up to me, clearly furious that I'm not begging or pleading for him to stop. He leans into my face, his coat pressing into my bleeding back.

'Put your number in,' he says angrily in my ear.

'You've still got one more.' My whole body is shaking. I'm in agony. But I will not let him see it. I will let no man see me buckle. 'Get on with it and get away from me. I'll take another hundred and still refuse you.'

He steps back.

Crack.

He put a lot more force into that one and I let out the slightest whimper before swallowing it down so no one can hear it.

He tosses the whip to the floor and storms off, followed swiftly by the three Grey Coats he came with.

Cass reaches me first. He unties my hands and takes my weight as I slump into his chest. Tee, Winder and Elder aren't far behind.

'What the hell did you do?' Cass asks angrily. 'You stupid idiot.'

'Enough, Cassius,' Elder scorns. 'Now's not the time. Get her to her room. I'll be there soon with some cream and medicine that will help.'

'Put your arms around my neck and wrap your legs around my waist,' Cass says, 'I'll carry you.'

I take back my weight and straighten myself up, holding the front of my t-shirt close so I don't end up half naked. Blood trickles down my skin and the pain has me dizzy.

'I can walk,' I say with a strain, wiping the tears that spilled over despite myself. 'I don't need to be carried like an infant. I'm fine.' I look at Noah who glances back at me over his shoulder before he vanishes out of sight.

Then I throw up all over the floor.

After my back was washed, dried and smothered in cream by Elder Eight and my friends, Elder hands me his *"medicine"*. A bottle of whiskey which I drink till my throat burns. It takes the edge off. I slump onto my bed topless, face down to let my back have some air. They kept asking what I'd done. I told them nothing. They kept pushing. And I kept refusing. After a while the boys leave. Elder too. Not before wishing me a solemn happy birthday.

Alone with Tee, she curls up beside me on the bed to sleep with her fingers gripping mine.

Thing is, this is no big deal. Not really. We watch someone get flogged almost daily. It's remarkable I've not been hit sooner what with my temper. Tee hasn't. Not once. She's too good. Too sweet.

As Tee snores, I can't get a wink. My ribs ache. My back throbs, but it's not bleeding much. He held back for most of it. Could have been a bloody sight worse. The Commander prides himself on his lashes. He gave Cass his scars. Noah wasn't that hard on me, except for that last one. I won't scar too bad. I'll just be sore for a few days.

It's hot and stuffy, even with the window open, but Tee's sleeping peacefully for the first time in months. Usually, she tosses and turns. The last few weeks have been the worst. The build-up to our evaluation has been hard. On all of us. But tonight, she's out like a light. The assignments are over. All tests completed. Tomorrow, she'll put her name in that box. Noah's lottery. But his threats and that nasty streak I've never seen before are playing heavily on my mind. I don't want to be his wife. Now more than ever. And I certainly don't wish Tee to be with a man like that either.

All I want is that damned Red Coat. I've earned it, God-damn it! Noah can't force me to give it up. I won't let him. There's never been a female Red Coat. There's never been a female anything of note. They say there's no rule against a woman filling these positions. It's just that there's never been one good enough.

What a load of crap.

I roll onto my side with a deep sigh. The more I think about what happened with Noah, the angrier I get. If it were anyone else who had kissed me like that, I would have cut their hands off. But I'm the one at risk now. I was the one lashed.

Screw this.

Lying here going over it all again and again will do nothing but frustrate me. I slide away from the sleeping Tee, gingerly pull a sports bra on, some shorts and trainers, and head out the door.

I need to clear my head.

I always love the eerie quietness that the early hours provide. I walk along the Soldiers Road via the stables, checking in on Hanzo as I go. He's sound asleep. I replenish his hay and clean his water before carrying on towards the main gate at The Wall.

'Morning, Owl,' I call up to the woman above me on lookout. She peers down and waves.

'Morning, Scar. Bit early ain't it? Even for you.'

'Can't sleep.' I shrug. 'Can I come up?'

'Course!'

I head up the narrow and steep steps carved into the stone. It's the only set of stairs along the whole wall. The wall which stretches on for a total of twelve miles. At every mile, there's a guard on watch, and lengths of rope to shimmy up and down. But other than that, there's no other way to get on top of the wall.

'You alright? I heard you got punished?'

I turn and show her my exposed back. She sucks in a sharp breath through her teeth.

'I'm fine. His strike was weak. Barely made me bleed. Much going on?' I ask her, looking over the edge into the wastelands. I've always hated that phrase. Like the world beyond our care is a waste. It's not. It needs saving. That's all.

'Nah...' she sighs, tucking her thick jet-black hair behind her ear. 'Quiet as a mouse tonight.' She leans over with me and looks out into the darkness. I can't see a thing down there. But she insists she can. 'Oh... we have a straggler.' She grabs her bow and aims an arrow down below. Her eyes narrow as she pulls it further back. And then... *whoosh*. She lets it loose. I hear a low grunt followed by a slight thump as her target hits the floor.

'Seriously?' I look at her in amazement. 'How do you see them in this light?'

'It's a gift,' she says with a wink, stashing her bow and resting her back against the wall. 'But you have your own gifts. I heard about your kill count today. That's amazing. You're gonna have cadets fighting to the death to join your unit.'

'Well, hopefully I'll be a Red Coat and in charge of lots of units.'

'Gotta dream big, huh? So, you not being able to catch some zees got anything to do with your coat? Or your girl putting her number in that box later?'

I sit on the wall, letting my feet dangle over the edge. 'Maybe. I've tried talking her out of it. But she's as determined to put it in as I am not to. What about you?' I ask. 'You putting your number in? You're eligible, right?'

'Course I'm eligible!' she replies indignantly. 'How old do I look to you?'

'I'm not familiar with the rules to be honest.'

'There ain't many, Scar. How can you not know the rules? Gotta be female. Aged sixteen to twenty-five. No Elders, Grey Coats or Red Coats are allowed.'

'Well, that's cos they're men.'

'Yeah but even if there was a woman among them, not allowed. And no physical deformities. So yeah, I'm eligible. I'm twenty. I'm hot and I'm just a humble Green Coat. But in answer to your question... no. I will not be putting my number anywhere near that box. I like my life. I like my job. And I am not giving it up to live in an old mansion with the sole purpose of popping out the next messiah,' she states.

'Wish Tee felt the same.'

'If Tee doesn't win, she'll be put up here, right? She wants a Green Coat?' She gestures to her green jacket with the wing emblem sprawled carelessly on the floor. 'She's a fantastic archer. They'd be stupid not to put her up here.'

'That's the hope.'

Owl Graduated three years ago and she spends her days sleeping, and her nights on the wall shooting the odd arrow at the rare target that manages to get past the various traps and deterrents surrounding The Haven. Her skill with a bow isn't what makes her stand out. It's how she seems to be nocturnal. Even as a kid, she would be a dozy cow all day and full of beans at night. So, when she graduated, she was put up here for the graveyard shift.

'How's the book I got you?' I ask, gesturing to the tatty old novel sticking out beneath her coat.

'Oh... it's fab!' she whispers happily, scanning the area to make sure we're alone before reaching down and scooping it up. 'It's almost finished though.'

'If I get a chance, I'll see if I can smuggle in another one.'

'You spoil me.' She tucks the book back out of sight. It's most definitely not an approved book. But Elder Eight gave it to me to read, and I thought it was terrific. Full of magic and adventures. So definitely not Verity approved. Noah would go spare if he saw it. Even more so than how he was earlier. Like me, Owl doesn't hold much stock with the religion here. But she has respect for the mission and the work. Like the majority of us really. I always think it's a lot to ask us to fight and die for a god that does neither of those things for us. But I'll do it for people.

For our people.

'You off for a run?' she asks.

'Yeah,' I reply.

'Is that wise? Cass popped up a couple of hours ago and told me to send you away if you turned up. He said you got punished and took a tumble on assignment. You sure you're up for it?'

'I'm a bit stiff, so I'll probably be a bit slower than usual. My head's a bit noisy tonight. Need some space to try and quieten it down. Ignore Cass. He's a worrier. I'm fine.' I get to my feet and do a couple of stretches as she picks up her book.

'Oh!' she says suddenly before I head off. 'Can you take this and give it to Bowzer as you pass him? He's at the fourth mile marker. If I ask the others to pass it down, it'll only get eaten before it gets to him.' She hands me a single bread roll. 'He gave me his yesterday cos I forgot mine. It's a little... hard, but I'm sure it's fine.'

'Owl... it's stale,' I tell her, looking at the rock-solid piece of bread. 'And there's a bit of mould growing on it.'

'Yeah well, he can soak it in water and scrape off the bad bits. Have a good run, yeah?' Her nose disappears in her book, and I head off.

The wall is four feet thick, so there's plenty of room to run along it. At every mile, there's a guard like Owl. All Green Coat graduates. They walk up and down, making sure that nothing unwanted lingers by our border for too long.

I run past two guards who all say a happy hello and offer the briefest bit of small talk as I pass. Mainly congratulations on my performance in the final assignment. I've been doing this almost every morning for the last three years. Not usually this early. Or late. But no matter what time I come up here, they never seem to mind. They actually seem happy to see me. They use me as a transport system down the line if they need something passed to a friend without it getting eaten or pinched on the way.

The fourth guard I pass is Bowzer. I toss him the roll and warn him of the choking hazard as I carry on. The fifth guard, Tan, a girl with the darkest suntan anyone has ever seen but who turns snow white in the winter, hands me a letter to give to Dash. A girl stationed on the fifth mile who rewards me with a sip of her water. The sixth guard is an Elder. Elder Ten. He's in his mid-fifties and was a child when the world ended. He insists on carrying on with the watch even though he has no need to. He reached retirement age a decade ago. He has a filthy sense of humour and is very funny. He's always happy to see me and he's very good friends with Elder Eight. He jokes that the only reason he stays up here is to see me, and to make sure his best buddie's favourite cadet is okay. As I pass, he always tells me a riddle.

'What's in a man's pants, that ain't in a girl's dress?' he calls after me as I pass. I turn and run backwards as I think. He throws a green apple in the air teasingly. 'Get it right and bring me back something for my collection... you can have this!'

'You're on!' I call back before turning and running on.

The sun's just below the horizon. The dark sky is gradually getting lighter. I pick up the pace and finish the last two miles at a sprint. When I reach the end of the wall, I sit and catch my breath.

The wall was built right into the ocean. The final half mile is mostly submerged beneath the water. It's like I'm walking on the waves standing out here. Targets can't swim, they don't float and they can't climb. So there ain't no way they're getting past the wall.

The sea's calm. The sound of the waves breaking on the beach is the most relaxing sound I've ever heard. All along the shore, boats are anchored and ready to be used in case the wall is ever breached. There's enough for everyone and then some. A mile or so away, barely in view, is the main jetty and the border of Noah's mansion. Sometimes when I run out here, I find him walking along the beach. He likes to train out here and always brings an extra sword for me. Just in case I turn up. He's the best swordsman I've ever known and is the only one who I've failed to disarm. Even when I've really tried. He's just too good.

Memories of Noah and how he turned so cruel are trying desperately to swamp my thoughts. But I can't let them. He frightened me. He's never done that before. But he's not here this morning, so I watch the sunrise completely alone and relaxed. I wonder what lies beyond the ocean. What the other countries are like. I hope that there are survivors out there too. Maybe another girl is watching the sunrise over in France, wondering the same thing.

After a few minutes rest, the sun has risen enough to give me some decent light so I get to my feet.

'This is gonna hurt,' I mutter to myself, looking down at the waves. I raise both hands above my head and dive head first into the sea. The cold water is refreshing, yes. But the salt water burns the marks on my back. I emerge with a large gasp and curse loudly with a scream as the gentle waves lap over the wounds, cleaning them and washing off the dried blood. Once the pain settles, I float for a while and let my body cool down and rest.

I swim back to shore on the inside of the wall and take another few minutes to catch my breath on the beach. My clothes are already starting to dry as the heat begins to stream down once more.

I find a lovely pink and white shell to return to Elder Ten for his collection, and climb the rope signifying the final marker before running past all the same guards I did on my way down. Whereas my day is just beginning, theirs is coming to an end. They'll head back and have their dinner as we have our breakfast. When I reach Elder Ten, I hand him the shell and give him the answer to his riddle.

'Pockets,' I say a little breathlessly, holding out my hand expectantly. 'What's in a bloke's pants that ain't in a girl's dress? Pockets.'

Laughing, he hands me the apple. 'I'll stump you one of these days, Cadet.'

'You can try,' I call back as I carry on. 'See you later, Elder.'

'Take care, Scarlett. And tell that Elder of yours to come see me soon.'

'Will do.'

When I reach Owl, she's doing her hand over to Halo who nods at me politely and congratulates me on my high kill count.

'Walk back together?' Owl offers, throwing her bow over her shoulder. I lean over the wall and see three targets below being tossed into the back of a cart by three young Brown Coat Cadets. I spent a year on zombie clean up when I was fourteen. We all do. They're taken away and burnt far from here. The smell they produce as they turn to ash had us all vomiting for the first few weeks.

'Sure,' I reply, following her down the stairs. 'I'm starving.'

'ARE YOU SERIOUS?!' Cass's voice carries clear across the forecourt as Owl and I head towards The Academy. I look up and see him leaning out his bedroom window, shirtless, pointing angrily at me.

'Damn...' Owl mutters, looking up at him and chewing her lip. 'He's stunning to look at. Even when he's yelling.'

'Yeah. Shame he's a bossy and overbearing idiot. Otherwise he'd be perfect.' I look up at him. 'What have I done now?' I call back, throwing my hands in the air. 'You literally haven't seen me today. What could I possibly have done to annoy you?'

'WHAT PART OF RESTING YOUR RIBS CONFUSED YOU?' he hollers. 'RUNNING ALONG THAT WALL AIN'T RESTING! YOU WERE LASHED YESTERDAY. FOR GOODNESS SAKE!' He looks at Owl and moves his angry pointer to her instead. 'I TOLD YOU NOT TO LET HER UP THERE!'

'I AIN'T HER KEEPER, CASS,' she hollers back. 'YOU KNOW BETTER THAN ANYONE THAT TRYING TO TELL HER WHAT TO DO IS A WASTE OF BREATH!' She nudges me with her elbow, stifling a grin. 'Good luck with that, Scar,' she laughs before carrying on inside. I look back up to the third-floor window where Cass is currently leaning out with a face like thunder.

'I've told you... I'm fine!' I insist. 'Stop clucking, Cass. Your feathers will fall out.'

A couple of young cadet's giggle as they watch us. Cass narrows his eyes on them, and they stop straight away.

With an additional glare from me, they scarper.

He simply wags his finger, beckoning me inside, and then disappears.

'Eurggghhh,' I groan loudly as I head up to meet him.

Inside, Cass pulls on his black vest as I walk into his room. I look briefly at what I'm sure is the most perfect male body to exist, despite the numerous scars, before glaring at his annoyed face.

'Sit,' he orders, pointing to his bed.

I do as I'm told and sit. Only because that run has knackered me out. Winder comes out of the bathroom and throws me a wink.

'Morning, Scar. Good run?'

'How did you know I went for a run?'

'One, you stink. Two, you're covered in sweat. And thre e...' He nods to Cass who's currently digging through a large wooden chest in the corner of his room. 'His voice carries.'

'How did you know I went for a run, Cass?' I demand.

'Because, Scarlett. I know you.'

'Morning,' Tee says happily, walking into the room. 'How's the back?'

I toss her the apple I won from Elder Ten. 'Fine. Scabbed over and fine.'

'Ohh yummy,' she chirps. 'The apple. Not the scabs. Obviously.' She busies herself cutting it into four. 'What was it this morning?' she asks. I repeat the riddle.

'Obvious...' Winder laughs. 'A dic-'

'Pockets!' I interrupt, making Tee laugh.

She throws us each a bit of apple before taking a seat on Winder's bed. 'Winder, will you do my hair? I love the way you plait it.'

'Sure,' he says, sitting behind her and braiding it. She sits patiently as he does it. As he has for so many years. She smiles contentedly as he works. And he runs his fingers slowly through each strand with extra care and attention. He adores her. And she feels the same.

Maybe in another life...

'Right,' Cass says with a mouth full of apple and standing over me holding something in his hand. 'Let me look at you.'

'Not that thing again,' I groan.

He gets on his knees and takes a closer look at my ribs. 'Well, if you didn't keep getting injured, maybe you wouldn't need to keep wearing it.' He does a double take at my face. 'What's that?' he asks, gesturing to my lip.

'My face,' I reply with a shrug.

'Your lip wasn't cut when I last saw you. What-'

'Slipped on the wall this morning is all,' I say with a light air.

'What's wrong with her lip?' Tee asks in a worry.

As he opens his mouth to argue, I look into his eyes and silently tell him to drop it before Tee gets in a flap.

'She's fine, Tee,' he says, thankfully letting it go. 'I'm gonna check your ribs aren't broken. And then I'm gonna clean your back again.'

'I've already told you-'

'I'll give you a foot rub, in addition to the back rub I owe you,' he sighs. 'How does that sound?'

'When?'

'Your back when it's healed, and your feet? Whenever you like. But after a shower. Preferably.'

'Fine,' I sigh, lifting my arms and wincing as I do. 'But only cos your foot rubs are even better than your back rubs.'

'Eat your apple,' he laughs.

He runs his fingers over every single rib, taking his time and being as gentle as can. He leaves a trail of goose bumps in his wake but doesn't mention them. And I love watching the deep concentration on his face as he works. I could look at him doing this for hours.

Finally, he comes to the same conclusion I did.

'Nope. Not broken. Just bruised.'

'Like I said,' I mumble, as he wraps his hideous elastic belt around my chest.

'Luckily, that prat only lashed your shoulder blades so the brace won't agitate the wounds. He didn't go too hard on you. Doesn't look too bad. Tight enough?' he asks, securing the belt. I inhale and exhale.

'Perfect.'

'Here.' He hands me some folded clothes and gestures to his bathroom. 'Go get washed, and we'll head down for breakfast together. And here...' He plonks my kicks on the pile. I look at the clothes he's handed me. They're mine. He did my laundry again. 'And... I'm sorry about yesterday,' he adds. 'I would never risk your mark intentionally. I was just worried about you and I tend to say shit I don't mean when I'm angry. But I am sorry.'

I rest my hand on his chest as I make my way into the bathroom.

'You're totally forgiven. And I'm sorry I thumped you.'

'Forget it. Now, go get ready.'

'Thanks, Cass. You always look after me.'

'Someone's got to. You sure as hell don't look after yourself.'

After breakfast and morning prayers, we grab our weapons and our coats before heading down to meet Elder Eight in the courtyard out front. In the lobby, standing to the side in a small huddle are four *Mr Greys*. I look over, and one in particular watches me as I walk past them to the door.

I wonder if it's Noah.

No one bats an eye at their heavy presence this morning. After all, Noah and his group are due today, so they're checking everything is safe and to a satisfactory standard for *God's representative on earth.*

Pffft.

'Nervous?' Winder asks me quietly, glancing briefly in their direction. 'Gonna be a bit weird, him coming to-'

'Later,' I say quietly, taking his arm and leading him quickly on.

Outside, we head over to Flash and Titan who are already waiting for us along with six other units, all under the wing of Elder Eight. There are usually six members in each unit. Sadly, three of the units have lost one of their members. They were good guys. Crap fighters... but sweet enough to know as people.

We all share a courteous nod and some light-hearted conversation when we get the chance. But the only real friendships we have are with our own units.

Flash heads straight over to meet me, walking past Cass with his head down and leaving Titan behind.

'I am so sorry,' he says quietly and in a panic. 'Scar, what happened yesterday will never happen again. I was just overwhelmed.' He stumbles over his words and is visibly shaking. His skin is pale and his lips are dry.

'Are you alright?' I ask, resting my hands on his shoulders. 'You look ready to pass out!' I rest my hand on his forehead. 'Are you sick?'

He glances at Elder Eight who is busy talking to a few of the other Cadets.

'He said he's going to talk to you about my performance. Please don't get me in trouble. He wants me reassigned. Don't tell him I screwed up. I'm begging you.'

'Who the hell do you think you're talking to?' Winder snaps, shoving him hard in his shoulder. 'This girl has kept your arse safe for the last twelve years. She defended you yesterday against Cass and a well-deserved beating. You think she would screw you over now?' he barks. It's not very often I see Winder annoyed. But Flash gets under his skin. 'Man... just get back over with Titan before I slap you.' He gestures to Titan who shrugs apologetically. Flash looks pleadingly at me one last time and opens his mouth. 'Did I stutter, Flash?' Winder thunders. 'Go!' He shakes his head and leaves.

'You're too hard on him. You and Cass both.'

'Nah, you're too soft. That's the problem.' He pokes me in the chest. 'You're too soft on everyone. Prat almost got you killed.' We turn to face Elder Eight as he starts loudly clearing his throat.

'Alright you lot!' he calls, twirling the ends of his moustache between his fingers. 'It's another roaster of a day I'm afraid. So take water with you on assignment. You two...' He points to the two teams on his right. 'You're on shore duty. See if anything worthwhile has washed up and clear out the traps.'

I like shore duty. You walk up and down the coast picking up any driftwood or other goodies that may have come ashore and checking all the boats are still seaworthy. Cleaning out the traps ain't as fun. Untangling writhing corpses from barbed wire or scooping them out of the pits we dug is really, really gross.

'You two...' He gestures to the teams on his left. 'Wall breach check. Exterior. And you two...' He points at us and the unit next to us. 'Clean up the exterior. Three-mile radius. No further.' He points to Jazz, the blonde lad who tends to take charge of his team. 'North. And you...' He points at me. 'South. But before you go... a word, Cadet 5-3-6.'

'Am I in trouble?' I ask.

'No more than usual. Off you all go then,' he orders the rest.

Flash gives me another desperate glance as everyone starts to head out.

'I'll get Hanzo sorted for ya,' Winder says, giving me a kiss on the crown of my head and ruffling my hair before following Cass and Tee towards the stables.

'Alright, Kiddo?' Elder says gruffly as I reach him.

'Perfectly fine, Elder. Yourself?'

'Bloody peachy. You gonna tell me what got you strung up yesterday?'

'Disobedience. Apparently.'

'Not gonna tell me, huh?'

'It's fine. I got it handled. Was that it?'

'No. I wanted to bend your ear.'

'About what?'

He begins to walk away from the others. I follow. 'About Cadet 5-8-5,' he starts. *Oh crap*. 'Your... *Flash*. So named for his speedy retreats, I'd say.' He scoffs and shakes his head. 'Now, from what I saw, and from what I've seen, your friend prefers to stay out of the line of fire and depends on the rest of you to pick up the slack and save his skin.'

'Elder, I-'

He holds up his hand to silence me. I hold my tongue.

'I'm not asking you to betray your friend. I was like you when I was a Cadet. I protected the ones that needed protecting. But there comes a time when we have to start looking after ourselves. You're graduating in a matter of days. So is he. Beyond the wall you have to be capable. And that muppet ain't capable and I'll be damned if I allow him out there with you, only to let you down and get you killed. You all work together very well. You're a fantastic team. But when you're assigned your ranks and when you leave the training behind, you'll be out there for real. You'll all depend on each other to have each other's backs. Yesterday, you, Winder, Tee and Cassius were as one. You and Cassius particularly. You killed what was coming after him, and he killed what was coming after you. It was like a ballet.'

'A what?'

He waves his hand dismissively. 'If you were with a cadet like Flash, he would not have protected you. You know that, don't you?' He waits for me to argue. But I don't. He's right. 'Now, I think he should be reassigned-'

'I disagree, Elder,' I say firmly, folding my arms across my chest as I stop walking. He stops with me and looks curious. 'I believe he would serve better being awarded a Green Coat.'

His eyes widen in surprise before he laughs in my face.

'The Green Coat is given to archers.'

'He can use a bow. Tee taught him.'

'He can *barely* use a bow. Tee's a great teacher... she ain't a miracle worker,' he says, mimicking me and crossing his arms while smirking.

'He's a good fighter. You've seen him in controlled circumstances. On paper, he passes every test. But when he's out there... he's afraid. That's not his fault.'

'And you ain't scared when you're out there?'

'Are you?'

He laughs a jolly laugh as he whacks my arm.

'Flash would love being a Green Coat, Elder. He would be thrilled,' I tell him.

'I couldn't give a hairy, stinkin' turd what he wants or what would make him happy, Kiddo,' he scoffs as he starts walking away. 'My priority is the unit's survival. I'm reassigning him.'

'Do it for me?' I call after him. He stops and turns back to face me. 'He'll die if you reassign him. Without us looking after him... he won't last a day out beyond the wall. Or he'll get one of us killed.' He watches me closely as I hold my nerve. 'Please, Sir. I'm asking as my personal favour.'

'Your personal favour... hmm? You know you only get one from me. Sure you wanna use it for him?'

'Please, Elder. I don't want my friend to die. Please give him a Green Coat.'

'And what about you?' he asks, still not convinced. 'Still want that Red Coat?'

'Of course.'

'Course you do,' he says proudly, his chest puffing out a little. 'I expected nothing less, and if it were my decision alone, you'd have it. I understand Cass is hoping for that too. Shame they only award one per graduating class.'

'I'm better than Cass. And if I had a penis between my legs, I'd get it no problem.'

'Part of me wondered if you were gonna accept the Grey Coats offer. I know they spoke to you a few years back and you said no. But they'd still have you like a shot.'

'And be cooped up in The Haven all day every day? No thanks.'

'What about the Canaries? If you want adventure, that's the place to find it.'

I laugh. Hard. 'I'm restless, Elder. Not suicidal.'

He laughs that deep, throaty laugh again and gives my shoulder a friendly whack making me groan as he jars my ribs.

'Glad to hear it. Now, get to work. I know you love being on clean up duty. And don't worry about Mr Flash. Whatever happens, I'll make sure he doesn't get reassigned.'

'Thank you, sir.' I call after him. 'Thank you so, so much!'

'Waste of your favour if you ask me,' he grumbles. 'Get to work, Kiddo.'

CHAPTER SIX

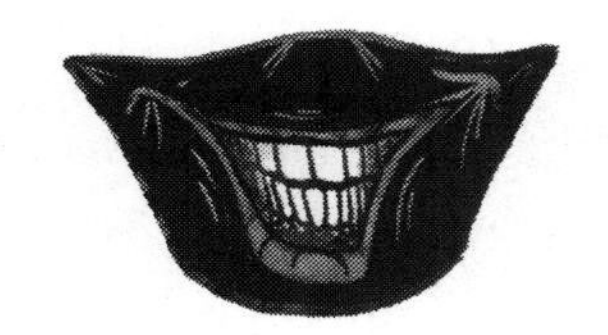

'It's a bit rubbish that when we graduate, we have to move to a new house,' Tee moans as we approach a still writhing Class Three, currently tangled in a spiralling barbed wire trap. I reach back and draw my Katana before driving it through its skull. It falls still and drips coagulated blood on the ground, narrowly missing my shoe. My second katana is on my back. Tee's bow across her chest. Cass has his Haladie daggers in his belt as he pushes the cart we use for shifting the killed targets. And Winder has his axe casually thrown over his shoulder. Our masks hang around our necks, and as ever, we're dressed for battle even though we're on sodding clean up duty. My wrappings are secure, the laces on my Nike kicks tied tightly and my brown coat fits as snug as ever. Not as snug as Cass's rib support though, which is making me sweat like crazy.

'I'm personally looking forward to the move. The Warren has less damp,' Cass replies, lowering the cart and heading over to help Winder untangle various limbs. 'It makes my throat scratchy.'

'The rooms have bars on the windows,' she argues.

'Well, yeah.' He shrugs. 'It was a prison, Tee. But we get our own rooms when we move, and they've made it quite nice. You know... for a prison. Man, this thing's arm is really stuck.'

'Move. I'll hack it off,' I offer. A quick swipe and the body falls free to the floor. Tee grabs its legs as I grab its head, all the while breathing through my mouth. Damn, it stinks. Cass keeps glaring at me as he picks up the severed arm. He definitely has something on his mind.

'Spit it out,' I tell him, hurling the Class Three onto the cart with the other four we've already collected. 'You'll give yourself a nose bleed, else.'

'I bet you didn't say a word to Elder Eight about what Flash did in the assignment. Did you?' he accuses, glancing over his shoulder to Flash and Titan who are out of earshot clearing another trap.

'What I did or didn't say is none of your sodding business,' I reply, as he tosses me the severed arm which I add to the cart of corpses.

'He doesn't deserve to pass,' he states, scooping up other various limbs scattered on the floor by our feet. 'He'll get someone killed out there. The bloody coward. Can you believe, he actually thought he had a chance at being a Grey Coat once upon a time?' He laughs at the idea. To be fair, it's a laughable one. 'You have one hell of a short memory. Or don't you care he almost got you killed-'

'Damn, let it go! If anyone should be pissed about what happened, it's me. Not you. Just get over it.'

'You're so... argh.' He waves his hands dramatically in exasperation, making Tee and I laugh. 'Fine. Whatever. He screws up and gets everyone rallying around him. I stick up for you, and you punch me in the face. How's that fair?' He turns and starts storming off, muttering incoherently as he goes.

'Stop acting like a baby,' I call after him, laughing at his pouting.

'I'm not acting like a baby!' he barks back.

'Yes, you are,' I chuckle.

'No, I'm not!'

I run over and jump on his back. 'Aw, Cass. Don't be pouty.' I ruffle his hair.

'Get off, you silly cow.' But he's smiling and holding me in place.

'Baby wanna bwottle?'

'Shut it.'

'What about a wittle kwiss.' He starts laughing as I kiss his cheek over and over.

'Geroff!'

'Anyway, as I was saying. A frickin prison!' Tee carries on complaining about where we'll be moving on to as she moves onto the next Class Three tangled in the next wire trap.

I look down at Cass, and he looks up at me. Both of us have a smile and he holds my legs a little firmer as I still cling to his back. But then his smile starts to slip.

'Who hit you?' he asks quietly, looking at the small cut on my lip.

'No one that matters,' I reply.

'I think that if he's still walking after laying a hand on you, he might matter just a little bit.' He blinks a couple of times and his playfulness is replaced with a solemnness. 'Do you love him?'

'Who?'

'The man you let get away with hitting you? It's gotta be love if you didn't break his neck.' I slide down his back, and he turns to face me. 'Whoever it was, you tell him that if he ever touches you like that again, I'll kill him.' He kisses my forehead before heading over to help Tee. My skin tingles at the warmth his lips leave on my skin as I watch him go.

Stop it, Scarlett. Stop looking at him like that!

I pull out my binoculars and look over at the next trap.

'Can I borrow your bow?' I ask Tee when I catch up with her. She hands it to me without hesitation as well as her quiver, and takes one of my swords instead.

'I'm gonna talk to Elder Eight later,' Cass says, still not letting it go. 'I won't have Flash put with me out there. I need people I can count on.'

'There's no need to talk to Elder Eight,' I reply, sliding Tee's bow over my head. 'Trust me, Cass. Elder knows what he needs to know, and Flash will get exactly what he deserves after graduation.' I start to head over to the next trap.

'She grassed him up?' Tee gasps.

'Where are you going?' Cass calls after me.

'To the next pit.'

'On your own?'

'Oh will you give it a rest?!'

'I'll go with her,' Winder says, jogging after me.

Together, we make our way across the dry land with the sun beaming down hard on us, past the three-story building that used to be an office block. All that remains are the metal support beams and the stubborn cement still clinging onto the bones of the building. The dry dirt leads us to tarmac as we cross a dual carriageway, weaving between the shells of deserted cars. I peer inside them. But everything's gone. They've been stripped bare. We took it all years ago.

'It was him, wasn't it?' Winder asks, walking beside me. 'Noah hit you. And he was the one that lashed you, wasn't he?'

'Yep.'

'Was I right? About the lottery?'

'Sure was,' I sigh. 'He wants me to put my number in, and he wasn't happy when I said no.'

He looks concerned. And rightly so. Noah can really mess up my life if he wanted to. Or end it. I tell Winder what happened in my room, and how I ended up tied to the pillar. Winder knows all about Noah. I admitted it all after he saw us together on the beach one morning. Obviously, it had to have been the morning we kissed that he chose to follow me out for a run. Noah has no idea he knows. If he did, I dread to think.

'What a dick. A hypocritical dick. I should tear his stomach out through his mouth for touching you like that.'

'Best not,' I laugh. 'Not unless you want to end up dead. It's just so stupid that Noah would think I'd want to get married. We kissed. Twice. In like... two years! He knows how much this life means to me. He's thick if he thinks I would ever give up a lifetime of work to sit at home and pop out kid after kid.'

'He's not thick, Scar. You would be foolish to think Noah's anything less than a very clever and cunning man. With a hell of a lot of power. He's possessive and used to getting his own way. He wants you because he can't have you.'

'And he never will.'

We reach the pit. A ten-foot by ten-foot hole in the ground where we toss a few bloody rags to lure the zombies to fall in. There are two clawing at the sides. One has no nose and no lips. The other is missing its bottom jaw completely. Their grey leathery skin hangs loosely off their bones which stick out. And they absolutely stink.

'What are you gonna do?' he asks. 'About our Lord and Master?'

'I can handle Noah.'

I let loose two arrows and hit the Class Threes right between the eyes.

'How exactly? He can easily force you to marry him, Scar.' Winder jumps in and starts tossing the corpses out. 'You said no, and he lashed you.'

'He lashed me because I hit him. I don't think he's accepted my no just yet.'

'You hit him to get him off you,' he argues. 'No man touches a woman without their permission. That's assault. Sexual assault. And if I'd have been there when he did that, I'd have introduced him to my axe.'

'Winder, please don't get involved. I can handle Noah. I don't want to start worrying about you as well as myself. If he thinks you know about us... If he thinks anyone knows about us... He'll react. Violently. Now. Can we talk about something else?'

'Did you really tell Elder Eight what happened on assignment with Flash?'

'Do you think I would?' I ask, a little offended that he thinks I'd be so heartless. He shrugs. 'Great. Thanks for that.'

'So, did you?'

I reply with the same, irritating shrug which makes him roll his eyes. I reach down so he can take my hand and climb back out. I swear and grab my ribs.

'Oh bugger, I forgot you hurt yourself. You alright?'

'Fine. I forgot too, apparently.' I straighten myself up and look to see where Cass and Tee are with the cart. They're still loading various pieces of the second target in, so we take a seat in the dirt and have a sip of water while we wait. After a cursory glance at the Class Three by my feet, something catches my attention.

'Winder?'

'Yeah?'

I shuffle closer to it. 'Something's off with this Zom.'

He shuffles closer too. It's a man. Well, it was. And he's certainly dead. But it's what he's wearing that's odd.

'He's a policeman.' Winder notices.

I flatten out his shirt.

'A German policeman,' I add, noticing the badge. 'What the hell is a German policeman, still in his uniform, doing in England fifty years after the outbreak?' We look at each other utterly confused. 'We didn't get any refugees from Germany, did we?'

'Not as far as I'm aware. How weird.'

'Are you gonna be much longer?' I call through the bathroom door. 'Tee? What are you doing in there?'

'It's open you know,' she calls back.

I open the door to find her smoothing down her long brown hair in the sad little shard of mirror we have stuck to the wall. She looks more nervous now than she does out there beyond the wall.

'You ready?' I ask. 'Ya know, it doesn't matter what you look like. It's a lottery.'

Looking in the mirror nervously, she shrugs. 'It can't hurt.'

'Are you sure about this? Once your number goes in, that's it. No taking it back.'

'It's the only chance I have of getting out of the army,' she says quietly, still smoothing down her perfect locks.

'Tee, if I asked you not to put your number in, would ya?' I ask apprehensively.

'Why would you even ask me not to when you know it's what I want? When it will save my life?'

'Because...' I sigh and slump back against the wall. I want to tell her the truth. But her knowing will put her in danger. 'I don't want to be without you. I don't want-'

'Well, not everything is about what you want!' she barks angrily. That's very unlike her. 'You know, everything you do, I support. I accept. I never tell you what to do. All your flaws, I embrace.'

'My flaws?'

'Yeah. You're rude and arrogant. You're hostile too.'

'I'm not hostile!' I snap.

'You wound up Winder all morning before the evaluation, telling him he was slow and not as good as you in hand to hand. You goaded him into a bet you knew he wasn't gonna win all because you wanted an edge.'

'What edge?' I laugh angrily, shaking my head.

'You bet his breakfast he wouldn't win and of course he didn't. More food means more energy. And for the final assignment, the more energy, the better. You got two portions and he got a tiny apple. You didn't think that him not eating enough would affect his performance, did you? And what about Flash, huh? Telling Elder Eight what happened. We have a code.'

'Hold on a minute-'

'And now you don't want me to put my number in because you don't want to be left on your own. You're selfish, Scar. Just... selfish.'

I look at her stunned. 'You really think of me like that?'

'You know how scared I am every time I go beyond the wall. You know how much I would rather stay safe, have a family, a husband, some kids. And you know that if you seriously asked me, right here, right now, not to put my number in, I wouldn't. Even though it would make me sad and resentful towards you. I wouldn't. I would live a life of fear and pain and die in the dirt because I love you and I would do anything to make you happy.'

'Tee, I-'

'And!' she snaps, cutting me off. 'Do you know that you have not once, *not once* told me you loved me? You call me your sister. You say you'd do anything for me. But you have never said that you actually love me.' She folds her arms and glares at me as I stand completely shocked and speechless at her uncharacteristic outburst. She's just scared. I know that. I'll let her vent even if it hurts my feelings, I'll take it. 'I love you, Scarlett. Say it back.' She watches me with expectant and angry eyes. 'Well? Say it!' The silence in the room is deafening.

'You know I can't say that back. You shouldn't even say it.'

'Oh what... because of the cadet curse?' she scoffs. 'That's such a cop out. Like telling someone you love them will actually curse them and they'll die. You're just scared. Say it.' She waits. But I refuse to say it. I can't. Everyone knows what happens if those words are said. Call it superstition. But I ain't risking it. Finally, she scoffs and shakes her head. 'Ask me then. Ask me not to put my number in.'

'Tee,' I hold out my hand. 'Can I come with you to enter your number?' I ask.

She sighs and nods. Clearly, she needed that. I head over and give her a hug.

'Sorry, Scar,' she whispers. 'I didn't mean that.'

'Forget it. Come on.'

'I really didn't mean it.'

'I know,' I lie. 'C'mon.'

'You still thinking about that Class Three in the German uniform?' she asks as we leave our room, keen to change the subject. And I'm keen to move on too. Her words cut far too deep.

'A bit,' I admit. 'Just seemed odd is all. How did a German zom get all the way over here?' I ask for the hundredth time. 'He was still in uniform!'

'Don't call them that, Scar. It's really disrespectful.'

'Sorry. Target. How did a German target get here?'

'He was wearing his uniform when he came over from Germany before the outbreak, obviously,' she says. 'Stop worrying about some random Class Three.' Her anxious expression has sod all to do with the policeman from Germany.

'You're right.' I reply with a forced smile, clasping her hand tightly as we walk through the halls. 'It's probably nothing. This is much more important. Are you excited?'

'I think I'm gonna pee a little.'

'Don't do that. No one wants to marry a girl that smells of wee.'

At the bottom of the main staircase, we find Winder and Cass chatting together and waiting for us.

'You sure about this?' Winder asks Tee as we join them. She just looks at him with wide eyes. All it would take would be for him to say, *"No, Tee. Don't do it."*. And she wouldn't. And there wouldn't be any of the anger she just threw my way either.

But he won't. And neither will I.

Again.

'Oh no. She ain't blinking,' Winder says. 'That's never a good sign.'

'She's fine,' I tell him. 'And she's sure. Come on.'

We all head to the open double doors which leads to the main hall. It's a massive room with a high, arched ceiling and the remnants of a beautiful painting of a night sky still visible above us. The three chandeliers were removed shortly after the Cadets went squish beneath the one in the lobby. There are four ornate fireplaces in here. In the winter, they light them all. More often than not, we all gather in here for warmth and sleep on the floor together. The winters are as brutal as the summers. Snow falls thick and fast. We collect wood all year round getting ready for it. We never cut down trees, so we only burn what we find. Which is what salvage duty is mainly for. The room is filled with odd-shaped tables with mismatched chairs and stools. At the far end of the room is a long table where all the Elders sit. But now they're all standing to the sides in deep conversation. As well as a fair amount of Grey Coats.

The sound of girls chatting excitedly and giggling incessantly is unbearable. It's my idea of hell in here. Give me the groan of a zom or the sound of my steel striking flesh over this girly crap any day. Tee's hand, which is currently squeezing the life out of mine, gets even tighter.

'Are you sure you won't do it with me?'

'Positive. C'mon.'

She glances up at me.

'Scar, being out there frightens me so much. If I ever screwed up and one of you got hurt because of my weakness, I would never forgive myself.'

'Is that why you're doing this?' I turn and face her. 'To try and protect us? Because if it is, then you're making a mistake. You have never let your fear overwhelm you. Not once! I trust you completely, Tee. We all do.'

She reaches out and rests her palm on my shoulder.

'The scar I left right here proves you wrong. I could have killed you.' She pales as she recalls the day she accidentally shot me and her head shakes swiftly from side to side as she decides, with impunity, that she will never let that happen again. 'I'm putting my number in. It's best for everyone. C'mon.'

Her legs looking a little stiff as she walks and together, we take our place in the crowd as Elder One, the head honcho of the Elders, stands at a small podium. He makes all the final decisions on what coats we end up with. He chooses who does what and when. Where Noah rules the rest of us, Elder One rules the Elders. He has short grey hair. His face is clean shaven, and he looks beyond stern. He *is* beyond stern. When I was ten, he and a grey coat caught me taking the lords name in vain. Rather than a lashing, he made me run ten miles in the middle of winter. My little legs nearly fell off. Wouldn't have been so bad if the ground hadn't have been so damn icy. I slipped and slid all over the place. Spent more time on my backside than actually running. Took hours to finish.

Utter bastard.

Think I would have preferred the lashings. But Elders don't lash. They may pass on your crime to the Grey Coats if they see fit. But normally they deal with it themselves. It's when the Grey Coats interfere you worry. My back aches just thinking about it.

Elder One clears his throat and welcomes us all in his holier than thou tone. Telling us all of the honour and responsibility that awaits the lucky lady who wins the lottery. He goes on and on about, well... Noah. And how great he is. How wonderful. And how the chosen girl will be the vessel for the next "*heavenly representative*".

Snore.

He says all the right things. But I see the slight roll of his eyes. I sense the edge to his tone.

He thinks it's all as crap as the rest of us. But like the rest of us, he plays along. For the greater good.

Elder Six, a young man compared to the others and relatively new to his position, wheels out a large sealed box with a slit in its lid before returning to the side. He took over from a man we called Turkey. He didn't have a chin.

Odd man. He died last year beyond the wall. He was a good guy. Bit strange towards the end. I think a person can only see so many deaths before they start to lose grip on reality. And Turkey certainly lost his. He started to think that The Grey Coats were infected. Got him in a fair bit of trouble. But everyone knew he was bonkers. One day, he led a team to clear out traps, and jumped in one.

Not a good way to go.

'This is where you will put your number in,' Elder One explains to the giggling masses. 'You may only enter your number once. When you have done so, you must inform your Elder. We don't want anyone being volunteered unknowingly. We will be checking each slip put in. If you put your number in more than once, you will be disqualified. If you put your number in and do not tell your Elder, you will be disqualified. Tomorrow night we will have an assembly which you must all attend, even if you are not graduating. In this assembly, I will clarify the different roles available to you in the Army, and you do get a say to some degree in which role you would prefer. As you know, yesterday the final unit of the year completed their final assignment. There are a total of thirty-six graduates this year.' There's a round of applause. 'As well as discussing the roles available, we will also be welcoming Lord Sands and his entourage to our home. We'll be disclosing ranks the following day for the graduates and the lottery winner will be announced the next morning.' He opens his arms wide. 'Have at it, ladies. And good luck.'

The high-pitched screeches of these girls are like nails on a chalkboard. Despite that, I take Tee's hand and head towards the crowd surrounding the box. As we walk, and as they see me, they all part and let us pass. Right up to the box itself. We stand there, the room a little too quiet as the girls wait patiently for us to do what we need to do.

The paper in Tee's hand is neatly folded. Her number is written in perfect handwriting.

'I'm putting my number in.' She looks from the box to me, as if seeking my blessing. I smile reassuringly, giving it to her. She leans over, rests her paper above the slot, and with a deep intake of breath, she drops it in.

I mean, what are the chances she'll win anyway?

The sun is just about to disappear, and there's a pleasant breeze gently blowing as I sit beneath the trees. It's a scary time. Graduation. It's a big and sudden change after everything being the same for my entire life. I'm feeling very overwhelmed.

'Mind if I sit?'

I turn and see a *Mr Grey* behind me. I can't see his face, but the voice definitely belongs to Noah. He lowers his hood and sits opposite me right here on the ground. After a cursory glance, I know we're alone. Not even his Grey Coats are nearby.

'What can I help you with, Lord Sands?' I ask.

'Wow,' he laughs. 'That's a cold reception. Are you mad at me?'

I busy myself with a leaf and spend far too much time folding it unnecessarily again and again.

'I'll take that as a yes,' he sighs, before snatching the leaf from my hand and tossing it on the ground. 'Yesterday got out of hand and I overreacted. I made sure I didn't hurt you too much but you needed to be punished. You can't behave that way. Not with me. Hey. Look at me,' he orders. I do. Reluctantly. He sighs again, a deep and very fake sigh. 'I'm going to ask you one more time. Put your number in the lottery.'

'I can't do that,' I reply.

'You can,' he says plainly.

'I don't want to then.'

'You think you know what's best. But you don't. I do. I insist-'

'Please don't make me, Noah,' I ask desperately. 'I'm begging you. I'll do anything. Please don't force me to do this.' I hate myself for begging. But I genuinely have no other choice. 'If you make me do this, I will never forgive you. You'll have a wife that resents you. That will hate you. Is that really what you want?' With a deep breath, I compose myself quickly and sit a little straighter. But he saw my brief moment of weakness and looks a little sad himself. He rests his hand on my cheek.

'I'm also sorry that I hit you yesterday,' he says, his thumb tracing the split on my lip that still stings. 'You upset me, and I reacted badly. I promise you, it will never happen again.'

'I appreciate that. And I'm sorry I hit you too.'

'Apology accepted. So, you don't want to get married. Tell me what you do want,' he says. 'Tell me exactly what you want for yourself and your friends, Cadet. And maybe I can make it so the woman I love can be happy.'

I rest my hand on his, glad that the old Noah, the kind Noah, has come back. 'I want to be a Red Coat,' I tell him. He nods knowingly. It's of no surprise to him whatsoever. It's all I've wanted for years.

'What about your friends?'

'I want Winder, Titan and Cass to get Black Coats. I want us to stay together as a unit. And I want Tee and Flash to get a Green Coat.'

'I heard Tee put her number in tonight. Don't you want her to win my lottery?' I remain silent and try not to give anything about how I feel away. 'I get it. I wouldn't want to watch my best friend with someone I care for either.' That's not it at all. I don't want her with a bastard like him. Not now I've seen that nasty streak. But I keep my mouth shut. 'So you want the Red Coat. Your friends by your side. And you'd rather see Tee stay in the army than have the chance to leave it because you don't want her to be with me. That is incredibly selfish. Poor Tee,' he tells me, his eyebrows raised. There's that word again. Selfish. 'Cassius wants a Red Coat too, right? But you said you want him to have Black. Very, very selfish.'

'It's not like that.' I try to defend myself, but he tuts and wraps his arm around my shoulders.

'Aw, my poor girl,' he coos, guiding me to his chest. 'This is such a hard time for you. So many choices and changes. Such threats of loss that only a warrior could ever experience.' He kisses the top of my head and rests his chin there. 'My dear sweet Cadet. You can have your Red Coat. I can ensure it. If you are certain that that's what you want.'

'You can?' I gasp, sitting up, completely taken aback.

'Of course. I love you. I want you to be happy. So, I can get you your Red Coat if that's what you really want.'

'It is! Oh, Noah... it really is!'

'But there would be conditions,' he adds.

'W-what conditions?' I ask, apprehension clear in my words.

'In exchange for your coat, I will place Flash, Titan, Tee, Winder and Cassius...' he strokes my cheek. 'In the Canaries.' He watches me as I slowly sit back, freeing myself from his gentle embrace.

'But... that would mean-'

'They would live out beyond the wall for months at a time. You would hardly see them. And as you know, the survival rate for a Canary is... bleak... at best. But you would be happy, right? With your Red Coat? Seems appropriate. What with you being a selfish bitch and all.' He watches me closely, waiting for a reaction but I'm stuck in stunned silence. 'Or...'

'Or I put my number in. Right?'

He nods. 'Be my wife. Cassius will become a Red Coat. Winder and Titan will become Black Coats. Flash can be a Green Coat and spend his days safely on the wall. And Tee will become a Grey Coat. I can have her positioned at my house. She'll never see a battle or bloodshed. She'll never have to leave The Haven. She can live in our mansion with us by the sea. You'll see Tee every day, and she'll be as safe as can be. What do you say?'

'Canaries are volunteers or criminals sentenced to time beyond the wall. My friends have done nothing wrong to warrant a conviction. And they won't volunteer for that. Everyone knows it's suicide out there.'

'I'll get them in the Canaries, Cadet. Accept my proposal, or they'll die. Mark my words.'

'Why are you doing this to me?'

'Because I love you.' He gets to his feet and looks down at me still on the floor. 'I have the power to make you and your friend's existence an enjoyable one. Or... I can make them miserable.' He pulls his hood up. 'I can make them dead. Your choice.'

'Noah.' I stand and feel my anger bubbling in my chest as he threatens my family and me. Although I can't see his face, I know he's smirking. 'If you do this, you realise that you will be forcing me to be physical with you against my will.'

'What are you on about?'

'Everyone knows what's expected of your new, young wife. In Elder One's own words, the lucky girl will be the vessel of the next holy representative.'

'Cadet... what-'

'Kids! Noah. Which means sex. If you force my hand, then the only reason I'll be sleeping with you is that you threatened to effectively kill my friends if I didn't. You know what that's called, right?'

'You're so dramatic,' he laughs.

'It's rape, Noah. You'd be raping me,' I bark in a desperate attempt to stop this from happening.

He stalks towards me, clearly enraged. Undoubtedly enraged when he grabs me by my throat and gives me a shake.

'You ever, EVER say that to me again,' he pulls down his hood and shoves his face into mine. 'You even think it... I'll have you lashed for impure and slanderous lies. You hear me?'

'You're not the man I thought you were, Noah. You're not a good man at all.'

He lets me go with a shove. 'I have always been a good man to you! I am no rapist, Scarlett. Contrary to popular belief, my life's mission is not to fornicate and breed. I have great plans for this town and the people within it. And you are the only one who can do the job that being my wife will require.'

'What do you mean by that?' I ask uneasily.

'I'll expect to hear that you have submitted your number by mid-day tomorrow.' He gives me an arrogant, lazy kind of shrug that sits well with his cocky, self-righteous half grin. 'If I haven't, well, you know what will happen. Have a lovely night, Cadet.'

He pulls up his hood and leaves me filled with a new-found hatred, showing me the winged V on his back as he saunters away.

He really has no idea who I am. He thinks he knows what I'll do.

But he's right about one thing. I am a selfish bitch.

No one... I mean *no one* will stop me doing what I was born to do.

I was born to fight. And I *will* fight.

He thinks he knows me. He thinks I'll marry him in order to save them all.

Well, he can think again.

CHAPTER SEVEN

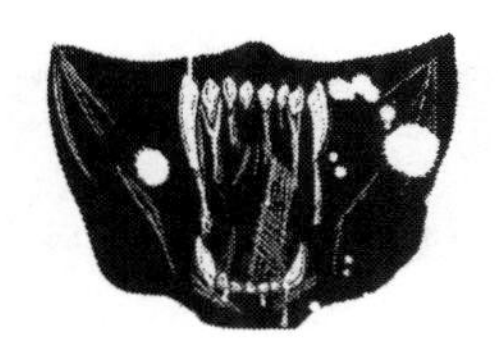

Deep in the woods, between Elder HQ and The Academy, set off the Soldiers Road by about half a mile, is a small cottage.

My favourite cottage.

Elder Eight's cottage.

No one else lives nearby so it's as quiet and peaceful as could be. He always says that after spending all day teaching a bunch of army brats, he likes the quiet. It's not what you'd expect a man like him to live in at all. But he inherited it from the man who was Elder Eight before him. And so on. And so on.

Personally, I like it. It's a three bedroom, two-story stone cottage with a slate roof and two chimney breasts. It has a little wooden porch out front with a wooden stoop and next to the white door is a rocking chair. As I head up the steps, the wood beneath my feet creaks and groans. I don't knock. I never knock. If he's up for company, he'll come out. If not, he'll tell me to sod off through the door. I sit on the steps and rest my shoulder against the wooden bannister with a sigh. Sure enough, the front door opens and he takes a seat next to me. Without saying a word, he hands me a glass filled with amber liquid. Alcohol is strictly forbidden, but Elder Eight has spent so much time working beyond the wall with his Cadets, he knows where to find the stuff and how to keep it hidden. Before he was an Elder, he was a volunteer Canary. Worked out beyond the wall on and off for five years. Then he was handed the Elder title and took over training instead. He's actually eligible for retirement. But he says he's not ready. He told me once that he'll stop fighting the fight when he's dead. And not a second sooner.

'Do you know how many Cadets I have pestering me to be put in a unit with you?' he asks.

I shrug, completely disinterested.

'Well it's a lot. They don't even care if you get the Red Coat. They want to work with you no matter what.'

'Humph.'

'You here for another book?' he asks. 'I have a great one for ya. If you fancy talking rabbits and insane men wearing stupid hats.'

'Maybe another time,' I tell him, downing the whisky.

'Wanna talk about whatever's goin' on in that noggin of yours?' he asks, downing his own drink. I shake my head and shift, resting my head on his shoulder. He wraps his arm around me and gives me a little hug.

The man taught me to read. Right here on this porch. Three nights a week, every week, for two years. He'd sit in that chair and teach me. He called it an investment. Can't have a Red Coat that can't read.

'You don't need to sit with me,' I tell him. 'I'm happy enough alone.'

'You say that. But if you meant it, you'd be with that little apple tree instead of here drinking my whiskey. Or running yourself ragged along the wall.' He taps my temple with his finger. 'Is it getting a bit loud in that old head of yours again?'

'A bit. Yeah,' I reply, looking into my glass. 'Just a lot happening. It's a bit overwhelming.'

'You don't get overwhelmed,' he says. 'Not unless that...' He taps his own head. 'And that...' He rests his hand over his heart. 'Starts to disagree. You sure you don't wanna talk about it?'

I shake my head.

'Are you in trouble?'

I give a deep sigh and settle further into his shoulder. 'I just need a safe, quiet place for a little while. And here with you on this porch is the safest place I know. Is that okay?'

'Course. My porch and my whiskey are always here when you need it, Kiddo.'

'And you, right?'

'Course,' he exhales. 'I'll sit with ya until it all quietens down a little in there and you feel ready to face whatever it is again.'

'You might be here a while in that case.'

'I have nowhere else better to be.'

'Thanks, Elder.'

'It's my pleasure.'

We sit on his porch in utter silence. And it's not uncomfortable. It's not forced.

It's home.

Has been my whole life.

It's almost midnight when I head back to the Academy. But not to my room. I go to Cass and Winder's instead. The door's slightly ajar and the last of a candle is about to burn out. As I expected, Tee is half hanging out of Winders bed fast asleep as he snores away next to her. When I'm not with her, she can't fall asleep. Winder's the next best thing, so she says. More often than not I find her in here when I'm late. Winder's hand is close to hers. Almost touching.

I'm about to leave, now that I've seen she's okay I'll head back to my room and get some sleep. But Cass pulls back his blanket and taps the empty space next to him. I linger in the door fiddling with the hem of my top.

'Scarlett... come to bed,' he whispers.

I go and slide in beside him and he sleepily puts his blanket over me.

'You alright?' he asks quietly.

'Yeah,' I whisper. 'Fine.'

'Where'd you go?'

'For a walk.'

'Did he hit you again?'

'There is no *he*, Cass. I told you. I went for a walk is all.'

He rolls onto his back and exhales deeply as he looks up at the ceiling. 'I wish you'd stop lying to me. Knowing you don't trust me hurts my goddamn feelings.'

I sit and swing my legs over the side of his bed. He sits beside me in nothing but his boxer shorts. When I go to leave, he takes my hand, keeping me sat beside him.

'What's wrong, Scarlett?'

'Nothing.'

'Please, just tell me what's going on.'

'Do you remember the night we snuck over the wall and went to the pier together a few years back?' I ask. He nods and looks at his hands, not wanting to meet my gaze. 'Can I ask you something about that night?'

'Do you have to?' he asks uncomfortably.

'Did you turn me down because I'm not a good person?'

'What? No!' he replies adamantly, careful to keep his voice low so he doesn't wake the others.

'So you just, aren't attracted to me then?'

'It's not like that.'

'Is it cos I'm selfish?' I ask.

'He called you that, did he? Your secret fella who likes to hit you?'

'Tee. Tee called me hostile, arrogant and selfish.'

He guides my face to his. Goosebumps erupt all over me as they always do with him. 'You are the best person I know,' he says with complete conviction. 'The absolute best!'

I lean in and kiss his lips thinking that right now, I have nothing to lose in trying once more to kiss him. But he dodges me.

I'm clearly not the best person he knows then. Or I would be good enough for him to kiss back.

'Sorry. I shouldn't have... Night, Cassius.'

I get to my feet and leave. And he lets me go without a word.

Well, that's definitely made up my mind.

Tomorrow, I'm requesting my coat and leaving them all behind me.

I'm better off alone anyways.

'QUIET!' Elder One hollers, raising his hands in the air. The packed-out hall falls silent. I lean against the wall with my arms folded across my chest, resenting the fact that I'm forced to be here. I know exactly what coats my family and I will be getting so this is all a waste of time. Down the very front, gathered in a protective huddle are a dozen *Mr Greys*. In the middle, the top of Noah's head is visible. He's not hiding today. He looks back briefly and his eyes land on me straight away. And he finds my hate-filled stare amusing.

'Now, before we get started, we have a guest with us today. Our Lord and Commander, Noah Sands.' Elder One gestures to Noah and the hall breaks out in enthusiastic applause. He heads up and stands before us all. He smiles so charmingly as he looks at all the faces watching him. The girls all whisper and giggle like infatuated children. Even Tee grabs my hand and squeals. I glare at him when he makes eye contact with me, lingering at the back. He starts to talk. But I can't hear him over the anger-filled blood pumping through my entire body. He's such a smooth talker. Only now does it piss me off. But he won't be that way for long. I laugh to myself at the idea of his face when he realises he hasn't got what he wants.

Despite his threats.

'Ow, Scar!' Tee hisses, snatching her hand away from my grip. 'I need that to shoot with!' She rubs her hand and returns her attention to Noah.

Someone whacks my arm. A young cadet I don't really know gestures to the door where Cass is trying to get my attention. He motions for me to come see him. But I'm even less motivated to see him than Noah. I look back to the front of the hall and again, I'm tapped by the young Cadet. With a shove, I send him flying on his arse, knocking a few other cadets off balance as he falls. A few people look at us. None more than Elder Eight who slightly shakes his head in warning. Noah continues to talk. I continue to ignore Cass, and now the others have all shuffled away from me in case I go for them next. Even though the room's crowded to capacity I have a good meter of empty space around me now.

A balled-up piece of paper smacks me in the side of my face.

Slowly, I turn my head and see Cass beckoning me over as Winder scrunches up another sheet ready for launch. I weave between the crowd leaving Tee watching Noah like a love-struck fool.

'What?!' I whisper angrily when I reach him.

'We've got the afternoon off,' Cass says quietly, grinning like a mad man. I see the excitement in his eyes and the hope that I'll let what happened between us yesterday go. 'Me, you, Winder and Tee. After this, we're free as a bird. You know what that means?' He raises his eyebrows suggestively, and I can't help but let my anger at him ease. After all, I can't get mad at him for not wanting to kiss me. Considering my dilemma with Noah, would be a tad hypocritical. Plus, we're not gonna be hanging out much in the future. Might as well enjoy the time we have left together.

'We'll make our declarations and go,' I whisper. 'I'm gonna beat you this time,' I tell Winder.

'In your dreams, loser,' he laughs.

We all turn back to Noah's speech. Noah notices Cass standing beside me. That wipes his smirk clear off his face and he continues his talk a bit colder than previously. Once finished, Elder One retakes the stand.

'You all need to find your Elder. You will sit down with him in private and discuss your preferred coat. Now, bear in mind that a lot of you will have no choice in what you receive. But some, those who have excelled, may request a preference. There are thirty-six of you joining the army this summer. And there are four positions to be issued. The Red Coat.' The crowd breaks into fierce whispering and my heart hammers at the words. 'There is only one Red Coat to be awarded. And they will be in charge of the units as a whole. By wearing the coat, they will stand out as the best of the best. The exceptional. It is the highest honour any of you could ever hope to achieve.'

Cass gives me a playful nudge.

'The real question for you all is where do you want to fight. Behind the wall? Protecting our borders and our people from the inside? If so, and if you are an archer, request a Green Coat. Or do you want to fight out there?' He points to the window. 'Do you want to chase the enemy rather than wait for it to come to you? Because if you do, request a Black Coat.' He scans the crowd for effect. He makes no attempt at all to hide the fact that he believes, like me, that we should all be out there taking back out country. But the wall and the people do need protecting.

Someone's gotta do it. I know a lot of Green Coats. I think they're all brave and fantastic people.

'And, let's not forget the Canaries.' The room falls absolutely silent. There's a heavy tension as he brings up the unit no one likes to talk about.

'Now, I know that there is a big taboo around this unit. But we do still open it up for volunteers. So, if you want to join them... tell your Elder.'

'I thought the Canaries is where they put the undesirables?' Winder ponders.

'It is. But you can volunteer too,' Cass says, whispering so as not to interrupt Elder One who is still talking about things to consider when making our choice.

Choice. Ha! As if we have any choice.

'It's where they send the *"criminals"*.' Cass explains. 'You know, the soldiers who have sex out of wedlock. Or commit a crime like stealing or blasphemy. They usually get a sentence. Like three months beyond the wall or a year. Depending on what they've done. No one sane volunteers. It's suicide.'

Elder One finishes his talk with a simple statement.

'Tomorrow, you will be awarded your ranks. Once your ranks have been issued, there is no turning back. No backing out. If you do, it's desertion. And you know the consequence for desertion.'

'Yeah. Death,' Cass mumbles to himself.

We're told to go queue up outside our Elder's office. Winder goes in first. Followed swiftly by Cass. Neither takes long. They both know what they want.

I'm next.

I go in.

Elder Eight is sat in a small room behind a simple wooden desk. There's a single chair opposite and a pile of papers to his left. I assume it's the cadet's preferences.

When the door closes, I head over and sit. 'The coats are awarded before the lottery, right?' I ask him in a rush.

'Yes,' he replies suspiciously. 'Why?'

'So the ranks we all get will be guaranteed no matter what? No one can take them away or change them. Right?'

'Once they've been issued... they can't be changed,' he confirms. 'Whatever you or your friends are issued with tomorrow, that's it.' He holds out his hand for my paper. But I keep hold of it. 'You're starting to worry me, Kiddo. What's goin' on?'

'It's a bit of a long and... sensitive story.'

'Good job I ain't got anywhere else to be then. Isn't it?' He drags around his chair and places it opposite mine. 'Start talking,' he orders.

'First, I need you to promise that you will do something for me.'

'Well, that depends on what it is.'

'I need you to get Tee's number taken out of the lottery.'

His brow furrows even further.

'Why exactly?'

'If I tell you, it will put your life in danger, Elder. I will tell you if you need me to. But please keep what I tell you to yourself. If he finds out you know, he'll kill you.'

'Who?' His arms fold across his chest and he nods for me to continue as I hesitate.

'It's Noah Sands. We can't let her anywhere near him. She will be much safer on the wall as a Green Coat. Trust me.' I shudder at the idea of him hurting her and manipulating her as he has tried to do with me. 'And you better take this.' I hand him the piece of paper with the coat I'm requesting. He reads it, and slowly, his eyes drift up to me.

'Explain. Now.'

I do. I explain exactly what my actions will mean for the others and I confess everything that has happened between me and Noah Sands. All of it. Including his warnings that he would silence anyone that finds out about us.

He is not happy.

Not happy at all.

Outside, enjoying our afternoon off, all four of us race our horses along the beach, their feet splash in the waves as they go. Tee's up front, followed by Cass. Winder and I bring up the rear, running neck in neck.

'Come on, slowpokes!' Tee shouts back, laughing as she gains another foot in the lead. 'You know what the loser gets!'

'That's you, Scar!' Winder says, giving his horse another nudge to pick up the pace.

'Not this time,' I reply. 'Come on, Hanzo!' Hanzo kicks it up a notch.

Cass gives a loud, hearty laugh as I appear by his side.

'Go on, girl!' he bellows.

The horses enjoy the sprint as much as we do. Usually, we trot in a bid to conserve both our energies. But we're not on duty. Not this afternoon. I mean, we're still fully armed and dressed in our leathers and masks. But we're not looking for a fight. We're looking for fun. And when Tee reaches the Cessna 172 light aircraft that's half buried in the sand and partly submerged by the waves, she jumps off and faces us with her arms in the air.

'WINNER!' she cheers. 'Suck it... bitches! HA!' She claps her hands together and starts wiggling her arse in her usual victory dance as Cass reaches her laughing. I finally get there and turn to face Winder who's pouting as he joins us last.

'Aww. Did I beat you?' I mock, sticking out my lower lip and trying not to grin. Too much. 'Looks like you're the loser this time, Winder.'

'Shut up,' he grumbles as we jump down. He takes Hanzo for me as I join Tee in her victory wiggles before taking her hand and heading to the pier just behind the wreckage.

It's barely standing. But it's secure enough. It's a raised structure that extends out into the ocean a good thousand metres. But of course, half of it has fallen into the sea now. Most of the well-spaced pillars have rusted and crumbled into the water, taking the ornate cast-iron railings and wooden planks with them. It's spent the last fifty years being battered by extreme weather and received no care or attention whatsoever. But that's the veranda. The part we're interested in... is the amusements. That part of the building is over the beach. Not the water. So it's relatively safe to be in.

Relatively.

We climb the steps and open the heavy, arched doors to the lobby. The horses come in with us. Tee stays with them in the entrance as the boys and I head inside to check we're alone. We always lock this place up when we leave. We don't want it to get overrun with zoms. It would suck having to clean it all out again. My fingers slide in through the knuckle duster on my right-handed katana before I unsheathe it. Then, we sneak inside. The floor is a mix of yellow and blue chequers, red and white stripes, and pink and orange stars. When we first found this place all those years ago it was filled with targets that had been locked inside for decades. We had to clear it out.

Not a pleasant afternoon.

But once we did, we'd never seen anything like it. It was called an arcade. Kids used to come here and play games. They'd put money into slots and try to win toys. Or put pennies in the top in the hope that more pennies would fall out the bottom. Must have been nice. A bit different than spending your youth learning beheading techniques.

We all split up. Cass to the right. Winder to the left. And me straight through the middle. Our standard battle formation. We head past the two-player shooter. Past the whack-a-mole. Past the dance mats, fruit machines and teddy bear grabbers. All are covered in a thick layer of dust and grime. Some with dried blood.

After a few minutes, Cass calls out, 'Clear!'

'Clear,' Winder replies.

'Clear,' I agree, replacing my katana. 'Tee, you can come in.'

With the horses locked up safely in the entrance lobby, the others gather in the far corner. I slide over a service counter to the stock room, scoop up four cans of soda and pull out a sealed jar of peanut butter before heading back to the others. It's amazing this stuff is still okay to eat and drink.

Winder's already lying on his belly down the end of the bowling alley standing the pins. The single lane tucked away to the side is the cleanest and most cared for thing beyond the wall. We don't get to come here very often. Five times a year perhaps. But we've done the same thing on our afternoons off since we found this place six years ago.

Cass inspects the petrol generator we put here last year.

'It's almost out. I think this will be the last time we can use it,' he says sadly. That fits well, I think to myself. This may be the last time we all get to come here together anyway. Not that they know that of course. The image of Elder Eight losing his mind after I told him my situation sends a chill down my spine. He was so cross with me about Noah, and livid about his ultimatum. And he didn't hold back on how awful and cruel he thought my chosen path was.

But sometimes you have to do what's best for you and not everyone else. I look at them all and know that they'll be fine. They'll have each other.

'I vote we use it for Dance Revs,' Tee says enthusiastically, returning my thoughts back to our last afternoon together.

'Agreed,' I say, handing her one of the cans of soda. Winder grabs a rag and broom. He lost the race, so he has to prep the lane.

Them's the rules.

I hand him and Cass a can of soda each. We gather in a circle, open them up and raise them high.

'To surviving long enough to bowl another game,' Winder toasts.

'To surviving long enough to graduate,' Cass says.

'To refined sugar and E numbers that mean we can still eat and drink this stuff fifty years later!' Tee chuckles.

They all look at me, waiting for my toast.

'To us.'

'To us,' they all cheer, clinking my tin.

'Right!' Cass says, wiping his mouth and taking hold of his bowling ball. 'Let's bowl.'

We spend a fair few hours here. The horses rest. And we play. We bowl game after game after game. Each one is more competitive than the last. Until we get bored of Cass winning and start making trick shots. We bowl backwards. Being held up by our ankles. Blindfolded. And when we get tired of that, we fire up the generator and connect Dance Revs. There's plenty of abandoned money in here. Thousands of pounds I'd say. Completely useless now. Well, not completely. We put a load of pound coins in and fire up the dancing machine. Tee and I go first. The music kicks in and we stumble over our feet as we try to keep up with the arrows. The loser - that would be Tee - gets hauled off by Winder who attempts to defeat me.

'You ain't gonna win!' I laugh, striking every single pose. 'I'm a swordswoman. Ain't no one can move their feet better than me!'

'C'mon, man!' Cass cheers, clapping his hands to the beat as Tee dances wildly beside him. 'Kick her arse!'

'Not gonna happen!' I chuckle, moving my feet easily.

'Get off,' Cass pulls Winder off and jumps on himself. He starts leaping around, slamming his feet onto the arrows and keeping up a lot better than the others. But he still ain't a patch on me. Winder grabs Tee and starts dancing to the music, hurling her around like a ragdoll as she whoops and roars with laughter. Cass turns and faces me. Still moving his feet but not paying any attention to the game.

'Dance with me.' He takes my hand before I can give it, and we dance our own dance. Jumping around and slamming our feet down. We swap. He takes my place. I take his. He takes away all the awkwardness I felt at his rejection last night. And when he starts singing the song, we all join in.

We have another soda.

We dip our fingers in the peanut butter.

And when the generator gives out, we head to the very back of the Arcade where tucked away, is a crazy golf course. Cass throws his club over his shoulder and tosses a golf ball playfully in the air before catching it.

'Let's golf.'

We play the course. Shooting through a stationary windmill and the open jaws of a plastic shark. Winder kicks his ball in after his thirteenth attempt on a par three, and finally, we watch the golf balls roll between a clown's legs and into a basket with the others we've sent there over the years.

There's a moment of silence as we all stand around them.

Six years of games.

Six years of stolen afternoons where we could actually be what we are. Youngsters that want to have fun. But when we leave here today, we start our careers as full-time soldiers fighting an impossible war. A war that will kill us in the end. We're paving the way for the graduates yet to come. For the boys and girls who haven't been born yet. We've only just started this fight. There are decades of battles and rebuilding ahead. It's like we're all thinking the same thing.

We may never all be here together again.

Winder wraps his arm across Tee's shoulders.

'Come on, Q-Tee. Let's get the horses ready.'

'We'll come,' I tell him, picking up my coat.

Cass wraps his hand around my elbow and stops me. 'Actually, I wanted to talk to you.' He looks at the other two and then back at me. 'In private.'

Oh no.

I nod, despite filling with nerves. 'Course.' I look at the others who linger. 'Um, we'll meet you guys back at home.'

Winder leads Tee away. But not before looking back to his best buddy with a confused expression. He's not the only one. I watch them leave, and we hear the doors close.

'You kissed me,' he says as soon as they shut.

I fill with embarrassment and annoyance in equal measure. I thought he wanted to forget about it. I thought he'd want to pretend it didn't happen. Just like the last time I tried to kiss him.

'Can you look at me, please?' he asks.

'I'd rather not,' I reply. 'I'm sorry I kissed you. I shouldn't have done it and I promise I won't do it again. Okay? Can we just pretend it didn't happen?'

'Why did you kiss me?'

'Because...' I sigh and run my hands through my hair, still unable to turn and face him.

Because I thought I might not get another chance. Because I thought that if you kissed me back, it would stop me doing what I've just done with Elder Eight. And because you're the only person in the whole world I ever want to kiss.

'Because I'm an idiot.' Is my chosen answer. 'I won't do it again. I got it, Cass. You ain't interested. Let's go back home and pretend this never happened. Please?'

I make my way to the door.

'Did you kiss me so I wouldn't request a Red Coat?' he asks. 'So I'd remove myself as your competition?'

I stop and turn.

'Excuse me?'

'Well, did you?'

I storm up to him and before I can think it through, I slam my fist into his jaw. And without a word, I turn and head to the door.

'Do I take that as a no?' he calls after me, rubbing his jaw.

I'm so filled with rage. I'm shaking with it. Why does everyone think of me this way? I'm selfish? I'm hostile? Screw them! I grab one of the small stools placed beside the penny machine and hurl it at his head. He ducks and it crashes into the fruit machine behind him causing several coins to tumble to the floor.

'Because I requested the Red Coat,' he says defiantly. 'You won't manipulate me into giving up on my ambition, Scarlett. Not again!'

'Again?!' I almost screech at him. 'What the hell are you on about? I have never-'

'So, it was just a coincidence then, was it?'

'What?'

'That two years ago, I get asked to join The Grey Coats, which would have meant I would need to leave The Academy and my unit for training. And then that evening, you try to kiss me!'

'You want to join the Grey Coats? Then go and join them!' I yell. 'I couldn't give a crap if you join the sodding Grey Coats! Why the hell would I care?!'

'Because *you* have to be the best!' he argues. 'And of course I don't want to join the Grey Coats. They just hide behind the wall, tormenting everyone and wasting their unbelievable skills. That's not the point, Scarlett. My point is that you always have to be the best. And you can't bear the fact that anyone else might be better than you. Especially your friends!'

'Why would you even think that?'

'Let's look at the facts. Most recently? Winder! You took his breakfast on assignment day! I mean... how selfish can you get?'

'Because breakfast was porridge that day!' I bark. 'When he eats porridge, he gets all sluggish and gets a stitch in his side. Every single bloody time! He might be strong as an ox, but he's as stubborn as a mule and has the digestive system of a new-born baby. He wouldn't listen when I told him not to eat it. So I made a bet I knew I would win and took it from him. I went for a run early that morning specifically to win an apple from Elder Ten so I could give him that instead. Was that selfish? Doing a seven-mile run on my assignment day so my friend won't be hindered on the biggest day of his life?'

'I didn't know-'

'Was I selfish when I stayed up all night with Tee the night before her Archery exam twelve months ago? When she kept missing and lost her confidence? I stood in front of her target and made her shoot. I told her I trusted her completely. I took an arrow in the shoulder and made her shoot again. That girl hasn't missed since! Was that selfish?' I turn but only take a few steps before I spin and carry on yelling at him. 'For the record, I had no idea they approached you two years ago. That is not why I kissed you. And stopping you getting a Red Coat is not why I tried to kiss you last night either.'

'Then why-'

'Because I like you, Cass. Alright!' I bark at him. My face flushes with heat and I know I've gone scarlet as I have so often around him. Hence the name. 'I more than like you, okay? I... I...'

'Do you love me?'

'I don't love anyone. Love is a luxury we can't afford,' I snap, crossing my arms across my waist and looking at the ground. 'But if I did... ya know... ever love a man.' I give a small shrug, my gaze still firmly on the floor. 'It would be you.'

'Scarlett,' he whispers longingly. Painfully.

'But none of that matters because you clearly think very little of me. So forget it. Just,

urgh. It doesn't matter anyway.'

I turn and storm to the door. I've never, ever felt like this before. There's a pain in my chest. In my heart. And it feels like something's trying to crawl up my throat. I need to get out of here. I need to get away from him. I yank open the door.

He reaches over my shoulder and slams it shut from behind me. I spin and shove him away.

'You want to fight me?' I snarl venomously at him as he staggers back. 'Take your best shot. I'll crack open your goddamn skull-'

He moves quick, and before I can finish threatening to kill him, he kisses me. I push him off and touch my lips which are still warm. His chest is rising and falling hard and fast, as is mine.

'What the hell are you doing?' I whisper.

'Something I've wanted to do since we were kids. And I'm sick of pretending otherwise. You confuse the hell out of me, Scarlett. I have no idea why you do half the shit you do. You scare me. You make me nervous and you infuriate me. But I want to spend the rest of my life being confused, scared, nervous and infuriated by your actions and always left in awe of you. Kiss me, Scarlett. Because if you don't, I think I'll go insane. I won't go another day pretending I don't love the bloody bones of you, woman. Kiss me!'

'You... you love me?'

'Of course I love you,' he sighs. 'It's always been you. Always and forever.'

I toss my coat to the floor, and we both collide into each other. Our enthusiasm is matched only by our passion. My arms wrap around his neck as his wrap firmly around my waist, and neither one of us hold back. Our kiss is almost violent. The need we suddenly have for each other is years of yearning reached boiling point, and soon we crash to the floor an entangled mess of limbs, tearing off each other's clothes.

Right now, we're exactly where we're supposed to be. With each other. But tomorrow, everything will change.

And I know that Cass will never forgive me for what I've done.

I wake when the sun rises, still wrapped in Cass's arms on the floor. He pulled his coat over us at some point in the night. As I shift, his hold on me tightens a little as he mumbles my name in his sleep.

What the hell have I done?

I'm filled with such a pang of heavy guilt it's almost crushing me. And what's even worse is that I regret it. I regret sleeping with him. It will only make what's about to happen to them all so much harder.

I take a deep breath and bury my face in my hands. Well, it's done now. Good job, Scarlett. Really well done.

I need to get out of here. I sit up and grab my clothes. My sudden movement has him bolt upright, grabbing one of his haladie daggers and looking for a threat.

'What's wrong?' he asks, scanning the room but finding nothing more than me scooping up my clothes. There's a confused furrow on his brow. 'What's the matter?'

'This shouldn't have happened,' I tell him, pulling on my top and leggings. 'This was a huge mistake.'

'A huge... what?' He jumps up and pulls on his trousers. 'What the hell does that mean?'

I avoid making eye contact as I grab my coat and walk out into the main amusements. The slam of the door hitting the wall tells me he's coming after me.

'I asked you a question! What do you mean, *a huge mistake*?' He runs after me and snatches my coat from my hand.

'Give me my coat,' I demand, spinning round and holding out my hand expectantly.

'Tell me what's wrong and I will,' he says, pulling it out of my reach as I attempt to grab it. 'You don't get to sleep with me and then storm off.'

'*Get* to sleep with you?' I snap. '*Get!* Oh well, thank you for the privilege, Cassius. I'm so honoured.'

'I didn't mean it like that and you know it. We just slept together, Scarlett. We made love-'

'I need to get out of here.' I turn and head to the door. When he grabs my arm, I shove him away from me. He staggers back, looking a mix between furious and really, really hurt.

'What did I do wrong?' he asks. 'Why are you so angry all of a sudden? Are you scared of someone finding out? Because no one will. I swear it.'

'Damn straight they won't,' I reply. 'I'm still furious with you. How could you think those things of me?'

'I... I...'

I roll my eyes and turn. He has no explanation other than that's what he really thinks.

'Later, Cass.' I get to the door and pull it open.

'I'm sorry. I thought the worst of you because I never thought for a second that you would genuinely want me.'

Hanzo lifts his head and gets to his feet when he sees me. Cass is hot on my heels.

'You're ambitious. Beautiful. Kind when you want to be. But you're so distant. The only person you seem to really care about is Tee. Her and the army. And then you try and kiss me, and I can't understand why you would risk your position in the army, risk being sentenced to the Canaries, just to kiss me. Not unless there was a reason.'

I look at him as my hand rests on the door handle. 'There are some things in this world, some people, that are worth losing everything for, Cass. Some are even worth dying for. Just because I can't show how I feel, doesn't mean I'm incapable of feeling it all together.'

'Then how do you feel towards me?' he asks. 'Because, I love you, Scarlett. Do you love me?'

'I don't believe in love, Cass. You know that.'

'Because of the stupid curse?'

'Because we're gonna die and we're gonna die bloody. I can't love *anyone* knowing that. What would be the point?'

'The... the point? The point is to live, Scarlett. To live your life with feeling and passion. For more than just killing dead things. To do more than simply exist every day, just waiting to die.'

'That's all we have, Cass. We won't live to see the world return. We're barely the start of its revival. This is it for us and I for one have accepted that. Love is unnecessary and dangerous.' I swallow hard and lower my gaze. 'And painful.'

'Do you love me?' he pushes. 'Despite the pain?'

'I'd die for you, Cass,' I tell him. 'In this life, the way I am, that's the absolute best offer I can make another person.'

'I don't want you to die for me. I want you to love me the way I love you. Scarlett. I want you to live every single day with me-'

'Well,' I sigh, looking at him one last time. 'I'm afraid it's too late for that.' I walk through the door and let it slam closed behind me. Quickly, I mount Hanzo.

He comes running out the door after me. 'What does that mean?' He grabs Hanzo's reigns and looks up at me. 'Does this have something to do with the guy you've been hanging around with in secret? Because I don't care about that. I don't! We're together now. We can be in the army and together. No one has to know. We can have it all!'

'Bye, Cass.' I lean down and kiss his lips. 'You're gonna make one hell of a Red Coat. I wish I were gonna be around to see it.' I kick Hanzo, and he sets off at a sprint, leaving Cass behind.

'SCARLETT? WHAT DOES THAT MEAN? WHAT THE HELL HAVE YOU DONE? SCARLETT... YOUR COAT!'

Hiding out here in the woodland alone where no one can find me, I take some time just to let myself try and relax. That is until I hear footsteps heading towards me. I jump to my feet and draw my sword.

'Easy, Cadet. It's only me,' Elder Eight says gruffly, trudging closer. 'I suppose I can't call you that anymore. You're a graduate now. Speaking of which, I come bearing gifts.' He holds up a package wrapped in brown cloth and tied together with string.

'How did you know I was out here?' I ask.

'I know more than you think,' he says, handing me the package and plonking himself on the ground. I sit beside him and cross my legs. 'Like the fact that you and your Cassius stayed beyond the wall together all night,' he concludes unexpectedly. I freeze. And he laughs. 'What? You think you're the only Cadets to act on the feelings they have for each other? I'm personally amazed you two waited this long.'

'I'm so sorry. Please don't report us. We didn't mean to. It just sort of-'

'Calm down. Don't give yourself a nose bleed. I know first-hand what living and fighting with someone in close quarters can lead to.'

'Elder...' I gasp, trying not to grin. 'You had a sweetheart?'

'Well.' He shrugs. 'That's not really your concern.' He looks at me and smiles through his thick moustache. 'She was a lot like you. Hard headed. Dedicated. Loyal. A real stunner.'

'What happened?'

'She died,' he says abruptly. 'You know they're all looking for ya, right?'

He moves on so fast, my head is still spinning.

'Did Cass make it back okay?' I ask.

'He did. Which reminds me.' He gives me a hard clip across the top of my head.

'Ow!' I complain, grabbing the spot he hit. 'What was that for?'

'Riding back without your damn coat on! What if you'd come across a target? You could have been bitten.'

'Sorry,' I grumble, rubbing my head. 'What happened today? Did you get Tee's number out of Noah's lottery?'

'Of course I did. We can't let her end up in his hands. I didn't report to Elder One that she even entered her number so if she is chosen, it won't be valid.'

'Well, that's a relief.'

'Tee and the others may be sorted, but you're still in a pickle. After Cassius knew you'd made it back inside the wall safely, he went looking for ya. When he couldn't find ya, he came and saw me.'

'And?' I ask nervously. 'What did you tell him?'

'I congratulated him on becoming the Red Coat,' he says.

I look at him and smile fondly. 'You accepted my request?'

'Of course I did, Kiddo,' he sighs. 'What other choice did I have? You would never request that Red Coat knowing what would happen to the others, and I won't allow you to be forced into marrying a man you don't want to marry.'

'Thank you,' I tell him with the deepest sincerity. I reach out and take his hand. 'Thank you, Elder.'

'I would say my pleasure, but this is far from the future I wanted for you,' he says, nodding to the brown package in my lap.

'Was he pleased?' I ask. 'Cass? Was he pleased when he found out he got the Red Coat?'

'He was thrilled. They were all very happy they got their chosen coat.'

'Did you tell them about me?' I nod to the package in my hand. 'About the coat I have?'

He shakes his head. 'I told them it was up to you to tell them. They knew your appointment was at three so they hung around. But when you didn't show, they decided to charge around the whole damn Academy yelling your name for a good hour. Last I saw, they were heading to the wall to see if you're up there. Here. I'm assuming you haven't eaten yet.' He hands me a bread roll from inside his pocket which I eat despite the knot in my stomach. 'I took the opportunity to come and see ya. Knew you'd be out here.' He looks at the small apple tree I've been growing for the last five years. 'Looks very healthy.'

'I water it every day like you told me to. Still hasn't grown any fruit yet though.'

'It will. When it's ready. Like all things, it does what it needs to do in its own time.' He pats me on my back making me wince from the wounds Noah inflicted on me. 'You have to tell them, Scarlett. They deserve to know.'

'I can't,' I admit sadly. 'I just... I think if I see them again, I won't be able to do what I need to do.'

'Hate to break it to ya, but that ship has well and truly sailed. You've been assigned. If you wanna change your mind, the only way to do that is stick around for the lottery results tomorrow afternoon.'

'Yeah... I'd rather die.'

'And you probably will wearing that.' He jabs the package and laughs as my insides squirm. 'I'm taking command of your first mission. Before you argue and insist I'm too old,' he says, holding up his hand as I attempt to do exactly that. 'It's done. We leave at five am. I've already taken the liberty of having your bags packed. You're to meet me at the gate wearing that.' He taps the parcel in my lap. 'I'll have your horse ready. I suggest you spend the remaining time with your friends and explain what the hell you've gone and done.' He gets to his feet, but before he leaves, he looks down at me. 'Tell your man you love him if you haven't already.'

'I can't even tell Tee I love her,' I say sadly. 'Never mind Cass.'

'Take some advice from me. You regret what you don't say a hell of a lot more than what you do.'

'How long will we be gone?' I ask.

'Long enough for Noah to calm down I hope. You've done the best that you could to protect everyone. Yourself included. Staying here... you'll be forced to be in a relationship that will demand children. That's not right. The path you've chosen instead won't be easy, but it will be bearable.' He turns and heads back towards his cottage. 'And don't stay out here alone all night. You need to rest. We have a big ride ahead of us tomorrow.'

'Yes, Elder. Thank you, Elder.'

I open up the parcel and see my new coat. He's cut off the sleeves for me. Good old Elder Eight. I run my fingers along the collar, feeling the thickness and toughness of the black leather. I stand and slide it on. It reaches my knees. It's beautiful. And it fits perfectly. The small badge sewn into the lapel tightens the already impossibly tight knot in my gut.

Shit... this is really happening.

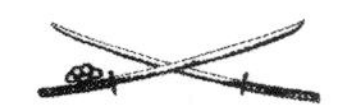

When the first glimpse of sunrise peaks over the horizon, I say goodbye to my apple tree. My one and only place of solitude.

'Grow some apples for me when you're ready. No rush, little tree,' I tell it as I put on my back harness over my new coat and stow my swords before heading towards the main gate.

It's still early. I don't see anyone as I walk through the woods. But when I reach the Soldiers Road that leads straight from The Academy to the main gate, I start to see others. As I walk, they smile at me, their eyes flick towards the badge sewn into my lapel and their smiles soon disappear. My heart is beating like the clappers. Dread and fear flow through me like never before. I've seen and done so much. I've faced zombies for god's sake, but this is the most afraid I've ever been.

'Scar?' a familiar voice calls after me. I turn and see Flash jogging up to me from the direction of The Academy. I quickly cover my badge with my hair. He looks thrilled as he gestures to his new green coat. 'I'm on wall duty this morning!' he says happily, coming to a stop as he reaches me. 'I got a Green Coat. Can you believe it?' he beams.

'That's great, Flash.' I wrap my arms around him and give him a hug. 'I'm so happy for you.'

He looks at my black coat as I let him go. 'You got Black!' he says happily. 'That's great! I mean, I know you wanted the Red, but Black's still really good. Hey... Winder and Titan got black too. Cass got Red! Tee will be with me on the wall, she got Green as well. You know everyone's been looking for you, right?'

'I heard. I just needed some space.'

'There were some Grey Coats looking for you too. Is everything okay?'

'Yeah, Flash. It's all-'

'Err... what is that?' he says suddenly. His attention firmly on my lapel. His smile goes completely, and suddenly he looks furious at me. 'What the hell is that, Scar?'

'It's none of your business,' I tell him, placing my hand uselessly over the badge. 'Listen, I have to go. But I'm really happy for you and the others.'

'Hang on a minute!' he snaps, grabbing my hand and stopping me from leaving. 'Do the others know about this? Do they know what you've done?' He glares at me showing me he does have the ability to feel something other than cowardice. He's pretty angry.

'I really have to go. I can't be late. My unit's waiting to go-'

'You're leaving now?' he says horrified. 'As in right now? I'm fetching Cass. You can't go. He won't let you.'

'He doesn't have a choice.' But he's sprinting back to The Academy before I can stop him. 'Ahh, bugger.' I turn before breaking into a sprint towards the gate.

'Morning, Kiddo,' Elder Eight calls as I approach. 'Where's the fire?' He hands me Hanzo's reigns as I skid to a stop beside him. 'He's all ready for ya, and a bag of your stuff is secured to the saddle.' I jump up on Hanzo, muttering my thanks while watching the still empty path leading back home. I have a few minutes till Flash gets to Cass and tells him. 'How did it go with the others?' he asks.

'It didn't,' I tell him, feeling very flustered. 'I stayed out all night cos I'm a coward. But Flash just saw me, and he's gone to fetch them.'

'Oh dear...' he chortles, not caring one bit I'm obviously keen to get a move on. 'Well, let me introduce you to the others.' He gestures to the two other cadets on their horses all wearing the same coat as me. I've seen them about, but never really spoken to them. 'This is Chilli.' He gestures to a man in his mid-twenties with a shaved head, light blue eyes and a very cocky smirk. 'He's usually a Black Coat. Apparently, he's good with a sword.' He gestures to the blade he has attached to his belt.

'You're not a graduate?' I ask. He shakes his head and chuckles to himself. 'What did you do?'

'He got a little hungry and helped himself to one of Elder Three's secret strawberry plants. He's been sentenced to a year of service.'

'For stealing a strawberry?' I gasp.

'Was a mighty fine strawberry.' Chilli smirks proudly.

'And what about Elder Three? What happened to him for growing an illegal strawberry plant?'

'Not a thing. That's what,' Chilli scoffs.

'Indeed,' Elder Eight sighs. 'And this is Loom,' he says, gesturing to the other guy. He has odd coloured eyes. One's blue and the other is green. He has long black hair tied back in a bun. 'He's a volunteer and an axeman.' Sure enough, strapped to his back is an axe. A double-headed thing with a steel handle.

'You volunteered?' I ask. 'Why?'

'Kinda personal,' he replies gruffly. 'I could ask you the same question. Why has the great Scarlett joined the Canaries?'

'Kinda personal too. Elder, shall we head off?' I ask hopefully, worried about what and who may very well be appearing very soon.

'Okay,' he says, looking at the gate and getting ready to order the doors open.

'WAIT!' Someone calls from behind us. 'HOLD UP, WOULD YA?'

We all turn to see a woman sprinting after us, pulling a horse alongside her and carrying half opened bags over filled with clothes.

'WAIT FOR ME!'

She approaches Elder, severely out of breath and utterly flustered.

'What do you want?' Elder asks bluntly.

'Here...' She hands him a piece of paper which he takes and reads as she catches her breath.

Elder lifts his gaze and a look of disbelief meets her.

'You're volunteering?' he asks. She nods, kneeling down and stuffing her belongings back into her luggage. 'Why?'

'Well... Let me start with telling you about when I was seven-'

'Elder,' I interrupt, glancing over my shoulder. 'I really have to go. The longer we stay, the more time others will have to try and stop me.'

He nods and stuffs Sky's paper into his pocket, gesturing for her to get on her horse.

'We're leaving now?' she asks, glancing over her shoulder. 'Don't we usually get a send-off or something?'

'Not this time.' He turns to us. 'This is Sky. She's an archer and if you ask me... a little insane.' He points to the girl with dark brown hair that reaches to her shoulders. Well, it's all brown except for two large chunks at the front which are pure white. She waves and smiles at me far too eagerly. 'She's a graduate and apparently a volunteer.' He looks at me with bemusement at her sudden appearance.

'Wasn't expecting to leave this soon,' she laughs, pulling herself onto her saddle. 'Are you sure we're supposed to leave so quick?'

'If you don't wanna come,' Elder replies. 'I can tear up your letter.'

She shakes her head and looks at me.

'No. No. I'm totally up for this! What you doing here, Scarlett?' Sky chirps. 'I had you pegged for the Red Coat. Or at least a Black. Were you naughty?' she asks, raising her eyebrows suggestively and wiping away the thick layer of sweat on her brow.

'She's a volunteer,' Elder tells them all. 'She's a dab hand-'

'She's a kick-arse swordswoman!' Chilli says. 'She fights with two mean katanas and has the highest kill count of any graduate yet. We know who she is, Elder Eight. She's a legend!' He looks back at me with an impressed expression. 'Gotta say, I feel much better knowing you're out there with us.'

'That's great. But I would really like to head off before we have company.' Either Noah or Cass.

'Right you are,' Elder says, mounting his horse which has bags and boxes attached to the saddle. I notice a crate holding pigeons, but I'm too keen to leave to ask about it. 'Suppose there's no time like the present. It's dawn. Means we can see where the hell we're goin'.'

Sky gasps and giggles wickedly. 'You swore!'

'Goddamn straight I did,' Elder grumbles. 'If I'm living out beyond the wall for a whole bloody year, you better believe I'm gonna be swearing.' He looks up to the top of the wall. 'BOWZER?'

'ELDER?' A head pops over the edge of the wall.

'READY WHEN YOU ARE.'

'YES, ELDER.'

Bowzer disappears, and the heavy doors begin to open. They grind and groan as they move. We all turn and face them. My hand settles on the little yellow bird that's been sewn onto my jacket as I take a deep, readying breath.

'Canaries!' Elder eight calls proudly. 'Say goodbye to home. We won't be back for a while.'

'Maybe ever!' Sky giggles maniacally.

I'm ready. Ready to leave. Ready to maybe never come back. If that's what it takes to keep my family safe and me out of Noah's grasp, I'll go out there to die with a smile on my face.

Then I hear it. I hear him.

Cass.

He's yelling my name in the distance. I turn and see him sprinting towards me. The others following close behind.

'SCARLETT!' he bellows. 'WAIT! STOP!'

'We can wait,' Elder says kindly. 'You should say your goodbyes.'

'SCAR!' Tee screams desperately. 'PLEASE! DON'T DO THIS! YOU'LL DIE OUT THERE!'

I feel it. The same as I did back in the arcades. Only now I know what it is. They're sobs crawling up my throat. Weird. I've never cried before. I don't like it. The pain I feel tearing up my heart. It's heartbreak.

But it's done. I couldn't change it even if I wanted to.

Yesterday, I put my number in Noah's lottery. So he awarded the guys the coats he promised. But no one, not even Noah, knew I volunteered for the Canaries. Elder kept it entirely to himself and Elder One.

If I stay, I'll have no choice but to marry Noah. And that's not an option. This way, everyone else gets their coat, and I still get to fight.

'Scarlett, say goodbye to them,' Elder Eight encourages.

'SCARLETT... WAIT!' Cass yells. 'DON'T YOU DARE DO THIS! I MEAN IT!'

I turn to the gate. 'Go.'

'You can't just-'

'PLEASE!' I yell. 'Please, Elder. Just go!'

'As you wish,' he sighs sadly.

He gives his horse a kick.

And we all follow suit.

The sound of thumping hooves slamming into the hard ground echo around us as they kick up dust. I don't look back. But Cass's final words follow me.

They follow me for months.

I dream about them every night.

Every... single... night.

'IF YOU DO THIS, I WILL NEVER FORGIVE YOU. DO YOU HEAR ME?! IF YOU ABANDON US JUST TO DIE OUT THERE, I WILL HATE YOU FOREVER!'

CHAPTER EIGHT

I hit the dirt and sigh with utter bliss.

Oh god... lying down feels good. So, so good.

The ground's hard. There's a rock in my side. And I'm pretty sure that someone has peed nearby. But it's the most comfortable I've been in days. I'm off my feet. My eyes are closed and I am gonna get some sleep!

Finally.

It's actually cold. And getting colder every day. I pull up the collar of my coat to shield my eyes from the rising sun, roll onto my side, snuggle into my arm and yawn deeply.

Finally, sleep.

'Scar... hey, Scar... you awake?' I keep my eyes closed as Sky whispers in my ear. I will not be kept awake again as she babbles on and on about the theory that the zoms might be aliens from outer space or that maybe we could develop a way to train them into doing menial tasks for us.

She'll give up. She'll leave me be. She'll-

'HEY, SCARLETT!'

'WHAT?!' I sit up and glare at her smiling face and sparkling eyes. 'What do you want?!'

'Ohh,' she giggles. 'You get so mad when you're tired. Like a big grizzly-'

'I've been up for twenty-three hours straight. I have three hours in which to get some sleep. So, this better be bloody important, Sky. Like world-ending kind of important.'

She scratches her head and her eyebrows squish together. 'But... the world has ended. How can it end again-'

I take a long and deep breath, pinch the ridge of my nose and shake my head. 'What do you want, Sky?' I ask tiredly.

She looks so excited and leans in close. 'I just thought you might like to know...'

'Know what?' I groan. 'Sky, I'm really-'

'The rules are you or Elder has to help.'

'What are you babbling about?'

'If you'd rather Elder help me-'

'Sky! Stop being so-'

'There's a Class Two out there,' she tells me teasingly.

'A Class Two?' I feel a grin creep across my lips. 'Really? We haven't seen one in weeks. You sure?'

She nods slowly. 'There it is... I love that smile. Come play, Scar. Come play. Come play...' She starts bouncing up and down like a child. In her lap is my back harness complete with katanas. 'C'mon... you're not *that* tired, are ya?' she asks, holding them out to me teasingly.

I take the harness and excitedly jump to my feet. 'Let's go.'

The structure we're currently using as a base camp was in ruins well before we screwed up the planet. Hundreds of years before, in fact. It was a circular keep. A stone fort a couple of metres thick and about eight metres high. Feeling a little like home, it forms a complete circle. Except for the one archway on the east side letting us in and out.

It's in fantastic condition for... well, ruins. It fits perfectly with what we need. It's on a high mound surrounded by a deep, dry ditch. We can see about a mile in all directions before the view is obscured by hills and woodland. We're overlooking a river which we've been using for fresh water and amazingly... fish! Yeah, there are fish here. And the woodland's alive. The trees and the grass are green. We couldn't believe it when we started to see the environment change the further south we travelled.

And we've travelled a lot.

Nine months of searching towns, villages and farmlands. Of travelling through deserted train stations with the derailed carriages left to rust. Exploring long abandoned theatres, the stage now only playing to forever empty velvet seats. Of taking refuge in the old banks that are still fortresses of brick and iron, burning the former world's wealth for warmth and light. Nine months of sleeping in shifts. Of sleeping on the ground or in trees with one eye open.

Nine months of being a Canary.

We're three hundred odd miles from home, down the very end of the country. Cornwall. And it's not a wasteland like it is back home. It's recovering. Healing.

The sun has only just started to rise as Sky and I head towards the arch. I see Chilli exactly where I left him after he relieved me of watch a few moments ago, but now he's standing with a bow and arrow poised and pointed into the distance.

'Morning, Sky. Morning, Boss,' he greets cheerfully, not taking his eyes off his target.

'I've told you to stop calling me that,' I remind him, pulling out my binoculars and taking a peek at where he's looking.

'I waited like I promised. You know, I could just let this baby fly. You don't need to go down there.'

'Where's the fun in that!' Sky gasps, leaning in close and inspecting his stance. 'Lift this arm a little,' she instructs, tapping his elbow and helping him adjust. 'That's it. Top finger to the corner of your mouth... perfect.' She nods and beams very proudly as he follows her instructions.

'How are my feet?'

'Big and smelly.' She shrugs, adjusting her belt so it sits comfortably on her hips while ensuring her sword is secured to it. He takes a double glance at her.

'Damn, Sky. You look...'

'You like it?' She asks, twirling and holding out the hem of her skirt. 'I finished it last night. It was a plain black skirt but because it was all torn up, I used some other fabric-'

'That she found in that camper van with the three corpses last week,' I add, still looking through the binoculars at the target.

'Yeah, but it wasn't dirty. I checked. No blood or goo or anything.'

'But it stunk of death,' I sneer.

'Not after I aired it out.' She dismisses. 'Anyway. I used that to give it some layers and to make sure my arse is covered. And check out the buckles!' She sticks out her leg to show him how she's used the old buckles she's been collecting to bring her outfit together. Below that she's wearing black ankle boots with the slightest heel and thick, baggy socks that go over her knees. They don't stay up alone so she's hitched them up with make-shift suspenders. His eyes widen as he catches a glimpse of her thigh. I'm getting used to her odd sense of style. The way she paints the lids of her eyes to match the bright colours she adds to her various skirts and tops. How she dyes the white streaks of her hair fantastic colours with things she finds lying around. And how she makes jewellery from clock gears. She has a bracelet on her left wrist that snakes up her arm in a stunningly intricate pattern. She finds it impossible to sit still. She has to be doing something all the time.

Sky is oblivious to Chilli's stares, but notices the lack of concentration he's giving to his aim. So she smacks his arm.

'Focus, Chilli!'

'S-sorry,' he stammers, his cheeks a little redder than before. I give a slight laugh and roll my eyes.

'You set?' I ask, securing my harness. She looks me up and down very smug.

'What do you think of Scar's new and improved outfit?' she asks. 'I spent days putting it all together.'

'She looks even more terrifying than usual,' he admires.

'Watch it,' I warn, drawing my katana and twirling it quickly in my hand before pointing it at him. 'Sky says I look hot.'

'And you do,' he says with a grin. 'But in a... *look at me wrong and I'll cut you*... kind of way.'

'I can live with that,' I shrug.

My brown leggings were far from adequate out here. So they've been replaced by a pair of ribbed leather trousers Sky found and mended for me. My red Nike kicks and less-than-cream wrappings are still a firm part of my outfit but the main addition to my wardrobe is a black leather corset with buckles holding it together up the front. Beneath which is a simple black long-sleeved top made out of something Sky calls "wet look material". Over that I have my black leather Canary coat that hangs down to my knees. The sleeves still cut off and the cuffs Cass made me protect my forearms.

I have to admit, I like her style.

'I could make some awesome cuffs for your arms if you'd let me. The ones you have are-'

'Staying put,' I say simply, running my fingers over the leather cuffs. Chilli's in baggy, dark-green khaki trousers but still wearing the army issue boots he left home in. He's in a light-grey T-shirt he found in one of the old houses we slept in a week ago with the letters *"FBI"* printed on it. And underneath, the words *"Female Body Inspector"*. We're all wearing our black coats, proudly boasting our Canary status on our lapel.

'Ready?' I ask Sky.

'Yes, boss.' She pulls out her sword and gives it a cumbersome twirl.

'Sure you wouldn't rather use your bow?'

'Why? You're teaching me blade skills,' she insists. 'How better to improve than by taking on a Class Two with my instructor.' She gives it another spin, and drops it. 'Oops.' She giggles, quickly scooping it back up.

'Chilli. Keep your aim on the target at all times. If one of us signals, you let the arrow loose.'

'Or if she drops her weapon again,' Chilli murmurs, watching Sky still attempt to spin her sword.

'Yeah. Or that.'

'I only ever dropped it once in battle,' Sky huffs.

'Three times.' Both Chilli and I correct her at the exact same time.

'Like I said. Keep an eye on the target, Chilli. Just in case. Got it?'

'Got it, boss.'

'I've told you. Stop calling me that, the pair of you.'

'Kiddo?' I turn and see Elder Eight approaching. He's stretching out his arms after an uncomfortable sleep. 'Have we got company?'

'Yes, Elder. Class Two approaching.' I report.

He stands beside Chilli and looks Sky up and down. 'What the hell are you wearing?'

'You like it?'

'No, Sky.' When her smile falters, the corner of his moustache twitches. 'I love it. Glad to see you bringing your personality into your wardrobe. I loathe the forced uniformity back home.'

'Ohh! Can I make you-'

'No!'

'It would be-'

'Go.' He points into the distance. 'Keep hold of your sword and follow her instructions, you understand?'

'Absolutely, Elder,' she says thrilled, her mind clearly made up that she's gonna create something for him anyway. 'I'll follow every word.'

'Good job. Because it's brought a posse,' Chilli tells us. I take a look through the binoculars. There are three slow and cumbersome Class Threes meandering out from the trees and making their way towards our original target.

Handing the binoculars to Elder, I pull up my mask and Sky pulls up hers too. After seeing mine, she insisted someone decorated hers. So Chilli drew a mouth that's been sewn up. Seems appropriate. She loves to talk. Even when we outright tell her to shut up.

'Where's Loom?' Elder asks.

'On watch on the other side of the fort,' Chilli replies.

'Ready, Sky?' I ask.

'Absolutely.' She nods.

'Shall I come too?' Chilli asks. 'Now there are more? I could fetch Loom to watch over-'

'The girls have it in hand,' Elder says. 'Off you go, you two. Have fun.'

'Oh, we will,' Sky giggles.

We head down the mound. Sky is close by my side as we make our way towards the Class Two which is currently facing the opposite direction and just standing there, looking into the distance.

'Remember what I told you?' I ask as we walk. 'About team work? Formation? Coordination?'

'Yes, boss.'

I wish they'd stop calling me that.

'Good. What do you want? Class Threes or the Class Two?' I ask.

'Two of course.'

I'm a little sceptical. But if that's what she wants... 'Right. It's gonna be quick and very strong.'

'I know.'

'They can jump-'

'I know! I know!'

The Class Threes slowly turn as we get closer, whereas the Class Two spins quickly. Its bloodshot eyes shine in the dull morning light as it throws back its head to let loose a high-pitched shriek that just carries on.

And on.

And on.

As the other three gurgle and groan before staggering towards us, Sky's target digs its feet into the ground and sprints straight at us full pelt. I can't see her mouth under her mask, but I know she's grinning as much as I am.

We charge forwards.

'I wanna fly!' she laughs, before falling back.

'Alright...' I carry on, her following just a little behind me. The Class Two's getting closer, closer... closer. I stop, turn and crouch down. Sky continues and leaps. When her foot lands in my cupped hands, I stand and launch her into the air. Wahooing, she somersaults over the Class Two, lands, spins, and stabs her blade through the back of its neck. I see the tip sticking out. It stops and looks down at it.

'Why would you stab? What the hell are you thinking?'

'Crap. I'm sorry. I wasn't... Crap!'

When she retracts it, it turns. She looks nervous and backs up a little as it faces her. Its leathery skin is a mix of pale-green and blue. It clings to its bones and muscles. The ribcage is half visible, and the skin from its lower jaw and down its throat is gone. And my god does it stink.

'Gross,' she mutters. 'Don't you have some Class Threes to deal with, Boss?' she snaps, annoyed when she sees me hovering. 'I got this!'

It lunges for her. She dodges and swipes her sword across its neck, and then again across its abdomen. But not deep enough.

'Class Two's skin is a lot thicker,' I call over. 'You need to-'

Whack.

It slams its arm hard into her chest and she soars backwards before landing on her back and skidding across the dew-covered grass.

'Ouch. You alright, Sky?'

She gets on her hands and knees, lifting her arm briefly with a groan. 'Fine,' she gasps, catching her breath. 'I'm fine.'

It's screeching again and digging its feet in ready to attack. She pushes herself up and gets ready for it, sword in hand and determination in her eyes.

The three Class Threes are heading straight for her too. I run forwards to intercept them, unsheathing my swords as I go. The fingers of my right-hand slide perfectly into the knuckle-dusters.

The first one has its arms outstretched. Its eyes are firmly on Sky as she fights the Class Two. The Class Three doesn't see me. Not until I jump between them. I swipe my sword and sever its outstretched limbs. It doesn't even flinch, but carries on charging forwards. I jab my second blade upwards through its skull until the hilt connects with its jaw. It falls still and silent. I use it as a shield against the second one that's right behind it, and as it tries to get through the corpse to me, I bring my second blade around, slam the knuckle-dusters into the side of its head and shatter its skull completely. When I pull my katana free, they both slump to the floor much deader than they were before.

The third one comes at me.

'SCARLETT!' Sky screams. I turn and see her Class Two charging at me as she tends to another winding it must have given her. I manage to barrel roll out the way before it reaches me, and it ploughs into the last Class Three instead. Back on its feet and looking straight at me, it screeches and then charges once more. The Class Three has no idea what happened and is slowly getting back up. The Class Two is rabid! I'd say... angry? I swipe with my left. It dodges. I have no choice but to back up as I take another swipe with my right.

It dodges.

I continue backing up. It opens its arms and hurls itself forwards. I duck and it grabs nothing but air. I thrust my sword upwards as I crouch below it. The tip of my blade pierces its side. Holy hell, its skin is really thick! No wonder Sky barely made a scratch. I thrust upwards, pushing myself off the ground hoping to get enough momentum to make it through its body. I run at it, pushing the sword in deeper and deeper, but it's like pushing a butter knife through rubber and hardly goes anywhere. It just gets pushed back.

The remaining Class Three is coming. I crouch and with my free sword, I side swipe and cut through the Class Three's legs, just above the ankle. As it falls, the Class Two wraps its fingers around the sword I have dug into its gut and yanks it out before snatching it from my hand completely and tossing it away. It lunges and I trip over the pair of severed feet behind me, landing hard on my back.

The Class Two reaches down, its mouth open wide and going for my face. I have no other move. I hold my sword tip up so it impales itself through the chest. But it keeps pushing, its body sliding down my steel. I slam my foot on its chest beside my blade and push it back up as hard as I can. Meanwhile, the legless Class Three has dragged itself next to me. Its bony and rotting fingers claw at my coat. It opens its mouth wide and slams its face into my stomach. But it finds nothing more than the leather of my corset and the metal of its buckles.

Thank-you-Sky!

It's snorting and snarling like a pig in dirt as it tries desperately to chew through my armour.

'SKY?' I yell. 'WHERE THE HELL ARE YA?'

I hear a high-pitched battle cry and then in a completely insane move, she jumps on the back of the Class Two, wraps her legs around its neck and just starts slicing and stabbing at it with her sword. All the while screeching like a nutter. It tries to grab her, but she dodges its attempts. It slides further down my sword another inch as she moves. Her weight is forcing it closer and the Class Three's pulling itself up my torso.

'GET OFF IT!' I order. 'YOU'RE TOO HEAVY!'

She's too busy being insane to pay attention to me and it slides down even further so it's less than an inch from my face.

Right, that's it!

'Get off the damn target, you idiot! AND KILL THE CLASS THREE, SKY! NOW!' She does exactly as I instruct and leaps off her original target with a flip. I slam my elbow into the Class Three's face hard a couple of times and when it's off me, I move to the side, wedging the handle of my sword into the dirt and hauling myself out from beneath the Class Two before running to where my second Katana lies abandoned. Sky grabs the footless creature and drags it away before driving her sword straight through its forehead. The Class Two has got to its feet, my sword still embedded in its chest. I snatch up my lost katana and get ready. It screeches as it runs at me. Its mouth wide. Its eyes hungry and its body nowhere near injured enough to slow it down. I hold my ground as it gets closer... closer... closer! Before it can grab me, I drop to the floor. It trips over my body and lands face down in the dirt. I launch myself up into the air, my sword above my head and the blade down, ready to strike. With the momentum of my leap behind my thrust and using every bit of my weight, I drive the tip straight through the back of its head, burying the blade not only through its skull, but also into the dirt beneath, right up to the hilt. Putting a foot each side of its head, I yank it out and severe the head completely before booting it far away for good measure.

Chilli and Elder clap and cheer up on the hill as I take a second to catch my breath before rolling the corpse over and reclaiming my other Katana. I look over to Sky who lingers by the Class Three anxiously as I wipe clean my swords.

She looks ashamed of herself. She should be. I'm not impressed by her performance.

Not. At. All.

'That was not good enough, Sky. It should never have got away from you like that.'

'I know,' she agrees. 'I'm sorry.'

'And for future reference, when there's a target on top of someone and that person is trying to push it off, don't jump on and add to the weight of it.' I flick my swords clean of the last of the goo and point the tip in her direction. 'That's really bloody stupid.'

'I didn't think. I'm sorry.'

'I know you didn't think. That's the problem with the way you fight. You don't plan ahead. You just react. You're reckless and careless and half-assed.' I take a final look around to make sure the area is clear and that everything is dead. It is. I point to the corpses with my blade.

'Get rid of them and get some sleep. No more costume making. Sleep. You clearly need it. That was absolutely pathetic.' I walk past her and snatch her sword away. 'You fight like a child. Stick to your bow from now on. You clearly don't know how to manage a sword yet.'

I leave her there telling herself off a lot worse than I ever would.

'Good work, Kiddo,' Elder says as I walk past. 'Nicely done. Get some rest. We're heading out to your next location in a few hours.'

'Yes, Elder,' I reply, trying to hide my annoyance at the mess of the fight.

'You shouldn't be so hard on her,' he adds as I pass. 'It was a difficult Class Two.'

'They're all difficult. Don't matter what Class they are. The problem wasn't them. It was her. The way she fought. Cass and I would have done that a hell of a lot cleaner.'

'Well, Cass ain't here, Kiddo.'

'Don't I know it.' I return to my spot on the floor where I curl up and close my eyes.

Don't I know it.

I wake exactly where I was when I fell asleep. I haven't moved an inch. As I sit and stretch, I notice that Sky is curled up in a ball fast asleep a few metres away. Her face is completely obscured by her hair as she hugs her bow like a teddy.

'Up already? There's some grub for ya,' Elder says gruffly from behind me. I turn and see him sitting a few metres away, nodding to some cooked fish laying in the pan by the still lit fire. 'And don't give me your usual - *"I'm not hungry, let someone else have it"*- crap. Just eat it. I cooked it specially for ya. I know it's your favourite.'

I take a seat on the grass beside him and pick at the meal. He's hunched over, scribbling away on a small strip of paper with a folded map by his foot. To his side is the cage that once contained eight birds. There are only two left now.

'Sure you couldn't try and get a bit more sleep?' he asks. I shake my head. 'Fair enough. I know not to try and make ya do something ya don't wanna do. Waste of energy and oxygen. How do you think she did earlier?' he asks, tilting his head towards the still sleeping Sky. 'Really? Now you've had a sleep and some time to calm down.'

'She did well,' I admit with a guilty sigh. 'Perhaps I was too hard on her. Her skill is getting there. But she's too reactive. Not a planner.'

He shakes his head and chuckles. 'That's Sky alright. Very reactive. She doesn't think much about what's next. Just the now. I mean, look at how she joined us in the first place! Running up to the first Canary unit she could find with only half her stuff packed and no idea what she was getting herself into.'

'She had it tough at The Haven. No one understood her, that's all. Yeah, she's a bit odd. But damn, she's loyal and sweet and hardworking. Brave and stupid in equal measure. But It can be taught,' I tell him. 'Discipline can be taught. I'm very pleased and very proud to have her in the unit.' I look over at her. 'I really like her. I really do. I like all of them.'

'That's handy, since you're stuck with 'em,' he chortles.

'Boys still on watch?'

'Yep.'

'They eaten?'

'Yep.'

I peer over his shoulder to see what he's writing. He sees me looking before covering the writing with his hand, shielding it from view.

'Tell me the information I need to enclose,' he orders, gesturing to the slip of paper.

'Another test?' I laugh. 'Alright. For lack of a better phras e... I'll bite. It's a letter back home telling them of our unit's progress which will be sent by one of the carrier pigeons. So you need to include our current location. Number of surviving members of the unit. Points of interest discovered. And any concerns we feel that they may need to know back home,' I tell him before taking another bite of the salty fish.

'So what would you put in *this* letter?'

'Well, it's our penultimate one. So, I'd tell them that we're all still alive. Where we are. That the climate here is cooler and the land greener. Much more hospitable and fertile. That we have found three locations since the last bird that they should send a unit to in order to salvage, and include the co-ordinates for those locations, as well as their risk factor.'

He nods approvingly and hands me the strip of paper as well as a folded paper map of the country.

Canary unit 63.
7/8 bird. 5 alive. S3 Current location. Fertile land.
3 salvage locations. S4. Hsp. T7. Factory. L.5. Ind est. Risk factor 3.

'What does it say?' he asks.

'That we're on the 7th bird out of eight. That will tell them that we're soon heading home. 5 alive. No one's dead.'

'Which is a miracle,' he laughs, picking up some of the food from my plate and helping himself.

'They'll look on the map they have back home and see where we are.' I pull over the map by his feet and open it up so I can point to the grid reference S3 where slap bang in the middle is our fort. 'Fertile land tells them that we're in hospitable environments. The three salvage locations are marked out in the letter.' I point to the reference locations on the map where we found a hospital, factory and industrial estate. All of which had fantastic supplies. Too many for us to carry alone. 'And telling them that the locations are a risk factor three.'

'What are the risk factors?'

'Four is little to no risk. Three is secured, but may be breached before next visit. Two is very dangerous. Not secured and large amounts of targets. One is don't even bother. Unless you have a death wish.'

He nods again, looking very pleased.

We spent a month clearing those three locations and sealing them up. They shouldn't be over-run anytime soon. So when another unit comes out to salvage, it should be clear for them. I instantly think of Cass leading his units to the hospital we found and stocking up on the bone saws, scalpels and medical supplies. There was so much stuff in these three locations. Clothes. Furniture. Weapons. Seeds. Herbs. Dry food. Metal. Plastic. We've found lots of places like that on the road. Good job too... or else we would have starved. The country is full of lifesaving and convenient supplies.

And zombies.

And destruction.

And corpses and skeletons.

The ones that died human.

So many bodies. Too many. Some were just... so small.

The loss of life that happened fifty years ago really hit home when we stumbled across a school. The teachers sealed the doors shut and they all became trapped. Everyone was hugging each other. We all saw their bones, still sharing a final embrace. I couldn't get over how small they were.

We had nightmares for weeks.

We avoided going too close to London as we travelled south. Cities are absolutely teeming with targets.

But when we passed, we soon realised there was absolutely no point in being worried about London. All we found was a crater.

There was no London. It was gone.

Plymouth was just a burnt husk buried under metres of rubble and ash. Bristol too. It was all destroyed. We found old newspapers in deserted houses with headlines telling of the horrors of the final days. Of how people were eating people. Of how cities were overrun with the dead. Of how the British government bombed their own people in a bid to try and stop the zombie population spilling out into the towns and countryside. We read that they didn't even give the survivors a chance to evacuate. That they just blew them all away.

A necessary sacrifice.

For the greater good.

And a dozen other fancy ways of telling the nation that they murdered thousands of innocent people.

I nod and pass back the paper to Elder Eight. 'It's ready to send.'

He pushes my hand away and gestures to the birds. 'You do it.'

I open the cage and scoop up one of the pigeons before securing the letter to its leg.

'You're training me to take command of this unit,' I say simply. 'Only you and I are allowed to take on a Class Two, to handle the birds, to-'

'If you're gonna continue stating obvious facts, I'm gonna get bored and fall asleep,' he tells me, gently placing some of the fish into the waiting beak of the pigeon and softly stroking the top of its head making it coo affectionately.

I finish securing the letter.

'There's never been a female Canary leader.'

'Or a female Red Coat. Or a Female Elder. Like I said, Kiddo. If you're gonna keep spouting stuff I already know-'

'Then why choose me to train up? Why not Loom? He's smart. Capable.'

'Cos you're the right person for the job. You got the brains. The sense. The skill and the level-headedness to keep not just yourself, but everyone else alive too. The others, bless 'em, are lacking some, if not all, of those skills.' He glances affectionately at Sky. 'They trust ya. The team have chosen you to lead them without any instruction from me anyway. You will make... you *do* make... a fantastic Canary Leader. Even without a penis. Isn't that right, Peggy.' he coos to the bird, chuckling away to himself.

'Why thank you,' I laugh.

'Don't thank me, Kiddo.' He lifts his gaze from the bird and focuses on me. 'Just don't die.'

I let loose the bird in my hand and it flies up high into the sky.

'I bet your people back home watch for those birds every day,' he says.

'I doubt that,' I scoff. 'The way I left things... they hate me for sure. But Tee's on the wall. So, she's safe. Winder and Cass have the coats they wanted. So they're happy. I can live with that. That's... that's enough. I'm more worried about facing Noah than them,' I admit. 'He's not gonna let what I did pass. Elder... I'm afraid of what he's gonna do when I go home.'

'Me too, Kiddo.' He taps my knee. 'Me too. But maybe we should talk about this another time.' He nods to the still sleeping Sky. 'Best no one else knows about that particular mess. The more they know, the more at risk they'll be. He's a vindictive little twerp. The more they know, the more at risk they'll be. He's a vindictive little twerp and he meant it when he said he'll kill anyone that finds out about you two, I'm sure. He won't risk losing the loyalty of his *"flock"*."

'Of course,' I whisper. He slaps me hard on my back as he watches the bird disappear into the distance.

'Good work with the pigeon. One last mission and then we get to send the last bird. When that one finally flies...'

I watch the pigeon soar into the endless sky. 'It means we're going home...'

CHAPTER NINE

Bags packed, horses saddled and weapons holstered, we leave this particular camp for good. It's time to move on. And we're all a little sad about that. This place was one of the nicer homes we've made on the road. Lots of open space. A secure wall. As much fish as we could catch. A nice change from abandoned homes, ditches or the husks of old lorries.

But it's nearly time to start heading back to The Haven. Chilli's sentence is almost up and everyone is getting a little worn out. Plus, the weather is starting to turn. Seasons aren't as they used to be. There's no gradual descent into a mild winter. When it starts to get cold, it means that snow is coming. And no one stays beyond the wall when the snow falls. Not if they don't want to freeze to death that is.

But... there's just one more place we need to check out first. One final mission.

The idea of facing the mess I left back home fills me with dread.

I'd rather just carry on exploring the country. That's the coward in me talking. I'm more afraid of returning to Noah than being out here. Part of me thinks that once I return, I'll never be released. That he'll drag me down the aisle kicking and screaming.

And I know Noah will use my friends to get what he wants from me.

But you never know. Maybe he'll kill me. Maybe he's moved on. And I'll just have three furious, betrayed and unforgiving friends – or ex friends – to worry about. Either way, the time has come to turn around. So, we agree to take a direct and known route back home. We know safe places between here and The Haven. We've secured a fair few so we can reuse them if needs be.

The plan is to ride back east and make for home.

With one detour.

And I'm seriously hoping it's worth it. Cos otherwise, I'm gonna end up with four very pissed off Canaries. And that's almost as scary as Noah.

Almost.

I'm sure it will be worth it.

As we ride, we keep our pace easy. We don't want to tire out the horses and we don't want to have to stop too often to let them rest. We're attempting to make our way back to a previous camp sixty miles east of here. It was a church once upon a time.

Still is I suppose. It offers sanctuary and protection. And peace to contemplate on ones sins and regrets.

But no one goes there to pray. Not anymore. We dragged out the bodies of the faithful who had locked themselves inside fifty years ago.

And starved to death by the looks of it.

If anyone ever needed proof that there is no god, they just need to look at what happened to his followers. To children. To the elderly. To families huddled together in a final loving embrace, knowing death was coming.

We've seen so much in such a short time. We've visited towns no living person has set foot in for half a century. Life just stopped one day. And we see that day. The plates from the final meals. The books left open and unfinished. The photo albums flicked through one final time.

Their blood still stains the ground and will never be washed clean. The ground is steeped in it. The soil drenched. Sometimes, the air stinks of death and it's almost impossible to breathe.

We all understand now why Canaries can sometimes be a little... off.

A zombie is one thing.

But a dead person is another entirely.

As we travel, we avoid towns and anywhere we might get cornered. It's not too difficult to be honest. There's miles and miles of nothing but farmland all around us. But of course, we still come up against plenty of targets. Not enough to cause too much trouble. Usually we don't even have to get off the horses to kill them. Sky's a very good shot. Even while riding. Just like Tee is. She just lets an arrow fly and scoops it back up as she passes. Every time I hear an arrow fly, I feel a strong sense of nostalgia for my lovely Tee.

God, I miss her.

'Alright there, Kiddo?' Elder asks as he rides beside me. 'You're looking a bit lost in thought.'

'Apart from a dead butt-cheek, I'm fine. You?'

'Both butt-cheeks are alive and kicking,' he chuckles as we lead the others along the main road. 'We're gonna have one last stop before we carry on to the church. And it's your turn to get some rest.'

'Got it,' I agree, careful not to meet the hard stare he's giving me.

'I mean it. You need to rest.'

'I said I got it!' I snap as he continues glaring.

'Don't you bark at me like a dog,' he warns gruffly.

'I'm just getting a bit sick of you guys telling me what I should and shouldn't be doing.'

'We want you to eat and sleep. Not asking for the world. You kept watch at the last stop. So you rest at this one.' Pointing up to the hill on our left, he calls back to the others, 'We're gonna stop up there for an hour.'

'About time,' Sky groans loudly. 'My arse lost feeling over two hours ago.'

We head up the small hill, at the top of which is the ruins of a little hut. All that remains are barely three walls made of large, grey stone, but the building itself is of no size at all. You couldn't even lay down in there. There's no roof anyway. None of us have a clue what the hell it was for. But it's up on a high hill and gives us a good view of the surrounding area. So, we head up and dismount. On the other side of the hill, at the very bottom, is a Class Three stumbling about. I reach for my sword to deal with it, but Elder wraps his hand around my wrist and nods to the little hut.

'I got it,' he says quietly but with a sharp edge to every word. As he withdraws his sword, he orders, 'Get in there and sleep.'

'You withdrawing your weapon for me? Or the Class Three?' I ask, snatching my hand away.

'Depends on if you head to the hut, or the target.'

I head towards the hut.

'Wise choice.'

'I'm getting real sick of this. I know when I'm tired and when I need to eat. I'm not a child.'

'Then stop behaving like one.'

The others are purposefully avoiding looking at us. Busying themselves with unsaddling the horses and unburdening the weight of their own weapons.

'Well, even if I was behaving like a child,' I yell back. 'I don't need or want you to parent me. Okay?!'

He storms up, stops me in my tracks and says with a low growl, 'I get that you're anxious about heading home. But don't lash out at the people who are just trying to look out for ya. Your shitty attitude is starting to grate and you're pushing everyone away so cut it out. Got it?'

'Got it,' I reply curtly.

'You better have.'

I head up to the remains of the little stone hut, place my hand on the wall and leap over. I sit with my legs tucked up tight and my head resting on my knees, and close my eyes. Dread fills my chest as I think of the gates back home.

But my dreams are filled with Cass's kiss as we collided in the amusements. His fingertips stroking my skin as I lay in his arms. His mouth whispering that he loves me as we make love.

And the venom in his voice as he yells that he hates me.

'Wakey wakey, girls.' Chilli pops his head over the wall and grins. He tosses me a flask of water and laughs at the curled-up ball beside me that is Sky. I'm amazed she even fits in here! Her face is covered by her hair and she's snoring so loud, I can't help but wonder how the hell she didn't wake me sooner. 'To someone that doesn't know that noise, they'd think there was a Class Two snarling away in here.'

I pat her head affectionately before getting to my feet. 'Let's let her get a little more rest. C'mon.'

I climb over the wall and head towards the others who are busy getting the horses ready for the next leg of our journey.

'Got some rest?' Elder asks as he tightens the straps under Hanzo's belly.

'Yep. I'm good. Sky's still asleep. Listen. I'm-'

'Never need to apologise to me, Kiddo,' he grunts, knowing that that's exactly what I was about to do. 'Just look after yourself. That's all I'm asking. Carry on breathing, and me and you will get along just fine.' He nods to the east. 'Fancy doin' a scout for us?'

'Bet your arse I do.' I beam.

'Thought you might. Have a look, see if you spot any signs of a horde. And take a few minutes to clear your head. Then get yourself back on the ground in one piece with your head in the game.'

I head over to the giant electricity pylon at the far end of the field. I love these things. I grab hold and start to climb the lattice tower. Right to the very top where a dozen or so powerlines link it to another a mile or so away. They go about sixty metres up and when you're at the top, you can see for miles. An endless canvass of hilly ground, tall untamed grass and abandoned farms. I feel like I'm on top of the world when I'm up here. Like nothing can get me. Not Noah. Not the zoms. Not even death. Unless I slip of course. The wind blows my hair across my face. The white fluffy clouds above me feel so close I wonder if I could touch them. And it's peaceful. Tranquil. I search the area with my binoculars. No sign of a horde. We've come across three in total. Mass gatherings of the undead that roam the country. I'm talking hundreds. Not sure why they do it. But they're not something you want to come up against unawares. We ended up on a roof top for two days as one passed us a few months back. Nothing seals a unit's bond like taking it in turns to use a chimney as a toilet.

I take my time up here. The wind and the height reminds me of the calmness I would feel while running along the wall back home. But it's cold. And too long up here seizes up my fingers. After a few minutes, I return to the ground and report to Elder that the path ahead is clear. Elder turns towards the hut. Putting his fingers in his mouth, he lets loose a loud sharp whistle that hurts my ears. Sky's head pops up from behind the wall. Her hair's a mess, her eyes wide, and she looks around like a confused rabbit.

'We're leavin'!' Elder calls over.

Wiping some drool from her chin, she nods and leaps over the brick and skips towards us. Her skirt flouncing around her as she does.

'For the record,' he says quietly. 'I've been looking after you for well over a decade. Just cos you're all grown up and graduated don't think for a second I'm gonna stop.'

'I don't want you to stop,' I add, flooding with affection for the old man. 'I'm just really worried about heading home is all. It wasn't personal. I just reacted. My temper seems far shorter than usual and it wasn't exactly long to start off with.'

He pats my shoulder and gives a small, sentimental nod. 'It's cos you're scared. An emotion you ain't used to.'

'Well, being scared sucks.'

'Yep. Sure does.'

We all mount up and head out. Elder and Chilli go up front. Sky and Loom in the middle. And I follow behind on my own. It's rare to get any time alone living like this. This is the most I can expect to get. Sky and Loom are talking in quiet whispers. And when they both turn to look back at me, I'm pretty damn sure they're talking about me.

'If there's something you wanna say, I suggest ya say it.'

Sky sweetly smiles and shakes her head. 'Nope. We're good.'

'Then eyes front, Canaries.'

We turn off the main road and head down a small country lane. This is something I'm not happy about. The road we took last time was further along. But the sun is setting and it's later than we thought. We need to get to the church before the sun sets completely and this shortcut Loom found will shave off an hour. The last thing you want is to be out in the open after dark. Targets don't sleep, and they prefer the dark.

The lane's thin with high verges either side. The trees that line it have grown over the road and made a canopy overhead. Beams of light from the setting sun cast a low orange hue all around us. I have to stretch out my fingers to get some feeling to return. When the hell did it start getting so cold? It wasn't this cold last night. We all have thick woolly jackets packed away. I think tonight will be the first night we have to pull them out.

Soon, the lane gets so narrow we're forced into a single line. I bring up the rear as Elder leads the way. The hooves on the tarmac echo loudly all around, and reverberates off the verges which are now higher than our heads. The trees are gone, but we're still very enclosed. We all watch the ground above us nervously. So much so, no one seems to be looking where they're going. My hand is ready to reach for my katana. Sky's just ahead of me, her hand resting on her bow. This is not a good situation to be in at all. No one can see what's above us. And we're making too much noise.

I knew we should have taken the longer and known route rather than this shortcut.

A gust of wind moves the branches. The leaves rustle and the bark creaks. A strange grinding, groaning noise travels through the air and a twig snaps. Sky moves quickly, pulling off her bow and loading an arrow. She aims it upwards, but there's no way she can see anything. A zom could literally land on our heads and there would be nothing we could do to stop it chowing down on our faces.

'Screw this,' I hiss, jumping down and fastening Hanzo's reigns to Sky's horse.

'What are you doing?' she whispers, bow and arrow still poised.

'I'm gonna walk along the top and keep watch. Last thing we need is for a horde to wander over the top and trap us in the valley of doom.' I turn and climb up the verge using the roots to pull myself up. 'Great shortcut, Loom.'

'It's another three miles to camp,' she calls after me. 'Scar, you can't walk the whole way. You need to keep your strength!'

The others have all turned to watch me. 'Yeah, well, my strength won't matter if we get caught off guard and something tumbles over the verge. Will it?' I get to the top and straighten myself up, brushing off the dirt from my climb. Another great thing about all this leather, it's so easy to wipe clean. I take a look around.

'Woah!' I mutter quietly. The field I'm in has an old wind farm in it. A dozen or so of the tall poles with three propellers still stand. Dirty and grimy. Rusted and weather beaten. A few have toppled over and lay at odd angles across the ground half submerged in long grass. Some are missing their propellers. One has landed on another and looks like one good gust would have them both down. Another has crashed through the old farm at the far end of the field. And one still turns. Slowly and begrudgingly. The groans of the gears travel through the air and echo in the vast emptiness around us with every gust of wind. That's what we heard.

'What's up there?' Loom calls.

'Nothing. Just an old wind farm.' I call back. 'It's clear. For now. But it's really crap for visibility in this terrain. I'll walk alongside you guys and keep an eye out.'

'Fine,' Elder grunts, urging his horse to continue. 'You wanna walk? Walk.'

'I don't particularly wanna walk. But I don't wanna wear a zombie as a hat either,' I reply. Chilli snorts a stifled laugh and lowers his head as Elder glares at him.

Half a mile down the road, I spot a couple of Class Threes stumbling about by a knee-high wall not too far away.

'Got a target,' I tell them all.

'How many?' Elder asks.

'Just the one,' I lie as a third head appears from beyond the wall.

'Need a hand?' Sky asks hopefully.

But I shake my head. 'Nah. I got it. Just keep going. Me dealing with it will be much quicker.'

Plus... I'm kinda bored and stressed, I add in my head. Drawing my sword, I head away from the verge and towards the wall.

'Ya know,' I say quietly as I walk. 'I think you would like to be out here with me. Sleeping under the stars. Seeing the world. What's left of it.' I pull out my second katana and give it a playful spin. 'No one telling us what to do or who we can be with.' I give a whistle to get their attention. All three turn, and as usual, their gurgling and snarling get more rampant when they see me. 'Except Elder of course. He tries to tell me what to do, as per usual. But he means well.' The first one charges at me. I swipe my right blade hard straight across its gut, just deep enough to make his insides spill out on the floor. It trips over its own intestines and lands face down in its entrails. The second one clambers over it. Its arms are stretched out and its toes squelching in guts. I cut the extended limbs off with two hard blows and then kneel so I can do the same with the feet. It lands beside the other one who is still trying to get to its feet, but getting caught up in its innards. I laugh as they stumble about, still trying hard to get to me. The third is drooling thick, stringy black goo from its mouth. It dangles all the way to its navel.

Gross.

I pull back my blade and thrust it straight through the front of its forehead. The arms fall limp. The growling stops. And the bloody phlegm detaches and sticks to its chest. I give the blade a shake, making it sway a little.

Kinda looks like it's dancing.

Then I retract my weapon and let it crumple to the floor.

'Oh Cass,' I sigh, looking down at the two still rolling about on the floor. 'I miss you.' I slam my foot down hard on one and decapitate the other. It still chomps. I stab it between its eyes and then line up a shot. I take a couple of steps back to give me a good run up and then boot it as hard as I can towards two trees on the other side of the wall. The head soars through the air spinning wildly as it travels. When it sails between the trees, I raise my hands in victory, the tips of my blades pointed high to the sky.

Gooooaaaaaallllll!

Perfect shot.

I flick the blood clear and re-sheath my swords before turning back to the lane. Loom is standing there watching. He shakes his head looking disgusted at my behaviour before climbing back down to the others. As I approach, I hear him report that I'm fine. Just blowing off steam.

'Zombie head football?' Chilli asks.

'Yep,' Loom replies, sounding as disapproving as he looked. 'Sometimes I think there's something wrong with that girl-'

I clear my throat as I stand above them.

'Problem?'

He glances at me only briefly before urging his horse onwards.

Like I care what he thinks.

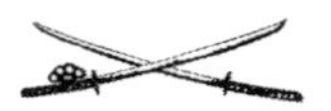

Finally, the verge begins to drop. The lane opens up and the border of the old church comes into view. The others dismount and lead the horses off the road and up a small path towards a little wooden gate where they meet me. I open it up and let them all pass before closing it behind us. Following a small stone path through the thick blackberry bushes, we turn a bend and finally see it.

'The church,' Chilli sighs happily. 'About bloody time.'

'And *Just* in time by the looks of it,' Elder adds, looking at the sun which is now so low in the sky that in another ten minutes it will be gone altogether. 'Let's get inside, do a sweep and light a fire. It's gonna be a cold one tonight.'

He ain't wrong. I can already see my breath in the air.

The church is made of red brick with a steep slated roof. And for a building in the arse end of nowhere, it's a pretty good size. The reason why we chose this particular building as a camp was for the design of it. There are large windows all around, but they're thin, tall and a good five metres above the ground, so, apart from the main door which is made from extremely thick, heavy wood and metal hinges, there ain't no getting in. It's a gothic, solemn and foreboding structure surrounded by hundreds of weathered gravestones. On each and every corner of the building are beautifully carved stone crucifixes. And right at the very top, on the highest point at the very front and centre, is a giant, stone lady with enormous wings. Her head is bowed as she looks down to the doorway, welcoming us in.

From inside his pocket, Elder pulls out the heavy, metal key he took last time we were here and puts it in the lock. I don't know why we all watch him with bated breath, and I certainly don't know why we all breathe a collective sigh of relief when he turns it in the lock. But I certainly *feel* relieved. He turns and looks at me.

'Check the exterior?'

'On it.' I pat Hanzo as he passes and start my walk around the exterior. A single lap is all I do. And as expected it's all fine. The walls are intact. There are no zoms. So, I head inside.

Closing the door behind me and turning the key Elder left in the lock, I head inside to find the others.

Down the very middle of the building are lines of wooden benches that are bowed and rotted. The first night we stayed here a few months back, Chilli sat on one. It creaked loudly and then splintered under his weight.

Very funny.

Either side are aisles made of red and cream tiles laid out in a mosaic pattern. The walls were plaster once, but it's nearly all crumbled away now, leaving a pile of debris on the floor and the bare stone behind. But it's the ceiling I love. It's a huge cylindrical dome shape with the faintest reminder of a beautiful painting that was once there. It's faded. But I can still make out the halos of the angels and the beautiful bodies of the divine. The colours are peaceful. If a colour can be called that. My world is filled with harsh colours. Blacks. Reds. Greys. Greens. Whites. Red. The ceiling has pastel pinks. Pale blues. Subtle yellows. Even though there's not much left to see, I still think it's stunning. As I head down the aisle towards the great big wooden altar at the far end, Chilli is kicking the crap out of one of the pews, breaking the wood down and tossing it to the side. I scoop up a handful and carry it to Sky who's busy building the fire at the front.

'Here.' I hand it over and carry on past the altar and towards the large stained-glass window above it. I stand there, looking up as the last of the light shines through it. The mix of yellows and blues are pretty. But it's the pure white dove with its wings spread wide that I love. In its beak is an olive branch and for some reason, it makes me feel warm. On the inside.

'Why do you do that?' Loom asks from just behind me. I turn and see him watching me with his hands tucked into his trouser pockets.

'What? What exactly am I doing that's caused that frown on your brow?' I turn completely and fold my arms across my chest.

'It's not what you're doing now,' he replies, looking a little unsure that he should say anything at all. His eyes flick briefly to the sword over my shoulder. 'It's...'

'What?' I ask. His eyes narrow a little. He's desperate to say something. But he won't. He never does. He looks at me like this sometimes. Like I'm beyond his understanding. But he never follows through on what he's thinking. 'Loom. What's the problem?'

Everyone in the church stops what they're doing and watches us.

'It's just... I think your behaviour is... out of line.'

'My behaviour?' I ask. 'What behaviour?'

'The way you are with the... ya know... the-'

'Zombies?' I ask. He flinches at the word and his nose scrunches up in distaste. 'What? Has my behaviour put you in danger?'

'No-'

'Has my behaviour put any of our missions at risk?'

'No, Scar. But-'

'But what?' I take a step towards him. He takes one back, like I'm a threat. And that really pisses me off. 'I don't like your derisive glances and the way you're backing away from me, Loom. What exactly is it about my behaviour that you don't like? Spit it out.'

Elder's got to his feet. But he doesn't intervene. He just watches and waits. The building is so quiet we could hear a pin drop.

He raises his hand and steps back. 'Never mind. It's not important.' He turns. 'Just forget it.'

'Stop!' I order as he takes a step. He does. 'Turn around, Loom.' Again, he does. He sighs as he looks up at me.

'There's clearly something on your mind. If you have a problem with me, you need to tell me.' I look to the others too. 'This is an open forum. Everyone can speak. We won't survive for long if we start resenting or harbouring unpleasant feelings for each other so... tell me. What's up?' I lower myself down onto the step and sit. I find that when trying to confront an issue, standing above the person I'm dealing with comes off as confrontational.

'It's just... sometimes...' He's really struggling.

'Oh for god's sake, man. Just spit it out,' Elder grumbles.

'Sky... you snore,' I tell her. 'Like an animal on heat. It's unbearable. And my god, can you talk crap. Zombies are not aliens. We are not a test site. The rest of the world is not unharmed and your outfit although very pretty, is not combat effective. Plus... you're a little bit mad.' Her face falls a little. 'But I love mad. I love your optimism and unwavering joy. And your quickness to forgive is admirable.' I add. She beams. I look at Chilli. 'Dude. You need to wash more. You stink.'

'Harsh!'

'And seriously... stop pissing close to where we sleep. I know it's a pain in the arse to walk a few extra metres, especially in the dark, but if I wake up to the whiff of your piss one more time, I'm gonna punch you in the face.' He looks like he's trying to come up with an argument. But he's got nothing. 'However. You are a great laugh. And you sure can cook.'

Everyone gives a slight chuckle. But Loom still looks uncomfortable.

'Elder...'

He raises his eyebrows, daring me to say something. I grin.

'You're perfect.'

He frowns, but has a playful smile.

'Damn straight I am.'

'But you don't half moan. And just because we can't hear your farts, doesn't mean we can't smell them.'

Everyone laughs. Even Loom and Elder. So I look to him again.

'Loom. I'm short tempered and rough around the edges. I'm bossy and overbearing. I know that you don't like how I am with the targets,' I tell him. 'I know it upsets you when I-''Play with their corpses?' he finishes. 'Cutting them up and kicking their heads about? Yeah. I think it's sick.'

'But they're corpses. They're dead things. They're-'

'They were us,' he says simply. 'Scar, they were people. I saw you after we cleared out this place. The way you treated the bodies of the dead so carefully and respectfully. But with the targets, you're just plain sadistic.'

'The bodies we cleared out of here were people, Loom. Targets aren't people. They're the things that killed those people,' I tell him. 'The monsters out there? What you see walking and biting is as far from human as can be. It's death wearing a skin suit. That's all. I love your idealistic views on the world. I do. But in this respect... you're wrong.'

'If I get bitten,' he argues. 'And I turned. You would happily lop my head off and play football with it?'

Chilli raises his hand. 'For the record, if you didn't play football with my severed head, I'd be a little offended.'

With an eye roll, I return my attention back to Loom.

'It wouldn't be you. I would be killing the thing that took you away from us.'

'But if I got bit-'

'Let me be clear.' I get to my feet and look at them all watching me. 'I think the world of each and every one of you. I would, and I have, risked my life to ensure you keep yours. But, the minute one of you is bitten... You. Are. Dead. End of story. I will not hesitate in severing your head from your body and booting it as far away from us as possible because if I don't, you will kill someone else. And I will not let that happen.' The room falls quiet again. 'So, Loom, if you are bitten, I will put you down. Even before you turn. Because that's what will keep everyone else safe. And it's exactly what I would expect any of you to do to me. They are not human. They are the thing that killed the human. They are just wearing the decaying corpse of a human. That - is all - they are. They deserve no pity, nor mercy. No dignity. Because they took all those things from the person they are wearing. I am sorry if I offend you with the truth. But that's the way it is.'

'And if it was Cassius that was turned into a Class Three, would you treat him the same way?' he asks. 'Would you cut off his head and kick it about for pleasure? Would you spill his guts just to watch him slip about in them?'

I feel the all kindness I have for him slip from me in an instant. Even the others glare at him.

'Loom, Enough,' Elder says. But he pays no mind.

'What about Tee? Would you kill her before she even turns? Could you look into those big brown eyes that would be filled with fear, and kill her so heartlessly? Or is it just us that you don't care about killing.'

'You're out of line!' Chilli snaps. 'How dare you talk to her like that. They're her people. Her family. Apologise now!' He attempts to charge forward when Loom remains quiet. But when I hold up my hand he stops. I walk down the steps. My feet echo on the stone and Loom blinks at each and every one. I stop just in front of him. I can see how much of an effort it is for him to hold eye contact with me. His breathing is jagged. He's even shaking a little. And his eyes keep flicking to my hands and the hilt of my katanas.

He's afraid of me.

'I'm sorry,' he says in barely a whisper. 'I should never have said that.'

'Yeah well, you did. You think I don't imagine that? Watching the people I care for more than anything suffer? Watching them die? But you see, the question of what I would do if any of you lot got bit, is completely irrelevant,' I tell him.

'How so?'

'Because if Tee, Cass, or any of you get bit, then that would mean I would already be dead. So what I would do is completely irrelevant because I wouldn't be able to do anything.'

'I don't understand-'

'Because the only way a target would ever get close enough to bite any of you,' Elder says sounding very annoyed. 'Would be if that girl was already dead. She'd die before she let a single one of you get bit. Just as I would. If you haven't learnt that yet, you're a bigger moron than I gave you credit for.'

Sky points at me while glaring at Loom hatefully. 'She gives you her food. She takes your watch when you're too tired. She-'

'It's alright, guys. He has a right to speak his mind. He thinks I'm disrespectful. You're probably right. I've had people I care about much more than you think much worse things of me. But as long as you're breathing, I'll fight to keep you safe. But when you stop, when you start biting, I'll show no mercy, dignity or kindness. Because they never show us any. They tear us apart. They eat us alive. They kill children. They have us living in goddamn cages. So you can think I'm a bad person.' I shrug. 'I don't really care. This ain't a popularity contest. Hate me if you want. But know that I'm a damn good soldier and that I'm ready to die for the cause.' I jab him hard in the chest. 'I'm ready to die for any of you.' I take another step closer. 'And if you ever talk about Tee or Cass like that again, I'll knock your fucking teeth out. I have enough nightmares as it is from all the shit we've seen out here. And more from what I've left behind at home without you adding to it.' I barge into his shoulder and head to the door.

'I'm sorry, Scarlett. I didn't mean-'

'I'll be on watch if you need me.'

'Kiddo, you don't need to do a watch. We're perfectly safe in here.'

'Well right now, it ain't safe for Loom's face if I stay in here.'

I slam the door hard behind me and head out into the dark.

CHAPTER TEN

A few minutes after I left, Elder joined me. He's obviously rummaged through my bags because he's dug out my thick, woolly jacket and thrown it over my shoulders before plonking himself on the raised tomb beside me. I put my arms through the jacket and pull up its hood, glad for the warmth. The temperature has fallen dramatically. The weather changes quickly. Winter is around the corner. I can taste it. I can feel it biting at my skin. If we get caught out here in a snow storm, we'll freeze to death. Or starve to death. I think of the snow storms we've had in the past. Everything back home slows right down. The others and I would take our blankets down into the great hall to sleep. Along with a few hundred other Cadets all desperate for the warmth of the fire they would light in the enormous fireplace during the worst of winter, when the snow fell thick and fast. Inches of it. When it's that bad, we don't go out beyond the wall. It's far too dangerous and the horses struggle.

Many times, a snowball fight has been known to break out in the military village. Sometimes, even the Elders would join in.

Snow days are the best.

'You alright, Kiddo?' Elder asks as I quietly chuckle at the memory of a Grey Coat taking a snowball to the back of their head and throwing a hissy fit.

'You know, I'm not a kid anymore,' I sigh, stretching out my legs in front of me and leaning back on the headstone of Joseph Miller. Whoever he was. 'I wish you'd stop calling me that. Makes me feel ten years old.'

'You'll always be my Kiddo, *Kiddo*,' he says, nudging my elbow as he laughs to himself. He leans back with me, his legs outstretched too as he lets out a deep, tired breath. 'He didn't mean what he said ya know. He doesn't think you're disrespectful. None of them do.'

'I don't really care what he thinks of me.'

He glances at me sideways with one eyebrow raised, clearly disbelieving of my words.

'What did the others call you?' he asks. '"*people I care about have called me a lot worse*", you said. Was that the reason for the late night visit you made to my porch the night before you told me you wanted to join the Canaries? Did you guys have a fight?'

'Tee and Cass said I was selfish. And Cass even thought I kissed him purely to stop him asking you for a Red Coat.' I shrug and snuggle down into my collar. The thick wool is scratchy and smells musty. 'But screw them, right?'

'Riiiggghhhht...' he says slowly. 'I assume we're taking watch?' he asks, moving swiftly on. Thankfully. 'A very unnecessary and pointless watch I might add. The church is a fortress.'

I nod and fold my arms across my chest to try and keep warm.

'I need some air and some time alone.'

'I'll sit with you,' he says, settling his hands on his lap. 'Keep you company.'

'Not really how the whole... getting some *"alone time"* works, Elder.'

'You just focus on working it out. I'll make sure you don't get eaten alive in the meantime. Just pretend I'm not here.'

'Work what out?'

'Whatever it is that's making your head noisy again and has turned you into a grumpy, insufferable git. You see, when your head gets noisy, you get careless and distracted. Always have. Ever since you were a kid. Now, when you get angry or annoyed, that's fine. You channel it and use it to your advantage. Makes you a fantastic fighter. Sometimes, Cass would wind you up before a fight to give you an edge. Not that you noticed. You just thought he was being an arse. But when you get emotional, your thoughts get noisy and drown out your senses. You don't focus. You lash out and attack the people that are just trying to help ya. So, you work it out and I will look out for you while ya do.'

'You think you know me so well.'

'I *know* I know you so well,' he huffs. 'There's no *think* about it. Besides, I like sitting outside looking up at the stars.'

'I overreacted with Loom, didn't I?'

'A tad. But to be fair, if anyone ever said anything like that about the people I care about, I'd break their nose. Putting an image of that in your head is wrong. You handled it better than I would.'

'He just mentioned the wrong people for his example. That's all. The idea of one of them being bitten...' I shudder.

'I get that. Losing the people we love is never easy.' He slumps a little and sinks into himself.

'What was she like?' I ask, looking over at him past my hood as he looks into the sky above. He moves his head to face me. 'The woman you loved. The woman who died. What was she like?'

His eyes soften in the moon light, and a slight but sad smile appears.

'You remember me telling you that?'

'Of course I remember. It's not every day your Commander, the toughest man you know, tells you he was in love. I'm desperate to know what she was like.' I nudge his shoulder.

He takes a deep breath. 'She was... brilliant. Clever. Witty. And my god, what a temper.' He laughs affectionately as he recalls. 'She was in my unit. We grew up together. Much like you and Cassius. She was a better fighter than me. Braver than me.' His smile fades a little. 'She was the other half of me. When she died, I think I died a little too.' He looks back to me and puts on that solemn smile again. 'Which is why I still think that you should have said goodbye to Cassius. If I was in his position and she left the way you did, I would have gone mad. And worse. Been heart broken.'

'How did she die?' I ask, not sure if I'm overstepping and steering the conversation away from Cass. 'If you don't mind me asking.'

'She died because of me,' he says quietly, looking up at the stars.

'Was she bitten?'

'No,' he says absolutely. 'No way. Like you, if she was bitten, I'd have been dead before that could have happened.' He turns to face me and with the help of a deep, courage-inducing breath, he admits, 'She got pregnant. As is the way when two people... well... you know. Get close.'

'You had a baby?!' I gasp.

'She was just starting to show. We had no idea what to do. Our relationship was illegal and we were kids ourselves. They would have taken the baby away from us as soon as it was born, and we would be in serious trouble. Probably sentenced to a lifetime in The Canaries. But then, she started bleeding. Out of nowhere. The bleeding never stopped. I lost them both. Just like that. I was so grief stricken, but I couldn't really mourn. If they ever found out I was the one who got her pregnant I'd have been banished for good. So, I volunteered for a few years with the Canaries to try and work it all out. Back then you could do that. Volunteer a year or two.'

'Bloody hell!' I breathe. 'I'm so sorry. That's awful!' He gives a small, single nod and clears his throat as if clearing the need to cry.

'They see us a number, Kiddo. Not people. You need to remember that. We're expendable. Every single one of us. You... you're not though. You're important. To me. To Noah. And to so many others. The Cadets back home, they look up to you. You're strong. Caring. You fight for the ones who can't fight for themselves.'

'I think you hold a higher opinion of me than you should.'

'I think you are blind if you don't see it. Noah wanted you as a wife not just because of your pretty face. You have the respect of every soldier, both graduate and cadet alike. I wasn't joking when I told you I was inundated with requests from Cadets to be placed with you. I got dozens! And the Grey Coats, they wanted you too. Noah wanted you to be his wife and ensure the loyalty of the soldiers. I think that in the last few years, as The Grey Coats have grown in number and vindictiveness, people have started to have less faith in The Verity. He'll do anything to keep power.' He looks nervously at me. 'If you approve of him. Stand by him. Follow him. The others will too. That's what I think he believes anyway.'

'Guess we'll find out when we get home. Looks like winter is on the way. We may end up snowed in. And all this, coming out here, it may all have been a waste of time. If he threatens my family again, I'll have no choice. I may just have delayed the inevitable. Noah can be very persistent.'

'He's a right little prick, that one. Gods representative, my backside.'

I can't help but laugh. Elder's complete disregard for the religion has always made me feel a comradery with him. I rest my head on his shoulder and look up at the sky with him as I have so many times before. He's never been this close to any other Cadets. Not that I've noticed anyway.

'I'm really sorry about your lady and your baby,' I tell him.

'Thanks, Kiddo,' he says, patting my arm.

'For the record, I think you would have made an amazing dad. You sure look after me brilliantly. Even when I tell you not to.'

'That means a lot. Thank you.'

'You're welcome.'

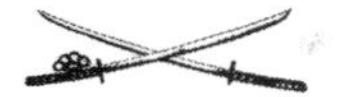

The muffled whisperings of Sky and Elder wake me from my brief and uneasy sleep. The sun was starting to rise when I closed my eyes, and as I open them, it's barely up. They don't notice me stirring. I'm still in the graveyard, curled up in a ball with my hood over my face and my head snuggled into the crook of my arm. My right side is stiff and aches from the contorted position I've worked myself into. I'm about to stretch it out when I hear Sky say my name in a hushed angry whisper.

'If there's something we should know,' she says. 'Then you need to tell us. Is Scar in danger?'

Elder groans, 'We're all in danger, Sky. We're not on bloody holiday out here.'

'I know I'm not the sharpest tool in the pond,' she hisses, ignoring Elder's snort of derision. 'But I know that there's something bad waiting for her when we get home and I demand to know what it is so I can protect her from it.'

'If you think that girl needs protection, you don't know her.'

'Let me tell you what I know about her.' I don't open my eyes. Mainly because I don't want to embarrass her. And I'm kinda curious as to what she's gonna say. 'I've seen her face Class Twos alone and not bat an eye. I've seen her sing while surrounded by slobbering, biting monsters. I watched her use her foot to stop me getting bitten.'

'Yeah, she wasn't happy about staining her kicks on that one,' he laughs.

'But she didn't even hesitate or flinch at shoving a part of her body into the mouth of a zombie is what I mean. When we ran out of food she didn't panic. When she dislocated her shoulder, not a word of complaint.'

'What's your point?' he groans tiredly.

'My point is you two don't whisper as quietly as you think ya do. She's not scared of anything out here. But she's terrified of going home. Every time we talk about it she flinches and leaves the conversation. And her mood since we turned around has been really shitty. We're all thrilled to be heading back. Excited. Not her. She wants to stay out here. What could possibly be scarier back home than what we've faced out here?'

'It ain't my place to say,' he replies. I hear him get to his feet. I peek out from my hood and see her grab his arm to stop him. 'I suggest you remove that,' he warns in a low menace I've not heard very often from him.

Not only does she refuse to let him go, but she stands nose to nose with him, looking firmer and more serious than I have ever seen her.

'I didn't grow up with friends, Elder Eight,' she states in a low tone that I would never thought possible for her to produce. 'Everyone thought I was weird. They all said my head was in the clouds. They laughed at my white hair and they called me weak because I let one of *them* scare me so much it changed colour.' Sky briefly told me the story of how her hair turned white. She was cornered by a couple of Class Twos on her first time out. She almost died. Scared her half to death and her hair drained of colour. 'She's the only person who's ever treated me as an equal. As a friend. I will protect her. But I can't if I don't know the threat.'

'There's nothing to concern yourself with,' he snaps, yanking his arm free. 'If she needs your help, she'll ask. But I wouldn't hold your breath.'

'What did she do to Noah Sands?' she asks as he starts to walk away. He slows and stops before slowly turning to look back at her.

'What do you know about it?'

'He's not going to let what she did pass? She's afraid of what he's gonna do to her when she goes home? I heard you two before we left camp. Like I said. You don't whisper as quietly as you think.'

'Neither do you,' I tell her, sitting up straight and lowering my hood. She loses her steely resolve with Elder as I glare at her. Her gaze meets the floor in embarrassment. 'Don't you ever talk to your superiors that way again. Understand?' I order.

'I just want to help,' she complains.

'Then help me get breakfast started.'

'Scar, if Noah's a risk to you, then let me help.'

'You wanna help?'

She lifts her head and nods eagerly, rushing to me. 'Yes! I want to help, Scar. Let me help.'

'Then help me get breakfast going and forget you ever heard us say that man's name. Got it?'

'I just-'

'You got it? Or not?' I jump down from the tombstone and give her a little poke in the chest. I know she's only trying to protect me. *Temper, Scarlett.* But if Noah knows that anyone else has discovered the truth about us, he won't hesitate in silencing them. Permanently. 'Well?'

'I got it. Jeez,' she replies, rolling her eyes and kicking the dirt.

When I head towards the church she follows close by my side.

'You being a bossy cow ain't gonna stop me looking out for you,' she grumbles.

'I know,' I tell her, wrapping my arm around her shoulders. 'Wish it would though. And for the record, you are weird. But I love weird. And I also adore your hair. Screw what others say about you. You just do you, Sky. Because you're brilliant.'

She absolutely beams at me. With a glance to Elder, I see him laughing to himself as he watches us leave.

Inside, Chilli and Loom are talking. From the looks of it, heatedly. They go silent as soon as I walk in.

Great. It's awkward.

'Right!' I call over. 'Breakfast and then we hit the road.'

'We still going to that flower place then?' Chilli asks, pulling his angry and furrowed brow away from a flustered Loom and showing me his over-the-top boyish smirk.

'Yep. It's a couple of hours ride from here. Toss me the saucepan, would ya?' I call over. 'I'll fetch water from the well so we can get breakfast started.'

Although I have my hands held out ready to catch it, Chilli shoves the pan in Loom's hands and nods him in my direction. He gets to his feet looking every bit the uncomfortable prat he is, heads over and hands it to me.

'I'm really sorry,' he says as I take it. 'I was out of line with what I said about your people.'

'You're my people too, Loom.' I remind him. 'And I was out of order as well. No more zombie head football. I promise. Tell you what. I'll just kill them and destroy their brains like any other normal girl. Deal?'

'Deal,' he laughs.

'Good. Then *you* fetch the water and get breakfast started.' I give him back the saucepan. 'I'll do a sweep of the perimeter. I slept funny and need to walk the knots out of my muscles.'

'Anything to get out of cooking, huh?'

'You know my view on things.' I nudge him. 'Men do the cooking. The women kill the undead.'

'Don't I know it,' he chuckles, spinning the saucepan playfully as we separate.

Walking around the edge of the grounds is a welcomed break from the others. Last time we stayed here we camped for a week. There are three villages surrounding us. All with houses and little shops full of supplies. Not to mention the fresh water from a pretty little well.

I follow the fencing which turns into hedges and then a waist high brick wall. The blissful silence and rare moment of serenity is interrupted in a manner I'm becoming all too accustomed to.

Someone yelling.

The panicked hollering has me filled with adrenaline and sprinting in the direction of the well where Loom is currently bellowing for help. I see the well in the middle of an open field as always. But there's no Loom. Nowhere. But I can still hear him. The others pile out of the church doors and stand beside me, all of us ready with our various weapons and all of us completely baffled as to where the hell he is. I'm panting. But not through effort. Through fear. Loom's in trouble and out here? That's deadly.

'Is that Loom?' Sky asks. She does a complete three-sixty and throws her arms in the air. All we see are empty fields. 'Where the hell is he?'

'LOOM?' I call out. 'WHERE THE HELL ARE YA? LOOM!'

'OVER HERE! HELP ME! MY FINGERS ARE SLIPPING.'

His fingers?

'THE WELL!' he shouts. 'HURRY!'

We sprint towards him. The idiot's fallen down the well? I'm out ahead, desperate to help him, my eyes completely on the stone wall of the circular well and stupidly not on where my feet are going.

'I'M COMING,' I tell him. 'Hang on, Loom.'

'Scar! Wait!' he calls.

'I'm coming - Oh shit!' The ground suddenly disappears from beneath my feet and I fall like a sack of bricks into a ditch. I reach out and grab at anything I can get my hands on to stop myself from falling. Especially when I see what's at the bottom of this pit. In a quick move, I slam my sword into the earth and anchor myself from falling any further. Opposite me, Loom is hanging by his fingertips.

'Good move, Boss.' His voice is strained and he's red in the face from the effort it's taking to keep himself from slipping. 'You're quick with that sword. I'll give you that.'

'Err, thanks. What the hell is that?' I look above where there are two small holes in a light canopy above us.

'Someone covered a ditch over with a lid of twigs and leaves!'

We both look down. 'What the hell are they doing down there?'

The five Class Threes below reach up and wrap their disgusting fingers around our ankles and start to pull. With every kick to get them off, we slip a little more.

'GUYS?! GET YOUR ARSES OVER HERE!' I yell, reaffirming my grip on the hilt of my katana. 'AND WATCH OUT FOR THE HOLE!'

'Hole? What- *Woah*!'

Elder grabs Sky by the scruff of her neck and stops her from crashing through the fake floor above us. They use the heels of their boots to smash it away and clear their view. As they all stare at us in a state of disbelief, Loom starts to slip. Chilli grabs his wrist just before he plummets down and hauls him up.

'Where the hell did this come from?' Elder asks.

'A great question,' I reply, still dangling and being yanked by several undead hands. 'Shall we discuss it here? Or maybe you could... I don't know... PULL ME UP?!'

He snaps back to the situation. 'Of course. Sorry, Kiddo.' He leans down and heaves me up quickly and rather violently. I go soaring through the air and he lets me land in an inelegant heap on the floor.

'Ow.'

But no one pays the slightest bit of attention to me. Why should they? They're all peering into the ditch. I join them. The five Class Threes are clawing at the sides, shoving and pushing each other in order to try and get to us.

'Did one of you dig this?' I ask, peering down at the pit.

'Not me,' Elder replies.

Loom glances at Sky. 'Did you?'

'No,' she says with an anxious swallow. 'You?' she asks Chilli, who shakes his head. We all look at Elder. But he just looks into the hole suspiciously, his thoughts racing.

'We're well over two hundred miles from any known scouting locations. Who the hell dug this if not one of us?' I ask. 'Can anyone see a blood rag?'

We all look. But can't see anything.

'Who would put a lid on a zombie trap?' Loom whispers.

I nudge Sky and nod to the contents of the pit. She pulls out her bow. It takes a minute for her to kill them all with very little fuss. Loom and Chilli then jump down, masks up.

'No blood rag,' Loom calls up, kicking the top soil about with his feet. 'It's not one of our traps.'

'Unless one of them ate it. Perhaps another group of Canaries made it out this far and dug it?' Chilli adds.

I feel something plummet in my gut as I look closer. 'What the hell...' I mutter. 'You see what they're wearing?'

The boys flip them over. They're all on their backs, mouths open, bile and pus leaking from their eyes and ears.

'It's army uniform.' Elder kneels down with me to get a closer look. 'All five of them are in the exact same army uniform.'

'We don't wear that,' Chilli states as Sky helps heave him out of the ditch before reaching down to give Loom a hand out. They brush off their clothes and lower their masks. 'That's not Sainted Army garb.'

The dark green mixed with light green in a rough pattern is very odd. I've never seen anything like it. I just thought it was weird that they're all wearing the same rags. But Chilli's right. That's nothing like what we wear.

'Not our army, Chilli,' Elder clarifies. 'It's the old army. Back from before the outbreak. These guys are all soldiers from five decades ago.'

'Weird,' Chilli says very casually with a disinterested shrug. 'You want me to go burn them? Or bury them?'

'Chilli... it's more than weird,' I state.

'How?' he asks. 'The world's full of zombies. They fell into a zombie trap. What's the big deal? It's what's supposed to happen when you make a trap.'

'So, who the hell made *this* trap?' I ask, gesturing to the ditch. 'It wasn't here last time and we didn't make it! And look at where it is. Right by the well. And concealed? Why conceal a zombie trap? They didn't fall through the roof. We did. The only holes in it are the ones that we made.'

'Probably another group of Canaries made it and couldn't be bothered to fill it in. Or maybe we just didn't notice it before.'

'It wasn't here before, Chilli. Stop being dense.' He goes red as I snap an insult at him. 'Don't you think it's a coincidence that all five of them that just so happened to be in it, all wearing the same thing?'

'They travel in groups sometimes. It's not that strange.' His tone is less certain as he takes another look at the hole, scratching the back of his head. 'I mean... what else could it be?'

'And why are they still even wearing clothes?' Sky asks. She gestures to the almost complete pair of green combat trousers on the one nearest her. 'Most of the one's I've seen are naked or at least wearing a lot less and in much worse condition. But these...' She stands and looks at all five. 'These clothes don't look too bad.'

'Thinking up your next outfit?' Chilli teases her.

'And what if I am?' she argues back. 'Green looks good on me.'

Despite Chilli and Sky bickering off to the side, I get to my feet and glance at Elder and Loom. All three of us share a silent look of deep concern over the mystery of the zombie pit.

'Okay,' Elder puts on his usual easy going yet authoritative demeanour. 'Boys, go and sort breakfast. Sky, finish the sweep and watch out for any more... zombie traps. Kiddo and I will bury the biters.'

Everyone nods and does as instructed. They head back to the church together muttering theories. Once they're clear, he stands close and looks me dead in the eye.

'This is very worrying,' he says quietly.

'You're telling me. Of all the places in the world to find a trap with five relatively clean Class Threes, what's the likelihood of finding it in a site we stayed in a few weeks ago?'

'There are three other Canary groups. I know each of their leaders personally. And none of them would ever come out this far. And none make traps like this.'

'Did you put this location in the pigeon letter you sent back when we last stayed here?' I ask.

He nods slowly and we both look down at the pit once more.

'You know as well as I do. This isn't a zombie trap, Elder. This is a People trap.' I look at him. 'This is a Canary trap!'

'We can't be certain of that,' he says, clearly not believing a word he just said. 'Nonetheless. We should get them buried and get out of here. Quickly.'

'Agreed. Let's get the hell out of here.'

CHAPTER ELEVEN

'What. The hell. Is that?'

'That, Chilli... is a giant greenhouse,' Elder replies, jumping down from his horse and heading towards the balcony ahead of us. We all climb down and follow his lead. 'Would ya look at that...' he mutters, letting out a long appreciative sigh and gently shaking his head side to side. 'Absolutely stunning. Have you ever seen anything so... beautiful?'

At the end of the balcony we all stop and marvel at the scene before us. We're standing along the top of a huge dugout pit. Below is a meandering path leading left to right then right to left, all the way down to the very bottom where at the base are two large dome shapes, covered in moss.

And they are huge!

Probably sixty metres high and two hundred metres wide if I were to hazard a guess. One of them has caved in. The roof is half missing. But the other has lush green foliage spilling out the very top through open slits in the domes.

'I've never seen plants like that!' I say in awe. 'Maybe in the illustrated version of the Jungle book. But not in real life.'

The leaves are thick and must be a minimum of three meters wide.

Loom notices a plaque to our right, wipes it clean of dust and grime, and starts reading aloud.

'Apparently, this place was used to grow plants from all over the world. The dome things *are* greenhouses. Just like Elder said.' He looks over at the large one spouting green. 'That one is from the rainforests, the other is from the Mediterranean. They called it... *The Eden Project.'* He glances at me over his shoulder. 'Well done, Boss. Good call on deciding to come here. Can you imagine all the stuff that's growing in there?'

'Why do you think I wanted to come here? We can harvest seeds and take them home.' I lean over the vista point. Along the paths there are several Class Threes aimlessly wandering about. Arms by their sides, their heads lolling as they continue with their incessant gurgling. Flesh hangs off their thin and decaying corpses. Bile drips from their orifices onto the floor. 'I count twelve. But there will be some more inside the collapsed Mediterranean dome I imagine. And see over there?' I point into the distance to my left. And then to my right. 'There are two smaller buildings. I can't see doors from here, but there may be more in there too. Loom, can you grab my brown satchel?'

'Yes! I love your brown satchel,' Loom says excitedly as he rushes over to Hanzo to fetch it. I open it up and pull out the only other piece of weaponry I love as much as my Katanas. Well, almost as much.

My slingshot.

The handle of which is made from an old Smith and Weston pistol I found a few months ago. No ammo of course. But I don't need bullets. I have something so much better than a shell containing gunpowder.

I climb up onto the ledge of the balcony, the satchel thrown over my shoulder and the slingshot firmly in my hand.

'Let's see what we can lure out.' I dig my hand into the satchel and pull out a balloon which I filled with my own blood. I got the idea from the incident during final assessment. Those suckers really went crazy for my blood. I pop it into the slingshot, take aim and let it fly. As they balloon soars high through the air, the others run to the edge of the balcony to watch. It carries on and lands with a splat in front of the dome.

'Great shot!' Chilli admires. 'Can I have a go?'

'Go bleed yourself if you wanna play with my slingshot. You have any idea how long it takes to make these things?'

The balloon has exploded on the concrete and the smell of my blood attracts every single one of the Class Threes in the vicinity. They turn and smell the air. Their gurgling turns to that chilling screeching as they make their way quickly towards the red puddle on the ground. Most fall flat on their faces to lick it up.

'I really love your blood bombs,' Loom says with a smile. 'You're right too... look at them all come scurrying.' He nods to the building on the left and at the additional Class Threes stumbling towards the blood. They bump into each other and trip over their feet. Some are missing arms. One has the flesh missing from their thigh, showing their bones. I pull out my binoculars.

'Another eight...' I count as they appear.

'We can take them on,' Sky says, retrieving a bow from her quiver.

'Hold it, Sky. Wait for it...'

'Wait for what?'

'Just wait.' They all stand silent. After a minute or so, Loom goes to talk. 'I said wait!'

There it is. A high-pitched shriek followed by a loud smash as a Class Two comes charging out of a building towards the blood. It tosses the others out of its way as if they're nothing more than bowling pins at the end of an alley. When it reaches the blood, it gets on all fours and starts lapping it up.

'Good call,' Elder says quietly.

'Well, it seems to be a trend. Where there's a fair amount of Class Threes, there tends to be a Class Two lurking about. That's twenty Class Threes and a Class Two in total. Here...' I hand Loom the binoculars to hold as I pull out another blood bomb and let it loose towards the building on the right. When it lands on the floor, Loom hands me back the binoculars. We watch in silence as more Class Threes appear from the back of the structure.

'There must be a door to that building around the side, out of sight.' I hear another high-pitched scream. I scan the area but can't see it. 'And there's another Class Two somewhere.' I sigh, looking to the second dome where the roof is half destroyed. 'Sounds like it's in there. Stuck I'd imagine if it can't get to the blood.' I look around us, taking in the details of the area. 'There's no point in attempting to secure the location as a whole. We don't have the time or resources. Not if we want to get home before the snow starts. It's far too large an area for us to build any kind of wall that will be of any real defence against any Class of zom. But...' I gesture to the dome that is lush with life. 'That *must* be kept secured. That's our mission here. Get down there and check if it's been breached. If it has, we clear it and seal it. Agreed?' I look at each and every one of them in turn. Including Elder Eight. They all nod their agreement.

'I can get up on the roof of that building on the left,' Sky says, pointing to the structure. 'I've got thirty arrows. I can put down as many as possible. But once that Class Two sees me it's gonna come straight for me. And it will be able to get up to me. Those things can jump pretty damn high.'

An image of the Class Two leaping on me during evaluation springs to mind. It cleared the first floor easy.

I look to Elder Eight for further instructions. But the team are all watching me. Waiting. Elder simply waits too. He's handing it all over to me. A final test maybe?

'Alright. Sky, you follow this ridge up until you're directly behind the building. Then climb down and get on the roof. When you get up there, take out as many Class Threes as you can as quickly as you can. There's no point taking on the Two. Arrows rarely go through the skull anyways. Best not to waste them or piss it off. Me and the others will head down in the standard formation. Three up front. One behind.'

'I'll keep up the rear and get the stragglers,' Elder says. 'You, Loom and Chilli take point.'

I nod. 'Loom to the right. Chilli to the left. Me front and centre. As we go, keep an eye on your arrow recovery.'

'I'll collect them and get them to Sky,' Chilli adds.

'I'll deal with the Class Two,' I tell them. 'Seal the horses up in the foyer building behind us. Give them enough food and water for a few days. Just in case we get stuck. We'll let them have a good rest while we work. They'll be safe in there.'

Everyone goes to sort the horses as Elder joins me at the edge.

'I think we should add this to our list of possibilities,' I tell him. 'What do you think?'

'Hmmm, being on low ground ain't that great. If we do build a secure wall like the one back home and it's breached, everyone would have to climb up the hill to get out. It's not practical.'

'True,' I agree. 'But, if we build the wall from the coast which is two miles south of here…' I point towards the direction of the sea. 'And then go around this place and along for another mile or so before building it back towards the water, we would have plenty of warning from the Green coats on the wall about a breach. And, we could separate this section. Build another wall between this and the land up to the water. Only use this location for growing. No one would sleep here. Just work. That greenhouse dome is filled with life. We can't abandon it.' He nods slowly, thinking it over. 'There are miles of empty farmland surrounding this place. And only three small villages between here and the water. The houses are in good condition. We wouldn't have to do much maintenance.'

'I have to say I agree,' he says. 'I'll add it to the list. We'll need to check for a possible water supply.'

'Judging by those plants, I'd say there's water here somewhere.' We look back out to the giant dome. 'Elder, this would make an excellent settlement. Much better than The Haven.'

'Ready?' Chilli calls over as he pulls up his mask. Sky painted his. It's a set of teeth with a strawberry lodged between them in honour of his crime. Beside him, Loom has his double-bladed axe in his hand. He pulls up his mask in preparation for the fight. His *"Knight in shining armour"* mask. Sky painted it to look like one of those metal helmets on a suit of armour from way back when. Sky stands beside him with her own mask up and every single one of them is watching me. Waiting for my instruction.

For me to lead them.

'I told you they've chosen you,' Elder whispers quietly before taking his place beside them. He draws his sword and pulls up his own mask. Sky drew on a bright red version of his handlebar moustache for him which he thought was hilarious.

'Okay... Sky, get to the roof of the building,' I tell her. 'The rest of us will head down slowly, give you time to get there. And keep an eye out for any other targets we didn't see.'

She nods and sprints off. I turn and head towards the meandering path. The others follow.

It's times like this I always think of my people back home. Of what they're doing right now. I imagine Tee on the wall. I bet she's got close to Owl. They'd make great friends. And then I think of Cass leading his units to locations of recovery and cleansing. The locations of the places we've seen in our long tour of England will be given to the Elders back home, and they'll decide which areas are worth sending a unit to. We provide details of distance to the point of interest and conditions they can expect to find. They'll use that info to decide how many units to send. How long it will take. How many carts they should bring in order to carry stuff home. And so on.

But Elder and I have bigger plans.

We want to create another Haven. Expand our safe zone. Building one down here, in the south of the country, means that we reclaim more land. That the Canaries won't need to spend almost a year out in the wild to gather intel.

Imagine!

Setting up towns all over the country. It's logical! Elder agrees. But convincing everyone back home may prove difficult. They're safe and comfortable in their little cage made of stone.

Especially Noah. Lord of us all.

So, Elder and I have kept our idea to ourselves until we can figure out a way to pitch it to the others back home.

As we reach the end of the path, I see Sky on the roof. Her bow poised and an arrow just waiting to fly. Her face is nothing but focused on her lethal aim. She may have her head in the clouds, but hell, she's one serious archer. I pull up my mask, unsheathe my katanas and give them a playful spin in my palms.

God, I love this.

The targets are all gathered in a circle, clawing at the ground, desperate to try and get even the slightest bit of my blood from the blood bomb. But the Class Two keeps tossing them away so it can lick it all up itself.

I raise my hand and Sky lets the first of her arrows fly. Then another. And another. All strike the heads of the Class Threes she aims for. But the Class Two notices and stands up. It turns and sees us approaching. It throws back its head. Its grey skin is pulled tightly around its ridiculously large muscles. Its fingernails have grown well over two inches and looks like sharpened bone. It digs in its feet, bends its knees, and sprints towards us. The Class Threes following it close behind.

'Death or glory,' I mutter.

'Their death... our glory,' I hear Cass reply in my imagination. *'Kick their arse, Scarlett. Then get yourself home to me.'*

CHAPTER TWELVE

We all charge.

Weapons ready and hearts full of determination. The two armies collide like waves on a cliff. I hear the others shouting and grunting as they swing their swords and axes. I hear them cutting through rotted flesh and brittle bones. I hear the squelch and splat of the blood and limbs they hack free.

I thrust my left blade through the gut of a Class Three, and as another approaches from my right, I swipe straight across its neck, severing its head completely. Heaving my still embedded blade in my left hand upwards, I split the corpse in two from the belly up. Just as the Class Two reaches me. I raise up my weapons in a cross above my head and strike them down. But before I get a chance to introduce its dead flesh to my steel, it body slams me hard and knocks me to the floor. With its full body weight on top of me, my arms are pinned to my chest. But what's worse is the way I've landed has my crossed blades an inch from my neck. As it keeps lunging at me with its teeth, chomping over and over, the blades get closer and closer.

An arrow lands straight in its eye.

Thank you, Sky.

I drop one of my swords and grab the arrow instead. I yank it out and thrust it upwards through its jaw at an angle to clamp its mouth shut. And then I slam my fist, as well as the knuckle-duster, straight into its face again and again and again until I get it far enough off me that I can buck it off. I snatch up my second sword, jump to my feet and attack.

I strike.

It dodges.

I strike again.

It bloody dodges.

I lift up both my blades ready to cut its sodding head off when I feel a set of teeth clamp down on my shoulder. The smell of death and rot comes with it. A Class Three tries desperately to get through the thick wool of my jacket as well as the leather of my coat beneath it.

No way that's gonna happen.

The Class Two claws at its own face, digging its razor-sharp nails into its flesh as it tries to get rid of the arrow keeping its mouth sealed shut.

Suddenly, it grabs its jaws with both hands and wrenches it open, dislodging the arrow and breaking its bones in the process. It wiggles its jaw side to side, lodging the bones back in place before sprinting to me with a snarl. I slam the knuckle-dusters into the face of the Class Three and kick the Class Two hard in the chest before it can reach me. As it staggers back, I take the seconds I've bought myself to turn and slice off the head of the hungry little shit that was trying to nibble my shoulder. I turn back to the oncoming Class Two, duck down low and... *swipe*. Off with its feet. It falls with a furious screech beside me. I jump up and take two more of its weapons away.

Swipe... swipe.

Off with its arms.

I stand over it and try to stifle my smile as I cut the suckers head clean off. But no time to gloat. I stab it through its temple, flick my blades clean - well, *cleaner* - and turn to help the others with the remaining Class Threes.

Chilli has a fist full of arrows and is currently sprinting towards Sky who is crouched low with her arm outstretched, ready to take them. He uses an old, silver table to leap high into the air so he can reach her. The exchange is quick. Seamless. She's back on her feet letting loose arrow after arrow as Chilli runs straight back at the Class Threes, his sword ready and a look of severity on his face that turns him into an entirely different person.

To my right, Loom is dismembering target after target with his double-sided axe. The blade never stops moving. It's like watching Winder. But less ginger.

'Quit daydreaming, Kiddo!' Elder bellows from behind. I turn and watch him effortlessly bring down his sword on a straggler. The head rolls down the hill and lands at my feet. Its jaws are still snapping. They stop after I stick it with my Katana right through its temple. 'Get to bloody work!'

'Err... guys?' Sky calls. I don't even need to look in her direction to know what's got her attention. The dome to the right, the one with its roof caved in, it's spewing zombies! Somehow, they're climbing up the sides from the inside and falling down on the outside. One, then another and another tumble over and land on the floor with a thud. Their legs may be broken. Their torsos twisted and their arms mangled. But they have their eyes on us and they're coming. There's one hell of a crash as the side of the dome breaks apart under the pressure and an army of undead, starving monsters spill out.

'Holy hell... there's hundreds!'

Chilli, Elder and Loom finish their kills and join me, their weapons ready. Even Sky has jumped down to join us.

'There's too many,' I tell them. One thing I've learnt quickly out here, know what fight you can win, and leg it from the ones you can't. 'Abandon mission.'

'We need to get back up the hill!' Loom says. We turn, but more have appeared from behind us and are heading at us from over the ridge. We're completely penned in and there are too many to fight. 'What the hell do we do?'

'We climb!' I point to the dome on the left. 'We climb up the foliage and slip inside through the vents at the top.' I shove Sky in that direction as she stares at the oncoming army of death in horror. 'GO! NOW!'

We all run like hell, slicing and hacking at the ones that manage to reach us, and dodging the rest.

'LOOM, LIFT!' He turns and cups his hands. I leap and he catches me before throwing me high into the air. I toss a blood bomb as far away from us as I can. It lands on the ground and explodes. It drives them crazy, and a few turn their attention to that instead of us. But most prefer the very alive humans to the bag of week old blood. Loom grabs my arm as I land and pulls me towards the dome. I kill one on my right. He kills one on his left. The noise they're making is almost deafening. The smell is more than I can bear!

Ahead, Elder is helping Chilli reach one of the large, thick leaves dangling above him. He grabs it and pulls himself up the side of the giant dome, using that and the vines as rope. The next to reach the side is Sky. She glances back at Loom and me over her shoulder.

'Scar!' she screeches. Elder grabs her before she can turn on her heel to help us, and hurls her upwards. She latches onto the vines and watches us below with dread. Elder looks back at us.

'HURRY UP!' he yells. 'STOP BLOODY DAWDLING!'

'GET UP THERE!' I order him. 'NOW! DON'T WAIT FOR US!' He stows his sword, swears under his breath, takes a few steps back and then sprints at the side of the dome. He leaps and grabs a thick vine.

But the horde around us is getting closer no matter how fast we run.

I slam the butt of my hilt into a dead face. And then stab at one over my shoulder. Loom decapitates one on his left with a forceful swipe and then another as he retracts it. His arms move like a deadly pendulum, as he just keeps cutting down anything that gets in our way. An arrow hisses as it passes my ear and lands through the temple of one an inch from me. I grab the arrow before the corpse gets a chance to fall. A rotting hand wraps around my arm. Another whoosh and an arrow lands in its face. I look up. Sky's on the wall of the dome. Chilli has her by the scruff of her coat as she dangles there with her bow and arrow, letting loose arrow after arrow. She gives us more of a clear path, but there are still too many. I duck as one claws at my face, spinning and driving my blade up through its jaw before continuing my sprinting.

Stab. Kick. Swipe. And then... *screech.*

'CLASS TWO!' Elder bellows, pointing behind us. 'It's charging through the crowd of Class Threes. GET YOUR ARSES UP HERE, THE PAIR OF YOU!'

I've never heard fear in Elder Eight's voice before. But I certainly hear it now.

I grab a plastic tray left on the floor and use it to slam into the face of a Class Three that's got far too close. And then another. And another. Until it shatters in my hands.

The dome is close. Ten metres maybe.

To our right, the screeching's getting louder. I see the Class Threes being tossed out of the way as the Class Two barges through. It's getting real close, real fast.

We reach the dome. Loom turns and cups his hands.

I sheath my swords and run towards him. My foot lands in his palms and he tosses me up. I grab one of the vines and look back down below.

'GET UP HERE!' I yell at him. Sky shoots the last of her arrows, giving him the space and time he needs to do a run and jump up to the vine beside me. He misses a swarm of hands by inches.

He sighs with relief, puffing out his cheeks with wide eyes.

'That was bloody close, huh?'

'Are you okay?' I ask him. 'Are you hurt?'

'I'm fine. You?'

I nod. We look at the mass of dead below. In the not too far distance is the Class Two still steaming towards us. And now we're up high, we can see what exactly had Elder Eight sounding so scared.

'Oh my god!' I whisper. 'What the hell is that?' The Class Two is huge. Seven feet tall and built like a gorilla. Not only that, but it's covered in spikes! Long poles with sharp edges are sticking out from all over its body, but not a single one is near its head. I'd say someone must have tried to take it down and failed miserably. I feel the material beneath us. The walls that make the dome isn't glass. It feels like plastic. It's strong. It can easily hold our weight and a lot more besides I imagine. But the spikes sticking out of that monster look very, very sharp.

'We can't let it touch the sides. Those spikes could tear the wall and the insides will be compromised,' I tell Loom.

'Well you ain't jumping down there to face that thing,' he insists with a horrified scoff.

'Hold me.'

'Hold you?'

'Yeah. Grab my waist and don't drop me. What do you think I meant? A bloody snuggle? I need both my hands. Quick! Before it gets any closer!'

He reaches over and takes hold of me around my waist as instructed, pinning me close to his body and wrapping his leg around mine to keep me close.

'I sure hope this vine stays attached. Or we're both screwed.' he mutters. He ain't wrong.

'Bet you're glad I skip the odd meal now, ain't ya?' I laugh, pulling out my slingshot and loading it with a blood bomb.

'Your pillow talk leaves much to be desired. Snuggle buddy.' He nods to the horde below. 'Focus.'

I aim it at the Class two and fire. It slams into its flesh; the bag explodes as it hits one of the spikes. A couple of the Class Threes turn and look at it with what I imagine confusion for the dead looks like. But it keeps coming. The Class Two makes its way through. The others start sniffing it. I smile and let loose another, feeling more confident in my plan. It hits it square in the face. It slows and starts licking itself so fiercely, it slices its tongue on the spikes protruding from its body. But it's the reaction of the Class Threes around it that I'm interested in. They're turning to face it, their noses in the air.

'You clever thing. It's working...' Loom whispers, as the vine starts to groan. He reaffirms his grip on me, pulling me in tighter. 'Hit it again.'

I pull out another and hit the Class Two in the shoulder. It's almost completely covered in blood now and the others can't resist. One sinks its teeth into its shoulder. The Class Two pulls away and growls at it. I send another which hits its stomach. Another Class Three grabs at it. Then another. It snarls and snaps its jaws at them. It tosses one away, but it's soon replaced by another, hungry and chomping. I reach into my satchel for the last blood bomb. I load it, and send it through the air. It hits it and the air fills with the excited grunting of countless starving, blood-thirsty monsters that can't tell the difference between my blood and the Class Two it's soaked in.

'You bloody genius!' Elder laughs as they all turn on the Class Two, and soon it disappears beneath a pile of zombies. The screeching and the sound of tearing flesh echo off the hillsides surrounding us.

Loom flinches. But I find it the best sound ever.

'Thanks for the hug,' I laugh. 'And such a gentleman. Barely any groping. You really are a knight in shining armour.'

'Anytime,' he chuckles, blushing ever so slightly. 'But if you don't mind, this vine is about to snap.'

I reach over and take a vine of my own and look up at the three others above who stopped to watch. They're all beaming, and Elder Eight looks as proud as I've ever seen.

'Let's go see a jungle.'

CHAPTER THIRTEEN

In the roof are countless open triangular windows, some of which have been torn from their hinges by thick vines. Elder Eight reaches down and hauls Sky up the last stretch. Chilli helps Loom on his final effort to reach the top and when Elder extends his hand to me, I take it gladly. The fight alone was tiring. That climb must have been almost a hundred metres. We're all exhausted! I slump a little when I reach the top and rest my forehead on Elder's shoulder as I catch my breath.

'Holy ja-moly. This is a big greenhouse,' I pant, looking down through one of the windows. 'That is a looong way down.'

Below is the most green I've ever seen. Leaves of all shapes, sizes and colours obscure whatever lies below. There's a chill in the air out here, but there's a warmth emanating from inside and a smell of damp and rotting vegetation that's oddly enticing.

I look at them all. 'Is everyone okay? Anyone hurt?'

They all tell me they're fine, just exhausted and pumped up on adrenaline. Which is a huge relief.

'You?' Elder asks.

'I'm good,' I reply, waving my hand dismissively.

'I'm not,' Chilli wheezes, his head low and his shoulders rising and falling at speed. 'I'm absolutely knackered. Chr ist... I can hardly breathe.'

'Well,' Elder grumbles. 'I hate to break it to ya, but we've gotta climb down the bloody thing now.'

His words have us all groaning.

'Right...' Elder is attempting to sound filled with energy and enthusiasm. 'Let's get inside and see what we got.'

Chilli slides through the window first, followed closely by Sky. Loom is next and then finally Elder Eight. I watch them all grab hold of various foliage, trunks and vines, before sliding in myself and shimmying down the trunk of a tree of some kind. Every muscle in my body is screaming for rest. But thankfully the adrenaline is still pumping hard, giving me the energy I need not to fall to my death.

'You alright?' Sky asks quietly as I begin to slow. She eyes me nervously, setting her sights on my hands which are white from how hard I'm holding onto the trunk. 'You ain't gonna fall, are ya?'

'I'm fine, Sky. You just concentrate on where your feet are going.'

'You fought hard and you haven't slept much in the last couple of days. You sure you okay to do this climb?'

'That's because you kept me awake again talking about building a rocket and starting a new life on the moon,' I sigh. 'Like I said. I'm fine.'

'You haven't really eaten either,' she mumbles.

'Enough, Sky. Stop. Now is not the time to scold me. Okay?' She's right though. Annoyingly. I'm running on fumes. I haven't slept more than four hours in the last three days. I didn't eat before I left camp because the knot that pit by the well created in my stomach made it impossible. I really hope I don't fall. After everything I've been through, falling to my death would just be embarrassing. I take a deep breath and carry on with the climb.

'We could ya know...' she grumbles to herself as she continues shimmying down. 'It's possible. There must still be rockets-'

'Wait...' I stop climbing and so does she. 'Can you hear that?' We listen. Her eyes narrow as she hears it.

'Is that water?' she asks excitedly.

We look below and see the others have stopped too. We all hear it. The sound of cascading water. We continue down, albeit a little quicker and filled with a little more excitement.

The lower we get, the more we all gasp in awe. And when my feet finally hit the ground, I'm far too excited to give in to my desire to curl up in a ball and sleep.

We stand in a line and marvel at it.

At our beautiful and miraculous find.

The floor is thick with mossy grass and ankle high, vibrant green plants. There are trees reaching up high above us, their leaves stretching out far and wide. Vines connect them all and stretch across the floors like a web. And there are birds and insects making so much noise, it's like a choir made from nature. Like they're all singing to welcome us into their paradise. Their songs echo off the odd plastic material of the dome walls and makes it so much louder than it probably is. But it's not annoying or overwhelming.

It's heavenly.

Compared to the usual grunting and screeching of the dead we have to put up with out in the world, this is bliss.

I look at the faces of the others. And they feel it too. Their amazement and joy is as clear to me as any one of the other emotions I know from them all so well. Usually I see determination. A fierceness. A readiness to die. The thrill of the hunt. The excitement of the kill. Even fear. But now they look lost in wonderment. And I'm lost too.

'When we were forced to listen to all those stories of how the world began back at the orphanage... How the Elders described Eden...' Loom walks a few steps ahead of us, his eyes wide and a small, but blissful smile on his face. 'This is exactly what I imagined. They sure got the name of this place spot on.'

Sky's hand wraps around my wrist and she starts to run. I stumble, she pulls me along so quick.

'What the hell?' I have to jump over trunks and stones as she continues guiding me somewhere. She's giggling like a nutter and keeps a tight hold on my hand. 'Sky! What-' She turns around a bend and stops before pointing up above us.

'Bloody hell!' I gasp.

On the other side of the structure is a waterfall cutting a path down from the top of the dome. The water rushes over jagged boulders and lands in a purpose-built stream which runs underneath a wooden bridge, and then travels like veins in all directions, reaching all parts of the dome. This is the source of the water noise, and this is the best thing that I could have hoped for.

'ELDER!' I holler. I needn't have yelled. He followed us right along with the others. He looks up and starts laughing. I can't help it! I laugh too. 'There's water here! Look at it!

There's water!' I'm borderline hysterical with joy! I take a sip. 'It's fresh! We can drink it!'

'And fruit!' Loom calls from behind us. We turn but can only see some leaves above us start to shake. He leaps down and lands in front of us with something in his hand.

'Is that...' Sky snatches it out of his hand and peels it. She bites. 'It's a banana!' she gasps. 'I've read about them! Scar, look! Look!' She thrusts it into my hand and I take a bite. All I can manage is a low moan as I taste it for the first time. It's sweet and unlike anything I've ever eaten before. I hand it to Elder and he has a bite too. And then he hands it to Chilli.

'No need to share, guys,' Loom says, as he pulls out two more from his pockets and tosses them at Sky and myself. 'There are hundreds!' He points upwards and sure enough, nestled close to the trunks of the trees are more. Countless more. 'This is unbelievable!'

'It is all very exciting. And better than we could have ever hoped,' I tell him, handing my banana to Elder Eight. 'But first things first. We need to make sure this place is secure. Priority number one. Check the structure. Loom, Chilli, you walk anticlockwise around the wall. Elder and I will go clockwise. We'll meet in the middle. Sky, I want you to get up as high as you can and check the roof. And also try to get a lay of the land. Get up to the top of that waterfall. It seems the highest point.'

'Sure thing, Boss.' She peels her banana and happily skips off, bow over her shoulder and an empty quiver. We'll have to spend some time replenishing her arrows. Luckily, there are plenty of supplies in here to do that. A very happy

Loom and Chilli head off towards the wall. Stuffing their faces with banana and laughing triumphantly.

'They're happy.'

'They bloody well should be!' Elder says, heading off and nodding for me to follow. 'This is a big win, Kiddo. A very big win. Look at what you've found!' He opens his arms wide, his handlebar moustache stretched across his face as he grins.

'*We* found.' I correct him. But he shakes his head.

'*You* found it. You wanted to travel south when I said north. You found this place's details in the tourist centre I said was a waste of time to visit. You persuaded us to carry on when every single one of us wanted to stick around North Wessex. And you are the one that found the locations we've added as possible settlements. No other Canaries have ever made it this far and lived to tell the tale.'

'Which is why our pitch to the others back home has to be accepted. If we can set up more settlements in different parts of the country, we wouldn't have to spend so long out here just to get from one end of the country to the other. We have a fortress in the east. We need one in the south, the west and the north at least!' I argue. 'How can we ever hope to reclaim this country if we hide away in that tiny little corner all the time.'

'Hey, I agree,' he says. 'Scarlett, you have found three fantastic locations that would be perfect to build on. That holiday village in Longleat forest. That island a few miles off the coast of what was left of Portsmouth. Now this one! None are a quick fix to this apocalyptic mess. But they're certainly places and outcomes worth fighting for.' He throws his strong arm over my shoulders. I feel ready to buckle under the weight of it. 'Can you imagine, clearing that island! We wouldn't need walls at all. It would take years of hard work. But we could do it! I'm so proud of you, Kiddo.' I look up at him as he smiles at me. 'Cass and the others will be so proud of everything you've achieved.'

'As long as they're still alive, that's more than enough for me.'

He gives me the slightest one-armed hug before steering us left as the others go right.

'See ya in a while,' Chilli calls back with a mouth full of banana before they disappear into the jungle.

'Be safe, boys!' I order back.

Elder and I walk side by side and do our best to follow the walls. It's impossible to see through the thick layer of moss and plant life that has grown all along the inside. It covers the lower half of the wall completely. But we take our time and inspect it as much as we can. I run my fingers along as much of it as possible. Not necessarily feeling for damage, but feeling nature itself. I stumble over a root but quickly straighten myself. I feel Elder watching me. And sure enough, he's got something to say.

'You're not looking after yourself nearly enough. You don't sleep. You barely eat.'

'Not this again. Christ. Are you and Sky on a harassment committee or something? I appreciate your concern. But I'm fine. Honestly.' I stop and look ahead with a sigh. 'The rest is a rock face. It follows the wall around for as far as I can see. Unless we learn to rock climb, there's no way to check it.'

'Yeah well... unless those Class Threes learn to climb the dome or do another body wall like they did in the other dome, I think we're safe. So, let's be careful not to spill our blood or make too much noise, and they should leave this place well enough alone.' He reaches up and grabs a couple of bananas. 'Eat,' he orders, thrusting it in my face. I take it and we continue walking. Eating and laughing as we go.

'This place is unreal!' Chilli chirps as we rendezvous.

'Is it secure?' I ask.

'Oh yeah. The main entrance to this place was sealed up from the outside and the walls are completely intact. No sign of any zoms either. Looks like it was locked up to keep it safe. But never mind that. Look at what we found.' He shakes a bottle he has in his hand. Elder Eight charges past me, pushing me unceremoniously out the way and almost leaps on the poor guy.

'Oh, you amazing, beautiful creature...' he says in a low, seductive tone, taking the bottle in his palms and licking his lips.

'Why thank you, Elder. You're rather beautiful yourself,' Chilli chuckles.

'Not you, ya twit. This!' He holds up the bottle with gentle hands and even more wonderment than he had when we first got in here. 'Rum... oh my dear friend. I've not seen you since I was a young Canary. I do enjoy whiskey. Port too. But rum... that's my real love.' He gives it a kiss and then points at us all with the bottle firmly in hand. 'Right.

Let's find that arrow-wielding nutcracker. We're gonna set up camp, gather some grub and drink this bad boy.'

'But... we need to come up with a plan on how to get out of here,' I remind him. 'We're surrounded by the undead. The horses are sealed up in that-' But he's already turned on his heel and started heading towards the waterfall. 'Elder! We have to make a plan! Elder!'

'Not tonight, Kiddo. Tonight... we celebrate!' He lifts the bottle above his head and yells out happily, 'Tonight, we drink. RUM TIME!'

Chilli and Loom stand beside me as we watch him almost skip away.

'Probably best not to tell him we found three cases of that stuff,' Loom adds with a laugh.

'Hell no. He'll never want to leave,' I reply with a soft chuckle. 'Come on. You heard the man. Rum time.'

With an enormous grin on each of our faces, we follow him to find Sky.

As we reach the waterfall, Sky gives a high-pitched whistle. Looking up, we see her right at the top. She waves her arms and squeals gleefully before heading down to meet us.

'You would not believe what is in here,' she says. 'There was some kind of bridge that looks like it went right across this place. It hung from the ceiling.' She points up to a few long pieces of wire cable dangling above us. 'It must have collapsed because there's metal steps laying across the ground over there.' She points to the right. 'It's under a load of undergrowth. And there's a roof of a cabin or hut in that direction.' She points towards the left. 'And over there...'She points to the doors of the dome. 'Over there is a truck-'

Elder slaps her hard on the back. 'Take us to the cabin.'

'But... there's a truck. It might still work considering it's been locked up in here,' she says. 'We could use it to escape.'

'And maybe we can use the wire and metal from the staircase for weapons,' Chilli says.

'Yeah...' Loom agrees. 'We could use that to turn the truck into a battering ram or something.'

'And Sky's out of arrows,' I tell him. 'We need to make some more. There's plenty of-'

'CADET'S! ATTEEEEN-TION!' Elder bellows, making us all jump. His tone is exactly as it was when we were back in training. Its arrival has us all standing in a line, backs straight and palms flat against our thighs. Our reaction is instinctual. Like breathing. He stands in front of us and looks at us each in turn with those analytical and judging eyes we all know so well. He then starts slowly walking up and down.

'Now. I want you all to listen to me *very* closely,' he says. 'And I don't want to hear any of you to say a single goddamned thing till I'm done sayin' what I gotta say. Got it?' We all nod once. 'Good. Now. We have been out in the wild for nine months and three days. We have slept under bridges. In caves. In a camper van that was previously filled with corpses which I swear, I can still smell in my leather coat. We have destroyed the skulls of hundreds of freaking zombies. Washed a ton of coagulated blood from our hair. Wiped our backsides with leaves. Been bitten by fleas. Stung by wasps. Chased by wolves and hunted by the undead. And I'm pretty sure that I slept in a puddle of Chilli's piss three nights ago.' He glares at Chilli who stifles a chuckle. 'We have not had a single moment of real peace, rest or relaxation in the whole nine months and three days we've been out here. The horses are sealed up safely with food and water. Enough to last for four days. So... we are goin' to that cabin Sky has seen. We are gonna gather food that is growing in this dome. We are gonna all sleep at the same time. We are gonna sleep for many, many hours. A whole day in fact. We're gonna take off these goddamned leather coats. Put down our weapons and rest. But first...' He holds up the bottle and gives it a gentle shake. 'We are gonna drink the entire contents of this bottle of rum. I want to hear every single joke you know. I want to hear the best anecdotes you have. Then... and only then... when we have done everything I have just said... will we figure out how to get out of here.' He looks at us all in turn, daring us to argue. 'Have I made myself perfectly clear?' he asks.

I raise my hand slowly. He stares daggers at me.

'Kiddo?' he growls. 'You have a problem?'

'No, Elder. Just thought you might want to know that the boys actually found three cases of the rum. So...' Elder breaks into an enormous, heart-warming smile.

'Perfect,' he says. 'Absolutely perfect.'

The first thing we did when we reached the little bamboo cabin was take off our coats, our weapons and our shoes. Well, it's only polite when entering someone else's house. And it's bloody boiling in here! We're all sweating like crazy in this humidity. We stand in the doorway in our socks, vests and trousers, and have a good look around this odd little structure.

The wide, wooden planks that make up the floor are thick in dust. It puffs up into the air and lingers with every footstep. To the left is a double bed made of crates pushed together. In the far corner is a shoddy shelving unit made of logs tied together with thick string. I press my foot harder on the planks, pressing my body weight onto it. They creak, but hold. Knowing it's safe, I head inside.

The shelves hold pots, pans, plates and bowls. Next to that is a chest. Inside which are cooking tins, magazines and something I know Elder will simply love. I pick up the deck of playing cards and toss it at him. He catches it and chuckles.

'Right!' He grins. 'Chilli, fetch the rest of that rum. Sky, grab some more bananas. Loom, help me sweep these floors, would ya? This dust can't be good for our lungs.'

'Yes, Elder,' they all respond.

'What about me?' I ask.

'Kiddo, sit your backside down and take a breather. Before you fall over.'

'I can help.'

'Please, Boss,' Chilli says as I go to argue. 'Let us look after you for a change, huh? Sit. Drink. Relax.' He winks before heading to the door. 'Because if you're not on top form when we try and get past that horde outside, pretty sure we'll all be torn to shreds. No pressure.'

Loom grabs a couple of brooms from the corner and hands one to Elder as Sky heads out to find some food.

'Fine,' I groan, knowing I'm beat.

I pick up something sitting on a makeshift coffee table called a *"Guide book"* and lay on the bed. Book in hand, back against the wall, and feet well and truly up, I take that breather they're all so keen on me to have. As they sweep, I flick through it.

'What does it say?' Loom asks, cleaning the floor with very little enthusiasm.

'That the hut was built to demonstrate how people live in a real rainforest,' I tell him. 'According to this, this whole dome was designed to be a rainforest ecosystem. Whatever that means.'

'It means they made the atmosphere hotter than normal and more humid so plants that normally couldn't grow in England can thrive,' Elder explains, tossing the broom to the floor and plonking his arse on the bed beside me. 'That'll do. What else does it say?' He puts up his feet and leans his back against the wall just as I have, and gestures for the rum. 'C'mon and sit down, Loom.'

Loom heads over with it in his hand and passes it to Elder before sitting on my other side. We're all chilling with our feet up as Elder opens up the rum. He takes a sip and moans in pleasure before handing it to me.

'It says that the dome's completely self-sufficient. It collects rainwater and has access to an underground stream,' I tell him. 'And, there are over a hundred different types of fruit, vegetables and herbs growing in here. As well as rice plants.' I take a sip and cough as I swallow. 'What the-' cough, splutter, 'That's strong!' I hand it to Loom, as Elder chuckles to himself. I continue to flick through the pages. 'There are recipes in here.'

'Really?' Loom says, leaning over and having a look. 'Recipes?' He takes a sip and gives a little cough as he swallows, but that doesn't stop him having more.

'And all the ingredients are in this dome,' I add, handing it over and pointing out a particularly delicious looking one. 'You think you can make it?'

'Of course. I can make anything.' That's true. He's a fantastic cook. He can make roots taste like... well... not roots. He has another sip and takes the book. 'I'll fetch the ingredients and we can have a real meal tonight.'

'Want some help?' I ask.

'Nah. You stay put.' As he heads to the door, he looks back and points at the bottle. 'Drink. It will help you sleep.'

I doubt that.

I hand the bottle to Elder and sigh deeply. He's watching me closely.

'You're gonna overheat,' he says, gesturing to my leather trousers and corset.

'You're right.' Sitting, I unbuckle my corset and toss it to the floor next to the rest of my leathers.

'You should take off those cuffs too.'

'Nope. Never,' I reply, running my fingers gently over the edge of the leather. 'I never take them off. They've saved my life more times than I can count.'

He takes a sip before getting to his feet.

'They remind you of Cass. Don't pretend otherwise. I'm gonna leave and give you some privacy so you can sleep.

I suggest you take off your trousers so you don't overheat.' He picks up his jacket, folds it up and lays it on the bed as a pillow. 'Sleep. That's an order, Kiddo.'

'I appreciate your concern. But honestly, I'm fine. I could do more sweeping if you wanna put your feet up.'

'Scarlett.' His hand lands firmly on my shoulder as I attempt to stand. He holds me in place and glares at me. 'Lay down and sleep willingly. Or I will knock out and you will sleep forcibly.' Part of me kinda believes him. I lay down and rest my head on his coat. 'Good. I'll wake you up when there's food. You want a drink? Water? Rum?'

I shake my head. 'I'm good. And feeling quite looked after. Thank you.'

'You're worried about Noah. I get that. But this distraction is goin' to get you hurt. Or killed.'

'I'm not worried.'

'Lying won't help-'

'I'm terrified,' I admit in a whisper, knotting my hands together in my lap. 'Elder... what if he forces me into marriage when we go home. What if he threatens Winder, Tee and Cass again? If I have no choice, if it's the only way to keep them safe... I won't be able to say no, will I? He hates Cass. He loathes him and I worry that if he hasn't already, he'll kill him. I hate to admit it. Especially to you. But Noah frightens me.'

'I've never heard you say you're frightened before. Does he scare you more than that horde out there?'

I nod. 'A lot more. Those monsters will just kill me. Noah can lock me up for the rest of my life. Force me to be his wife. Force me to give him children. He could sentence my friends to The Canaries.'

'You'll kill him before he ever gets to lay a hand on you. Or them. Of that I'm certain,' he replies.

'And then I'll be executed. No matter what, he'll win. And I'll lose.'

He kneels down and rests his hands over mine. 'We have no idea what's waiting for us when we go home. For all we know, he's moved on and chosen another girl to marry. Cass and Winder are probably loving their time in their unit. Doin' what they do best. And Tee is up on that wall. Safe and sound. And all of them are missing you like crazy. Right now, there's nothing you or I can do about what may or may not happen back home. All we can do is survive the here and now. And you won't survive if you keep yourself up at night worrying about the people you sacrificed everything for in the first place. *They're* safe. They have their coats. They have each other. The protection of the wall. That's why you did this. You can't give any more than you already have. They wouldn't want you to die out here to protect them.'

'But what if Noah's hurt them while I've been away.'

'And what if he hasn't? Hmm? There's no point worrying about something that may not have even happened.'

'What if he forces me into marriage? What if-'

'What if? What if? What if?' he sighs. 'Focus on the facts. We're trapped in a rainforest. A bloody rainforest! There are hundreds of Class Threes between us and our horses. They have four days of food and water until they die. If they die, we're stranded. We need to get to them while keeping this dome's integrity intact.'

'Then I should make arrows-'

'I don't know if you've noticed, but everyone is at their limit. We can't defeat what we need to defeat in our current condition. And you are our main fighter. We need you if we're gonna get out of here. So please, I know you care about your people back home. But these people need you too. We need you to help get us back home.' He looks me straight in the eye. 'Do you hear me? We need you. Alive. And strong.'

I nod and hold his hand as tight as he's holding mine.

'I hear you.'

He slaps a friendly hand on my shoulder and gets to his feet. 'And for the record, if you are forced to be his wife, I'll slit his goddamn throat before he gets a chance to consummate that marriage. I promise you that.' He's being deadly serious. And it makes me feel a lot better. 'Now sleep.'

He turns and heads to the door.

'Thank you, Elder. If I did believe in God, I'd thank him for sending you to me.' He watches me from the door. 'You've had my back since I was five. I'm only alive because of you.'

'That's not true.'

'It is. I was so afraid when I left the orphanage. If you weren't there, if you weren't the one that taught me how to survive, how to fight... well, I just want you to know. Cass, Tee and Winder...' Saying their names makes my insides ache. I have to swallow down a sob. 'They aren't the only ones I consider my family. You're my family too. And if you hadn't volunteered to come with us, I think I would have given up months ago.'

His face falls a little. I think he's angry. But then... there are tears in his eyes. He quickly clears his throat and gives a small, humble nod.

'You have no idea what that means to me,' he says. 'What you just said... I'm very touched. And I want you to know that I feel exactly the same.'

He does?

He clears his throat again and straightens up. 'But if you ever hint to giving up again, I'll kick your arse. Now, get some rest.' He gestures to the makeshift pillow and leaves. Quickly. Wiping his eyes dry as he goes.

As I lay looking up at the ceiling, the sound of the rainforest outside and the water tumbling over the rocks does very little to settle my nerves. Give me a zombie. Give me a weapon to clean. Hell, I'll sweep the floors. Anything to keep me from thinking of the people I left behind. Anything to keep me from the reality of what I'm going to return to. Noah and his wrath. How I betrayed Winder and Tee. How I left Cass so soon after sleeping with him. I don't want to go home. It will put us all in danger. But yet, I long for them more than I long for anything else in this world.

But I love *these* people too. Loom. Chilli. Sky... Elder Eight. They shouldn't have to suffer because I'm a coward. They need to go home. They want to go home. So... I'll get them home.

I close my eyes and much sooner than I expected, I fall fast asleep.

Sky's hysterical giggle wakes me up. I'm still on the bed, sprawled out on my back. And I am sweating hard. My mouth is dry and my head is thumping. I'm overheating, just as Elder warned me I would. This outfit is fantastic for fighting. But not for sleeping in whilst in a rainforest. I undo the buttons of my leather trousers and lift my hips so I can peel them off. I toss them on the floor and sit in my pants and my long black sleeved top.

I slept.

Not sure for how long. But it was deep and I feel better for it. And then I notice a fantastic smell wafting in from outside. Sky gives another giggle. I get to my feet and have a good stretch before heading out to see what's going on.

'SNAP!' Elder hollers as he slams his hand down hard on a crate he's using as a table, making us all jump.

'GODDAMN IT!' Chilli yells back. 'You're too fast!'

Elder chuckles and picks up the pile of cards between them triumphantly before they both continue slamming down card after card. Sky's on her knees watching them play with an enormous grin, her face etched with excitement.

'You're up! Sleep well?' Loom asks quietly. He's sat cross-legged on the floor to my left, stirring a pot that's bubbling away on a small fire. I head down the steps and sit on the very last one and leave the others to play.

'I did. Whatever you're making smells amazing.'

'You must be thirsty.' He hands me his flask. I open it up and drink till my belly's full. He doesn't bat an eye that I'm in my pants. We've lived in each other's pockets for months. Not much shocks us now. Even Sky's taken off her long socks and tucked up her top so her belly is on show. Everyone has a light sheen of sweat but they also look relaxed which is lovely to see.

'How long was I asleep?'

'Only a couple of hours.'

'Oh hey, you're up!' Sky chirps, making everyone look. 'Does that mean we can eat now?'

'Soon,' Loom laughs. 'Eat another banana if you're hungry.'

She jumps to her feet as the others continue playing and heads over to plonk herself on the step next to me.

'I was gonna try and take those trousers off while you were sleeping,' she says, sweeping my sweat-soaked hair from my face. 'But decided I valued my life and left them on,' she teases. 'You must be starving!'

'I am actually. So, what's cooking?'

'It's papaya risotto,' Loom tells me happily. 'Wait till ya taste it. There's beans, papaya, olives, rice... tons of stuff!'

'SNAP!'

With a loud swear word and after sending his cards in the air, Chilli gets to his feet in a huff.

'That's it. I'm not playing anymore.' He charges over to us and sits on the floor with his legs and arms crossed. 'He cheats. That's the only explanation.'

Behind him, Elder's chuckling away as he tidies up the cards. Scooping up his almost empty bottle of rum, he comes and joins us too.

'How's that dinner coming along?' he asks.

Loom has a taste and nods approvingly at his own creation. 'Ready.'

Sky scoops up a pile of plates beside her and hands us one each.

'Right,' Elder says in his usual gruff way, pulling out a new bottle of rum and unscrewing the lid. He points at Chilli. 'A joke or a funny anecdote. Your choice.' He thrusts the bottle in his hand. 'But I fully expect to laugh. Go.'

CHAPTER FOURTEEN

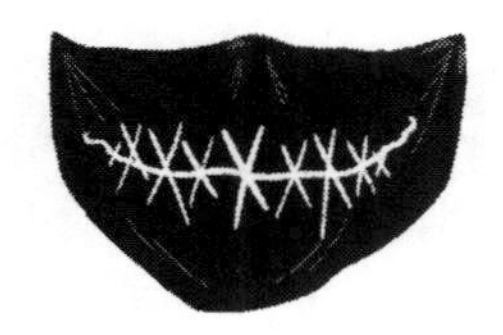

'Hang on. Run that past me again,' Elder groans. His eyes are scrunched closed and his fingers are pinching the ridge of his nose. 'Maybe I'm still drunk. Or maybe I'm just really, really hungover, but I don't understand what your crazy arse is proposing.'

'We take the railings from the fallen stairway,' Chilli explains. 'Attach it to the front of the truck. Add some spikes we can fashion from the branches. And drive through the horde out there. Right up to where the horses are. What's so hard to understand?' His eyes are bloodshot from all the drinking he did last night. And his skin is clammy from the heat. Each swallow he makes look like a desperate attempt not to vomit.

'Great,' Elder grunts. 'Let's charge up the battery with a non-existent power source. Fill up the tank with imaginary diesel. And then get the truck through whatever the hell that wall is made out of, all the while keeping this place intact. I apologise. You're not crazy. You're idiotic!' he barks.

'It's an organic truck!' Chilli argues, waving the guide book in the air. 'According to this-'

'He can read?' Sky groans with her head on her knees and her backside on the floor next to me. 'I didn't know he could read. Do you guys have to be so loud?' She grumbles as I gently pat her on the head. I told her not to drink that much. But would she listen? No. Of course not. She pathetically swats my hand away and moans. 'I think I'm gonna hurl again. Rum is the devil.'

'Yes. I can read. And I can hold my booze too. Unlike you, ya lightweight.' Chilli slaps the booklet over her head making her complain loudly before returning back to Elder Eight. 'According to the guide book, the truck was made with the same sentiment as the rest of this place. To be eco-friendly. It runs on organic material. It's an organic truck! All we have to do is fill it up with stuff off the floor. Leaves and rotten fruit, that kinda stuff, and it should work!'

'That's great,' Elder sighs. 'So we get it to start. How do we get it outside?'

'Well, we can create a pulley system. Use the cables from the fallen bridge to hoist it up... somehow.' He scratches the back of his head as he struggles to create a plan.

'A pulley system?' Elder stares at him like he's insane. 'The roof is over sixty metres high, ya numpty. And how are we gonna get it through the roof even if we do haul it up there? The windows are barely big enough to get *me* through, let alone a sodding truck.'

'We can remove one of the panels,' he says. I'm not sure if it was a question, but it certainly sounded like his resolve was in question.

Elder just stands there with utter disbelief on his face. Even Sky has lifted her head to scowl. Me and Loom have a bowl of leftovers in our hands as we watch the show before us trying hard not to laugh.

'What?' Chilli asks, his face going a little red. 'It could work. We could make the truck into a weapon and drive it down the side of the dome.'

'Or...' I take the guide book from his hands and flick through to a page at the back and show it to him. 'We could use the underground water system they set up.' I tap the page that has a map and details on how it all works. 'Behind the waterfall is a man-made grate. We take that off and climb down into this cavern here. See?' I point to the diagram. 'The water funnels through these tunnels. One goes to the other dome, the other goes to a lake outside.'

'A lake?' Chilli asks, peering at the book. 'I didn't see a lake out there.'

'It's behind that big building to the right where the Class Threes came from before the horde of dome zombies escaped. It's there. And the cavern connects by tunnels big enough to crawl through. I think we should try the tunnels first. If it's flooded or blocked, then we can rethink your truck idea. What do you say?' I look at them all in turn and they all agree. 'Great. I'll finish my breakfast. Sky... sleep off your hangover and then get to work on making arrows. Loom, would you give her a hand?' He nods and carries on shovelling food in his face.

'I'll give you a hand with the grate,' Elder says, still looking at Chilli like he's nothing short of bonkers. 'And Mr pulley system here can gather supplies for the trip home. Seeds and fruit. Bloody truck... down the side of the dom e... I mean really.'

'It could have worked,' Chilli mutters to himself as Elder clips him round the ear as he passes.

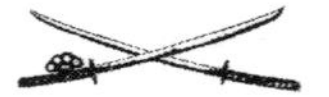

The grate still hasn't come off after an hour of swearing and shouting. From Elder of course. He's not renowned for his patience. And will he let me help? Course not. I've never heard such language in my whole life actually. And growing up with Winder... I've heard plenty. He must have called those stiff screws every conceivable curse in the English language and then some. If we were at home, he'd have racked up fifty lashes at least. I'm trying so hard not to laugh. Every snigger I'm not able to hold in gets me one hell of a stare as he stands waist-deep in water with his hands and torso reaching behind the waterfall. He's soaked through and keeps getting a face full of tumbling water. But when he slips over and disappears beneath the water completely, I can't stop my hysteria. He jumps up coughing and spluttering as I hold my sides.

'If you think you can do this better,' he snaps, tossing the screwdriver at my head. I protect myself with my arms so I don't get hit. 'Then have at it, you bloody idiot.'

Still roaring with laughter, I double over. His moustache has lost its shape and is sticking up all over the place. He stands there fuming as I fall off the rock I was sitting on and roll about.

'That's it. I'll be back at the hut,' he grunts, wading out the water. 'When you get this sodding thing open, come and get me.'

He storms off, squelching as he goes.

'Need a hand?' Sky asks as they pass each other. He barges into her shoulder muttering profanities to himself leaving her looking to me for an explanation. But I'm still wetting myself. 'What's so funny?'

Finally, I get the last screw loose and can lift the metal grate free.

'Good job,' Sky sings, taking the grate and tossing it to the water's edge before returning to my side. Together, we shove our heads under the cascading water and peer down the dark tunnel. It's brick near the entrance, but further in it becomes a cylindrical metal tunnel which dips downwards into blackness. It's big enough for us to all crawl through. Elder might find it a bit of a squeeze, but as long as it doesn't get any thinner, he should be alright. There's a couple of inches of water trickling steadily down the centre of the funnel, and so far, my plan seems perfect.

'ECHOO-ECHoo-EChoo-echooooo.' Sky watches with wonder as her voice slowly fades away. Then she looks at me with an excited grin. 'Don't you just love this job? Who else can say that they've spent the last twenty-four hours chilling in a jungle, drinking rum and preparing for a journey down a secret tunnel hidden behind a waterfall?!' She whacks my arm and leans in even further. I wrap my fingers around her elbow to stop her from going too far in and taking a tumble. 'It's a bit dark. How will we see where we're going?'

'We'll just have to feel our way. C'mon. Let's go tell the others the tunnel's open.'

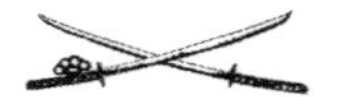

It's agreed. One more night and then we head out. We're all worried about the horses, even though they're locked up safe and sound. The sun goes down. The card deck comes out. Loom gets cooking. Elder and Chilli get drinking. Sky's singing made-up songs as she whittles arrows in the corner of the hut, and I'm not in the mood for any of it. As they laugh and joke and sing, I make my excuses and sit alone with my feet in the water, staring at the waterfall that conceals the tunnel out of here. The air is stifling in this place. I feel smothered by the thickness of it. Smothered by the walls. The ceiling. The birds that won't stop tweeting. The crickets that chirp incessantly. This place is amazing. A whole different world than the one out there. But it's still, just another cage. Like the walls back home are. The opening of the grate is right there in front of me. The way out. The pathway back to the real world.

What's wrong with me?

I want to get out of here and out there as soon as possible. I hate just sitting. Waiting. Every second I do nothing, we lose a little more of the world. I could just slide in through that grate. Blow off some steam. Be back before anyone even knew I was gone.

'Sort your head out, Scarlett,' I scold myself. 'Going out there and getting yourself killed won't fix this.' I lower myself into the water completely and cool off.

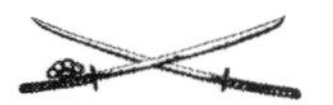

I head back along the path to the others the long way around, wringing out my top as I walk in my underwear. As I approach the hut from the side, I spot Loom and Sky cornering a rather red-faced Elder as Chilli relieves himself behind a tree in the distance. As Elder sits, the other two look very agitated. When they see me, they put on a forced smile and scatter, leaving Elder still sat on the floor looking a bit pissed off.

'What was that about?' I ask, putting my top back on and sitting beside him.

'Nothing,' he grunts, handing me the almost empty bottle of rum.

But a quick glance to Loom and Sky whispering in the distance while glancing at me anxiously tell me that it was something. I take a sip and look at Elder with raised eyebrows.

I just wait.

'Loom heard us talking about Noah,' he says. 'He asked Sky if she knew anything and of course she spilled the beans about what she knows and now they're sticking their beaks in.'

'Did you tell them anything?' I ask, handing back the rum.

'No.' He drains the rest and falls heavily on his back with his eyes closed. 'Now sod off. I'm trying to forget the fact that we have to leave this little slice of paradise tomorrow. Let me relax, will ya?'

Relax? More like drink himself into oblivion. As I watch him, his breathing gets heavier, slower and much deeper. Then... he starts to snore.

Well, a bottle of rum tends to do that.

I reach over and pick up my coat which is tossed over the steps of the hut. I fold it up, gently lift his head to give it to him as a pillow, and lay him back down.

'Thanks, kiddo,' he says sleepily.

'No worries,' I whisper back, patting his shoulder.

As he sleeps, I eat the soup Loom made and watch as he continues talking to Sky. I could go over there. Tell them to cut it out. But to be honest, I can't be bothered to get into it.

'Cards?' Chilli asks, sitting cross-legged in front of me and dealing them out. 'I need to practice if I ever want to beat the old man.'

'Sure. Why not.' I look over at Sky and Loom. 'Hey, you two! Fancy giving the gossiping a rest and having some fun instead?'

I like watching them sleep. Weird. But it's good to see them safe and comfortable. Dreaming their dreams. Not worrying. Not being tense. Sky's mumbling to herself. She always mumbles. I don't make out much. But she keeps giggling and saying - *"Cut it off. Cut it off"*.

She's an odd one.

I get up and have a stretch. We're heading out in a couple of hours. I should really get some sleep myself. As I turn to head inside the hut to do just that, Elder rolls over and mumbles a little himself. Curiosity gets the better of me as I linger.

What the hell does a man like him dream about?

His hand settles on his neck and he starts stroking it. When I look closer, I see a delicate silver chain. It's whatever's at the end of it that he strokes so gently. Then he mumbles my name.

Scarlett.

What the hell?

He falls still and quiet again. His hand falls limp by his side and he continues to snore. I take a look around. Everyone else is still fast asleep. I'm not proud to say, curiosity has definitely got the better of me. I tiptoe over and kneel by his side. My hand lingers just above his chest. The silver of the chain shines in the firelight. Slowly, I reach down and pull it out.

It's a necklace with a silver oval pendant on the end. It's tarnished and very, very old. I can tell that he's worn it for years. There's the faintest engraving on it. I lean in a little closer to get a better look. It's three hearts all entwined with each other.

It's beautiful.

As I look, I see a small catch on the side. I click it and the pendant opens.

Inside is a picture.

A photo.

I've not seen many of those in my time. But it's not the fact that I'm looking at a photo. It's what's in the photo that has me speechless.

'That's not possible.'

'You bloody WHAT?!' Elder bellows in my face and showering me with spit as I finish explaining why he just caught me climbing back through the grate. I'm soaked through and glad to be back in the warmth of the dome after being out there in the bitterly cold, soaking wet. But I needed to get out. I had to. I have no idea what I'm thinking or feeling right now. And for me, that can be dangerous. Explosive. Cass always said I had a temper like a wasp. 'What the hell were you thinking?' he barks. 'You stupid bloody fool!'

'I wanted to make sure the tunnel was clear,' I tell him, wringing water out from my hair and avoiding his stare at all costs.

'What a stupid, irresponsible thing to do,' he snarls. 'You leave without telling anyone. With no weapons and no back up. Through a tunnel that might not even be structurally safe-'

'Well, better it collapses on just me than all of us.'

'Better it bloody doesn't!'

'Let's agree to disagree.' Retying my hair and walking past him without so much as a second glance, I carry on. 'The tunnel's safe and big enough for us all to fit through. It comes out in a clear area. We can get back to the horses without-' As I pass, he grabs my arm roughly. I can't help it. I just react and shove him off me so hard he stumbles back and looks at me completely stunned. 'Don't.' I warn. 'Don't you dare touch me.'

'What the hell is your problem?'

'I have a right not to be touched if I don't want to be,' I snap back. 'Why do you think I volunteered to be out here in the first goddamn place! No man gets to touch me without my permission unless they want the sharp end of my sword up their backside.'

'Don't you liken me to him.'

'Liken him to who?' Loom asks the others quietly.

'None of your damn business,' I snap, before turning back to Elder. 'I'm just doing my job and getting you out of here and back home.'

'Your job ain't to get yourself killed, Kiddo.'

'Scarlett. My name is Scarlett. And your job ain't getting pissed and passing out, Elder Eight,' I argue. His brow furrows as he tries hard not to lose his temper. And so am I. 'We need to get back to the horses.' I look at the others. 'You all wanna get home, right? Chilli, your sentence is almost up. You can get back on the wall. Sky and Loom, you're keen for a break? Some time off before coming back out here? Winter's on its way. With any luck, you can have a few months off if the snow is bad enough. Well, pack up. Your wish is coming true.' I walk away. 'You're all going home. We leave in an hour. Pack your shit.'

'Don't you mean we?' Sky asks as I pass. '*We're* going home?'

'Yeah. Sure. Whatever.'

After shimmying through the tunnel, we emerge in the cold, fresh air by the lake. It's easy enough to get to the horses from here.

'Hello, beautiful boy.' I'm so relieved to see Hanzo and he's clearly happy to see me. I run my fingers through his mane and kiss his face over and over as he nudges me affectionately. 'I missed you too, buddy.'

'So what's the plan?' Loom asks, looking between Elder and me as he runs his hand along the side of his horse. The atmosphere is uncomfortable to say the least.

'Better ask Scarlett,' Elder says, not even turning to respond.

'We could go to the mortuary again?' Sky suggests.

'Oh really?' Chilli groans. 'That place is so creepy. Can't we go back to the church?'

'It's in the wrong direction. We need to start heading east,' I tell him. 'The mortuary's a seven-hour ride from here and it's in the right direction.' And we didn't put that location in a pigeon so it should be safe. 'We'll head there. Good idea, Sky. Everyone ready?'

'Ready,' They all reply.

We stick to the main road which cuts through the emptiness of the countryside and leads us clear past the small towns that surround us.

It's a quiet journey.

An awkward journey.

And a bloody cold journey.

The chill in the air has come as quickly as the heat did in the summer. But thankfully we're not too far from our destination now.

'Hello?' Sky says. I look over and see her watching me. 'You alright? You look a million miles away.'

'I'm fine.' I shrug, hating where my thoughts are right now. 'Just cold.'

'I know, right!' she says. 'I'm gonna have to put on some thicker socks.'

'Or some trousers.'

'Nah. I like wearing skirts while I can. Won't be allowed back home. Listen, what's going on with you and the Moustache?'

'Nothing.'

'Is it about Noah?'

'Sky, drop it.'

'Because if it is, you don't need to worry. We got your back-'

'Just drop it!' I almost scream in her face. 'Do you ever shut up? I mean seriously. You just talk and talk and I'm sick of listening to your nonsense. Stop acting like we're friends. We're not, okay! We work together so just stop!' Her whole face falls in a way I've never seen before and her bottom lip even wobbles a little.

Great.

I'm taking out my anger and upset on her. The one person who deserves it the least.

'I'm sorry. I didn't mean-'

'My mistake,' she says quietly. 'I'll err... ride on and make sure the mortuary's secure. *Boss*.' She gives her horse a kick and speeds off as I call after her. The others glare at me as they ride. Elder shakes his head disappointed in my cruelness. I was so out of line.

'Nice one, Kiddo,' he says. 'Real nice.'

'Crap,' I mutter. 'I'll catch up with her and apologise.'

I give Hanzo a kick and he speeds up. He's fast, but he's built more for distance than speed so we can't catch up as easily as I'd like. When she disappears out of sight round the twists and bends of the roads, I start to worry. She's on her own and upset. I'm on my own now too, having left the others behind. But the clatter of hooves behind me makes me turn. Elder Eight catches up.

'If whatever's crawled up your arse and pissed you off gets that girl killed, I'll never forgive you. Ya hear me?' he shouts over the sound of hooves.

'I know. I know! This is my fault and I'm gonna fix it.'

It's another twenty minutes till we reach the large metal gate of the mortuary. It's closed and I worry that she hasn't made it. I climb down from Hanzo and take hold of his reigns so I can lead him through the main gate. It opens with a groan and Elder follows me in.

I'm thrilled to see her standing with her face buried in her horse's neck safe and sound. What doesn't make me happy is the sound of her sobbing.

Elder climbs down before turning to me. 'You *better* fix this,' he says. 'She loves you and you treated her like something you scraped off the bottom of your shoe.'

'Don't lecture me on how I should treat people,' I reply. 'Coming from you, that's a load of hypocritical crap I'm not in the mood for.'

'What the hell is that supposed to mean?' he demands. I turn and head towards Sky. But he has different ideas and abandons his horse to follow me. 'I asked you a question!' he calls after me. Sky lifts her red and tear-streaked face to look at us. I carry on heading towards her, Hanzo's reigns still in my hand and Elder hot on my heels. As I reach her, I secure Hanzo with her horse and rest my hand on her shoulder.

'I'm sorry, Sky. I didn't mean what I said,' I tell her. 'I was just in a bad mood.'

'Hey!' Elder barks, snatching my hand away. 'You owe me a sodding apology too. What the hell is your problem?'

'I don't owe you jack,' I hiss, yanking my hand free. I look back at Sky who's watching us speechlessly. As another little tear slides down her face my guilt goes into overdrive. 'I really didn't mean what I said. I'm just tired and had something else on my mind. You are my friend and I love hearing your nonsense. Honestly. You always put a smile on my face. That reaction was on me and had nothing to do with you. The past few days have been hard for me and I've taken it out on you guys and for that I am really really sorry. You are so much more than just a friend to me. You're family.' I give her a smile which she returns before wiping her tears dry. 'Please forgive me.'

'Of course I forgive you!' she wails, hurling her arms around me and squeezing the life out of me. 'Let's never, ever fight again.'

'Great,' Elder says gruffly, pulling her away and standing in front of me instead. 'What ya got to say to me?'

'Nothing,' I bite back, busying myself with unstrapping my katana harness which has been digging into my side from the speedy ride. ''To you, I have absolutely nothing to say. We're done. I don't like liars. Cos you can't trust them. And trust is all I got.' I lay them gently over Hanzo's back and turn. But he grabs me and hurls me back so I land on my arse before standing between me and the building.

'We ain't done. And you ain't goin' nowhere unarmed. We haven't checked the perimeter yet.'

'I err,' Sky points to the building. 'I'll just head inside and wait for you guys to finish screaming at each other.'

'You don't need to go,' I tell her, getting to my feet and brushing off the dirt. 'Like I said, we're done here.'

'Yeah, I do,' she says. 'It's like watching your parents argue. Ya know,' she shrugs 'If we had parents *to* watch argue.'

'Yeah,' I sigh, glaring at Elder. 'Imagine that. Having parents.' I walk towards him and jab my finger into his chest. Right on top of the locket. 'Just imagine.'

His hand settles over the locket and a wave of realisation washes over his face.

'You saw the locket?'

'Yeah,' I sneer. 'I saw the locket.' I turn and start to walk away, heading towards the mortuary.

'I can explain,' he calls after me.

'No need,' I reply, not even turning to look at him. 'I get it.'

'I don't,' Sky adds.

I turn. 'You wanna know?' I ask her before pointing at Elder. 'He told me that he knocked up a girl back in the day but lost both the baby and the woman before it was even born.'

'Kiddo, you're out of line,' he warns.

'But that was a lie. She had the baby.'

'Stop...'

'And then he took a photo of them all looking *so* happy together.'

'Scarlett...'

'And then... he donated her. He donated his own child to the army!' I'm trying to keep my calm but I'm shaking with anger.

No.

Hurt.

I'm trembling with a sense of utter betrayal at the picture of the young woman with thick red curls who was the spitting image of me, cradling a baby girl.

Sky doesn't know what to say. It's the first time I've seen her speechless as she looks between Elder and me.

'Does the army mean that much to you?' I snarl at him as he just watches me. 'Did it mean that much, that you gave up your own kid for it?'

'You don't understand,' he says.

'Oh, I understand,' I laugh hatefully, throwing my hands up in the air. 'So, what happened to the woman who gave birth to your bastard daughter? Hmm? Is she still in the army too?'

'Can you let me explain?'

'No need.' I turn and look at Sky. 'Let's get inside.' I walk away from him, scared that if I stay, I'll do something I'll regret.

'Everything I have ever done, every lie I've ever told or choice I have ever made, has been for you. Because I love you!' he calls after me. I slow to a stop, Sky close to my side. 'I reached retirement seven years ago, but I'm still here. Still fighting. Because that's where you are. I'm out here because you are!' I hear him walking towards me.

'Oh my god...' Sky whispers. 'You're her dad?' She's not the quickest. But she's there finally.

Sky's watching him, but I can't bear to turn. He stops behind me.

'You're not a bastard, Scarlett. I married your mum. In secret. She gave birth to you and refused to tell anyone who the father was. I wanted to come forward but she made me promise not to. She knew that I could be executed if I did. When you were born, they took you away and sentenced her to a lifetime in the Canaries, and they put you in the military orphanage to grow up as a soldier. You know the rules we have to follow. It's not like we could be public about our marriage! We had to keep it all secret. When she fell pregnant and got arrested, he made me swear not to tell anyone I was the father. The sentence back then was death, do you understand me?'

'So you had to keep it secret. Fine. But you could have told me! All these years... and not a word.'

'I couldn't risk it. If anyone else found out, if the Grey Coats learned the truth, I would either be killed because of my crime, or I would have been sentenced to a lifetime in the Canaries and then you would have been all alone in the world. And if they knew that you knew, the same fate would have befallen you. I would never risk that. Never!'

'And you just left my mum to die out here alone? After she was sentenced to be a Canary?' I ask, still not able to look at him.

'No,' he says calmly. 'I volunteered. Back then, you did two year stints. I did two stints with your mum before I came back. That's four years.'

'I can count. And then what?'

'She didn't want me to leave her. She had this idea that we could run away and live out here on our own.' He turns me and lifts my chin so I look at him. 'But the orphanage had you. No way I could get you out. They guard it closely, scared that the parents will raid it and take back their children. So I refused to go with her. I had to get back to you. I needed to make sure you were okay. Four years was long enough.'

'You left her?'

'She should never have asked me to choose between her, and our daughter.' Both his hands settle on my cheeks as he smiles at me. 'My dear girl. She was never gonna win that competition.'

'I'll leave you two alone,' Sky says quietly, bowing out and heading towards the door of the mortuary.

'I loved your mum,' he tells me. 'Our love made you. And our circumstances took the chance of raising you as our daughter away from us. I may not have been able to be your father. But I had to have a hand in raising you. Seeing you grow. Watching you laugh. I couldn't get anywhere near you in the Orphanage so I missed your first steps and your first words. I was just a simple soldier and wasn't allowed anywhere near the Orphanage. I had to wait till you were put in The Academy at age five to see ya again. I knew I had five years to get to where I needed to get to. I worked my arse off. Got close to the former Elder Eight. And when he died, I was named his successor. I took his place. I made sure you were in my charge so I could have some say in the way your life turned out. But if anyone ever knew that I was your father, you would have been left completely on your own or even killed. I was about to finally retire. You were gonna get a Red Coat. Or a Black and I could take a step back. Cass had your back. He loves the bloody bones of you, any fool can see that. But then when your stupid backside volunteered for this nonsense, I did too. Cos that's what fathers do for their daughters. They support them. And they keep them safe. Even from the side lines.'

'You did all that for me?' I ask as I try my hardest not to cry. 'You turned your back on your wife and retirement for me?'

'Of course, Scarlett. You're my daughter. I taught you to read. Made sure you didn't get brainwashed by The Verity nonsense. Ensured you grew up strong. Loyal. Tough. That you had good people around you. I always have and always will choose you over everything else. Always.'

'What...' I clear my throat and shuffle my feet, nervous to ask. 'What happened to my mum? Is she still out here somewhere?'

'No,' he says sadly. 'No, Kiddo. She's not still out here.'

'She died on mission?' My voice starts to strain and my throat gets a little tighter. 'Did she-did she turn?'

'No. I told her I couldn't abandon you. That even if we could get you away from the orphanage, this world was no place to raise a child. If we didn't starve we'd be eaten alive or freeze to death when the snow started to fall.' He takes a deep, solemn breath. 'She took her own life, Kiddo. The night before she was due to leave on her third mission. The first one she would have faced without me.'

My lip trembles. I slam my hand over my mouth to stop it. I've never felt like this before. So vulnerable and... and... sad. Not just for the woman who I would have called mum who killed herself. But because of the grief I see so clearly in Elder's eyes.

'I'm sorry,' I whisper. 'If it wasn't for me-'

'None of this is your fault. Never apologise to me. It's me that should apologise to you.'

'You should have told me.'

He nods and lowers his head. 'I won't blame you if you hate me-'

I throw my arms around his neck and hug the hell out of him. His arms wrap around my waist and he hugs me back so tight, my bones crunch a little. But it's the best hug ever.

'Can you forgive me?'

'There's nothing to forgive,' I tell him. 'Even without me having a clue, I always thought you were the best dad I could have ever asked for. I'm sorry I was so cruel. It's me that needs your forgiveness. I acted harshly and said awful things. I'm so sorry.'

'It's alright. It's a shock. I get it. Now, Scarlett. There's something else I need to tell you.'

'What?'

He lets go and looks at me with the kindest expression he's ever worn. 'I wasn't entirely honest with you about what we have been doing out here.'

'What do you mean?'

'I've been working with others. Formulating a plan in which we get to leave Noah and the Grey Coats behind. Where The Verity doesn't rule over us.'

'You mean... treason?'

'The locations we've chosen. The ones that could be new Havens. Well, they will be. For us. We're leaving The Verity behind. It's time to break away and start over without their rule. Scarlett, they're up to something. Elder One and I... we discovered something terrible. Something-'

A high-pitched, shrill scream has both Elder and I turning to look at the open door of the mortuary.

'SKY?' I call out.

'HELP ME!' she shrieks in a panic. 'PLEASE! HELP ME, SCARLETT!' She's absolutely hysterical and the fear in her voice has us both sprinting towards her. When I get in through the door, Elder grabs the waist of my trousers and yanks me back.

'CAREFUL!' he hollers. 'The sodding floor's gone!'

The floorboards have been ripped up making a ditch into the basement. Sky's fallen in and is surrounded by the undead. She's holding one arm to her chest, and wielding a plank in the other as she lashes out at them.

'My arm's broken. I can't move it!' she cries. 'Help me!'

'Hold on!' I tell her as she looks up at me in terror, pleading for help. 'We're gonna get you out!'

She whacks the plank into the head of a Class Three that just stumbles before trying to get to her again.

'There's too many!' She clambers on a pile of bricks and reaches up to a support beam above her head, trying desperately to get out of their reach. But without two hands she can't climb or fight. One grabs her ankle making her scream. She whacks at it with the plank and backs up to the wall.

'I don't wanna die! I don't want them to eat me alive! Help me... please!'

'We're coming,' Elder tells her. As he goes to jump down, I pull him back. 'What are you doin'?'

'I'll fight them. You get rope or something to get us out.'

'You're not goin' down there! You're not even armed!'

'I'm not strong enough to lift you out if you go! Get the rope. I'll be okay.' I take his weapon and give him a shove as he stands, reluctant to obey. Without giving him another chance to argue, I pull up my mask and jump down into the pit.

He disappears from view as I land between her and the Class Threes. I try to swing Elders sword to sever the head of anything that gets too close. But there are too many. I have no swinging space and those I do strike are replaced with more. Their hands grab at me all over. Their jaws are wide as they come for us both. Sky whacks one in the face with her plank, dislocating its jaw and knocking a few of its teeth out.

But that doesn't stop it.

'Scar, we need to get out! There's too many!'

She's right. There are twenty at least.

I slam my foot into the chest of one too close and as it stumbles back, I get enough room to swing the sword and lop its head off. I look up. Still no sign of Elder.

'SCAR, LOOK OUT!' she screams.

I look just in time to see one lunge at me teeth first. I shove my wrist in its face so it gets a mouth full of leather cuff instead. But it's charged at me so hard, I fall back and land on the floor with it on top of me. Then they all start bundling me. The weight of them pushes the air out of my lungs as they all clamber on top of each other, desperate to get to me and Sky. I feel their hands and teeth biting and scratching at the leather protecting my body. I'm not sure if it will hold out against this many. My skin hurts as they chomp down, causing deep bruises. But they don't pierce my skin. Sky snatches the sword from my pinned down hand and starts hacking at them all the while screaming like a banshee. As limbs and guts and black goo go flying everywhere, I see a lone red brick a few feet away. I reach out, wrap my fingers around it tightly and slam it into the skull of the one still gnawing at my wrist cuff. It falls limp on top of me as its head caves in. I hit the one behind that, and the one behind that, until I manage to buck them off and get back to Sky. In a quick move, I pick her up and hurl her up onto the beam. She then stretches out her hand to me.

'CLIMB UP, SCAR!'

I put one hand on the beam and it groans under my additional weight.

'GET UP HERE!' she bellows.

'If I climb up there, it will break and we'll both fall.' I snatch the sword still in her hand. 'Just stay as still as possible and it should hold.'

'What about you?'

I turn and slash at anything that gets too close. They reach up for her, but she's just out of grasp so they turn their attention back to me.

I hack. I hit. I swing and I brawl. I yell and shout as I wield this heavy and cumbersome weapon.

'ELDER!' I call out, slamming the blade through a neck. 'HURRY UP!'

There's a groan. And not the type that comes from a dead thing. The plank holding Sky is giving way and I've ended up on the opposite side of the room. There's a loud creak. I look at Sky and she looks at me. Then with a shriek, the plank snaps and she crashes to the floor.

'SKY?' I scream. 'SKY SAY SOMETHING!'

She doesn't respond and the way they all lift their heads and sniff tell me she's bleeding. They turn away from me and start heading to her.

'SKY!'

Elder lands in front of her, my sword in his hand and a lasso in the other. He swings my blade with skill, killing anything that gets in its way. But it's a wall of monsters. He can't protect her, fight them all and get out.

I see a rusty nail sticking out from the wall and slam my hand onto it hard. And then I pull it down, cutting my flesh in a deep jagged cut. Blood pours from the wound and splatters the floor around me. It works and distracts them. I'm bleeding more than her. That's something.

'HEY!' I yell. 'COME HERE. COME TO ME!'

They all turn and start scrambling to me instead. Behind them, Elder is lifting a barely conscious Sky to her feet and looping the rope under her arms.

'HELLO?'

'LOOM!' Elder shouts back. 'WATCH THE HOLE!'

Loom and Chilli cautiously peer over the edge and survey the carnage below in shock and disbelief. 'What the...'

'PULL HER UP!' I order, bringing the heavy sword down again and again. My grip on the handle is slippery as I continue to bleed. They sprint to the other side and take the rope to heave her up. Once her feet leave the ground, Elder heads to me, cutting through whatever finds itself in his path. Sky is hoisted up and blinks us into focus. As she comes around fully, she starts screaming to be let back down so she can fight. But no one listens. She's no use to us. I swing too hard and the sword flies out of my hands as blood continues to seep from my wound, driving them all crazy. Elder doesn't slow or stop as he forges ahead. He scoops up his sword as he passes it and tosses me my katana which lands in my uninjured hand. Now I can really get to work. This is my weapon. My limb. I drive it through the gut of one and skewer another two behind it like a zombie kebab. Then I yank it up, splitting them both in two. I spin, slicing off the head of another two then reverse my swipe and take another.

This sword is so much lighter. Elder is causing some serious damage with his. Heads, arms and bits of flesh are flying all over the place. When he reaches me, he grabs the back of my head and plants a kiss on my forehead.

'You okay, Kiddo?'

'Fine. You?'

He nods and lifts his sword to bring it down on one behind me as I drive my sword upwards under the chin of one behind him. And when I see Sky's feet disappear over the edge, Chilli reappears with the rope in his hand ready to toss it back down.

'SCAR!' he yells, letting it go. 'GRAB IT!' The floor beneath him starts to groan. The beam that collapsed was holding up a large portion of the floor and without it, they're standing on kindling.

'GET AWAY FOM THE EDGE!' I yell back. 'BEFORE YOU FALL!'

'GRAB THE ROPE!'

A chunk of floor gives way and Loom drags Chilli away just in time. But he drops the rope. I rush forwards to get it back.

'SCARLETT! LOOK OUT!' Elder throws himself between me and a Class Three that leaps at me. He collides with it and lands in a heap.

'ELDER!' I rush over, swinging my katana wildly as I go. When I reach him, he's pinned beneath it. 'ELDER!' I haul it off him and hack its head clean off. 'You okay?' I ask, reaching down and helping him to his feet.

'I'm fine!' he says.

'There's too many. What do we do?'

He wraps his arm around me and pulls me into a hug. 'Elder One,' he says. 'You get back, you tell him our plan. You tell him about the locations we found. You tell him about Noah and his threats. You hear me? No one else. You trust him and you tell no one you're speaking to him. Understand?'

'What-'

'I love you. So much. And I'm so proud of you, Kiddo. You're everything a dad could ever wish for.'

'We're gonna get out of this,' I tell him. 'Why does it sound like you're saying good bye?'

'We don't have long. Fight!'

He lets me go and turns back to the battle. We both do. Side by side. Father and daughter. The floor is so littered with corpses we can barely stand. As we stumble and trip over the pile of bodies beneath us, we never stop fighting. We never stop swinging. And Chilli has Sky's bow, using it to fire arrow after arrow. We add more bodies to the heap and when the last one falls, I clutch my side and gasp for breath before raising my katana high above my head and letting out a victory cry.

'YEAH!' I bellow. 'THAT'S WHAT I'M TALKING ABOUT! WOOO!' I laugh, looking up at the others who are avoiding the edge and watching us with relieved smiles.

'HELL YEAH, GIRL!' Chilli applauds. 'GO, ELDER EIGHT! YEAH!'

'Yeah, great,' Sky breathes. 'Can you both please just get the hell out of there now?'

'Yeah, yeah.' I turn my attention to the floor. 'Do you see the rope?' I look around at the carnage. We're knee deep in bits of zombie. 'Elder, do you see the rope?' I look over at him. He's across the room with his back to me. I can see his shoulders rising and falling as he tries to catch his breath. His sword is still in his hand and he just stands there facing the wall.

'Elder... you alright?' I take a step closer. His breathing gets louder and more laboured. 'Elder?' I ask again.

He drops his sword.

'A-are you okay?' I take another step closer. His body starts to spasm and it sounds like he's choking. His head tilts back and he starts to violently twitch. 'Elder?' I hear the fear in my voice. The dread. The panic and the grief. 'Elder?' But he doesn't say a word.

'Scarlett,' Sky says slowly. 'Scarlett, get away from him.'

But I don't. I take another step closer.

'Elder Eight, can you hear me? Elder... Elder...' I take another step closer and rest my hand on his shoulder. His breathing stops. The twitching. The gurgling. It all ends as soon as he feels me touch him. He stands frozen, looking at the wall.

'Dad?'

CHAPTER FIFTEEN

He turns quickly.

I go to scream. But nothing comes out. My breathing and my voice get stuck in my throat as I stumble back, falling over the bodies of those we just killed together.

His eyes are pure white. His lips are turning black. There's thick, black blood and bile oozing from his mouth and his skin has already started to go grey.

He's been bitten.

It must have happened when he jumped in front of that Class Three meant for me.

He *was* saying goodbye.

He sniffs the air and catches the scent of my blood. All my training's gone out the window. I drop my Katana, fall on my backside and just scramble away as he throws back his head and lets loose the familiar high-pitched howl that comes just before they attack. Everything seems to slow down. I can't get up. I can't get away. I can't say anything.

My Dad's a Class Two zombie.

My dad is dead.

And even as he begins his descent on me, I do nothing but watch. In the background, I hear the muffled yelling of the others. But I can't make out their words. They sound a million miles away. All I can see, all I can hear, is the man that raised me from the age of five. The man that was there for me every day, who taught me how to fight, who gave me advice even when I didn't want it and who protected me from so much.

And now he's gone. He's dead.

But at the same time, he's not!

He's right there.

'SCARLETT!' Chilli yells. 'GET UP! GET YOUR SWORD!' The floor creaks and collapses as they go towards the edge. Elder is on all fours, scrambling over the uneven ground of bodies like a beast as he crawls closer. His teeth bared. Stuff oozing out from his mouth, eyes and ears.

'SCARLETT! FOR GOD'S SAKE! FIGHT!' Loom orders. Elder grabs my ankle. He's snaring like a monster. Barely recognisable. 'SCAR! GET AWAY FROM HIM!'

His other hand grabs my calf. I slam the heel of my shoe into his face and knock him back. But he just tries again. I keep kicking.

'DAD! STOP, PLEASE!'

Kick. Kick. Kick.

I've broken his nose so badly, it's just a hole in his face. His front teeth are gone. And with another kick, his jaw breaks. He screeches as I scream, but he keeps trying to get to me. To kill me.

'STOP, DAD! STOP!'

Kick. Kick. Kick.

'PLEASE!'

He lunges back, and then hurls himself forwards. His limbs scrambling like a spider as I stumble back.

'GET YOUR SWORD!' Sky shouts.

I roll over and claw myself away so I can reach out and grab my katana.

'ON YOUR FEET!' she bellows.

I get to my feet and turn to face him. He still tries to get to me. His face all broken. His body moving in sharp, jarring movements.

'Dad... you're still in there! I know you are.'

'NO. HE'S NOT. KILL HIM, SCARLETT!' Sky orders. 'KILL HIM NOW!'

I have my sword ready. He's getting closer. I back up more and more until I hit the wall. My hands tremble. My whole body does.

'I can't,' I admit in a terrified whisper. 'H-he's my... he...'

They're all screaming my name. Ordering me to kill him. But he's my dad. Even before I knew to call him that, he's always been my dad. His hand wraps around my leg as he pulls himself closer. His other hand grabs me and he drags himself up my body. The others continue screaming at me as Elder pulls himself to his feet. Now in front of me, he opens his wonky jaw and screeches before lunging at my throat. I close my eyes.

This is it.

This is how I die.

And I think... I'm okay with that.

Because I don't think I can live in this hell without him.

I don't think I want to.

My fingers relax their grip on my sword and I feel my body relax all over. We die together.

And that's okay.

That's okay.

'CADET 5-3-6. KILL THE TARGET. THAT'S AN ORDER!' Loom demands, mimicking Elder Eight's voice and tone to perfection. Before I know what's happened, my fingers tighten their grip and my body reacts. Eighteen years of conditioning takes over and I drive the blade of my sword through the side of Elder Eight's skull so far, the hilt becomes slick with his blood. His pale eyes just stare at me. His mouth agape. His whole body goes limp and he falls, bringing me and my sword with him. I pull out my katana and drop it to the floor so I can catch him in my arms.

No... No. No. No. No. NO!

I cradle him and let out a huge, loud, agonising scream that echoes on and on and on. I hold him close.

I rock him.

My Elder.

My friend.

My dad.

Gone.

CHAPTER SIXTEEN

The paper's in my hand. I've written the message. The bird's in the cage right in front of me. But I just sit here, limp and mute on the grass. Staring into the distance. Doing nothing. The air's bitterly cold. I don't feel it. My hand is bleeding. It doesn't hurt. I want to cry. But I can't. I want to scream. But I have no strength.

I'm empty. Completely empty.

'I need to send the bird.'

'Okay. But, Scar, you need to give me your hand,' Sky says gently. She's kneeling beside me with a first aid box in her lap. Her eyes are red and puffy from all the tears she's shed. But as she reaches out for the sixth time to tend the wound on my palm from the nail, I flinch, and she sighs. 'It needs stitches. Please.'

'I need to send the bird.'

'We can do that,' she nods with a little sniffle. 'After I've sewn up your hand-'

'I need to send the bird.'

I'm barely aware of the footsteps behind me. Or Sky looking upwards at someone over my shoulder.

'How's she doing?' Loom asks, his voice strained and overworked from his grief.

'She just keeps saying she needs to send the bird,' Sky replies. 'She won't let me fix her hand. She won't look at me. She won't let me clean the blood off her.' She stands up. Her legs are in my peripherals. I don't look at them. I just sit and stare out at the world. 'She won't even cry. I think she's broken.'

'Scar doesn't cry,' he adds quietly. Like I won't hear him if he lowers his voice. 'She never has. Not once. She's kinda known for that. And the loop? She's probably in shock. She'll come around. How's your arm?'

'It was just a dislocated shoulder. Chilli popped it back. It'll be fine. I'm more worried about her.'

He walks around and kneels in front of me in my direct line of sight. 'Scarlett?'

'I need to send the bird,' I tell him.

'I know. And we will.'

'I need to send the bird.' I look down at the paper in my hand. 'I need to... I need...' He takes my hands in his. I look him in the eye. 'When did I get out here?' I ask. 'We should get some dinner going or something, right? It's that time of day when we eat. Should we eat?' I nod. 'We should eat.'

'Scarlett, do you understand what happened?' he asks. 'Inside the mortuary, do you remember?'

'I'm not sure,' I admit, looking back over his shoulder at the building. 'You must all be hungry. We should make dinner.'

He lets out a deep breath and gets to his feet to talk to Sky.

'She's in shock. Definitely. She probably won't be able to process exactly what happened for a day or so.' They both look down at me. 'We'll set up camp nearby. Let her have some time...' Their voices fade and everything else seems to shift into focus. The grass beneath me. The sky above me. The chill in the air. The stench of death on my clothes. The pain in my heart.

I killed Elder Eight.

I stabbed him through the head and held him in my arms.

Loom got me out of the pit. I let him manoeuvre my body as if I were a doll. He carried me like a child outside and settled me gently on the grass. Tears streamed down his face. Chilli held Sky as she wailed uncontrollably.

'We really need to stop the bleeding so we don't attract any more... err,'

'Zombies?' I finish. I look up at them both. 'You can say it. He was a zombie when I killed him, right? When I murdered my dad?' As I talk, I feel nothing. The words should make me feel something. Shouldn't it? They both kneel down.

'He was dead before you put him down. You know that,' he tells me. 'You didn't murder him.'

'I stabbed him. I felt his blood on my skin.' I look down. Some of it's still there.

'Scarlett. You listen to me closely.' Loom rests his hands on my shoulders and looks into my eyes. 'Your father was bitten.'

'And I killed him.'

He shakes his head. 'No. You didn't kill your dad. He was bitten. He turned. You put him down before he could bite and turn you. That creature was not your father. You said it yourself, remember? The thing you saw was what killed him. It was wearing him.'

'I'm sorry,' I whisper.

'Sorry?' he asks. 'For what?'

'You were right. They deserve respect. I never thought... I never understood...' I look down at the paper in my hand.

Sky looks behind me and turns a little pale.

I turn to see. And what I see has me to my feet. Everything inside me stops being fuzzy and returns to the sharp, solid and absolute cruelness that has always been my life.

I watch Chilli carry out the body of my father and lie him down on the ground with the utmost kindness and respect. He gives him a small bow and then heads towards us, wiping a tear from his cheek as he does.

He's dead.

That's all there is to it.

But that's not the end of it.

Not by far.

Chilli stands before me. 'Scar, I'm so sorry for your loss. Elder Eight was a great man. And he loved you very much. Even before we all knew who he really was to you, we could all see how much he cared for you.' He reaches out and takes my hands. I feel something in his palm. When I look, it's my dad's locket. 'You should have it. We always called you his favourite, ya know? A Teacher's pet. You totally were his favourite,' Chilli says fondly. 'He called you Kiddo. We all call you The Moustache's Kiddo behind your back. In a nice way.' He then pulls me into a hug and tells me, 'Whatever you need. You got it.'

'I need to understand.'

I manoeuvre around him and head back towards the mortuary, glancing briefly at my father's body as I pass. Only briefly. It hurts to look.

Inside, I stand at the edge of the torn-up floorboards and look down at the carnage below. I have to admit, I'm confused. This floor wasn't damaged before we left. There wasn't so much as a scratch.

The others are all standing by my side looking down with me.

'Sky, when you came into the building, was the door locked?'

'I think you should have a lie down-'

'Sky. Answer my question.'

Loom gives her a small nod. She thinks for a moment, and then shakes her head.

'I locked it when we left,' I tell them. 'I know I did. A hundred percent. I locked that door and gave the key to Elder Eight for safe keeping.' I point to the floorboards. 'They've been torn up. Look.' The splintered remains of the planks litter the edge of the room. 'If it was a collapse, they'd be in the pit. Not up here. The floorboards were stripped and tossed to the side.'

'The hole is too big and purposefully round to be a collapse,' Loom adds. 'And unless a horde of zombies managed to open a locked door, all wander inside, pull up the floor, clamber down, and then close the door after them... this isn't an accident.' He looks at me with shock, his face turning a ghostly white as he realises, 'It's another trap.'

'Like the church. That pit by the well deliberately covered over. Two locations. Two traps. They're not zombie traps.'

'They're Canary traps?' Sky gasps. 'Bloody hell! Someone's trying to off us?'

'Someone seems to be,' I conclude. Elder's final words echo in my head. I know what he wanted. And I think I know that we all want the same thing. I've been with these guys long enough to know they don't respect The Verity. 'Can I ask you all a question?' I turn to face the unit. 'Do you believe in The Verity?'

'In God, you mean?' Chilli asks with a scoff. 'No.'

'No way,' Sky agrees.

'Not a chance,' Loom adds.

'Not God,' I clarify. 'I'm asking if you believe in *The Verity*? Their rules? The way they make us all live? I'm not asking if you believe in God. I couldn't care less if you believe in God or bloody unicorns. I'm asking if you believe in *them*? In Noah? Because I don't. And neither did Elder Eight.'

They all share nervous glances. A conversation like this could end up in some serious punishment back home. But we're not home. We're here.

'No,' Sky says first, glancing at the two others a little worried. 'I don't. You?'

'Me neither,' Loom adds.

Chilli sighs in relief. 'Not even a little bit. The whole system back home is just wrong.'

'Good. Then we're on the same page.' I take a moment to think. And they stand patiently as I do.

'What are you thinking, Boss?' Loom asks.

'Someone murdered Elder Eight,' I tell them. 'He may have been bitten. That I can understand. That I can maybe forgive. But someone human built this trap. Someone human made the trap at the church too. And whoever made them, they're the ones that killed him.'

'The only people that knew we were here are the ones that read the letters he sent back home,' Loom says.

'The church. Maybe. But we didn't put this location in the letters.'

'Then how did anyone know we'd been here?' Sky asks.

'Maybe we're being followed?' Loom suggests.

'Maybe. I don't know. But what I do know is Elder loved my mum. All he wanted was to be her husband. My father. That's not a crime. It hurts no one. And what happened? She got banished and driven to suicide. I got taken away from a family that would have loved me, and I was signed up for a fight before I could even walk. We all were. You,' I point to Chilli. 'You stole a strawberry and got sent out here while the man that grew it, illegally - which in itself is ridiculous - got no punishment whatsoever. Sky, you were so traumatised by an attack when you were little, your hair turned white! And who can blame you. A child up against a Class Two alone? It's a miracle you didn't die. And Loom... well, I have no idea why you volunteered, but-'

'I think this is my fault.' Loom stares at the ground, avoiding all eye contact with any one. 'I think your dad died because they were trying to kill me.'

'Who is trying to kill you?' I ask. He lifts his gaze and it lands on me. 'My Elder... The Elder I had when I was training... well... he used to come into my room, late at night. He wasn't entirely... appropriate.'

'Jesus...' Chilli whispers.

'It was just touching, ya know? But it wasn't right. It went on for about a month. Then, he stopped. Pretended like it never happened. He retired and I never really saw him after that. Then, a week before we left home, I went to the stables to check on the horses, and I walked in on him with a young cadet.' His face screws up in disgust. 'Fucking old pervert. He had his hand down the lad's trousers and I just lost it. I just attacked.'

'I repeat,' Chilli murmurs. 'Jesus!'

'The cadet said he wouldn't tell anyone and we just left him there. The next day, I heard that the old man was in a coma and that the Grey Coats would put whoever did it to death. I panicked and volunteered for the Canaries. What if they found out it was me?'

I close the distance between us and take his hands in mine. There's a deep and dark pain in his eyes. And guilt. How can he feel guilt for this?

'This isn't your fault. Even if this is in retaliation for your actions, it still wouldn't be your fault! What happened to you was awful, Loom. And you putting that old bastard in a coma probably saved a lot of others from the same pain you suffered! But if I'm honest, I think that perhaps, this is because of me. That this is Noah's doing.'

'Noah?'

'He wanted me as his wife,' I confess. 'I said no, so he threatened to kill everyone I care about unless I agreed. I joined the Canaries instead. If anyone gave the orders to have us killed, I would put my bets on him. Either way, this isn't on you and it isn't on me. It's on Noah.' I turn and face them. 'It's on all of them. They all sit under a tent and watch us fight so they can mark us. They take us from our families. They let us die bloody and screaming. They demand we do as they wish. To fight for them. Kill for them. As if taking our freedom and our lives isn't enough, they dare demand our bodies too? That...' I point to pit. 'That was an attempt to kill us by a human. It's wrong. It's us versus the undead. Not us versus other people. Sentenced to this because of stealing, of love, of having a baby, for blasphemy... Joining up because we fear those who are supposed to protect us and keep us safe from harm... it's wrong. I'll die to save my family. You guys. The people I left behind. That's the reason I want to fight. To get this country back. I don't fight for Noah or Elders or Grey Coats. The only threat anyone should face is from the targets. They should be the only thing we have to fear. But they're not! Back home, being eaten alive is the least of our problems! It's time you know what Elder Eight and I had planned. And what he told me just before he died.' I tell them of our plan to build more settlements. To spread the survivors beyond The Haven. And they're on board completely before I've even finished. 'I propose a world without the sodding Verity. Without the law of donation. Without worshipping a man who is more sinful and cruel than any other man I've known.' I look back down to the pit. 'No one knows about the dome. Or the island off the south coast. We didn't put it in the pigeons.' I turn back to them. 'I propose we leave the Verity behind and make our own life.'

'You want to set up a new base without them?' Loom asks.

'That's precisely what I want to do.'

'I like it,' Chilli nods. 'Where we can love who we want.'

'Where we're not forced to fight,' Loom agrees.

'Where we can have a family.' Sky nods.

'Where we can be free and focus on the real enemy,' I add.

'What do you have in mind?' Loom asks. They're ready to follow any instruction I give them. I see it in their eyes. I keep my promise to Elder and keep the fact Elder One seems to have something to do with this under wraps. After all, it seems that he tried to help poor Loom by sending him out here. 'We're going back. We're not the only ones who want out. We'll go back and tell the others that we plan to leave and if they want to join us, they can. And the person responsible for this...' I gesture to the pit. 'They're gonna pay. Big.' I look at Loom. 'If you don't want to return with us...' I look at them all. 'If any of you want to stay away from home, you can stay at the dome over winter. I can bring others back with me when the snow clears.'

'If we don't do something, more people will suffer,' Loom states. 'We need to return. Together. As a unit. People deserve to choose the kind of life they want to lead.' Loom stands by my side. 'I'm coming back with you.'

'And if Noah or the Grey Coats try to take either of you, they'll get an axe in their face,' Chilli states furiously. His hands tremble as he speaks.

'We have a mission now. It's bigger than us. We know where we can bring others to start over.'

'We're ready to follow you,' Loom states. 'Wherever you decide to take us. Boss.'

'Sure thing,' Sky nods.

'Okay,' I breathe, completely overwhelmed. 'We return home. Gather the people that want to leave. Serve some justice, and then we go.'

'That simple?' Sky asks. 'Who will we ask? What location will we go to?'

According to Elder Eight, Elder One is the man to talk to. But he also said not to mention that to anyone else. So I keep that little nugget of info to myself.

'We can figure the details out on the way back home. I'm going back. I'm gonna find out who did this to Elder Eight. And then, I'm gonna rip their spines out with my bare teeth.'

'I think she's at the anger stage of the grieving process,' Chilli breathes.

'Better believe it. Pass me the pigeon and then let's pack up. We're going home.'

'Yes, Boss,' they all reply.

Canary unit 63.
8/8 bird.
4 alive.
1 deceased.
We're coming home. 1 week out.

CHAPTER SEVENTEEN

Hanzo's getting a little tired. It's been six days of pretty intense travelling, only stopping for nightfall in locations that are unfamiliar and in most cases, unsecure. We can't be too careful. Nowhere we've been before is safe. And I won't risk losing anyone else out here, so everywhere we stop needs to be new. And therefore, cleared from scratch. It's hard work for such little rest. Two sleep. Two on watch. No more than four hours at a time. And as soon as the sun begins to rise, we carry on. Everyone is full of purpose. Worry. Anger. Grief.

And questions.

What's gonna to happen when we turn up with the dead body of an Elder?

Who's been following us?

Was it Noah? Grey Coats?

And for me personally, my question is why Elder One? The man's never spoken to me unless it's been to deliver a punishment or a scalding. What have they been planning? What was Elder Eight talking about?

The others are afraid that I'm returning to my doom. I see their side glances. Hear their secret whisperings. They're twitchy. Uncertain of my choice to go back. They continue to ask if I would be willing to stay out here as *they* return and find out what happened to Elder on my behalf. Sky was more than up for the idea of us camping out in the world together.

But I refused.

I need to find out who the hell's been following us. Why my father died in that pit. I need to see my family. Make sure they're okay. I need to hug the hell out of Tee and hear her sweet little laugh. I need to see Winder's beaming smile. I need to see Cass furrow his brow as I do something he disapproves of, before rolling his eyes and letting the corner of his mouth twitch into a begrudging smile.

And apparently, I need to see Elder One.

But I doubt they'll even want to talk to me. I broke so many promises to them. I swore not to abandon them. That I would always be there. I lied about Noah and the relationship we had in secret. I slept with Cass and then ran off with the Canaries without a word of explanation. My actions led to Elder Eight volunteering. If he hadn't, he'd still be alive and retired. They'll blame me for his death. They loved him too and they should blame me. It's my fault he was out here in the first place. If they didn't hate me, I'd be very surprised. But still, I need to see them. Winder doesn't need to smile at me. I just need to see him smile. Tee doesn't need to laugh with me. I just long to hear that giggle. And Cass, I just need to see those eyes. Even if they're filled with hatred. I just need to see them.

My fingers play with my locket I have around my neck. I've spent hours looking at the picture inside it. My mum had a beautiful smile. It must have been hard for Elder Eight. Looking at me every day. We're so similar in appearance.

'Earth to Scar,' Sky says playfully, trotting right along beside me as we ride east on horseback. She's not left my side since we got out of the pit. None of them have really. They're always watching me. Like they're scared I'm gonna snap. My reaction immediately after they pulled me out of that hole scared them. I was empty and they had no idea what to do.

But I'm better now.

'How's your hand feeling?'

'Fine,' I lie. It's throbbing and stings. Red is starting to seep through the bandage again.

'Will you please let me clean it up?'

'It's fine,' I tell her.

'You haven't been able to fight since Elder died,' she blurts out.

'Cos my hand hurts.' Truth is, every time I look at my sword, the sword I used to kill him, I feel sick.

'I know.' She nods. 'Which is why you need to let me look at it. What if we need your help fighting off a Class Two? What if-'

'My hand hurts. Okay? It will heal when it heals. End of.'

'Alright. Sorry.'

As we ride, she keeps talking. On and on she goes. I have no idea what she's talking about half the time. I just nod and give the occasional, *"yeah"*. I think she feels the need to fill the silence and to distract me. Distract us all from the loudest most painful thing around us.

The bundle that's draped over the back of Elder Eight's horse.

No one can look at it. No one wants to talk about it. I just hold the reigns of the animal carrying the body of my father and stare straight ahead.

Coming into view is the towering wall that protects The Haven.

'We're home.'

As we get closer, my heart starts to race harder. The wall seems taller than I remember.

Weird.

I clutch the reigns of Elder's horse firmly in my hand as we ride. The others have all gotten a little closer, like they're forming a protective barrier around me. And when the main gate with those stupid V's boasting The Verity's authority on the front starts to open, they all stop.

'What are they doing?' Loom asks. 'They never open the gate until they see who we are.' He climbs down and rests his hand on the handle of his axe. 'Scarlett, stay behind us.'

The others all climb down too and stand in a line ahead of me, all with their weapons ready.

'You are not to intervene,' I say firmly. 'No matter who comes through that gate or what they want, you stay out of it and let it happen.' I jump down and stand up front.

The gate has barely opened a crack when a single person squeezes through the gap and starts sprinting towards us, kicking up dust as they run.

'What the hell?' Chilli asks quietly. 'Who is that?'

Sky draws an arrow and points it at the oncoming solider who continues their solitary dash across the wasteland, on foot, straight at us. They're yelling something. But they're too far away for us to hear them. They're moving quick and shouting something in such desperation, I don't know if we should run away from them, or run towards them to help.

'They're yelling your name,' Loom realises, looking at me with a quizzical expression.

'SCARLETT?' they yell. They're so far away, I can barely hear them. 'SCARLETT?'

Sky pulls back her arrow ready to fire. But I lower it and shake my head. Because I think I know who it is.

'SCARLETT? IS SHE THERE WITH YOU?' She screams to us. 'PLEASE. TELL ME SHE'S THERE WITH YOU!'

'Tee...' I whisper. 'Guys, it's Tee!'

'Well, safe to say Tee's happy to see ya at any rate,' Chilli laughs, before looking to me. 'Well? Go on then. What are you waiting for?'

I thrust the reigns of Elder's horse into his hands before breaking into a sprint.

'TEE!' I call out as I run. 'TEE!'

'SCARLETT! IT IS YOU!' She sobs happily, running as fast as her legs will carry her. 'I KNEW IT! I KNEW YOU'D COME HOME!'

I see her tear-streaked face. Her beaming smile. Her relief at seeing me. I feel everything I see on her face and then some. I open my arms. She opens hers.

And we collide.

She grips onto me with everything she has. Her arms are vice-like. Her whole body swamps me. And I know I'm doing exactly the same to her. It would hurt if we both weren't so happy to see each other. She sobs into my neck, talking so fast I have no idea what the hell she's saying. I just hold her. Relieved to feel her hair in my face. To smell her scent. To have the full strength of her hug crushing my ribs.

When she lifts her head, I brush the hair from her face and dry her cheeks with my thumbs. I feel so awful for thinking for even a second that she would ever have it in her to hate me.

'I knew you'd come back in one piece,' she wails, 'You had to. Oh, Scarlett, I've missed you so much. You have no idea.' She pulls me back into a rib-crunching hug which feels so good, I never want it to end.

I bury my face in her neck and just breathe her in. This right here, this is home. 'Is everyone else alright?' I ask. 'The boys, are they okay?'

'They're all fine. But, Scar?' she asks. 'Your letter... who died? Your pigeon.' She looks into my eyes. 'Four alive. One deceased. There was no name. I've been sat up on that wall waiting for you to come back for days. I thought that maybe... it was you.' She glances over my shoulder to where the others are still standing. Her eyes linger on the empty horse carrying a bundle on its back. 'Scar... where's Elder Eight?'

'We-we...' I look over my shoulder at the body draped over the mare. 'We lost him, Tee. I'm so sorry.'

She pulls me back into her arms and once more I bury my face in her neck as she sobs desperately. But these are far from happy tears.

I tell her how sorry I am that I let him die. It's all I seem able to say.

I'm sorry.

I'm so, so sorry.

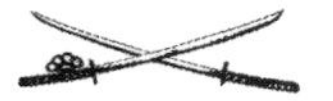

Tee holds Hanzo's reigns as I hold Elder Eight's, and together, we walk them back towards the wall. She's pulled herself together. Just about. But the odd sniffle and whimper doesn't go unnoticed. Our free hands grip onto each other. Her fingers are locked with mine. I'm as reluctant to let her go as she is to release me. Ahead of us, the others walk and lead their own horses. Each one of them looks back at us occasionally. Checking that I'm still there. That I'm okay. They eye her suspiciously. Looking her up and down with clear distrust.

'Wow,' Tee whispers. 'They seem really protective over you.' She looks at me with wide eyes. 'And very hostile. Are they going to attack me?'

'We've been through a lot,' I tell her. 'They won't hurt you. God, I have so much I need to tell you.'

Sky openly sneers at her. As I frown in her direction, she rolls her eyes and returns her attention to the road that leads to the gate.

'Are you sure?' Tee whispers. 'Sky looks like she wants to rip my face off.'

'Err, yeah. I'm sure.' I grip her hand tighter and show her a smile. 'She's harmless. Relatively speaking.' Her eyes shift instead to the increasingly bloody bandage wrapped around the hand I'm using to hold onto Elders horse with.

'You're hurt.'

'I'm fine.'

'You're bleeding.'

'I'm fine, Tee,' I insist a little sharply.

By the time we reach the gate, it's completely open. Sky and the boys head in first and just as I pass the barrier, I hear a joyful cheer before being body slammed with a hug by Owl who's just sprinted down the steps to accost me. Loom draws his sword and gets ready to attack but I shake my head and he holds his position.

'I knew you'd come back, you absolute nutter,' Owl laughs. 'I told Tee that you would, but she refused to budge from my post. Your girl's been up there for days.'

Tee won't release my hand and I can't let go of Elder's horse so it's a bit of an odd embrace. She lets go and holds my shoulders so she can get a good look at me. Her cheery smile soon fades.

'Hang on.' She looks to my side and that look of grief washes over her too. 'Elder Eight? He's the one that... he's not...'

'Yeah. It was him.'

'Oh... oh no...' she whimpers, her hand covering her mouth and her eyes brimming with tears. 'Oh, Scar...'

'I need to go report to Elder One, and...' I nod to the bundle on the back of the horse. I really can't take the look on her face and the sniffles that continue to come from Tee. 'I need to-'

'Of course,' She steps away and gives the saddest little smile while wiping a tear dry. 'Go and do what you need to do.' She throws a nervous glance at Tee. 'Have you told her about... ya know...?'

'I will,' Tee replies, looking between Owl and me with extreme discomfort.

'You need to tell her, Tee.'

'I just want her inside first.'

'So she can't turn tail and leg it?' Owl scorns. 'Like she ever would.'

'We'll see you later, Owl.' Tee gives my hand a light tug and we carry on heading down the path.

'What was that about?' I ask nervously. 'Why would I leg it?'

'Nothing.' She shrugs. That's a massive lie. I wait, watching her expectantly and she knows it. I only need to wait. She'll spill. But Sky doesn't give her a chance to spill on her own. She turns and walks quickly to Tee, stopping so close to her face their noses are almost touching.

'Tell her what you're holding back,' she warns. 'Or I'll make you tell her and you won't enjoy a second of it I promise you.'

Tee looks completely terrified. Without looking away from the girl whose face is in hers, she spills.

'Cass is really angry with her.'

'Is he going to hurt her?' Sky demands.

'N-no one knows what he's going to do,' she stammers. Releasing my hold on the reigns, I rest my bloody palm on Sky's chest and urge her back. She doesn't look away from Tee as she retreats a few steps.

'Don't corner her,' I warn. 'Never. You hear me? I told you. Whatever happens when I return, you're not to get involved. Now, Sky... Back off.'

'Just so you know,' Sky says to Tee. 'Anyone so much as looks at her funny, I'll tear their eyes clear out their skull. Got it?'

'I... err...'

'YOU GOT IT?'

'Sky!' I bark.

'I got it,' Tee whispers, squeezing my hand even tighter as I shove Sky further back and stand between them.

'That's enough!' I hiss. 'Tee's my sister. You'll treat her with some respect. *You* got *that*?' She looks down at my hand and glares at me. 'What?!'

'It's still bleeding. I told you, you need stitches. You need to-'

'I don't need to do anything. You need to take the horses to the stables and get them settled. They're exhausted.'

'But-'

'And then you need to get your arses to the main hall for some food before you get yourselves to bed. We will regroup in the morning. We discussed this. We don't want to draw attention to ourselves!'

'We're not leaving you,' Loom says plainly, his axe out and over his shoulder. 'It's not safe and you know that.'

'GO!' They all watch me. And I glare at them. 'Do not make me repeat myself.'

They obey with a distinct look of annoyance before they turn and carry on ahead of us. I know that if I'm approached by Noah, Grey Coats or even Cass, they'll fight. And my unit will lose. They know their new mission. That's all that matters.

'Wow...' Tee whispers. 'I take it you're the new Canary leader now Elder's gone then?'

I turn to face Tee, who still has her hand in mine. 'I need to know what I'm walking into. Please, Tee. Just tell me.'

With a beaten sigh, she spills. 'Cass says he hates you. He won't let anyone say your name and the other morning, we were sitting in the main hall having breakfast when we heard about the pigeon saying one of you had died. And he-he sort of...'

'What?'

'Said good riddance and stormed off. No one's seen him since.'

Ouch.

She goes on to tell me that after I left, they had no idea what the hell to do or why I did what I did. They went to look for Elder Eight but he'd gone too. Then they all got dragged to the lottery announcement where Elder One called my number as the winner of the lottery. She watches me for a reaction as she talks. My lack of shock comes as no surprise to her.

'You knew you'd be chosen. Didn't you?'

'I can't go into it right now. Please don't ask me to. What happened next?'

'Noah got mad. Like, really mad. He started demanding to know where the winner was. Cass stood up and announced to everybody that you'd left as a Canary that morning. Made a point of the fact that he knew and Noah didn't. There was this really awkward stare between them. Everyone could feel the hatred they had for each other. Then Cass went and said, *"Looks like she'd rather live out there, than be your wife, mate".* Noah ordered Cass be lashed and arrested. He wanted him executed, Scar.'

'What?!'

Nodding, she carries on. 'Cass went quietly. But everyone else kicked off. Even Elder One.' She looks at me with such a serious expression. 'They kicked off big time. Even he was surprised by how many people came to his defence.'

'What charges did he accuse him of?'

'Sex out of wedlock,' she tells me, still watching my face closely. I must have a great poker face because she doesn't pick up on anything. 'He said that Cass must have pressured you into degrading yourself and driven you to flee. That Cass was jealous of him. But Elder One demanded to know what proof Noah had to accuse him of such a thing. And then pointed out how strange it was that Noah knew anything about you or Cass, considering you'd never met. Which of course, now we all know you had met.' Again, she waits for me to add something or deny it all. But I don't, which in itself tells her something I suppose.

'Turns out Noah had no proof about any kind of relationship between you and Cass. And Cass wouldn't deny or confirm his allegations. He just smirked like a prat. And without you here, no one could do anything according to Elder One. But they dragged him off anyway.'

'And then what? Was he okay?'

'The morning after, he was back in the main hall for breakfast. He looked like hell. Beaten black and blue. Wincing as he walked. He wouldn't say what had exactly happened, but he said that he got a punch in.'

'He hit Noah?' I gasp.

'Dunno. That's all he said. Well that, and that you were a selfish coward. That you had got yourself into a mess with Noah and run off leaving him to deal with your crap. And that he never wanted to hear your name again. He said that we're not to talk about you. Or to you. We're to stay away.' She shrugs apologetically. But I'm just glad that Noah didn't have him killed.

'But you're here. Why wait at the gate if he's ordered you to stay away?'

'I'm your sister. I choose you over everyone else. I told him to get stuffed,' she scoffs. 'He may be the Red Coat. But he can't control who I choose to talk to.'

'Has he been awful with you?' I feel terrible.

'He's been so busy with the units, I've not seen him much. He's been okay. Winder and me just try not to talk about you in front of him.'

My whole-body slumps as my insides plummet. She pats my shoulder sympathetically.

Cass hates me. I got him hurt.

'He really said good riddance when he thought I was dead?'

'That's what he said.' She glances over my shoulder to the bundle; a haunted look etches over her features. 'But the look in his eyes when he heard...'

'What? What did he look like?' I hesitate to ask, but I ask anyhow. 'Happy? Sad?'

'Terrified. I think,' she says, her eyes returning back to me as she tries so hard to ignore what lies just behind me. 'I've never seen him look like that before. But Scar, if you had any thoughts of a good reunion between you two, I have to tell you-'

'I don't,' I tell her, swallowing my sadness. 'I know Cass. I know he'll never forgive me.' Her big eyes look into mine with a huge amount of sympathy. 'But I did what I had to do and I can't change it. Even if I wanted to.' My hand slides to her shoulder. 'As long as I've still got you on my side, I'll be fine.'

'Your side *is* my side,' she assures me, her hand resting on mine. 'I'm so glad you're home safe. Well,' she glances at my hand. 'Relatively speaking. Sky is right. Your hand is bleeding. You should get it seen-'

'CANARY 5-3-6?' The formidable tone makes us both jump.

'Ahh crap,' I mutter when I see five Mr Greys blocking our path. 'This can't be good.'

'Scar...?' Tee whispers as she steps a little closer to me. 'What do we do?'

'It's alright, Tee. Just keep quiet. I'll deal with it.' I turn to face them, stepping between her and the weapons they have aimed at us. They're all on foot. Two are pointing arrows at me. Two others have their swords drawn and the fifth is standing front a centre. 'Can I help you, Commander?' I call over, attempting to sound calm. I know it's him that spoke. I know his voice all too well. As ever, all their faces are concealed by their hooded coats. But that won't hinder them killing me where I stand with a more than perfect shot.

'Canary 5-3-6?' he repeats.

'You know who I am, Commander. Is there a problem?'

'You are to come with us. Right now.'

'Why?'

'Surrender your weapons, step away from the Green Coat, and put your hands behind your back.'

'I'll ask again. Why?'

The archers pull back their arrows a fraction as a warning. And when I stay put, they move their aim from me, to Tee.

'I will *not* ask again, Canary,' The commander states. I look at them each in turn. But I can't see a thing beyond their hoods. Noah could very well be among them.

I turn and place the reigns of Elder's horse into Tee's hand. What else is there to do? She trembles as she takes them.

'What do I do?' she whispers in a panic. 'Shall I fetch help? Your unit maybe?'

'Just, just take Elder Eight to Elder HQ. Tell Elder One that the Grey Coats have me. Only him, understand?' I try to pry my hand free. 'I have to go with them, Tee. Let go.'

'I'm not leaving you.' She tightens her grip. Her fingernails dig into my skin.

'Tee, you have to let me go, before they shoot you.' I take hold of her wrist. But she won't release me. 'Tee. Let go!'

'I just got you back. I can't lose you. I really can't!' she exclaims, tears brimming in her eyes. 'You don't understand. You can't leave me again!'

'Canary!'

'Yeah. Hold on, Commander!' I snap. Tee's breaking apart in front of me. Her nails are drawing blood. What the hell is the matter with her? Why does she look so frightened? 'Tee, listen to me. You have to let me go. Everything will be fine.'

'You don't know that!'

'Trust me. It'll be fine.' I manage to pry myself free before they do actually let loose an arrow. With a kiss on her cheek, I step away.

'Your weapons, Canary.'

'Yeah. Yeah.' I undo the buckle on my harness and hand my weapons to Tee. 'Look after those.'

'They can't do this!' she insists.

'Pretty sure they can, cos ya know, they are. Just, take care of Elder Eight for me. And make sure the others stay out of trouble,' I add. 'The last thing I need is for them to come charging after me.'

'Step away, Green Coat,' Commander warns Tee. She steps away, holding my weapons and the reigns firmly in her hand.

'On your knees. Canary. Hands behind your back.'

I lower myself down and put my hands behind my back. She doesn't take her eyes off me as one of the swordsmen makes their way over to cuff my wrists together.

'Everyone knows she doesn't want to marry Noah,' she says in a panic to the Grey Coats. 'He can't force her. Not now.'

Safely restrained, the commander stands before me. I crane my neck upwards and see the slightest smile beneath the hood.

'I think marriage is on the back burner now, Green Coat,' he scoffs. 'He has something else planned.'

'Gonna sentence me to the Canaries?' I laugh.

The next thing I see is his fist as it slams hard into the side of my face. I land on my side in the dirt as Tee screams. The Commander kicks me in the gut. Then again in the ribs, flipping me over so I'm on my back coughing and wheezing as blood fills my mouth. The Grey Coat who cuffed me grabs Tee as she tries to intervene.

'You can't do this!' she cries. 'STOP!'

'You embarrassed him,' The Commander snarls, lifting me by the scruff of my coat and giving me a rough shake. 'Your infidel friend laid hands on the most divine.'

'Yeah. I heard Cass got a punch in,' I mock, although my words slur a little.

'Yeah. Your man got a lucky punch in. *You'll* pay for that insult.' He reaches into his pocket and pulls out a pair of pliers. Big metal things made of solid steel. 'He punched him in the mouth. Knocked out one of his teeth.'

'You just punched me. So, who gets to punch you?' I laugh, but choke on my blood as I do.

'And so, the lord said...' He tosses me on the floor, winded and dizzy. 'If there is harm done, then the one that harms shall pay.' He kneels over me, a leg each side and my arms still cuffed behind my back. His fingers go in my mouth and he prises open my jaw, forcing the pliers in between my teeth. 'An eye for an eye.' He clamps the pliers around my back tooth. Tee is screaming so hard; the Grey coat covers her mouth. 'A tooth for a tooth.' His face scrunches up as he gets a grip. My legs are kicking out as I try to get him off me. I'm yelling a garbled yell past the metal and the blood. 'Welcome home, Canary.' He pulls. The pain as my tooth is yanked from my gum has me furiously yelling. More blood fills my mouth as he admires the molar he's just stolen. He laughs and slides it in his pocket then heaves me to my feet. I try to ignore Tee looking on in a helpless mess as I sway. The Commander spins me. I can tell he has a cruel smile beneath that hood. I spit blood in his face.

'What? Noah not brave enough to torture me himself?'

'Oh. He wants to torture you. He wants to break you. And he will. That was just my own personal welcome home. Come on. Let's go.'

Tee is thrown to the floor but she's soon back on her feet. Tears streaming down her cheeks but a fury like I've never seen in her eyes.

'Where are you taking her?!' she demands.

'Canary 5-3-6 is under arrest.' He throws back over his shoulder, already leading me away.

'For what?'

'For desertion of duty,' he says. 'And you know what that means?' He wraps his fingers in my hair and yanks my head so I'm looking up at him. 'The sentence for which is death.'

'DEATH?!' Tee screeches. 'YOU CAN'T!'

'Your sentence is to be carried out at first light. Until then, Lord Sands will keep you company. And he has much worse things than pliers waiting for you. I assure you.' He looks over his shoulder to Tee. 'Her execution is scheduled for tomorrow morning. Seven am. Attendance is mandatory. We'll see you then, little Green Coat.'

I'm dragged away.

'Go find Elder One, Tee!' I yell back. 'GO! NOW!'

End of part one.
Part two is available now.

THANK YOU.

Thank you for reading The Verity: Part One.
Please take a moment to leave a review with your favourite retailer.
Reviews are so important to indie authors, and they are very much appreciated.

Amazon
Goodreads
If you would like to know about upcoming releases, please follow me on Facebook https://www.facebook.com/HelloMJLawrie/
Or sign up for my newsletter through my website:

https://www.mjlawrie.com/

Also by

M.J.LAWRIE

The Last Witch Series

A dark, paranormal fantasy romance series.

The Verity Duology

A dystopian, romance, fantasy.

The Stolen Fae series

A dark, MFM, paranormal romance fantasy.

Printed in Great Britain
by Amazon

3cd9f298-b71c-4841-a67f-e26b17c07a03R01